The Pebble in my Shoe
Return of the Mods

By Paul Runewood

paulrunewood.com

All rights reserved. No part of this publication may be reproduced, distributed, or transmitted in any form or by any means, including photocopying, recording, or other electronic or mechanical methods, without the prior written permission of the publisher, except in the case of brief quotations embodied in critical reviews and certain other non-commercial uses permitted by copyright law. For permission requests, write to the publisher, addressed "Attention: Permissions Coordinator," at the address above.

© Paul Runewood 2022
Based on Screenplay 'Yesterday's hero' by Paul Runewood ©2012

The Pebble in my Shoe
Return of the Mods
By Paul Runewood

For Peter
For believing in me

-

In memory of my great friend
Ian 'Arnie' Russell

This is a work of fiction. Although its form is that of an autobiography, it is not one. Space and time have been rearranged to suit the convenience of the book, and with the exception of some public figures, any resemblance to persons living or dead is coincidental. Although it seems there's more truth in fiction than so-called factual books these days, please do not try to second guess the author. Just enjoy the story. The opinions expressed are those of the characters and should not be confused with the author's views.

CHAPTER 1.   Looking Back.

Ronnie Diamond, all middle-aged spread and receding hairline, hovered over an old record player, in the plush cream coloured living room of his country residence. Clumsily, he allowed the needle to skip, as it crashed down onto the vinyl. The sound of a familiar crackle emanated from the speakers, as the single whirled around the turntable. He was brimming with anticipation for the noise that would spring forth, like hearing the ping of the oven while awaiting a slice of freshly baked bread.

The song, a rhythmic upbeat punky number encapsulated, within its three verse, middle eight and double chorus assembly, every well-worn, lived-in emotion from Ronnie's teenage years. The youthful arrogance, the raucous excitement, the violent tension, the world conquering comradery, the heart pounding lust and the daring showmanship was all bound up in the frenetic beat of this three-minute wonder. He could almost taste his adolescence.

"I love this song… I fuckin' love this song," said Ronnie. Ronnie constructed a smile of drunken contentment as his right leg gyrated along to the music. It reminded him how alive he'd felt back then, as a tearaway, in the early nineteen-eighties, in the backstreets of the urban chaos that was his inner-London life.

Ronnie had been the leader of the Battersham Aces, a band of second-generation Mods. They were youth culture trailblazers for the initiated; at least that's how he saw it. He took another swig from a glass of whiskey. Partly singing along, partly lost in thought, he betrayed an edge of indignation. The room was immaculately orderly, except for the various albums and singles, with their eye-catching cover artwork, that were strewn across the sofa and along the floor, as if discarded by a burglar searching for something of a little more value. At that moment in time, those records were very much the pot of gold at the end of Ronnie's rainbow.

Every few years, he had spasms of nostalgia and was taken to go exploring the dark crevices of the loft, like an archaeologist returning to a familiar site seeking out undiscovered artefacts. Each time he would have to satisfy himself with the familiar old ghost of his younger self that lurked among some old trunks and dusty boxes.

Over the last few years, the visits had become more frequent, and as time went on, he found himself seeking out the company of this alter ego with more and more fervour. It was like the reawakening of a deep-rooted religious conviction.

On consulting his treasure trove of memorabilia, a conversation had begun raging in Ronnie's head, helped in no small part by the bottle of Glenmorangie he had been serenading. 'CDs are shit. CDs are for Coldplay losers in their company cars, for airless showrooms and monotonous hotel lobbies,' he heard himself think, as if in a heated debate with some kind of invisible entity who was desperately in need of Ronnie's unquestionable wisdom. He found himself agreeing profusely with himself.

"And don't get me started about digital downloads," he said aloud. "They swapped record sleeves for barcodes... fucking barcodes."

Ronnie continued, racking up the volume another notch with almost every sip of booze. A jolt of unfamiliarity mugged him, when his eyes met his reflection in the full-length antique mirror that stood in the corner of the room. In his mind's eye he was 20, 25 tops, and still in his prime. Like the reverse of an eating disorder sufferer convinced their skinny frame was the epitome of gross obesity, this aged coating had crept over him like moss on a neglected statue but remained mostly invisible to his ego.

The sound of the front door slamming shut was singularly out of step with the booming music. At last, he thought, someone to join his conversation. He had important things to say, he assured himself.

A few moments later he raised his glass and expelled a little "Hey, Hey," by way of acknowledging the appearance of Hazel, his auburn-haired wife. While he had taken on the appearance of an aging businessman, she was as pretty now as she had been when he first set eyes on her at the age of seventeen. Hazel was a little chubby around the gills now, but naturally beautiful, nonetheless. His age had plagued him like a bad smell, while she had only aged in weight.

Hazel stepped across the impromptu floor display to the stereo and turned the music down. Ronnie used the moment to calmly squeeze a cloud of melancholy into words.

"These songs used to fill me with, love, lust and laughter," he said.

His soliloquy was having no effect on his wife who, for the past few years, had grown accustomed to his little rose-tinted ventures into yesteryear. Slowly but surely, he was becoming a hostage to his history.

"Did you get my text message about the veal cutlets?" asked Hazel.

Ronnie ignored her interruption, continuing his sermon in the vain hope that she was keenly awaiting the punchline.

"Now, it's just the requiem of my youth," he lamented. Hazel turned up the corners of her mouth as she flushed his words away, in a moment of mild exasperation. He put down his glass and picked up an album cover and marvelled at it. His eyes flashed with an intensity that even the excess booze couldn't dull.

"If you really listen, for the briefest of moments, we're there," said Ronnie.

"We *were* there," said Hazel.

Delighted that she had tuned-in to his line of thought, he continued his elegy with a touch of theatrical whimsy.

"Those wild and belligerent teenagers..." He clutched the album ever-firmly as if hanging on tight to a fading memory, fearing it would slip through his fingers and disappear into the ether or desert him like his 28-inch waist and full head of hair had done so many years ago.

Swaying a little, he stammered, "Taking on the world."

"Listen to yourself," she said, dismissively.

She took no comfort from bursting his bubble, but Hazel knew she needed to nip his mood in the bud.

"You're working up a rant, and it can hardly be a new one," she said, as she prized the album cover from his hands.

"Name me a song, go on, just name me one song from the last ten years that would be fit to grace the track listing on that album."

She ignored him.

"You see, can't be done. Because there ain't one," said Ronnie, feeling pleased with himself.

She studied the album in her hands, it was in mint condition.

"Is this new then?" she said, instantly regretting that what would surely follow would be another political broadcast by the 'Back in the day' party.

"It's a re-issue; all the classics," he enthused, tuning in to the personalised music TV channel 'Ronnie Diamond, the early years' that was broadcasting in his head.

"I see a lot of those eighties bands are reforming now, doing the nostalgia circuit," said Hazel.

"They offered Weller a cool million, but he still refuses to reform The Jam."

A bewildered expression swept across her face.

"He said no to a *million pounds*?" She stopped short of calling him an idiot for fear of offending Ronnie. Weller had been a mythical figure elevated higher, at times, than even his own mother.

He quickly ushered out a loyal response in defence of his hero's character. Paul Weller was the Battersham Aces' unofficial mentor and president. There was a deep-seated loyalty that had remained with him through the decades. Even when his idol veered off the tracks and coughed up a long line of unremarkable recordings, Ronnie couldn't bring himself to criticise him. A slight on Weller was an affront to his own core being, akin to the tinge a parent gets when hearing unflattering remarks about their own child.

"It's called integrity," said Ronnie.

"I can think of another name for it," said Hazel.

He ignored her, throwing out his arms ostentatiously and declaring, like a town crier, "Wembley Stadium, Glastonbury, Reading festival, Hampden Park, you name it, they'd sell out in minutes."

Hazel shook the bottle of whiskey at him.

"I take it this is what's been oiling the wheels to nostalgia central?"

Ronnie, a cheeky glint in his eye, pleaded for her to join him, even though he was aware there was no way she'd agree. She knew that a drink-induced party for one was always in search of company. There was never any fun playing catch up with someone already three or four times around the track.

"I hope you're not too sozzled to make dinner. You did promise," she said optimistically.

Ronnie's mood soured.

"That about sums me up, eh? I used to love drinking, now it's an inconvenience to the bloody cooking schedule."

"I don't have time for this," said Hazel, as she walked out of the room shaking his current disposition from her head.

Ronnie ratcheted up the sound of the stereo and snarled along to the agit-pop tune now reverberating throughout their impressively large house. His tub-thumping moves were a blend of terrace fist-pumping and shadow boxing that, although a little unsure of its footing at times, now appeared more aggressive than celebratory. Songs about factory life, street brawls and tower blocks contrasted deeply with the picture postcard views of his extensive, well-kept, traditional English garden, visible through the living room's rear windows.

Hazel walked through to the adjoining kitchen and closed the door, attempting to shut out the noise of Ronnie's wannabe X-factor audition. His singing was well out of key with the youthful voices coming from the speakers. His father had been a drunk and notorious pub warbler who saw himself as Battersham's answer to Frank Sinatra but sounded more like Frank Spencer, albeit that none but the brave would chuck that appraisal into any conversation he was a part of.

Hazel took a cup from the cupboard, switched the kettle on and, just as it was coming to the boil, noticed the flashing red light of the telephone answer machine. She leaned in to listen to the message, above the din of Ronnie's one-man retro performance.

She straightened up, peered at Ronnie, who followed her gaze as she walked back into the living room, her face carrying an awful burden. She turned the music off.

"Oi, I was listening to that," he protested.

Even through the bibulous fog, and his boyhood reconstructions, he recognised a sincerity in her sombre expression.

"There's a message for you," she said.

Ronnie glugged some more Whiskey before Hazel pulled the glass away from him and placed it on the side, a gentle kindness carried in her voice.

"I'm sorry, Ronnie, it was Mick Macpherson.... Arnie passed away."

Ronnie's bravado had ebbed away the moment she'd taken his glass and he dodged eye contact for fear of the raw biting pain that two people can share at such moments. He released himself into the comfort in her open arms.

"I know," he quietly whispered.

She pulled back and looked him straight in the eye.

"You know?"

"I heard him," he said.

Hazel looked a little puzzled.

"Didn't you speak to Mick?"

"No," he said.

"Why?"

"I haven't seen him in over twenty years, what would I say?"

His reasoning was lost on Hazel.

"But you loved Arnie," she said.

"He was my best mate…. once upon a time," said Ronnie.

Her initial concern had been with Ronnie, but suddenly Hazel felt something pulling at her own conscience, as she drifted off into her own acknowledgment of the sad news, "Poor Arnie," she said.

"When we were young, everyone saw me as the face of the Aces."

"Yeah, you hated that," she said, sarcastically.

"I'm serious," said Ronnie. "It was always Arnie pulling the strings. He sorted the music, the scooters and the girrr....clobber. He was the kingmaker. We were just a bunch of street mutts, but that boy made us feel like we were back street heroes.... up until three o'clock this afternoon that's what we would have always been."

"But you never went down to see them?"

Ronnie was stumped and, in light of his old friends' death, felt a little ashamed. He tried to conjure up a passable answer.

"I don't know. We just lost sight of each other," he said.

Hazel was following her own train of thought.

"I don't suppose you parted under the best of circumstances," she said.

Hazel's comment jolted him, like somebody suddenly turning the TV off half-way through a football match. It was out of keeping with Ronnie's current mindset, His response was unnecessarily defensive.

"Mick, maybe, but I never had a problem with Arnie. Nothing major anyway," he said

They both sat back and allowed themselves to be swallowed up into the familiar comfort of their sumptuous couch.

"At the end of the day, we were all trying to find the escape route. You had to believe you could win out. There was some bitterness that some people got left behind. Hope can be a cruel playmate," he said.
"Everyone evolves differently, that's just life," said Hazel.
"We've been right lucky though, haven't we, eh?" said Ronnie.
"Luck never found a quitter, we earned our way here," she replied.
Happiness is relative and there was relatively nothing she wanted from her old life in London, except of course, Ronnie. There was a deep subconscious understanding, that had conjoined them right from the get-go. They'd shared a wild and very private intensity that on occasion could prove to be quite combustible. When they set-off from South London, she had been the calm wind in his sails and he, the firm hand on the tiller. Their journey thus far had been an eventful one, they'd ploughed on through stormy seas, shipped water and hung on for dear life at times, but in their shared imagination, they'd always managed to keep sight of dry land.
Tentatively, Hazel breached the subject of Arnie's funeral, hoping her husband wouldn't make a rash decision he'd later regret. Strange, she thought, how going to a funeral might be just what he needed to lift him out of the gloom he'd been heaving around on his back, over the past few months.
"Mick said the funeral is on Friday," she said. "Don't you think you should be there, y'know, say your goodbyes?"
"Of course, we'll be there," he said, as if the question had been a stupid one.
"Then why didn't you pick up the...ahh, I don't get you," she said.

She stood up and they exchanged piercing glances, like the hoisting of old tribal banners. Before she trudged out of the room, Hazel turned back to get the measure of him, lost half in booze, half in thought but still fully Ronnie Diamond.
"When that puzzle of a man first darkened my door all those years ago," she said. "I wish he'd come with instructions. Really I do."

CHAPTER 2.
Last Song for a Local Hero.

Battersham, with its eight housing estates and enclaves of terraced housing, now crammed in seventy-eight thousand people, twenty thousand more than when Ronnie and Hazel lived there. To the north, a steady spread of gentrification had set in. Ronnie helped build some of the riverside properties that were being touted at one million pounds apiece. Factories and churches made way for estate agents and wine bars. South of the borough, on the other side of the train lines that carried commuters into the city, from Surrey, Sussex and beyond, nothing substantial had changed. There were security doors on the tower blocks and all the second-hand shops had disappeared, but it was still the same place Ronnie had once called home.

A swell of young lads, in grey hoodies and charcoal coloured baseball hats, gathered outside the Thompson Crematorium, milling around the hearse as Arnie's coffin was carried out and placed on a trolley. None of them looked particularly healthy, coughing and spluttering like a small flock of filthy London pigeons.

"A right bunch of Chavies," Ronnie whispered to Hazel.

"You were like them once upon a time," said Hazel.

Ronnie flashed her an injured look, before giving the once over to a trampy looking lad, with jeans hanging down exposing his pants, who was swigging from a can of beer while observing proceedings from afar. Ronnie thought back to the way his own dress sense and persona had been

virtually one and the same thing at his age. He winced at any possible comparison between himself and this slacker.
"Nah, these boys could never measure up to the cut of my cloth," said Ronnie.
A Hoodie, with a tear drop tattoo under his left eye, talked with Faye, Arnie's widow, who was dressed in traditional funereal black. Touching fifty, and just over five feet tall, Faye was almost as wide as she was high. The Hoodie had succumbed to an awkwardness, not uncommon on such occasions, and didn't seem to know where to direct his gaze, so he stared at his own feet.
"I wanted to wear a suit today, like, 'cept my bruvver needed it, like, for this job interview he's goin' to. It was Arnie what sorted it out for him, the interview. He was gunna come too but I told him to go for the job, like," said the Hoodie, in broad, modern-day, cockney.
"Arnie would be proud of you," said Faye.
She handed him a carrier bag and he nodded his appreciation.
"He used to say never let the clothes wear the man," said Faye.
"He always seemed to know what to say, like," said the Hoodie.
"Yeah, he did. Although he did tell a group of girl guides that it was what was underneath that mattered, and an angry dad came looking for him," said Faye, with a warm smile.
"He always gave us a laugh, eh? Even when he never meant to," said Faye.
The sudden loss of her husband of eighteen years, felt like a cold steel blade stabbing intermittently at her heart but, in and around the hurt and uncertainty, she experienced a warm glow from the deep respect being awarded to him.

When she was a youngster, she loved nothing better than watching TV programmes that recounted the lives of the rich and famous. It never seemed to be about the destination, always the journey. In a way, she hoped Arnie's funeral would be exactly that, a tribute. It was a great shame, she thought, that he wasn't here to listen to the outpouring of affection endowed upon him. She pondered at the fact that it was the closest most of us ever get to some kind of communal recognition and yet they wait until we're not even here to voice it.

Approximately sixty people shuffled in and filled out much of the plain and somewhat sterile crematorium. There'd been funerals she had attended where half-way through the proceedings she'd stolen a swift look at the order of service just to check she was at the right ceremony, such was the discrepancy between what was being said and who it was being buried. She hoped there would be none of that hypocrisy today. He'd been a rascal at times, there was no doubt about that, but he had such a happy-go-lucky demeanour it had been impossible to stay upset with him for long.

At the front of the sparsely decorated, high ceilinged room, Arnie's coffin was perched on a wooden trolley. Hazel and Ronnie shuffled in with Guzzler, a chipper podgy fellow, who couldn't seem to stand still.

Guzzler had shared in many of Ronnie's youthful escapades. He never held grudges and spent most of his time living in the moment. When Ronnie knew him, his most pressing aspirations had always been where his next mouthful of chow was coming from. He'd been christened Guzzler at the age of eight, after being caught devouring his classmates' packed lunches in a school store cupboard.

He'd grown into that name ever since. It was only really his wife, Tracey, who called him Jason.

"See the big fella on the end with the girl with the bump," said Guzzler.

He pointed out a couple at the other side of one of the benches. Ronnie nodded.

"That's my Ian and his missus, Diane," said Guzzler.

"Grandad Guzz, it's got a nice ring to it," said Ronnie, with a little chuckle.

"You and Hazel got any kids?" asked Guzzler.

"No." said Ronnie, avoiding opening up to that line of enquiry.

"I still can't believe you're actually here," said Guzzler.

Ronnie nodded towards the coffin.

"I can't believe *he's* in there."

"They might fit his body in there, but never his heart," said Guzzler, incessantly hopping from one foot to the other, like a little boy waiting for the cartoon to end before rushing to the loo. There was anxiety underneath the front he was putting on. If he stood still, the magnitude of his best friend's departure may have proved too much for him.

"I make you right there, my friend," said Ronnie.

Hazel nudged him to be silent as the vicar made his way towards the podium.

The vicar opened his book and began to read a sermon. Ronnie was busy exchanging nods and catching the eye of various other attendees. Old faces from his past, some of which, he was forced to squint at, as he cross-referenced them with their younger selves in his memory. His attempts to exchange greetings with Mick, a wiry tall man with a weather worn face, drew a blank.

The vicar was in full flow.

"Do not be dismayed, for I am your God. I will strengthen you and help you; I will uphold you with my righteous right hand."

Guzzler pulled a face and then whispered to Ronnie.

"Arnie would hate all this. He used to say that the only religion worth a toss was football, and that only made sense after three or four pints on a Saturday afternoon."

Oxford, A bald-headed black man, standing behind them, chipped in with a voice that would give Barry White a run for his money.

"The God squad's in full flow today. I think they offer a discount now if they can do a sales pitch before they send 'em on their way."

Various people shushed them, and they all fell silent. Ronnie reached out and squeezed Guzzler's hand, an affectionate gesture that took him by surprise. Hazel was scrabbling around in her handbag as the main door clanged loudly, and a swathe of heads turned in unison to see a pretty blonde woman in a slender black suit jacket and figure-hugging pencil skirt stride in and find a space amongst the congregation. Like someone spraying bullets, the sound of her high heels on the wooden floor cut through the sombre peace of the auditorium. She was feigning apology as she found a vacant space on one of the benches. This was one lady who knew how to make an entrance.

There were some of Ronnie's ex-girlfriends, one-night stands and old flames present, but by the look on his face he hadn't quite blown out the pilot light on this one. Oblivious to the intrusion, Hazel pulled a tissue out of her bag and dabbed her eyes.

"Come and see what the Lord has done," continued the vicar in his lofty tones. "The desolations he has brought on the earth. He makes wars cease to the ends of the earth. He breaks the bow and shatters the spear; He burns the shields with fire. He says, be still, and know that I am God."

The expression of raw sentiment was draining away, as the impersonal nature of the vicar's words was having the emotional impact of someone counting sheep. Ronnie wondered to himself why, in this day and age, vicars didn't come with a mute button. After about twenty minutes, the *Lamb of God* closed his book and was replaced at the podium by a voice from lower down society's pecking order, but closer to the heart of today's ceremony. The Hoodie had no book or notes to reference. His hands became objects that were suddenly alien to him. Eventually he just stuffed them in his pockets.

"I just wanted to say something about who Arnie was to me, and to loads of others like me. Arnie helped me out when I was havin' it tough, like…"

He was interrupted in mid-flow by a loud course voice at the back.

"Speak up, mate. We can't hear ya."

This was proceeded by a few murmurs of disapproval at the interruption. The Hoodie took a deep breath and continued, albeit not much louder than before.

"He didn't preach or lecture, except for when he tried to get us to listen to his horrible music. He just wanted to see us make a go of things. Round 'ere that ain't always easy. He was a good 'un."

Ronnie and Guzzler exchanged glances. The Hoodie had got their vote.

"He gave us his time. He looked out for us when no-one else was bovvered. Now, whenever I hear the sound of a Scooter drivin' by, I will think of Arnie. He will always be our Modfather. He was a good 'un."

"And so say all of us," said a triumphant voice in the crowd.

Ronnie was choked up, catching the escaping tears from his eyes in a tissue handed to him by Hazel. The more he thought about Arnie, the more annoyed he became with himself for losing touch. When you have money, proper money, there's normally a way to change the outcome of important things happen. But no amount of lucre was going to resurrect his old pal.

Someone started clapping, a few heads turned to their neighbours, as if seeking approval, before the place erupted in rapturous applause. Ronnie and Guzzler clapped vigorously, releasing a little of the pent-up energy that had been desperately seeking a moment in which to escape.

"I don't think you're supposed to clap at funerals," said Hazel.

"I Know," said Ronnie, as they both continued to applaud.

The Hoodie left the podium, stopped at the coffin to pull a battered old pair of red, white and blue Mod shoes out of a carrier bag, placing them gently on top of the wooden box. Head bowed, he returned to the pews, where snivelling was audible in every direction. There was a brief moment of silence before everyone's eyes were drawn to the mechanised maroon curtains slowly opening to swallow up the coffin. Snivelling was temporarily replaced by a communal deep intake of breath. Hazel grasped Ronnie's hand.

Within the darkest moment of sorrow, the solemn atmosphere was abruptly upended by the sound of the most unexpected upbeat song ever likely to appear on a funereal playlist.

"De, de, de, de, de, de...Blue is the colour, Football is the game...." came the music.

The deep gloom of sadness was temporarily pierced, as wide grins and stifled chuckles accompanied the anthem of Chelsea Football club's famous song. Heads rose to look around in disbelief at the surreal nature of the anthem being pumped out through the hall's speakers.

Guzzler beamed.

"Typical Arnie. He could pull a cold beer out of a volcano, that fella."

Ronnie, Guzzler and Oxford needed no reminder of the words and proudly sang their hearts out.

"So, cheer us on through the sun and rain, 'cause Chelsea, Chelsea is our name..."

Hazel turned to Ronnie. "Only in Battersham."

With the football ditty in full pelt, the curtain began to close on a little man of great stature.

Like most of the nicknames doled out in Battersham, Arnie had picked up his in a joke about his diminutive comparison with the enormous muscle-bound film star Arnold Schwarzenegger. Nicknames have always been a bit of a lottery, some stick and some don't, but from that moment on, no-one ever called him by his christened name. The official records would state that Wednesday 18 May, Ian Russell, case number 114328002 was cremated at 11.40 am. But what really mattered was the assembled people present who were reflecting on a generous soul who gave everything he had and more to earn the moniker 'Our Arnie.'

Both Ronnie and Hazel's parents were dead. Working-class people weren't supposed to live forever. They'd give you a pension as long as you didn't abuse the privilege and overstay your welcome. Middle class folk were sent a telegram on their hundredth birthday; A working class centurion was more likely to receive an eviction notice.

She recalled a time when her father was out of work and caught in benefit limbo. He wanted to work but needed the money to see him through until he got paid, but the bureaucrats messed him around so much, he got neither the job or the dole cheque, and she found that soup was on the dinner menu a hell of a lot during that time. It was no laughing matter, but later he would joke about it being his gap year, particularly as the phrase was beginning to be banded about by middle class teens, who hadn't ever done a proper day's work but fancied a year off all the same. Hazel's Dad was a very practical man, a stoic who never made a fuss. His death was made starker by the fact he'd kept secret the cancer that had invaded his body, like a terrorist outfit, that took him down one organ at a time. One minute he was there, next he was dust. Right now, she'd give anything to be that girl hanging around his garage, while he tinkered with the various bits of metal and rubber that he would weld into, what he considered, a road-worthy motorbike.

As they shuffled along towards the exit, Ronnie stole a quick look at where Roxy had been seated and felt a twinge of disappointment that she was no longer there. Guzzler nudged Ronnie from his thoughts.

"Hope Faye's put on a decent spread. I am Hank Marvin," said Guzzler.

Ronnie gave his belly a pat.

"Some things never change eh?"

Ronnie and Hazel were slowly walking away from the crematorium when they were joined by Arnie's widow, Faye, who linked arms with Ronnie as they ambled along.

"How are you baring up? We were all so sad when the news came through," said Hazel.

"None of it feels real at the moment," said Faye.

"He'll be sorely missed," said Ronnie. As the words escaped his mouth, he thought how clichéd and small that phrase felt for such a colossal event.

"He missed you," she replied, adding guilt to all the other sensations that had been milling around since he stepped foot back on what was once, very much, home soil.

"I should have come around more. You never expect...well..."

"He'd be glad you came," said Faye. "You'll come back to the flat, won't you?"

Hazel was quick to confirm. "Of course, we will."

Like a film star on opening night, everyone wanted a piece of the widow and soon enough Faye was accosted by an old man in a trilby hat who clasped his hands around Faye's as they slowly wandered off, deep in conversation.

Ronnie and Hazel walked on. Ronnie acting like he'd been trying to assemble a jigsaw in his head only to realise that some of the pieces had fallen down the nether reaches of the sofa of his mind.

"I knew it would be different, but Battersham's really changed. It's kind'a disappointing and intriguing in one stroke. It's like opening your old photo albums and finding pictures you've never seen before," said Ronnie.

He motioned to the tower blocks which had a colourful plastic cladding added to their exterior. No doubt the work of some government turd-polishing department.

"Everything's been knocked down or coated in plastic," said Ronnie.

"I think that's what passes for urban regeneration these days," said Hazel.

"It's like a poor man's Legoland," said Ronnie.

Ronnie was scouting the area like a big game hunter, as he sought out old landmarks and reminisced about those features that had fallen foul of the planners. This wasn't the Battersham he missed; that would only come by re-engaging with the people, like Faye, Guzzler and Oxford. They passed a group of worshippers in long robes hurrying on their way to the nearby Mosque, jabbering loudly in an alien dialect.

There was a recognisable shift in the local demographics, there had been a large influx of new immigrants since he had lived here. He'd grown up in a multi-racial community as part of the ethnic majority. He had never really given it much thought, but now, on his return, he found that his tribe was now in the minority.

Bizarrely, seeing the religious attire of the worshippers. reminded Ronnie of the infamous fancy-dress pub crawls of his father which would now be considered extremely offensive. His dad and his friends would wear old bed sheets, dressing gowns or anything they could get their hands on, some even blacked-up on occasion. No matter what their chosen outfits were, someone always ended up in bandages by the end of the night.

"It feels so weird being back. I don't know what I was expecting but it wasn't quite like this."

"What did you think, there'd be Pearly Kings eating jellied eels and singing *Knees up Mother Brown* on every corner? We still lived here when all that went south," said Hazel.

Ronnie and Hazel made their way through an alleyway, Ronnie's eyes scouring the graffiti on the walls until he found an example of his own ancient handiwork. The word 'Aces' with a Mod target was barely legible, faded into the brickwork and covered in hip-hop tags. While she was almost retching at the dank smell of urine, he was off romanticising his days in the gang, like a piper on the battlefield carrying the tune while stepping over the slain corpses of his comrades.

They escaped the musty exterior corridor into an open space, that contained a communal garden, about half the size of theirs, that was supposed to serve the hundreds of families that surrounded it. There was more grass in the joints, being passed around by the youths sitting on the vandalised playground equipment, than on the adjoining green. Nothing grew right in the shadow of Chibnall House, an ugly foreboding concrete block of flats, with its garish newly adorned pink plastic trim. If you put this place under an X-ray you could still make out the tracks of Margaret Thatcher's iron fingernails, where she'd dragged them, like the claw of a bulldozer, through the very heart of the indigenous community.

"Funerals always attract more than just the sadness of those who have passed, you know what I mean?" said Hazel.

"Yeah, but it is good to see the old faces, makes me think how much I've missed them, y'know. I don't know why I stayed away so long," said Ronnie.

Hazel's face betrayed a restrained aversion to the deceit of his self-delusion.

"You do, Ronnie, you do," she muttered under her breath.

CHAPTER 3.
The Wake – Revolving Doors.

Outside the lifts at Chibnall house, Ronnie pressed the call button and listened for its familiar slow clunking sound echoing down the lift shaft, like the waking of an old mechanical giant. They were soon joined by Guzzler and Mick, a man whose gait was determined by how many grudges he was carrying at that particular time.
"Talk of the Devil… Well, if it ain't Battersham's most wanted," said Mick.
"McPherson," replied Ronnie formally.
With pleasantries exchanged they did what they'd always done. It was the verbal crossing of swords. Mick tapped Ronnie's girth.
"See, I heard you'd gained a few pounds since last I seen you."
He looked to Guzzler who was smirking. Ronnie acknowledged the throwing down of the gauntlet. He revelled in Battersham's reputation for cockney banter, sharp wit and cutting jibes, it was something he sorely missed since edging his way into the polite, beige-tinted, society of suburbia. Ronnie raised his eyebrows in the direction of Mick's hairline.
"What I've gained in pounds you've lost in strands."
"Bit bare up there yourself, mate," replied Mick.
"Now, now boys," said Hazel, keen to keep things on an affable footing.
Ronnie leaned over and gave the lift button another press.

"I see this lift still gets the huff," said Ronnie.

"It's her time of the month," returned Mick.

They were joined by Bulldog, a skinny chap hiding deep dark eyes under a pair of thick-rimmed tinted glasses. His hollowed cheekbones gave Ronnie the impression he'd aged twice as fast as everyone else. He wore a tie-less polo shirt with its top button fastened Mod-style.

"Fellas," he said, before taking another drag on a roll-up. He eagerly shook hands with Ronnie.

"Alright Bulldog," said Ronnie.

"Yeah, safe as," said Bulldog.

Bulldog gave Hazel a peck on the cheek. As brief as it was, it had been as welcome as a waft from a blocked drain. Coughing into her hand, she tried diplomatically to camouflage a wince at the awful stench of his breath. If he was kissing anything else tonight, she hoped it would be a toothbrush.

"Good to see the Bulldog's still barking," said Ronnie, clasping a hand across his old friend's shoulder.

"Oh, he's barking alright," said Guzzler.

Bulldog pressed Ronnie on his past aloofness.

"You're a hard man to track down. I spent ages searching for you on the internet..."

"I don't do all that social media stuff," said Ronnie.

Ronnie shrugged him off, recalling the avalanche of desperate messages he had ignored.

"I thought someone like you would be connected," said Bulldog.

"I have trouble enough dodging people in real life," said Ronnie.

Bulldog stubbed his fag out on the floor and pulled out his mobile phone and attached it to a selfie stick.

"Group up," he said.

"Give it a break, Bulldog," said Mick.

"A quick snap for old times, it's not every day we're graced with the presence of such esteemed company," pleaded Bulldog.

"You after a photo or a career change?" said Guzzler.

Mick turned to Ronnie and Hazel.

"One-man paparazzi is our Bulldog. He must have the biggest collection of pointless photographs on the planet."

Eventually they complied, and Bulldog showed Ronnie the resulting photo.

"The Aces together again." said Bulldog.

"And to think, all it took was for Arnie to kick the bucket," said Mick.

"Leave it out, Mick," said Guzzler, only too aware of the target of his bitter taunt.

The lift arrived and in the corner of the graffiti-laden metal box was a filthy Junkie lying half-comatose, like a discarded bin bag. They all piled in, Hazel and her queasy stomach trying to keep her distance from the dosser and the grimy walls.

The vagrant started to groan some inaudible nonsense, his arm out in a half-arsed attempt to beg. When out and about, Ronnie often put his hand in his pocket at such moments and thought about rolling off a twenty and dropping it in the Vagrant's lap. Done the wrong way this could appear vulgar, and he was conscious not to be interpreted as showboating in front of his old pals, some of whom might have been only slightly less desperate for the cash. Homelessness had been just as prominent when he'd lived around here. Tramps were as much a part of the street furniture as lampposts or post-boxes. Ronnie had stuck by the adage 'Never money up a scrounger - lest you want 'em hanging around ya.' Throw them a coin or two and they would haunt your every move or make out you were dear old mates whenever they spotted you in the street. It was the sort of thing that could cramp your style when taking a new girl out on a date. That said, Ronnie had often handed them his half-eaten fish and chips when crawling home from the pub.

"What did Arnie actually die of?" asked Hazel.

"He was working at the School," said Guzzler.

"Arnie was a Teacher?" asked Ronnie.

"Didn't you hear? He was head of his own department and everything," said Mick.

"really?" said Ronnie.

"Yeah, Mops and brooms," said Mick, chuckling.

"He was a Janitor," said Guzzler, a little put out at Mick's insensitivity.

The dosser was becoming more vociferous with his pleading, before Mick, who clearly knew him, promised him a few quid if he 'kept schtum.' From that moment on, he was as silent as he was malodorous.

"But how did Arnie die?" said Ronnie.

"A Vending machine fell on him. Crushed him," said Guzzler.

"Jesus," said Ronnie.

"That's so awful," said Hazel.

"I told him them Mars bars would kill him one day," quipped Mick.

They all struggled to stifle laughter. The lift arrived at the sixth floor and they all clambered out on to the landing leaving the grumbling Junkie in their wake.

"Stick him a couple of bob, would you Ronnie? I'd do it meself, but I woke up this morning and couldn't remember which one of my yachts I'd left me wallet on," said Mick, with a wry grin.

Ronnie obliged, but as he retraced his paces back to hand the vagrant some cash, he felt like he'd been mugged by the way Mick had played him. Arksdean had softened his senses.

In the narrow hallway of Arnie's flat, Bulldog was deep in conversation with Ronnie. Behind them in the kitchen, Hazel was chatting to Faye and her sister Joanna, as they uncovered plates of food and made tea and coffee for no-one in particular. The place was clean but sparse. It reminded Hazel of her own parent's flat where money had been so tight, you'd be up on a murder charge if you were caught helping yourself to an extra biscuit or flicked the electric fire on to two bars instead of the ubiquitous one. She hated it, but the experience certainly made her appreciate all the comfort she enjoyed these days. It was an uneasy feeling being so close to it now.

No sooner had they entered Arnie's flat, Bulldog began offloading an emotional cargo on to Ronnie. There was a mania about Bulldog's need purge himself of this burden.
"I just wanted to, y'know, about all the hassle I gave ya, I didn't mean to, what I'm trying to say is I'm sorry." said Bulldog.

It was a line of conversation Ronnie clearly didn't want to indulge.

"It's alright, mate. Don't worry about it," he said.

Bulldog spewed his words out in such a hurry that they almost tripped over each other.

"Ron, I was a bloody letch. I weren't a good mate. I'm ashamed. Y'know, all that badgering, the verbals and that..."

Ronnie held a palm up in a hasty attempt to stop Bulldog in his tracks, before throwing an arm around his shoulder.

"Whoa, whoa... I'm just glad you're through the other side..." He said.

Caution suddenly pulled Ronnie's words short. A shiver ran down his back that made him feel like the sucker who'd just spotted the swerve in the small print of a timeshare agreement he'd just signed. Was he being led up a path? The ones that ended with the pledge 'I'm doing ok, but if I could just borrow some money...' If Bulldog was on the highway to hell Ronnie had no intention of paying the petrol.

"How's it going, I mean, still fighting the good fight?"

He was almost as tentative as Bulldog in his probing. Like an evangelist, Bulldog delighted in extolling the virtues of his new lease of life.

"I'll admit it, I've walked with heavy footsteps," said Bulldog. "You see Smiffy, the crackhead in the lift, he weren't always like that. He used to run his old man's video shop. I was like he is now. I hit rock bottom and every day I thought about ending it, but I'm still here. Been clean for five years now.

"That's great, mate," said Ronnie.

"It's 'cause of me mum, really," said bulldog.

Ronnie was genuinely pleased and more than a little relieved his old friend wasn't going to hit him with the latest addict's begging routine.

"Five years? I'm chuffed for you, you're looking well, mate," said Ronnie.

He was being kind. Ronnie had seen healthier roadkill.

"Cheers, mate."

Bulldog pulled out his selfie stick.

"What's with all the photos?" asked Ronnie.

"Me counsellor, Karen, it was her idea. The demons hate happy pictures," he said.

He held it up and snapped a photo of the two of them.

Hazel was sipping timidly at a glass of wine as she chatted with Faye and Tracey, a middle-aged fat woman with red hair.
"So, what do you do?" asked Tracey.
"Work? I'm in insurance," said Hazel.
"They phone me more than my kids do," said Faye.
Smiling, Tracey mimicked an Indian accent while holding a phone to her ear.
"Ve heard you were in an accident and vant to help you claim tousands of monies..."
Hazel smiled.
"No, I'm not one of those miscreants. I specialise in Equestrian cover."
Tracey nodded, but couldn't think of what that meant.
"She insures 'orses, Trace," said Faye.
Feeling a little stupid Tracey batted her off. "I know."
"Do you ride?" Asked Faye.
"Not as much as I'd like to," said Hazel.
"Such beautiful creatures. When I was a kid, this Gypsy boy at school..." said Faye.
"They're called travellers now," said Tracey, interjecting with a faux reprimand.
Faye waved her jibe away.
"Whatever. Anyway, I was the only one who bovvered talking to him at school, this Gypsy traveller boy, so he let me ride his 'orse. It was a grouchy old fing, but it seemed to like me. Then one day his Uncle asked me to marry him, I mean I was only ten. I never went back after that."
Tracey smiled and theatrically placed both hands upon her heart.

"Life could have been so different, eh, Faye?" she said, chuckling.

"I could certainly do with some lucky heather about now," said Faye.

Hazel considered whether the time she'd spent here would qualify her for remission. She took a small sip of wine, placed the glass by the sink, and said her farewells. She gave them each a hug and Faye thanked her for coming. Hazel retreated out of the kitchen, exchanged a quick goodbye with Ronnie, who barely skipped a beat while holding court with his old compadres in the living room. Hazel was free. Liberated from the claustrophobia of duty. It wasn't that she didn't like them, or considered them somehow lesser than herself, it was just everything she had in common with them revolved around a shared upbringing that Hazel had long since filed away under 'ancient history'.

Hazel escaped through the front door and off into the walkway with its panoramic views of London.

Hazel mused over the fortunes people would cough up to attain such a view, but not the apartment or the location in its current state. It would take a lot to gentrify this part of the city, but she didn't doubt that it was on the radar of at least a few unscrupulous property developers whose biggest dilemma would be where, and how quickly they could dump the current set of undesirable residents. Their fate would, no doubt, be similar to those already ripped out of the riverside developments to make way for million-pound Thames-side penthouses. Most of those folks were offloaded to non-descript rabbit hutches in new towns at the back end of nowhere, many miles from their roots.

She walked to the lift, pressed the call button, then leaned her back on a wall and released a sigh of relief. She checked her watch then looked up as the elevator door juddered open, revealing the same filthy Junkie they saw on the way up. He was out cold in the corner of the lift. She turned her back and headed for the stairs.

Inside the flat, Tracey and Faye sang the praises of Hazel and how they'd always admired her, in a race to add ever-increasing layers of adoration.

Ronnie and Bulldog were let loose on Arnie's record collection, each record they pulled out of the box came with a boys-own tale. They both marvelled at the depth of his vinyl horde. Each song was a stepping-stone back to who they once were.

Ronnie left the front room and passed a huddle of folk in the hallway. Others were picking at the finger food in the kitchen. A group of younger people, on the stairs, were chatting to each other via the ever-changing screens of their mobile phones, as he passed them on his way to the toilet. No-one objected if you stopped to chat, but membership was only temporary to these micro social clubs.

On his return, Ronnie stopped off in the kitchen to load up on supplies. Apart from the frostiness of Mick, everyone had given him a genuinely warm welcome. It made him feel less distant from them, but he remained neither in their camp nor out of it.

Ronnie carried a bottle of beer and a glass of wine into the living room, where Bulldog was master of the decks, spinning tracks that had worn away more of his shoe leather than all the Postmen in the borough get through in a lifetime. Ronnie handed the glass of wine to Roxy and made a space for himself on the sofa, that hadn't previously existed, between her and Guzzler.

"So, where's Hazel?" asked Roxy. "Don't tell me. She took one look at this lot and decided to escape before it got messy?"

"Something like that," he said.

"Not daft, that one," she said.

"I looked for you after the funeral, but you did a vanishing act before I could catch up with you."

"You were looking for me? That's so sweet," said Roxy. Ronnie felt himself transform into a blushing adolescent.

"Well, y'know, I just wanted to say hi and that."

She smiled at him.

"I thought you might be holding court at the gossip fest in the kitchen," he said.

She leaned towards him and spoke into his ear, just loud enough to avoid competing with the record player.

"I've got better things to do with my life. It's all tea, cake and middle-aged spread in there." She patted her hand on Ronnie's thigh and he found himself lost under her spell, like a tongue-tied teenager.

"Anyway," she continued. "I'm happy where I am, thanks."

"You look amazing," he spluttered, just as the record had been whipped from the turntable, magnifying his statement.

"Thank you. You're not looking so bad yourself."

"Really, you haven't changed a bit," he said, a little quieter. A nervous energy had befallen him, a dry mouth encouraged him to take another sip of beer.

"I have to make an effort, it's what my clients expect," said Roxy.

Clients? He thought. Was she in the fashion industry, a hostess or even a high-class hooker? He was both ashamed and excited by his filthy flight of fantasy.

"That and the sea air…does wonders for your skin you know."
"You're no longer in Battersham then?"
She gave a chuckle.
"I ankled this place years ago. I've got a Beautician business on the coast, in Brighton."
Ronnie's eyes lit up. Brighton had been their Mecca, a mythical place of Mod folklore. It was the battleground of legendary rumbles against Punks and Skinheads, and where he'd enjoyed raucous nights jumping around to the best Mod bands of the time. Brighton held so many milestones in the memory. It was also where Ronnie and Roxy had spent more than a night or two of wild unadulterated teenage passion.
"Brighton? Wow… I haven't been there in ages," said Ronnie.
"You should come down. I'll show you around if you like."
"Really?" said Ronnie, hoping it wasn't a throw away offer said out of politeness.
"Sure…. anytime," she said.
For a moment Ronnie was hopelessly lost in her smile.
"I might just take you up on that," he said.
"You and Hazel fix a date and let me know," said Roxy.
The mention of Hazel's name rocked him from the cloud he'd been perched on. Roxy pulled out a pen and took his hand in hers. She could have used a scrap of paper or written on the order of service from the funeral, but instead she thought carefully about where best to leave her mark. She scribbled her number down, the pen just about holding out for the last digit before the ink supply dried up. He was a little drunk, a little excited and completely lost in the idea of Roxy in Brighton. Roxy took a sip of the wine and almost spat it back into the glass.

"Oh, god. What *is* this?"

Ronnie offered to get her something else, but when he motioned to get up, Roxy put an arm across him, insisting he remain seated.

"It's alright, I'll get myself an upgrade. Possibly something without that distinctive bouquet you get with Plonk de la River Thames, or whatever this rat juice is."

Mesmerised by the sway of her delectable curves, Ronnie couldn't keep his eyes off her as she glided towards the kitchen. Guzzler broke his trance with a chiding look. Ronnie feigned innocence, like a boy with a chocolate mouth insisting it hadn't been him who'd raided the biscuit tin. Guzzler had his number.

"Ease up, mate. Thoughts like that come with a price tag that even you might not be able to stomach."

Roxy confidently swaggered into the kitchen and swiftly dumped the remainder of her glass into the sink. Faye, Tracey and two other women were chatting in the kitchen. As a young woman, Roxy soon learned that if she wasn't going to be passed over or ignored in life, she had better find a voice. She made sure wherever she went, that everyone knew, you messed with Roxy Nostos at your peril.

"Hey, Faye. You okay? I just wondered if you had any Sauvignon?"

Faye smiled sweetly and turned to her friend, Tracey, and pulled a face.

"Sauvignon, Trace?"

Tracey drew a blank as she scanned the bottles of cheap wine on the sideboard.

"Or a Pinot Grigio, maybe, just whatever really," said Roxy, knowing her presence in Battersham wasn't always greeted with open arms, she was still trying to be diplomatic.

Tracey offered her a bottle of cheap plonk with a CostSavers label on it, but scouring the bottles from a distance herself, Roxy spotted a non-supermarket brand and vied for that.

"You keepin' busy?" said Faye.

"Flat out," said Roxy.

"You still doing the hairdressers?" asked Tracey.

"Beauty Salons, yeah, I've got two in Brighton now, one in Bournemouth and I'm opening one in Torquay soon."

"Torquay aye? You must be raking it in," said Tracey.

"I love it. I mean it's hard work, but I've never been frightened of that."

"Well done you, eh?" said Tracey, through gritted teeth.

Faye took Roxy's left hand and rubbed her wedding finger. "Not found your Prince Charmin' yet, then?"

She let go of her hand. Roxy smiled and picked up her wine glass.

"Oh, you know me, happy go lucky," said Roxy.

Roxy was used to this pantomime every time she'd returned to Battersham. It had upset her in the past but now she saw that bitter cloud as something that could only rain on them. As soon as Roxy stepped out of the kitchen, the knives were out.

"Four Salons? And have you seen the car she rolls around in? How did the likes of her manage that? That's what I'd like to know." Snapped Faye.

"Like she says, Faye, she's been flat out... on her back," said Tracey.

Swift and clean, the assassination satisfactorily complete, the two of them shared a little chuckle. "You are awful, Trace," said Faye.

Somewhere in the evening it had been decided that a visit to the deceased's lock-up was of paramount importance. A small party ventured out into the bowels of the housing estate, through a myriad of alleyways and past a boarded-up pub. Ronnie, Mick, Guzzler and Bulldog each stopped to relieve themselves under a heavily graffitied footbridge that rose above the train tracks. They casually sauntered on into a wide courtyard, circumnavigating a large disused industrial sized metal bin, the type they had all referred to as Daleks when they were young. Finally, they found themselves outside a rickety old, shuttered unit that someone had spray-painted a penis on. This was Arnie's lock up.

Guzzler slid the key into the padlock and pulled back the shutter. Behind him, Mick, Bulldog and a bleary-eyed Ronnie, gazed in awe as he flicked a switch and a much cherished 1963 Piaggio Vespa GS 160 MK2 Scooter dazzled into view. White with red trim, it was in pristine condition, dazzling like a magnified toy.

"It's beautiful," said Ronnie, mesmerised.

It instantly passed the auditions to star in this week's dreams. With a grinding clang, Guzzler let go of the chains and the shutter closed behind them.

"He loved that thing like a boy loves his dog," said Mick.

Ronnie's eyes were drawn to a red, white and blue target and Scooter design stencilled on one wall. It was unlikely to give the street artist, Banksy, a cold sweat, but it was a statement Ronnie appreciated none the less. In the corner, a mannequin was dressed in a Korean war U.S. Army green parka coat. Where a sergeant's stripes would have originally appeared, the sacred 'Battersham aces' woven patch was affixed in pride of place.

"Like Arnie always said, them days meant the most," said Guzzler

"Mick's still got his Scooter, ain't ya Mick?" said Bulldog.

"Me Scooter?" said Mick. "Yeah, it's like a lazy teenager... bit particular about when it wants to work."

Guzzler pointed to an old Lambretta that looked like it was winning the battle to relocate to the junk yard.

"Arnie was helping me get this thing going," said Guzzler.

"That thing should be on a life support machine," joked Bulldog.

"That ain't ever going to be road worthy. There's more life in that Lift Junkie than in that sack of crap," said Mick.

"We'll see," said Guzzler, defensively.

Ronnie swung a leg over, straddling Arnie's Vespa. He was pleased he'd successfully managed it in the one go, such was his state of inebriation.

"Ain't this the bollocks though, eh?" he said.

In his mind's eye he could visualise himself living the dream, leading a parade of Mods along Brighton's sea front.

"Arnie was always on about reforming the Aces. He said he tried to get hold of you a few years back, Ronnie," said Guzzler.

Ronnie looked embarrassed.

"He was forever talking up a ride-out to the seaside," said Guzzler.

"He also said he'd manage Chelsea one day," said Mick, sarcastically.

"Not a bad idea, though," charged a freshly enthused Ronnie.

"What? Us lot, a ride out to Margate?" said Bulldog, with more than a hint of scepticism.

By now, Ronnie was beginning to get high on the idea.

"No. Brighton. It's got to be Brighton," said Ronnie.
"I know drunk talk when I hear it... I invented much of it," said Mick.
"I ain't driven a Scooter in donkey's," said Bulldog.
Then Guzzler uttered the words that Ronnie knew would green light the adventure.
"We could scatter Arnie's ashes down there. He would love that."
There was a pause for consideration, Guzzler and Ronnie were sold on the idea but Bulldog and Mick, who was shaking his head to the contrary, were not so easily convinced.
"Don't listen to Mick, he can't leave Battersham without getting a nosebleed," said Guzzler.
Ronnie gestured at Mick.
"Come on, what ever happened to Mister 'Anything goes?'"
"Everything's gone," he said.
Ronnie pointed at Bulldog who was trying to re-light his roll-up.
"And what about his good friend 'the Care-Free kid?' I loved those blokes. I'd like to see them fellas again."
Mick might have been loosened up by the drink, but he played the evening like a police surveillance job. He felt he had Ronnie sussed. He could see how this would go. Talk was cheap, Ronnie would get everyone pumped up on the promise of the second coming, they'd sit up into the early hours recanting old war glories, making big plans and then by the morning he'd disappear like so much crematorium smoke, never to be seen again.
He didn't need us, he had his princess, his mansion and his pot of gold, thought Mick. When he reached the promise land, he didn't send word for the rest of the posse to join him. Twenty years of silence had proved that. No, things

needed saying and if there was one man on the manor who told it like it was, that man was Mick.

"You emigrated," Mick said to Ronnie.

Awkwardness played over Ronnie's face as Mick's verbal uppercut caught him off guard.

"D'ya go abroad then, Ronnie?" asked Guzzler, completely out of tune with the situation.

Bulldog looked at Guzzler, shook his head and groaned.

"Well I dunno, do I?" said Guzzler.

Ronnie, his ego deflating like a balloon that had just been acquainted with some drawing pins, withdrew himself from the seat of the scooter.

"Look, I know it's been a while," said Ronnie.

"A while?" Replied Mick. "Last time we saw you, Chelsea were shit, Thatcher was still terrorising people from Downing Street and Richard Branson was floggin' moody records down the Portobello Market."

"I always meant to keep in touch, but you know how it goes," pleaded Ronnie.

Ronnie's words slid off Mick like greasy eggs from a Teflon pan.

"No Ron. How does it go?"

"All I'm saying is I don't want it to be another funeral before I see you lot again,"

"Well, we ain't goin' nowhere," replied Mick.

CHAPTER 4.
Blocked Paths and New Adventures.

Hazel and Jane, a tall, willowy brunette, in her late forties, were sipping coffee in Hazel's plush modern kitchen. Jane was sifting through some of Hazel's surplus clothes that she was getting rid of. It wasn't that Hazel didn't like the clothes, she adored them, but she had finally given up on the idea that she was ever going to drop the two sizes she needed to fit into them.

The walls were adorned with framed photographs of the horses Hazel had either owned or ridden. A beautiful bouquet of Lilies, Roses and Carnations lay on kitchen table. They were a statement of apology from Ronnie. He rarely bought flowers for Hazel, and when pressed he would state that although he didn't often come home laden with bouquets, he'd bought her a massive garden full of the darned things.

When Ronnie and Hazel dropped anchor in the quaint old English village of Arkesdean, approximately twenty years ago, Jane became the keystone of Hazel's social circle. It was an open secret that she thought her husband, Anthony, was a crashing bore. She made up for his personality disorder by exuding hers and generally living it up at every opportunity. She was the epitome of the 'kept woman' and she loved it. She was probably the only woman to ever wear a Feminist t-shirt ironically.

"You sure you want to part with this? It's still got its tags on," asked Jane, as she measured up to a figure hugging electric blue dress.

"I hate to admit it but size twelve is an old companion I lost touch with years ago," said Hazel.

"Rubbish. You always look fantastic," said Jane.

Jane wasn't one of those people who punished themselves with a diet of fresh air and lettuce, Jane ate like a horse, yet somehow, she remained as lean as a Greyhound.

A clanking noise from outside drew Jane's attention.

"Ronnie's in the garage tinkering with his past. He's been stalking memory lane ever since they cremated Arnie, an old friend of ours from London," said Hazel.

Outside, a desperate looking Ronnie was attempting to resuscitate his old Vespa Scooter. It had once been his pride and joy, but after years of neglect, covered up in a dusty corner of their garage, he dragged it out into the daylight only to find it rusty and dated. It was a relic that didn't want unearthing and its exposure somehow diminished its legend.

As Hazel looked out from the kitchen window, she could see that the only thing holding it together was Ronnie's hope.

"If he gets that old death trap going, he might end up joining Arnie earlier than he'd imagined," said Hazel.

Jane placed a spangley top on to a small pile of clothes on the table and picked up a skirt.

"He's a man," said Jane. "First, it's sex with everything, then chips with everything and then everything gets a good dousing of melancholy. It's par for the course."

A 'bing' sound emanated from a laptop on the kitchen table, but Hazel ignored it.

It had taken a while assimilating in Arksdean, but early on she'd bonded with Jane, who was always on hand to give Hazel the lowdown on all the high-profile residents, describing them as if they were suspects in a murder case that she was charged with solving. Villages often have a reputation for being cliquey and Arksdean was more parochial than most. Hazel soon found that in this part of merry old England, snobbery was a religion, and in Arksdean they were mostly Orthodox.

Jane warned her about the travelling band of Gypsies who turned up each year with a new rouse to get their grubby little mitts into the pockets of the gullible and those who thought they were above such trickery. Her most stringent warning however, was reserved for the local Vicar whose wrath was fiercer than his masters' when it came to those who failed to succumb to the procuring of his tithe. Ronnie, who'd always fancied himself as street smart soon fell afoul of both parties.

Ronnie had the gift of the gab and could make friends in an empty field, but even he had to dial down his Cockney inflection. It wasn't something Ronnie took lightly. He was sick of the bad guys on British TV always having working class London accents. It seemed to be that if the writers or directors wanted someone to sound like an idiot or a psycho, they'd adorn that character with a Cockney accent. Neither of them were ashamed of their roots, quite the opposite, but even they realised they'd have to tolerate a few superficial compromises if Ronnie's local property career was going to gain leverage.

Hazel took a sip of coffee and flicked open the lid of her laptop.

"An old friend suddenly passing away could give anyone a little jolt," said Jane.

"It's just, we're different people now. I have nothing in common with them and frankly, I don't want them impinging on our life now," said Hazel, looking down at the screen as her Facebook page snapped into view.
"See, this is what I mean. I've just had a friend request from Bulldog," said Hazel.
Jane pulled a sardonic face.
"You have a friend called Bulldog?"
"He's about as fierce as a slightly miffed butterfly, but it's not the point, I don't really want him on my social media feed," said Hazel.
"Then don't accept."
"I always feel obliged. I hate to appear rude."
"I have to admit I have about thirty people on mine that would come last in a 'Spot the Jane' competition," said Jane.
Ronnie hated social media. It was a bug bear for him, and he had bored Hazel enough about it to know that her little forays online would be best enjoyed as a guilty secret.
Hazel summonsed Jane away from the garment she was sizing up and drew her attention to her computer screen.
"Get this... Bulldog turned up at the funeral with a selfie stick. I mean, come on."
Disparagingly, Jane pulled a face, "Yep, that's definitely weird," she said.

As dusk approached, Hazel looked out at a majestic sunset that cast its fiery glow over the surrounding fields. The thing she loved most was the sense of space. The 360-degree vista atop a hill, with the nearest neighbours out of sight and almost a mile away. She always found something in all the seasons to wonder at. When the snow came and cast out its pristine white blanket, it was as picturesque as any Christmas card she had ever marvelled at as a child. The contrast in London couldn't have been more vivid, snow there turned to black mush almost as soon as it had fallen from the sky, like its beauty was subject to an ugly tax. When it rained in Arksdean, she could almost feel the ground breathe and grow. Autumn, possibly her favourite season, was a blood shot riot of amber and gold. There was only one thing missing from the scenario and that was the sound of children playing, particularly their children playing.

Hazel's infertility was an enigma. All tests had shown that there wasn't any practical reason preventing her from falling pregnant. They had tried everything from traditional remedies and ancient superstitions to the rigorous demands of five sets of clinical IVF treatment. Nothing worked. Ronnie and his ego ensured everyone knew that he was holding up his end of the bargain. His merchandise had been drawn, cut and analysed to confirm he was among the top ten percent of fertile males in the land. It was like having the keys to a Rolls Royce that never left its parking space in the garage. Similar to so many other desperate wannabe-parents, the emotional burden of their predicament almost tore them apart.

Jane left, laden with clothing while Ronnie continued to tweak his Scooter in their double garage. He had his back to Hazel, who came out to discuss the evening's dinner plans.

"I see your ex was at the funeral," said Hazel.

As if on a high wire, Ronnie suddenly felt an urge to control his breathing, knowing even the smallest deviation in tone or expression could find him freefalling into an unwanted grilling that risked ending up in a slanging match or a two-week spell of freezing temperatures in the house.

"Roxy? Yeah, she was there," he said casually, busying himself as to avoid her advanced system of facial recognition. The CIA could learn a thing or two from her ability to read him. He tightened a screw on the engine panel.

"Have much to say for herself, did she? said Hazel.

"She said hello, that was about it," he said.

Hazel eyed him carefully. He stood up and attempted a smooth gear-change, briefly glancing at Hazel with an optimistic declaration.

"I think this is it," he said.

He mounted the Scooter and gave the pedal a strong kick. The engine made a brave attempt to appease him. A crunching noise was followed by the pathetic excuse for a bang and an exhausted puff of black smoke crawled out from its pipe and the machine returned to the slumbering state of hibernation it had enjoyed for many a year.

"Oh, bollocks," spat Ronnie, as the shape was suddenly lost from his shoulders.

"You sure you really want to do this?" said Hazel

Ronnie shot her the most cutting glare he could muster.

"all right, all right..." she said.

His lust for re-adventure was confirmed. She didn't want to appear like the spanner in his works, but she was clear this was an escapade she had no intention of riding pillion on. He would have to rekindle old friendships and see them for what they were before he could truly bury this ghost. She just hoped he could get out the other end in one piece.

He pulled his hand across his head and sighed, his earlier exuberance now vanished, like the boy who dreamed of a dog for Christmas and watched as it slipped its lead and ran off down the street never to be seen again.

Ronnie picked up his green fishtail parka coat from a nearby work bench and held it up to show Hazel. Once the crowning glory of his Mod uniform, it was a tattered shadow of its former self and boasted a large frayed hole in the middle of its back.

"The Scooter's fucked, Moths have eaten my Parka and I can't fit in to any of my old suits."

Hazel just about managed to stifle a laugh.

"What did you expect?" said Hazel.

"I don't know," said Ronnie, despondently.

"If this means so much to you, why don't you go and buy a new Scooter?" said Hazel.

"It's not the way, you know that. The old Vespas have style and class. They were crafted by Italians. There's no romance in the monstrosities they sell nowadays, assembled by robots for granny shoppers and traffic wardens. It's got to be authentic."

Hazel rolled her eyes.

Ronnie knew she had the power to sooth him with her words, the way a masseur could drain away the tension, but if that was what he wanted he knew he'd really have to work for it.

"Well, what do you want me to say?" said Hazel, already bored of the subject.

Ronnie looked into her eyes and saw an honesty that cut right through him and his aspirations. He cast out his line hoping for a second opinion.

"Do you think I'm just making a fool of myself?" said Ronnie.

Hazel curled up her mouth in exasperation. "Would it change anything if I said yes?"

CHAPTER 5. Missing Words.

A large canvas photo print of a dog was the only adornment to the pale barren walls of Mick's high-rise flat. His dog had passed away eight years ago but it was not the only thing that had died in there. As a young man he crashed through life like a one-man wrecking ball, but now life had sapped him of vitality and the only energy he had left was anger. He had prized his mutt higher than any human life he'd ever known, including his own.
A bright red sweatshirt lying crumpled over an armchair was an unwelcome intruder to his otherwise colourless existence. Everything was as faded and grey as its inhabitant.
Mick, wearing an old T-shirt, sagging Jeans and slippers, was plugged in to an ancient looking computer, engrossed in a controversial website. Neverbesilenced.com was hosting a videoblog from of an obese neo-con American, ranting about secret societies. While he listened to John Doh! Mick scrolled down the page and read the comments. These were an assortment of rant-extensions from the featured monologue, adorned with links to ads for penis enlargement cream and phoney Bit-coin opportunities.
User IC1 was warning that the whole conspiracy website was itself a Russian doll type conspiracy designed to muddy the waters by failing to distinguish between genuine government cover-ups, wacked-out loonies and UFO fantasists.

Mick's life was stale and had been for years. He wore his stagnation like it was his own trademarked brand. The high-jinks, daring-do and effervescence of his youth had faded into the threadbare carpet of his mid-life. Mick wasn't blind to the fact, he clocked it in every morning at the bathroom mirror and bade it goodnight, as he brushed his teeth, before he slipped in between the crumpled sheets of his loneliness.

On a stand, a few feet away from Mick, was a Telescope, fixed in the direction of the opposing flats. Why pay a TV license for all its voyeuristic nonsense when you could get the real thing for free. Recently he had grown a little bored of the telescope too. His regular peeping targets; a Spanish Nurse, the busty Barmaid from the nearby Lost Angel pub and a girl who worked the late shift at the local Betting Office, all occupied various flats adjacent to his block. He had mastered the longitude and latitude, he knew their coordinates like he was plotting the stars, but there was no escaping the fact that they were Amateurs and when he had them in his sights they always failed to adhere to the pornographic wish-script playing in his head. Mostly it just made him loathe himself that little bit more. The Telescope had been part of the unregistered spoils that came from a short stint working as a Repo man.

Guzzler was lolloping around on a ripped old leather armchair; he had a novel in his hand but had followed the words off the page and was frozen in a bubble of thought. He enjoyed daydreaming the way a tele-addict gets lost in the TV screen. He could pick up a novel, read a few pages and suddenly drift off into a completely different story of his own making.

Tracey bounded in, sirens blaring and all lights flashing, like a squad car in hot pursuit of a dangerous criminal.
"Your phone's off, I've been looking for you," she said.
Guzzler, jolted from his thoughts, quickly slipped a notebook, containing some of his recent poems, under his chair.
"Oh," he mumbled.
"What you doing?" she asked.
"Just pilfering a bit of silence from the day," he calmly mooted.
When Tracey's fuse was lit, she expected fireworks. His response was an affront to that.
She quizzed him. "What?"
It was more of an accusation than a question, but it was met with an open heart that went someway to disarm her.
"I come here sometimes when I'm sick of being Guzzler."
"'ave you been drinking?" she said.
"No." He said defensively. "Well, actually, yes, but just a little can to swig while I read me book."
He held up the paperback. She inhaled slowly and allowed the day's frustration to escape through the gaps in her crooked teeth, as she parked herself on the arm of his chair and began gently stroking his back.
"Is this about Arnie? It's one hell of an 'ole he's left, aye?" said Tracey.
If Guzzler had been forced to explain what love was, he thought to himself, then this was it. It wasn't flowers and selfie photographs or replicating tired cliché's across social media like a modern-day chain mail letter. It was this connection. This wonderful union that was ever-present but rarely seen with such clarity. She might have no understanding for his love of writing or share his appetite

for classic literature, but she loved him with her every breath she owned.

"I don't know what to do with meself, Trace. He was the only one who really knew me... the real me," he said.

Tracey looked a little hurt and Guzzler attempted to rectify that.

"Except you of course," he said.

"You know what he'd say. Don't ya? He'd say, don't be such a soppy sod, he would."

"That's easy for 'im to say, he's the one what's dead," said Guzzler.

Arnie had been the only one who indulged Guzzler's passion for words. Arnie loaned him Steinbeck's 'Grapes of Wrath' and it had spoken to him in a way that nothing else had before. Like a swimmer ducking his head into the sea, he found a whole new world under its surface. Orwell, Twain, Dickens and Camus each planted a seed in his head and thus grew a garden of literature. With each new book he felt himself grow a little. Some of his friends would think reading a five-hundred-page book as pointless an activity as train spotting.

There was nothing shameful about being a writer. Local people campaigned until the bitter end to save their Library. The problem was, if you told someone you were a writer, and they hadn't heard of anything you'd written, you would face derision. As if being unpublished and claiming to be a writer was somehow fraudulent. In Battersham, undiscovered creatives hid their talents like Tory voters hid their allegiances.

Guzzler didn't write to make money or become famous. It had become an internal necessity, a creative thirst that could only be quenched with imagination, guile and a pen and a pad. It helped him make sense of himself.

The people around Guzzler that did read, chose trashy novels rooted in another world. None of the characters in their books resembled anyone he could identify with. When he fell in love with literature, he felt a sense of urgency to catch up on everything he'd missed. It gave his reading an intensity that spilled over into his own writing. It was exciting but it was a happy secret he only ever discussed with Arnie. When the mundanity of life encircled him, he knew he could escape on the wings of his imagination. His own writing filled him with a barrel-load of emotions in which self-doubt always seemed to win out. However, it was never enough to stop him reaching for his pen when new ideas burst forth.

Guzzler hoped that one of his children might join him in this secret garden. He'd inherited his grandmother's old diaries in amongst a box of old tatt that had been unfavourably referred to as 'Granny's gumpf.' She died, aged eighty-nine, when he was sixteen and he rescued the box from being unceremoniously dumped in a skip. At the time he had been intrigued by the collection of mementos, but it was much later that he began to pour over the diaries like a pirate searching for clues to some long-lost treasure. The diaries, there were six of them, were more than just a record of old times. They were poetic, philosophic insights to the life of a deep-thinking woman who'd experienced abject poverty, disease and war, but had done so in a stoic manner that made Guzzler proud and also a little ashamed that his family had seen so little value in them. Like many people, particularly of their generation, his parents had lived by the motto 'destroy that which you don't understand.' Guzzler often wondered if one day, his own scrawlings would survive the bonfires of their ignorance.

Among the other lockups in their row, that hadn't been vandalised beyond use, was one, a couple of doors down, that was frequented by two lumps who stored their fishing gear there. When they couldn't escape from their lives and head off to the edge of a riverbank, they'd confer in their lock-up with some doorstep-sized sarnies and a can or two of falling down water. The last unit along the line was an open house for the living dead. Junkies would crawl in like Beetles, and if they were lucky, crawl out hours later.
"Maybe we should write a will and decide who we're going to leave our debts to," joked Tracey. Guzzler raised a brief smile. Tracey motioned to the gleaming Scooter in the lock up.
"What'll become of the chariot of fire, then?" she said.
"Dunno. Faye said I can drive it to Brighton," said Guzzler.
"What's wrong with your one?" Asked Tracey.
He pointed at his own dishevelled excuse for a Scooter, lying there like an abandoned tribute to a bad art installation.
"It's like comparing Roller skates with a Harley Davidson," he said.
"What do you mean, Brighton?" Asked Tracey, catching up with her own conversation.
Guzzler's weekend-away pitch was delivered in double-speed and with triple gusto. He wore his apprehension like a flashing bow tie. She could have read him in the dark.
"Ronnie and the boys, we're gonna do a weekend down there… In Brighton…Y'know… Like the old times… A reunion of the Aces. Ronnie said..."
Tracey pulled the plug. "Ronnie?" she said in a mocking tone. "You don't think Ronnie's coming back, do you?" She gave a sarcastic snigger as the sense of adventure drained from Guzzler's face.

"He's fixing up his Scooter and we're all driving down there," said Guzzler, pleading his case.
"Jason, that's never gonna happen. The new Pope of Suburbia swans up here preaching the gospel and kissing the tarmac. He'll never return, you do know that?"
"He has to come. We're gonna scatter Arnie's ashes down there," declares Guzzler, hoping his trump card will lend some much-needed plausibility to the venture.
"You better have a word with Faye then, 'cos I saw her tipping something off the top floor of their flats yesterday," said Tracey.
Guzzler looked crestfallen.
"Arnie's ashes?" he said.
"Well, I don't think she was emptying a hoover bag."

Head down, avoiding the cracks in the pavement, Bulldog made his way along the street to an unwelcoming concrete and glass block building. When he saw the padlock and chain barring the doors, he panicked. Amongst the scribbly illiterate graffiti on the wall, a sign advertised a drop-in clinic for mental health, alcohol and substance abuse counselling. Bulldog rattled the door, trying to peak within the tiny gap between the frame. A homeless man, secreted behind a pillar in the corner of the doorway, grunted at him.
"'s closed."
"But it's Thursday. I always come here on a Thursday," responded Bulldog, with an equal measure of anger and fear.
"It's closed down," said the homeless man.
"Oh fuck, no way." exclaimed Bulldog.
"Don't blame me you prick, blame the fuckin' government," said the homeless man.

Bulldog's anxiety was off the scale, he could feel his heart racing. He pulled out a packet of cigarettes but when he flicked open the lid, there wasn't even the remnants of a fag-butt to suck on. He fumbled for his mobile phone and selected a number. He clamped the phone to his ear while pacing in circles. He got no answer. In all the confusion and trepidation, he was struggling to think straight. He crammed his phone back in his pocket just as the door of an immaculate, top of the range, BMW car opened in front of him. A mixed-race man in his early twenties with a wide scar down his left cheek stepped out into the street, VIP-style, as if about to pick up an award at some red-carpet event. This wasn't the MOBO's, the prize he had come for was Bulldog, or at least Bulldog's custom and subsequently his enslavement. Bulldog glared at him. The man checked his smug reflection in the car window before he threw his arms open in a gesture aimed at Bulldog.
"They abandoned you, innit. You wanna get high? Go ahead. No-one watching but the blind eye," he said.
Bulldog, fidgeted, his eyes wide with an inner fear that painted vulnerability across his face. He bit his lip and turned his back on his tormentor and, head down, nervously walked away mumbling to himself. The drug dealer took a few steps in his direction, calling after him. Bulldog ignored him.
"You can't run away forever, ol' man," he sneered.
Bulldog winced at his words and turned to face him. The pusher opened the back door of his car and the dealer's beefy minder flashed him a glimpse of bags containing various compounds. Bulldog lightly shook his head but couldn't keep his eyes off the drugs. A scream of desire communicated from the veins in his arms straight to the

desire receptors in his head. Bulldog dug in, scrounging resistance from whatever inner resolve he could muster up.
"You got money? I do you a deal you can't refuse, bro?" said the dealer.
Bulldog found himself shaking his head, as if something other than himself was in control of his mental faculties.
"If you nah got no money, gimme your phone, old man, and you can have a lickle piece of heaven."
Bulldog didn't move, wavering on the precipice of his own conscience. Then suddenly, as if directed by an external force, a voice inside his head bellowed 'run'. Bulldog exploded into a sprint.
The drug pusher shouted after him. "You want it. You know where I am."
Bulldog tried to block out the words. He found a temporary friend in adrenalin, which flooded his body, as he made his escape. His face was contorted with a scream that would make Edvard Munch's famous painting look like a mild chuckle, but no sound came out.
Flustered, sweating and out of breath, he stopped at the entrance to a Supermarket, where he briefly composed himself and wheeled in an empty trolley. He rolled down each aisle powered by an intent that was slipping out of his reach. He felt his hands shaking uncontrollably. Randomly, he started loading the cart. Large items like washing powder, toilet rolls and cereal boxes were piled in. He grasped a bottle of vodka and placed it in amongst the shopping. In a crowded aisle he leant over the trolley and slipped the Vodka into his inside jacket pocket. Other shoppers were now staring at him as tears rolled down his ashen face. He abandoned the trolley at a nearby queue and bustled past an obese woman in an ill-advised tracksuit

combo, who was punching her number in on the card machine at the checkout.

"Sorry," mumbled Bulldog, as he squeezed through, but it was virtually inaudible.

He made a beeline for the store's toilets, almost knocking over a young girl in the process. The woman in the tracksuit made light of the situation with the checkout girl.

"Hope it ain't catching," she said.

"Yeah, and I hope he makes it...I've got to clean in there when I'm done here," said the checkout girl.

Bulldog slammed the cubical door shut and frantically pulled the vodka out of his jacket, attempting to break the security cap on the side of the toilet. After three manic attempts he smashed it open, glass and vodka exploding everywhere. He put the jagged neck to his mouth. He glugged it neat, like a man possessed. He stopped to spit out a shard or two of glass which splashed into the basin with a stream of fresh blood.

CHAPTER 6. Where Are Ya?

Mick's bleary eyes were still attempting a fresh calibration as he asked them to stare out at the housing estate through rain-splattered windows in his high-rise flat. The morning after the night before had taken on a different shape lately. He'd more or less ditched the pubs and spent most weekends in his flat, guzzling cheap booze, flitting between the living room, kitchen and various internet chat rooms that sucked him in, wound him up, raised his blood pressure and then spat him out, adding another dimension to the following morning's bottle ache.

Being a Sunday, Mick was trying desperately, but failing, to avoid thinking heavy thoughts, while his brain was in the clutches of a bout of Irish flu. In this frame of mind, one dark strand of thought could swiftly weave itself into a blanket of depression that, on some occasions, would insist on keeping him company for days on end.

Mick pondered at the heavy rain that was lashing down and wished it could somehow wash away his problems and the concrete eyesore before him and replace it with something else, anything else. Whoever designed this housing scheme hadn't intended on living in it, that was for sure. He remembered the streets of terraced slums that had preceded the high rises. They were small, and often dilapidated, with outside loos, but the material gains of central heating and modern toilet facilities came at the expense of community spirit, something the planners had clearly given little thought to. Ronnie's Dad, an ardent socialist, had insisted it was a master plan to destroy the working class.

Those old streets, where many families had resided for generations, had been neighbourly. He recalled the helping hand or corrective whack around the ear, that was readily applied to those in need. People looked out for each other, now they just looked at each other, mostly with suspicion. Tower blocks or not, hailing from Battersham really meant something to the teenage Mick, Ronnie, Guzzler and co. In fact, they often had fights in its honour, with lads from other areas, who were as identically poor as themselves. The idea seemed ludicrous now, but back then it was very much part of their identity and bravado of their culture. Had they been asked to intellectualise exactly what it was they were loyally defending or upholding, they would have probably been stumped, none of them were especially unintelligent, but it was the emotion of belonging that had galvanised that fighting spirit. Human history is littered with all manner of battles that were fought by respected and revered individuals for far more ridiculous reasons. Having a tough reputation had always been a highly sought-after vocation in working class areas and those who couldn't pass muster soon learned they had better brush up on their jokes, construct a shell or find themselves perennially crushed under the heel of contempt, in the stampede to survive. Without the casing of a reputation or an alto ego, bits of your life had a way of just breaking off. Mick learned how to throw a punch early on, but never found any appeal in the materially rewarding, but cowardly demeanour, of the bully.

The majority of Aces' rumbles had occurred as a result of teenage exuberance, where cuts, bruises and the occasional black-eye was generally the extent of the damage done. Bruised egos seemed to be the wounds that took longest to heal.

A knock at the door was a welcome distraction from the dark shapes shifting frantically in Mick's head, like a glitching computer game on overdrive. Although any delight on Mick's part was impossible to gather from the nonchalant manner in which he greeted Guzzler.
"I was down the Lost Angel last night, they said they hadn't seen you in ages," said Guzzler.
"Been busy, ain't I," said Mick.
Like most 'people of size' or whatever fat folk were called these days, Guzzler had been forced to develop a thick skin. Outwardly, nothing much seemed to bother him and at times, his visits to see Mick felt a little like care in the community. For a man who lived on the eighth floor, he always seemed to draw his moods from the basement.
Guzzler and Arnie used to try and coax Mick to attend one of Chelsea Football Club's home matches, where he could release the pressure. Along with rows and rows of other blokes whose dissatisfaction with their crappy lives could, for ninety minutes at least, be converted into a different currency, that of a ferocious tribal vitriol, to be directed at the faceless enemies returning the compliment at the other end of the stadium. To some extent, this safety valve had been disconnected since football's gentrification and the commercialisation created by corporate sponsorship, dubious oligarchs and billion-pound television deals.
On one occasion, some years back, Mick had jumped out of his seat to remonstrate with the ref, due to his failure to

award a stonewall penalty after a blatant foul on Chelsea talisman, Frank Lampard. Mick's behaviour had been greeted by calls, from their own irritated supporters sitting behind him, to sit down. To add insult to injury, a steward, who'd struggle to marshal paper coffee cups into a binbag, asked him to curb his colourful language.

Mick couldn't understand it, he had been blooded in the days when Chelsea played like chumps but were cheered on like champions.

The slow walk home that evening had been a long one and consisted mainly of Mick regurgitating his disgust at being told to shut up and sit down, and at the so-called supporters gawping at their ipads and mobile phones rather than the game being played out before them. It was like a radio news bulletin stuck on repeat. He ranted at everyone who would listen which pretty much amounted to himself.

Guzzler wandered into Mick's flat and perched on the edge of an armchair.

"Who's let the air out of your tyres?"

This was like slotting a pound coin into the defamation Jukebox. There was a brief inhalation and then he was off, knocking down targets like he was at the rifle range.

"They're building another fuckin' Mosque, ain't they? I tell ya. Right where the Disco Tavern used to be."

"Why do you even care? You used to call that place the numpty magnet," said Guzzler.

"I'd rather be kept awake by shit music than have all that fuckin' wailing and chanting morning, noon and night," said Mick.

The Driscoll Tavern, as it was formally known, had been the bane of Mick's life. You could have produced a double album of his rabid tirades on that subject. He was always banging on about how it was once an ecological freak show that enticed swathes of pond life from far and wide to come and drink overpriced cocktails, take LSD and dance to the loudest and most unimaginative, monotonous rhythms known to man.

A look of resignation spread across Guzzler's face. Perhaps at one time he'd have gone along with what Mick was saying, but Guzzler wasn't the same man today that he'd been twenty years ago. He was long done with group think. He realised that the current line of conversation was destined to go in circles, so he signposted an alternative route.

"Have you spoke to Ronnie?" Asked Guzzler.

Mick shot him a look of contempt and Guzzler realised that line of enquiry was equally contentious. Guzzler pulled a crumpled piece of paper from his pocket and picked up the phone and dialled.

"Hello Ronnie... Yeah good. Good...."

The convivial nature of the exchange playing out in front of him was too much for Mick, so he snatched the handset from Guzzler's grasp.

"Ron, it's Mick."

Mick hadn't snatched the phone eager for a conversation, he simply wanted to read out Ronnie's charge sheet.

"You were all for swearing oaths and building club houses six weeks ago..."

Whatever Ronnie was saying to placate him, it wasn't working.

"That's great but it was your idea... Guzz has got the ashes and everything."

Guzzler gulped awkwardly as he offered a not all together convincing thumbs up gesture.

"You comin', or not?... I mean, *I* ain't bothered...yeah..." said Mick.

He allowed a brief moment for Ronnie to make his case before putting the phone down.
"What'd he say?" asked Guzzler.
"He's been busy," said Mick.
"But is he comin'?" pressed Guzzler.
"We'll see."

CHAPTER 7.
Seal the Deal and Pay Your Dues.

Ronnie flicked the venetian blinds closed, while his work colleague, Grace, wrestled the cork from a bottle of Champagne. Ronnie knew a public show of celebration at an Estate Agents was about as popular as a politician's expense sheet. His company, Diamond's Estate Agents, had concluded business on six premiere league properties that week. The combined deals would be worth over fifty thousand pounds to them. The business required extremely delicate handling, to see off the competition from some heavy-weight rivals, who were also in the race. They had to placate one of the original buyers after Grace had facilitated a gazumping. The stress had dominated the mood in the office, like an electric forcefield.

Grace, an officious looking woman in her forties, handed Ronnie a glass of bubbly and he knocked it back in one go, he felt it race around his veins, like a pinball, unknotting his pressure points and exploding in his head like an endorphin grenade. He gathered his small team of staff around him and delivered an impromptu speech.

"We've all heard the clichés about teamwork making the dreamwork, etcetera. but I do want to say that our little team is sitting up there at the top of the league. Managing to get these deals done and dusted with no loose ends, the way we did, was exceptional."

He could have been speaking at a Cheshire cat convention, even Grace, not one to wear her heart on her sleeve, was beaming from ear to ear.

"Duck End was a tricky old bird, but we stuck in there and got the pay off. And you know why we can compete with the big boys?... because we are the big boys," said Ronnie.

"And girls," said Isaac, his correction a virtue signal if ever there was one.

"Absolutely," said Ronnie, overriding any minor irritation the interruption had brought.

"It's a turn of phrase," said Avery, quietly directing a little derision at Isaac.

"So, here's to us," said Ronnie, as he raised his glass.

"To us," they all repeated.

While glasses clinked, and the seven people assembled chatted. These moments often served to repair any minor grumbles within the team.

Ronnie indulged himself in a refill. He was absolutely buzzing. Avery, a bright woman in her mid-twenties, who only needed to sniff a wine cork to become a little tiddly, joined him at the makeshift bar. She was the youngest, but yet his finest agent. She had the charisma and guile to deal with their trickiest clients. Some six-figure deals could be dependent on a hundred-pound offer for curtains, or blinds that would be no use anywhere but the house in question. She had a short brown bob haircut and electric blue eyes that could melt an ice cream from forty yards. For someone so charmingly pretty, Ronnie thought it odd that she remained single.

"Congratulations... big boy," she said teasing him as she brushed past him closer than she needed to, on the way to grasping the Champagne bottle.

"Easy does it, Avery," said Ronnie.

She giggled then downed another glass straight. Avery had made subtle moves towards Ronnie before and although he was flattered, it was something he had no wish to encourage. He'd seen the infidelity of some of his friends and colleagues. It always ended up punching holes in their lives, like a chimpanzee at the controls of a wrecking ball. The fleeting uplift of ecstasy soon made way for the poison that turned everything sour and, before you knew it, everyone was getting taken down.

Ronnie never forgot a particularly bad spell he and Hazel had endured, about ten years ago. They found themselves entrenched in opposing camps in a 'Battle Royale' that raged for months under their roof and far longer in his head. During the prolonged stand-off, in their war of attrition, she had attracted amorous overtures from someone at work. She used the situation as an opportunity to torment Ronnie and it had worked. His insides were blistering with heartache and jealousy consumed his every waking moment. In the old days, Ronnie would have stoked it out in the street with his perceived rival, but he was no longer a teenager and he had no proof that anything untoward had actually occurred. If he had made accusations, he knew it would have been the death knell to their marriage. It took him a long time, but eventually he traced the starting point of their fracture to a deepening selfishness that had started to fog his approach to life.

As Isaac drove Ronnie home, he was bemoaning his poor luck with women, particularly with Avery, who he had become infatuated with from his first day at the company. Ronnie was more concerned with the traffic jam they had joined. In front of them, a bus had driven the wrong way down a one-way street. It was nothing like the inch-by-inch drudge home, in the clogged arteries of the big city, but the little market town of Bawden ground to a halt at the smallest of things. Ronnie was pretty merry by now, sitting in the passenger seat of Isaac's VW polo, as they crept along, like a wounded snail. He gazed up at the architecture of the crooked old Tudor buildings that overhung the pavement.

"A lot of Women are attracted to power and status," said Ronnie, launching into an impromptu life lesson.

"With some, it's authority, others it's the power of laughter, of intellect or the appreciation of good manners and decency. But in my experience, they are rarely wooed by politics."

Ronnie thought about how that may be perceived as sexist. He hated the dominance of political correctness, but it crept in anyway because he knew the repercussions of being misunderstood could be damaging.

"Those that are interested," he continued. "Do not find social policy or world affairs an aphrodisiac. Kindness possibly, selflessness quite probably, but remember, there's no self-sacrifice in popular opinion," said Ronnie.

Isaac was hanging on his every word, hoping for the secret to unlock the door to a part of his life that had no key for. He was trying so hard to be the man he thought people wanted him to be that he left the real Isaac languishing in the shadows.

"Please don't take this the wrong way," said Ronnie.

"Of course not, Ronnie, I really respect what you -."

Ronnie cut him off mid-flow. He didn't know which were worse, bigots or arse-kissers.

"Pull over. Now," said Ronnie.

Isaac was flustered, he'd face the wrath of other drivers if he just stopped where they were, but Ronnie must have a good reason, he thought.

"Now," Insisted Ronnie.

Isaac anxiously pulled his car on to the curb.

"Have you got any cash on you?" asked Ronnie.

Isaac was a little puzzled, only a few hours ago he'd seen Ronnie whip out his wallet to pay for the Champagne, he must have had a good few hundred pounds in there, he thought to himself. Isaac pulled out his rather less impressive bundle. He had two fivers, a ten and two twenties. Ronnie took it and pulled all the cash out.

"Take this and give him the lot," said Ronnie.

Isaac sat there befuddled wondering what he was talking about.

"Give who?" he said.

Ronnie pointed to a homeless man in the corner of a shop doorway cuddled up with a mongrel dog.

A little perplexed, after flashing Ronnie a look of disdain, Isaac got out and did as Ronnie had said. He placed the money into the man's fingerless-gloved hands. And immediately got back in the car. As the drivers he inconvenienced passed him, one growled and two gave him thumbs up.

"What was his name?" asked Ronnie.

"Who? The tramp?"

"Did you introduce yourself?" Ronnie asked, as Isaac slipped the car off the curb and back into the line of traffic.

"No, I mean, I think I startled him," said Isaac.

"I'm sure you did," said Ronnie with a smile. "How did it feel?"

"Well, I guess he needed it more than me," said Isaac, telling Ronnie what he thought he should say, not what he actually thought, which was really 'Why don't you give him your own money? Or is that how the rich stay wealthy, spending other people's cash?'

"His name is Sandy," said Ronnie. "And the dog's name is Lucky. He used to like a punt on the horses... a little too much. Flutter after flutter he waved his wife, house and business away. He couldn't help himself. An addictive personality can bring you success in everything, even failure."

"I thought he was just a drunk, y'know," said Isaac.

"He is a drunk, now," said Ronnie.

"So, won't he just piss my money up the wall?" Asked Isaac.

"Your money? It's his now and he can do with it as he pleases."

"But they say never give the money to tramps, you should give it to charity."

"You mean those charities that weigh out over a hundred k each to their CEO's?" Asked Ronnie.

Isaac fell silent, but Ronnie wasn't finished.

"Sandy might get himself some food, a bit for Lucky, or he might kill himself with booze. One way or another, two winters from now, if the dog survives that long, it's going to be looking for a new owner anyway. Every day you're outraged about some injustice or other, desperate to be seen on the side of equality. And that's great, we love you for that, we're none of us monsters. But actions speak louder than words and there's a man and his dog within reach of your help."

"You're right, Ronnie, you are so right," Isaac said, forcing a smile. He said all the correct things, but Ronnie knew underneath he would be irked with him.

As they arrived at the Diamond residence in Arksdean, Ronnie thanked Isaac and prepared himself to greet the guests that Hazel had invited from work. Honestly, he thought to himself, he'd rather grab a coat and go and spend the night in that shop doorway with Sandy, it might be cold, but he was sure the company would be more to his liking.

Isaac blew out his cheeks as he drove away.

"Why didn't you give him some of your mountains of cash, you preachy twat," he said to himself.

Something wedged in the crease of the passenger seat caught his eye. He stopped at the first junction, thinking he might have to return to the house with whatever it was that his boss had left behind. There, stuffed in the upholstery was sixty pounds. A feeling of private relief washed over him, as he quickly forced the cash into his pocket. It was followed shortly afterwards by a flood of guilt.

At Dinner parties, Ronnie often felt like the guest whose invitation was based on politeness alone. Some of Hazel's work friends were professional bores with expensively dull lives. This evening's ensemble was no different. Philip, Polly, Rod and Caroline had already joined Hazel around the dining table when Ronnie arrived.

The Champagne imbued earlier encouraged him to take a more cavalier approach to proceedings. He was in a playful mood, much in the way a cat can be when deciding to torment, rather than swallow, the mouse it has caught. Caroline and Rod, having recently arrived back from a fortnight's jaunt to Greece, were skimming through holiday photos on the large screens of their identical mobile phones in competition with each other for the commentary. Ronnie found it odd that there was absolutely nothing of them in the pictures. Rod boasted about their itinerary and how they crammed their days with whistle-stop tours of all the main sites. They'd breezed through every room in the National Gallery and seen everything from Breughel,

Rodin and Rembrandt to Greek masters such as Volanakis, Jacobides and Altamouras. They viewed the works of art like someone flicking through an Argos catalogue. They'd seen everything, yet, nothing. They lived their lives like a tick list, collecting foreign holidays like empty jam jars with exotic labels.

Hazel was only too aware of Ronnie's aversion to her guests. He was the oil to their Perrier water. She used her glances like a cattle prod to keep him in line, but tonight he was the one who was setting off charges.

"So, Rod, what was your favourite thing about Greece?" asked Ronnie.

"Well, I, umm…"

"The weather," charged Caroline, delighted with herself for answering first, as if in a TV quiz show.

"Yes, probably the weather and the vino," said Rod, concurring.

Hazel had told Ronnie that Caroline was a very different person when she was at work. She was kind, funny and thoughtful. Ronnie would have to take her word for it.

Philip and Polly were equally as non-descript. Ronnie rang an imaginary bell in his head every time Polly managed to twist the conversation in the direction of her time studying at Warwick University. She just about stopped short of having her history degree fashioned into a Brooch with matching earrings. Those few years weren't just the best days of her life; they were her life. After graduating, her entire existence had become a justification for what she couldn't do. She worked hard at it.

Philip was the breadwinner; he had an astute mind for numbers that had him perched in a relatively safe senior position in corporate finance. Polly, on the other hand was prepared to wait indefinitely for the right career opportunity to arrive. Despite the fact that she hadn't worked much more than a few months during the past two decades, she still required a nanny to help raise their three children. She was an illness wanting to happen, an affliction that would only be tempered by the oxygen of other people's sympathy. She clung to her ailments like a penniless mother clutches her food stamps.

Ronnie was in a gang of one. He fired off sharp, witty missives that only he seemed to find amusing. Hazel was usually able to contain him by using her daggered eyes as a remote control. Tonight, it felt like the batteries had failed.

"Hazel was telling us about your little gang, when you were teenagers," said Philip.

Hazel knew his patronising tone would rile Ronnie, but instead of biting, Ronnie took the opportunity to talk about his Mod days.

"You should have seen us. All skinny trousers and too much to say," chuckled Ronnie.

"Now it's all receding hairlines and too much to eat," said Hazel, mimicking a large belly.

"Must seem a bit daft now looking back," said Philip.

For most people, there was nothing particularly notorious about being a Mod. Ronnie hadn't borne the obnoxious attitude of a Punk, with their leather jackets and shocking green Mohicans or the fearsome reputation that came with the shaven head and bovver boots of a Skinhead, but he still felt that Mod was the pinnacle of that particular tree. If you hadn't lived it how could you even begin to understand what it meant to be a Mod, Ronnie thought. And so, Phillip's comment hit a raw nerve.

"Not at all," said Ronnie.

"It must have been a lot of fun," said Polly, sensing Ronnie's ire.

"I cringe whenever I see a photo from my teens. We all look so…silly," said Rod.

"Silly? I don't think so. They were the best days of our lives," said Ronnie.

"Best days? Oh, hardly," said Philip jangling his Mercedes keys. "My best days are now."

"If I had to choose between my old scooter back then or your Merc now, the Merc would come a poor second," insisted Ronnie.

"Alright Ronnie, we get the point," said Hazel, attempting to reign in her husband.

Ronnie refilled everyone's glasses with Wine and when he got to Polly's glass, he suddenly remembered they had some gin in the cupboard and, much to the chagrin of her husband, she made it clear that she'd be delighted to have a little tipple. Ronnie disappeared and came back with a large tumbler of it.

"Go easy, eh, Pol," Philip mumbled in her ear.

It was too late, the genie was out of the bottle. Polly was explosive TNT when she got drunk. No-one was safe, but the swing of her scorn was always angled in the direction of her husband. Fill her up with gin and she would demolish him like a stack of dynamite on a withering old industrial chimney. Philip was defenceless to her facetiousness, and he shrank along with his arrogance. Ronnie often wondered if Philip got a kick out of being humiliated. She was gobby and brash, but out of the two of them, it was Polly that always got the invitations, partly by way of the mouth-watering deserts she made.

Philip had disqualified himself from ever establishing his own viewpoint. He made politicians look honest, the way he weighed up the momentary balance of opinion. Inside his head, was a simmering cauldron of anger and frustration but there were padlocks on the zips that held back his fury. He seemed to Ronnie like a man who would, one day, snap and drive his high-performance Mercedes off a bridge. Right now, Ronnie felt like throwing Philip his keys.

CHAPTER 8.   Getting Mobile.

A large van, with the orange spanner logo of the Mobile Motorbike Mechanics company inscribed on its side, pulled away from Ronnie and Hazel's forecourt, and disappeared through the electronic gates and out on to the little country lane, leaving a whirlwind of spray and leaves behind it. Ronnie slowly edged his Scooter out through the garage door, intoxicated by this new sense of his old self. The once familiar smell of two-stroke oil and petrol in his nostrils ignited something inside him. His Scooter had been overhauled and had so many new parts, like Trigger's broom, it could hardly be considered the same machine, he had even replenished the set of mirrors fixed on either side of the handlebars.

Ronnie felt like a fraud for calling in the Cavalry. In the old days, him and his mates would roll their sleeves up and repair their machines themselves. It was a matter of pride and price. Although, thinking back, Ronnie had to concede that it had been mainly Mick and Arnie who had done the grafting. The only thing he'd really learnt was the most useful place to stand to be able to hand out the ratchets and spanners.

Ronnie's father had been the same when Ronnie was a child. He would take his old banger to get its MOT from some bloke he knew in a lock-up around Wandsworth. When he got there, he used to say to Ronnie, "Listen son, I'll be honest with you. I haven't got a Danny La Rue about cars, but *they* don't know that." He'd saunter in and collar one of the engineers.

"Oi Chief, the old What's it's playin' up. Give it the once over, will ya? I think the old frugal bearings are up the Swanny, and them there under pipes are a bit iffy too."

He would attempt to bamboozle them with a smattering of banter and gibberish and walk out feeling like he was head honcho for a Formula one racing team.

Crash helmet on, twisting the throttle, Ronnie was pumped up and raring to go. A holdall bag was attached to the back seat by bungee straps. For the first time in ages, he felt younger than the imposter he saw every morning in the bathroom mirror.

Hazel bounded out of the house towards him.

"You really going to do this?" She said, hollering over the pitter-patter of the engine.

"If this old thing can get me there," he said.

"What about work?"

"They know how to get hold of me," he said.

"I know you want to see your old friends, really I do, but…"

He deliberately revved the throttle, drowning her out.

Hazel shouted louder, "Have fun, but don't forget why we left all that behind, eh?"

He let the throttle settle, ensuring she could hear him.

"Why you gotta put a downer on it?" He murmured.

"Just don't cry to me if Bulldog picks your pockets and drinking with Mick leaves a sour taste in your mouth."

"Give it a break, aye? I never moaned when you and Jane went off to Portugal, did I?" said Ronnie.

She could have been talking Chinese for all the notice he was going to take. A bitter expression on his face, Ronnie revved up the Scooter in unison with the corners of Hazel's mouth. He drove off leaving her looking on with a sense of trepidation. An image of her mother watching her father, as he sauntered off with his wages to the betting shop resurfaced in her mind.

"Don't fuck it all up, you idiot," she said aloud.

He was too far gone to hear.

Ronnie had talked it over with Hazel a few times, but her answers never seemed to fit his questions. They seemed like parts to very different jigsaws. She had no problem with him going off on a jolly with his old mates, she just wanted the baggage he brought back to be restricted to the clothes and wash bag he'd stuffed in his holdall.

Ronnie was a dreamer; this was both the making of him and his biggest hazard. He'd broken free, and there was no knowing what cages he would rattle on this little escapade. The sleeping dogs didn't have a prayer.

Now that Ronnie was back in the saddle, thoughts of his irritation with Hazel soon dissipated. As if in sync with his mood, dazzling shards of light burst out from an overcast sky, gleaming off the wet tarmac. Ronnie was in his element, the wind in his face, cruising along the country roads on his Scooter. The hunt for the holy grail had begun. With each new mile on the clock, he eased himself into a comfort of old. In his mirrors he could almost see a convoy of scooters and old girlfriends, their fresh faces beaming as they nestled in behind him. A few choice glances in the reflections of parked cars and shop fronts convinced his ego that, once more he was the dapper leading man in the movie adaptation of his own life story. Hazel was concerned that hers was turning into a black comedy.

Crossing London, he stopped off in the West End for a quick shufti at the clothes shops along Carnaby Street. In the swinging sixties, it had been a beacon of high fashion, associated with famous musicians and film stars. The Rolling Stones, Rod Stewart, The Small Faces, Lulu and Twiggy were regulars. Trendy shops like Lord John and The Mod Male made it a Mecca for the London in-crowd. All that was before Ronnie was born. By the time his crew of South London oiks rolled up, in the early eighties, Carnaby had become something of a dive. Downmarket boutiques selling badges, hair dye and cheap replicas alongside Union Jack socks, London T-shirts and all manner of tourist tat.

There were a couple of shops where you could get half-decent clobber, but mostly it was only the cheap stuff that Ronnie could afford on his early ventures over the Thames to Carnaby. He remembered the odd scuffle with Skinheads, who dominated the flea-market that stood half-way up the pedestrianised street. It attracted urchins that could have stepped right out of a Charles Dickens novel. There had been one occasion where the Mods, Scooter boys and even Skinheads had joined forces to ambush a mob of Soulboys and Bodypoppers, after they'd beaten up a young Mod girl. That triumphant uprising was talked about for months to come but generally that kind of cross-cult unity was rare.

In comparison to those mostly threadbare days, when it came to clothes, Ronnie's budget was now virtually unlimited. He browsed through the racks at Targets, a side-street boutique peddling a niche line in everything from button-down shirts to Union Jack blazers. There was a grey-haired old Mod measuring someone up for a tonic suit and an Indian fellow who was measuring everyone else up for a fleecing. It was a market trader's credit check, a quick calculation on who to offer the hard sell and patter to. Ronnie avoided eye contact with the Indian, flicking through some books and magazines, while he waited for the store's more fashionable assistant.

The grey-haired Mod introduced himself as Pat Danson, he had the face of an old rock star, with contours that resembled an elephant's skin. Prior to any recommendations, measurements or purchases, they sounded each other out in a kind of authentication process. They each rattled off names, eagerly checking them off to verify their own Mod lineage. It was like the reading of an alternative family tree, Ronnie found long-forgotten names just flew off the tip of his tongue; Hodges, Pearcey, Geordie John, Aussie Adam, Squaddie Dave, Teardrops, Watford Pete, The McVicar brothers from Woolwich, Pondy from Southend, Big Ian, Little Ian, Fat Andy, Bank job, Peachy, Gary Walnut, Wattsy, Draney, Beano and Lightning Nige. His face lit up like a switchboard, every name a page from the Who's Who of 80s street life.

Ronnie chuckled when he realised Pat was talking about his old mate, Mick, when referring to 'Micky the hat'. Mick had worn a trilby, a relic of his Skinhead days, it wasn't really Mod uniform, but Mick wouldn't part with it. Pat knew of the Aces. It transpired that Arnie had frequented the shop sporadically over the years. Pat was genuinely sad to hear of Arnie's passing.

Once they'd done with namechecking the faces, they were on to Mod milestones. Pat went back further than Ronnie and had seen everyone from The Who and the Small Faces to The Jam, Secret Affair and The Chords.

"The Jam, Marquee, 1980," said Ronnie, delighted he got it in first.

"Yeah, the secret gig," said Pat.

"They played under the name 'John's boys.' I got a call at home from a mate, left me tea 'alf eaten, forty minutes later I was in the queue," said Ronnie.

Ronnie was proudly illustrating that he knew his onions.

"I got thrown out half-way through when it kicked off with some Skins," said Pat, trumping him once more in the credibility stakes.

They exchanged anecdotes about Bank Holiday ructions along the South coast of England involving police cells in Margate, holding pens in Brighton and magistrates' courts in Southend.

"There's still a half-decent little Mod scene, but it ain't the same," said Pat. "But then I don't suppose it ever could be. I mean, this new wave, they've gotta find their own way, make their own statement, if you get my drift."

"I really miss them days," said Ronnie.

He found that he was becoming more and more Cockney and his grammar was slipping back to his Battersham High School levels. It was the same with the voice in his head. He even began to think in Cockney.

"I've seen 'em come and go... Been a Mod all me life. They'll put a target on me gravestone and that'll do me fine," said Pat.

"I'll drink to that," said Ronnie.

By the time he'd left the store, Ronnie was well and truly keyed up. Brighton couldn't come soon enough. He was buoyed about meeting another brother-in-arms. He delighted at the instant comradery. It was like meeting a favourite old cousin. There, in a sea of nobodies was a fellow traveller, one of the enlightened, one of the chosen few. They used to swap notes on how nobody understood what it was like to be a Mod. The right to be seen and the fight to be heard. It was that mythical siege mentality that held the whole thing together. Ronnie was now in search of the source of that particular elixir of his old life.

CHAPTER 9.
Shark-infested waters.

Outside Mick's flat in Locke House, Battersham, two burly men announced themselves with the kind of knock at the door that would make a battering ram appear courteous.
"Repo, open up," one of them grunted.
Mick, crouching inside, in his pants and faded T-shirt, held his breath. He could see the two monsters of rock gnashing their teeth, via a strategically placed mirror next to his bedroom window. They were ugly brutes, both had noses that looked like they cushioned punches for fun.
"We know you're in there, MacPherson," one roared, as the other rumbled the door again.
"We'll be back later. You'll be listening for us," said the other Thug.
Mick, skulking behind a dusty net curtain, exhaled what seemed like a week's worth of bad air, as his tormentors trudged along his walkway to make some other poor soul's wretched life a misery. He knew only too well that a closed door was no defence against these Repo men.
It shamed him inside, as he thought back at all the underhanded, and devious ways, he had treated people, struggling in a similar fashion to his current predicament, when he had worked for blood money, alongside those Goons.
On one occasion, Mick froze to the spot, as one of his fellow Repo Men smashed up a flat in front of three

petrified children. It affected him so badly he couldn't sleep. A few days later, when the frightened expressions he saw in his nightmares started overwhelming his daytime thoughts, he resigned his post under a hail of derision. Being in debt is so fucking exhausting, he thought to himself, as he made his way into the kitchen. Flicking the switch on the kettle, he opened a near-empty fridge. Recoiling from the smell emanating from a carton of curdled milk, he realised he wasn't the only thing that was past its sell-by date. He would have to have his tea black. This wasn't a little rut he'd got himself in to, it was a man-sized crater, and he knew that those two goons would happily chuck him down it and shovel earth on top of him if he gave them half a chance.

Bulldog was virtually camouflaged as he lay like dirty laundry amongst the crumpled covers of a futon bed in his barren, dingy looking bedroom. A hastily improvised three-inch slit had been made at the bottom of the door to accommodate a food tray being inserted. This bedroom wasn't a sanctuary from a cold and indifferent world. It was a self-made trap to keep him from seeking out the pie-eyed piper of Battersham. He had got himself into a quandary and this room was a physical representation of that. Nowhere was safe, he couldn't even claim it as a refuge from himself. It was a place where he was mocked and plagued by his own deceptive shadow.
The night terrors were the worst. Giant beetles and cockroaches falling on him from every direction, accompanied by an inescapable gnawing sound that sickened him to the core.
A couple of lads he knew from the Mod scene did a bit of amphetamines, but when it came to drugs, Ronnie had

always insisted the Aces stay clean. You could barely cadge a joint in the nineteen-seventies on this estate, but by the late eighties, drugs, mostly in the form of weed and coke, were everywhere. Nowadays most people here took it as read that if you were over twelve and under fifty, you were more than likely dabbling in anything from marijuana to magic mushrooms. Toerags in tinted BMW's were driving around like mobile chemists, taking the temperatures of their patients to see how far they could push them before they'd burst, or their ill-gotten supply of money would run out.

Bulldog sat up and hugged his knees. His long-suffering mother was standing gazing out of the window, her yellow tipped fingers holding up the blinds, to peer out, hoping to catch a glimpse of the kind of luck that had avoided her for most of her time on this planet. She was a lifer, as much a prisoner to this hellish regime as her son. At least he experienced the occasional high. Other parents might have abandoned him and bailed out when the going got tough, but she resigned herself to battling his demons even when his own feeble defences had withered away.

The wrinkles on her face resembled the branches on a leafless winter tree. The blue in her eyes was fading like her stamina. She lived her life in a monotone hell of fear and hope, and hope could be a treacherous companion. No matter what, she could never turn her back on her son. She only had one son and, unlucky for her, that son became Bulldog. Memory was her faith. She had to believe the happy, kind and inquisitive little boy was still in there, lost somewhere in that bag of bones currently cowering in his bed.

"Aggsy says the centre's closed for good. It's the government cuts. They haven't said it, but you know they're only interested in flogging off the building," said Bulldog.

Bulldog's mum responded like her batteries had been super-charged on anger.

"With the swish of a pen, those bastards just sweep people off into the gutter. I don't know who is worse, the politicians or those bloody drug pushers, they certainly share a warped sense of morality," she said.

"I really don't know what to do," said Bulldog, as he started to make a roll-up from a small pouch of tobacco. "Have you tried calling Joe, or one of the other counsellors?"

"It just goes to an answer machine, referring you to your GP," he said.

"It's like the magic roundabout. Each door's a revolving one that dumps you out into the street, back where you started," she said.

She had jumped through so many hoops with him, the dizzying sensation felt immutable. She was sure the government pen pushers were deliberately nudging the most vulnerable over the edge. In her mind, it was all a cynical ploy to cut loose those without the strength to hang on as they navigated the emotional assault course that is the care system.

"It'll be alright, Mum," he said, without qualification.

She shook her head then turned to Bulldog, her face disfigured by the gravitational pull of misery.

"No, it won't," she whispered.

Her words hung there in the room like the discoloured air of a terminal illness. She knew in her heart of hearts that his high-stakes game of *Snakes and Ladders* was running out of safe squares and there was only one place the local reptiles would lead him. He was set-up to fail from the very first moment he showed his hand, when they'd placed the dice in his palm, and he'd taken his first tumble. He was a smart, caring and loyal son but he had 'lost cause' scrawled across his face in indelible ink. She could never imagine a time when he would be free from the shackles of dependency on the drugs, and on her.

"D'ya think I should go to Brighton with Guzzler and...Ronnie? said Bulldog, as if he had no more control on his own life than an eight-year-old boy.

She knew there was nowhere with absolute protection, like most Junkies, he could sniff out a drug deal in a force ten gale. His human magnetism attracted nothing but toxic matter. She presumed that Brighton would be no different from London, only he'd be unknown to the wolves and hyena's there and she knew Guzzler, Ronnie and even Mick, who she detested, didn't paddle in those waters. She would have to trust him.

"Go, son. Just go," she said.

Assuming the coast was clear, Mick ventured out from his flat, instantly finding himself being door-stepped. Mick's heart sank lower than his withering aspirations when he caught sight of Dunbar and Bains, two loan sharks in near-matching Leather Jackets, blocking his path. Avoiding the Repo Men only to bump into these two crocodiles was like dusting yourself down after successfully escaping over the prison wall, only to find the firing squad cocking their rifles.

The Repo Men were always desperate to unburden you of your possessions, whereas these psychopaths were praying for a non-payer. For Dunbar and Bains there was no line they wouldn't cross. When it came to violence, they were not even aware a line existed. Bains, the podgier of the two, was born with a nasty sneer that even the best surgeons in the world would struggle to alter. He was the ringmaster, a cunning orchestrator of sheer brutality. As the police presence receded on the streets of London, the government's cuts became more literal in these parts. Bains had filled the void with protection rackets, usury, and intimidation on behalf of his boss, Grev Goldman, an unscrupulous businessman who laundered his dirty money through a collection of Mini-cab firms.

"MacPherson... You've missed three payments," said Bains.

"Come on Bainsie, you know me, I'll sort it," said Mick.

"Mister Goldman has been very generous to you and he expects you to pay your dues," said Dunbar.

"You'll get your money," said Mick.

"You disappoint me, MacPherson," said Bains.

Far from being disappointed, the two henchmen savoured the moments of knee scuffing and bootlicking, that acted like an appetiser to a main course of barbarism.

Mick was like all of their victims, offering genuine pleas and unrealistic promises, in the vain hope it might buy him a pass. Best to worry about the details later.

"Come on, Bainsie, mate," said Mick.

"I don't give a shit if you have to car-jack the Queen of fuckin' England or rent your back door out to a troupe of male dancers. You get that money, and you get it quick," said Bains.

Dunbar grabbed Mick.

"Here's a little reminder of our terms and conditions," said Dunbar, as he smashed his fist into Mick's gut.

Mick fell to the floor and tried to protect his vitals as both of his tormentors lurched towards him, simultaneously kicking and stamping on him with bloodlust that would not be out of place among the pages of a novel, from the 'Gangster-lit' section, next to the colouring books in Waterstones.

"Leave it out," gasped Mick, in a futile attempt to wave the white flag of surrender. He got a smash in the face for his troubles.

Mrs Burns, a neighbour in her late seventies, opened her door and shooed them away like crows pecking at a half-dead rabbit.

"Clear off, you wrong 'uns," she glowered.

They stopped decimating him and calmly walked away, but not before Bains had sneered at the old lady. She wasn't easily intimidated.

"You don't scare me, you ugly brutes," she spat.

Bains smiled before sauntering off with Dunbar to find another poor wretch on their hit list.

With his dementors vanished, Mick pulled himself to his feet while his neighbour gave him the once over.

"What'd ya wanna get yourself involved with them bleedin' villains?" she said.

She tried patting him down where the dirt from the floor had marked his clothes, but he resisted in the manner of a boy avoiding his mother's impromptu face cleaning ritual.

"Come on, come and 'ave some Soup," she said.

She turned back into her tinsel Palace and Mick trailed behind her, still feeling like a bullied child who'd found a temporary refuge behind his granny's apron.

Mick hadn't been inside Mrs Burns' flat since he was a child. It was a museum to her life. There was barely any sign of the faded wallpaper under the gallery of photo frames from which both stern and happy faces gazed back at you. In amongst the photographs were some old postcards of Kew Gardens, Margate's Winter Gardens and the beach at Bognor Regis that had been put behind glass and hung on the wall, perhaps as a reminder of happier times or maybe a jolt of escapism that an old person might need to survive around here.

CHAPTER 10.   Being Guzzler.

As Guzzler and Ronnie walked past the Merryfield junior school, in Battersham, Ronnie's fingers wrapped around the chain fence and he paused to lean into the enclosure. He scanned the empty tarmac playground and visualised the chaos of playtime from his stint as a pupil there. The games where the rules changed mid-routine, the girls skipping, chanting poems about the black death, boys mimicking teachers, parents and pop stars. The shouting, singing and screaming, lung-busting sprints, the blood rush from hanging upside down from the climbing frame. Every day had been a happy riot, or at least that was how he chose to remember it. Most of the would-be bullies hadn't quite mastered their stock in trade at that age, so the School yard wasn't the war zone it turned out to be, a few years later, at Secondary School.

Ronnie pulled himself away, as his eyes followed the fence upwards to its barbed wire topping, an addition added long after he'd attended.

"That to keep 'em out or keep 'em in?" said Ronnie.

"Don't. You sound like Mick," said Guzzler.

They resumed their ambling pace along the road towards some high-rise flats.

"What's up with him? He trade in his funny bone for a long face?" said Ronnie.

"Muslims, Magistrates and Mother bloody Theresa... He's got a rant for all seasons," said Guzzler.

"He always was a bit of a moody sod," said Ronnie.
"I'm telling ya. He could put a frown on a birthday cake, that fella," said Guzzler.

A gaunt, weather-worn, old woman, hurrying along the other side of the street, lifted a hand of greeting to Guzzler without missing a step. She was hunched over as if the wellbeing of the residents in the surrounding tower blocks was a burden for her alone to shoulder.

Guzzler acknowledged her with a gentle waive. She careered on at pace like there were no brakes to slow her momentum.

"Jesus, the graveyard running an early release programme?" said Ronnie.
"You know who that is, don't you?" said Guzzler.
"One of the Adams family?" said Ronnie.
"That's Bulldog's Mum," said Guzzler.
"She looks a wreck,"
"A better soul you will not find." said Guzzler.
"She looks like she's been through the wars," said Ronnie.
"Having a Junkie son will do that to you," said Guzzler.
"It's a crying shame," said Ronnie, drawing his hand across his head.
"By the way, she absolutely detests Mick," said Guzzler.
"Why?"
"He was a Repo Man for a bit," said Guzzler.
"Mick?" questioned Ronnie.
"Yeah. And one of his first jobs was to reclaim some stuff from Bulldog. People round here have long memories for that kind of thing," said Guzzler.

They passed a little chorus of pre-teen yobbo's hanging around a wall, hoping to improve their street credentials by pretending to be tough. One lad, riding a bike with no seat on his seat post, circled the pair. To his dismay, neither of them gave them the time of day. Guzzler was, however, aware that Ronnie's fancy wristwatch would draw unwanted attention if he wasn't careful.

He nodded at the timepiece. "Nice watch."

"Cheers," said Ronnie.

"What d'you reckon it'd fetch on the black market?" said Guzzler.

Ronnie gave Guzzler a puzzled look. His street smarts had been blunted by the cordiality of life in the countryside.

"'round here, A watch like that, could come with an optional punctured lung or a black eye, if you meet the wrong people," said Guzzler.

"I better not meet the wrong people then, eh?" said Ronnie.

There was an almighty crash only a few feet away from them as an old Fridge landed on the grass and disintegrated.

"Fuckin' 'ell," said Ronnie, who's heart was suddenly running on double-time.

They both looked up at the flats, but the culprit had vanished.

"Hope that's not Mick's idea of a welcome," said Ronnie with a smile.

They approached Locke House. Identical to Arnie's flats, except the plastic trim wasn't shocking pink, but a nice shade of vomit green.

"Bulldog said he's been clean for five years," said Ronnie.

Guzzler gave him a questionable look.

"That bullshit, then?" asked Ronnie.

"Not exactly. I haven't seen that much of him lately, but I know he came off the Skag." said Guzzler.

"Fair play to him," said Ronnie.

"He was a right mess. There was only me and his Mum standing between him and an early grave. She got him off the Smack only for him to get hooked on weed instead. Some people can hack it, some can't. He nearly got sectioned," said Guzzler.

"At least he's off the Heroin," said Ronnie, not wanting to think Bulldog's drug problem could overshadow their glorious escapade to Brighton.

"Addiction never knows when it's beat," said Guzzler. "He has to start from scratch, every day, building defences. It wouldn't take much for it all to crumble."

Ronnie started to wonder if he'd returned to an alternative universe. Some of the lives didn't seem to fit their original profiles.

At Locke House a sign read 'Lifts out of use,' so they began to climb the stairs. The stairwell reeked of piss, vomit, and teenage boredom. Ronnie used to whizz up these stairs without breaking a sweat, now he was half-way up and wondered if he would need oxygen by the time he reached the eighth floor.

Guzzler knocked on Mick's front door, while Ronnie lingered awkwardly.

"I know he gives it the big 'un, but he ain't the Mick of old, he's vulnerable, Ronnie. Just remember that."

All of this negativity was not what he'd ventured back to Battersham for. He hoped Guzzler would keep any similarly down-beat exchanges to himself. Ronnie had brought his own fluffy white cloud and wanted to invite them aboard where they could revel in stories about their shared experiences of music, beer and laughter. He wanted the tales of how they'd got one over on the Old Bill and regularly stitched up the miser who ran the Off Licence. He yearned for yesteryear's buzz, the wind-ups and the banter, he didn't want to hear that the buzz had got grey and old. He stubbed that thought out instantly.

Guzzler knocked on the door again. He kneeled down to look through the letterbox.
"Come on Mick, it's me, Guzz."
Guzzler turned back to Ronnie and shrugged his shoulders.
"It's not like he wasn't expecting us," said Guzzler.

At Guzzler's place, the end house on a terraced row of six, Ronnie and Guzzler were sitting on the sofa eating microwaved Carbonara. They chatted about guzzler's children, now grown up and flown the nest.
After completing the washing up, Guzzler took Ronnie back to Arnie's den, stopping by at the local Off Licence to load up on beer. Crossing the estate, they were accosted by a small man with a shiny bald head.
"Well, I never, Ronnie fuckin' Diamond. How are ya, bud?"
"Yeah, good thanks," said Ronnie.
"Ronnie's down for a few days. We're getting the scooters back on the road," explained Guzzler.
"Yeah?"
"Yeah. We're off to Brighton." said Guzzler.
"Oh, mate. That brings it all back, eh?" said the bald man.
"Had some mad times, eh?" said Guzzler.
"Up until a few years ago, I had a Harley," the bald man said, proudly.
Ronnie was scouring his memory bank like a Google search engine but kept coming up with an error code. He had no idea who they were talking to, but the more they chatted, the more familiar his face became.
"Cor, we did some crazy shit together, eh? What was that dare? Remember, where you had to down a can of beer in one go then walk on the outside edge of Battersham

bridge? How we never fell into the Thames and got washed away, I'll never know," the bald man laughed.
Ronnie smiled, nodded in the right places and shook his hand before the bald man took off in the opposite direction.
"You still with that Harriet?" he asked, turning while still walking.
"Hazel, yeah, married twenty years," said Ronnie.
"You done well, my son. Give her me best," he said, and with that he was off.
"Who the bloody hell was that? Asked Ronnie.
"That's Andy 'Apples'. You know, used to run his old man's fruit stall up the Junction."
"Now you say it. He don't half look like 'is Dad," said Ronnie.
"Remember, we used to watch those dodgy blue movies 'round his house," said Guzzler.
"Oh yeah. He was the only one with a video machine. How long's he been a billiard ball?"
"Yonks…. I tell ya, he goes on about that Harley Davidson," said Guzzler. "What he didn't tell you was, it was a girl's Bike. All the other bikers used to wind 'im up rotten. Tie ribbons on it, stuff like that."
At the lock-up Ronnie continued to play catch up. Mulling over a group photo of the Aces and associates, at a Rally on Battersham Bridge. Guzzler gave him the run down, pointing out each of the characters he hadn't bumped into yet.
"Streatham Tony, he's..." Guzzler pointed to the floor. "Down under."
"He's not dead, is he?" said Ronnie.
"No, Australia. There's umm…" said Guzzler.
"Benji. Yeah, what happened to him?" asked Ronnie.
"Down under," said Guzzler.

"He's in Australia too?" asked Ronnie.

"Nah, he's a goner. Fell off a scaffold about fifteen years ago," said Guzzler.

"He was alright, he was. Really good at pool as I recall," said Ronnie.

Guzzler continued the run down. "The two Pauls. Small Paul went blind, lives in Putney. Tall Paul does security for Status Quo and the Rolling Stones, Coked off his nut most of the time."

"What's Little Darren up to?" asked Ronnie.

"Skag head." said Guzzler.

"Fuckin' hell, I remember when he used to fake drinking beer 'cause he hated the taste of it, He was about eleven at the time though," said Ronnie.

"Pete's doing all right. Works up Chelsea. Chauffer. Got eight kids."

"Eight kids?" said Ronnie, raising an eyebrow.

"They're the ones he knows about. More fertile than a lorry load of Rabbits that bloke. He only has to sneeze, and someone's having nappies delivered," said Guzzler.

Ronnie pointed to a lad with a wide grin wearing a target t-shirt.

"What about Chas?"

"No idea. I think he moved to Bristol or Bath, somewhere out west. In fact, I think he might be brown bread an' all," said Guzzler.

"It's fuckin' sad. Know what I mean?" said Ronnie.

"Yeah, they ought to have a health warnin' on this place." said Guzzler.

"Poor Chaz. His Mum was a dinner lady, always gave us double pudding," said Ronnie.

"And you remember Flat Dave?" said Guzzler.

Ronnie nodded.

"Him and his missus are banged up on some insurance fraud," said Guzzler.

It was like a list of condemned buildings all demolished or line-up to be pulled down. While looking at the photo, Ronnie realised he was in a club of one. His success suddenly felt like an embarrassment.

Ronnie remembered a boy at school who got a bit part in a TV advert. For a skinny little waif of a child, he became a little bit too full of himself. In Battersham, boastfulness was a currency only valid when applied to boxing or football. He got pelters in and out of school. He was mocked senseless. But the same lads who ridiculed him were the first to excitedly inform their family and non-school friends how great it was and that the boy in the advert was their best mate.

Ronnie wondered what it was that set him apart from his peers. Hazel would say otherwise, but he knew there was a large slice of luck involved in his success. It used to be a catchphrase around here, 'Be lucky' they'd say. Ronnie wished his old pals had caught a stronger dose of it.

Ronnie and his friends set light to their school ties on the last day of term, it was symbolic of their new-found freedom and a comment on how certain school names listed on a CV were as helpful as a blood stain on a white shirt, when it came to decent job interviews.

The reggae music that used to boom across the estate from a disused underground car park had changed to the brain numbing racket aptly titled 'Garage' music. Guzzler used to tell anyone who'd listen that a Nurofen salesman would clean-up if he went door-to-door on the estate when the Ragamuffin DJ's were doing their thing.

In the lock-up, Ronnie was on his fourth can of beer, when Guzzler moved the conversation onto Ronnie, Hazel and more particularly his house.

"Must be lovely having a big old house?" said Guzzler.

"It's nice, yeah. You ought to come up some time," said Ronnie.

Ronnie wanted to keep his head in the fog of old times, school days and tales of characters from the estate. He didn't want to appear boastful about his wealth, it would feel like he was rubbing Guzzler's face in it, and he'd take no pleasure from that. He wasn't excited about his success right at that moment, it didn't feel appropriate. He was compartmentalising, and in that life, there wasn't a coat peg with Guzzler's name on it.

"All that space and I bet you've got a great garden," said Guzzler.

"It's Hazel that does the garden thing, but yeah, it's a bit over an acre in size," said Ronnie.

"Our garden is a three-foot oasis of scrubland in a valley of concrete. The only thing that you could call real grass around here is bagged up and sold on street corners for ten quid a quarter ounce," said Guzzler, with a smile.

"We have all that shit up our end too. Gets everywhere, don't it," said Ronnie.

"It seems like everybody's self-medicating. Most of them just accept that their kids will end up doing it. It's like Russian roulette. Some can handle it, others can't." said Guzzler.

Ronnie felt his earlier invitation for Guzzler, Tracey and the kids to come and visit stick in his throat. He knew Hazel wouldn't want it either, but it didn't stop him feeling ashamed. Guzzler and Tracey had opened their doors, and their poorly stocked larder to him, without the bat of an eyelid. Yet here he was, with all his resources, reluctant to return the gesture. He'd come down to Battersham a little wary of being milked or taken advantage of, but Guzzler had treated him like he treated everybody, with openness and respect. If anyone was dipping pockets it was Ronnie.

"You know what I miss about Arnie?' said Guzzler.

Ronnie pulled his head out of his own thoughts and focused on his friend.

"All the random crazy stuff he did. He'd phone you up with some off the cuff idea, some mad plan for the day, and we'd be off on an excursion." said Guzzler.

Guzzler reached for a can of beer and offered Ronnie one, but a shake of his can told him he was losing pace with his friend, so he declined.

"Yeah, I used to love his spontaneity. Remember he led a mob of us on scooters, up to St. Ives in Cambridgeshire, wondering why we were the only ones there, when we should have joined thousands of other Mods, three-hundred odd miles in the other direction, at a Scooter rally in St. Ives, Cornwall," said Ronnie, chuckling.

Affection for Arnie was universal. They could always warm themselves on the tales of their adventures with him. Whenever there'd been ructions, he always seemed to find a solution.

"Did I tell you about the time we did a robbery?" said Guzzler.

"*You* did a robbery?" asked Ronnie, in surprise.

"It was one Christmas. Arnie was proper skint. We all was. He said he wanted to do a robbery, so he could get something nice for Faye. He roped in Bulldog and Oxford too. I mean, Bulldog would nick the steam off your coffee, but none of us were proper thieves. Oxford had a decent motor, so he was going to be the getaway driver. Arnie's plan was as sketchy as a two-year-old with a crayon. Bulldog half-inched some balaclavas from that Army surplus store up on Wandsworth hill. So, we're sitting there in a side street in Balham."

"Gateway to the south," jokes Ronnie, about Balham's self-appointed epithet. A place that doesn't have enough landmarks to fill even half a postcard.

"Yeah, Gateway to the south," continued Guzzler. "So, Arnie says all we've got to do is wait in the motor. I've got to keep my window open. So, he hops out. We're thinking he's going to have a shufti, check the place out. I mean, he ain't got a gun or anything like that. So, we're sitting there, adrenalin pumping, engine running, all wearing our balaclavas rolled up on the top of our heads like skull caps. We looked like the Sweeney, only Jewish. As conspicuous as a clown's red nose at a funeral. Me old ticker was doing overtime. A couple of minutes later, I catch sight of him running towards us and I'm thinking he's gone and pulled it off himself. He's got what looks like a big beige bag of money in his hands and it looks pretty heavy. We pull our balaclavas down, Oxford puts the car in gear. Then wham, a fuckin' Turkey, the size of one of them big old Television sets, comes flying through my window and lands on me lap. Arnie jumps in the car and shouts at Oxford to shift it. I tell ya, we were pissing ourselves all the way home. Tears coming down his cheeks, Oxford could hardly see to drive."

Ronnie and Guzzler are in fits of laughter.

"God love 'im. That was our Arnie," said Ronnie.

CHAPTER 11.
Goodbye, Battersham.

With Ronnie off to refuel his scooter, Guzzler was loitering with intent in his kitchen. Tracey was busy cramming clothes into a washing machine. He knew that disturbing her, when she was powering through her domestic hitlist, was risking being roped into chores he'd spent a lifetime attempting to sidestep, but today he was in a bind.
"What am I going to do? I can't go down there with nuffin'," said Guzzler.
"What you on about now?" asked Tracey.
"Brighton," said Guzzler.
"Come on, Jason. I feel like I'm your mum packing you off for a school trip. You don't want me to come and wave you off, do you?" she said, smirking at him.
"Don't mess about. Ronnie's planning some kind of ceremony in Brighton and I don't have Arnie's ashes, do I?" he said.
Tracey pressed the buttons on the washing machine, and it whirled into action. She staggered up on to her feet, sighing as she pulled a cigarette out of a packet on the side and lit up. Guzzler sheepishly followed her into the front room, like a nervous child at a birthday party. She gathered up some dirty cups and plates and handed them to him, shoeing him back towards the kitchen.
"Make yourself useful," she said.
"But what about -" said Guzzler.

"- I'll sort it."
He smiled like a boy who'd just been told he could have an extra ten minutes on the swings.
"Thanks, Doll face," he said.
Guzzler had mimicked an advert for cheese spread twenty years ago and the nickname had stuck, although he always felt embarrassed when it slipped out in company.
Guzzler placed the old crockery into the sink before filling the kettle. He flicked the switch on and helped himself to a custard cream biscuit. Tracey stubbed her fag out in a plastic container and busied herself about the flat emptying ashtrays. She opened the hoover and added clumps of dust and fluff to the merry mix. She returned to her husband and handed him a translucent Tupperware box. He wondered how she'd done it, maybe it had come from Faye after all, he thought.
"Happy now?" said Tracey.
"Thanks, lover." said Guzzler.
She took a sip of tea and analysed him. He was a big useless lump, but he had a good heart and his heart belonged to her.
"We used to always do the run to Brighton together," she said, in a gently accusing tone.
It wasn't exactly true. Tracey attended a couple of Scooter weekends, but that was at the tail-end of it. This was the *Jolly Boy's Reunion*. He felt certain that Ronnie, Mick and Bulldog wouldn't relish the extra company. Even so, he reluctantly offered up an invitation.
"You could still come? I mean, if you really want to."
"What? And have to look at Ronnie's stupid face when he realises that it was a time machine he needed and not a Scooter? Nah, you're alright," she replied.

She had no intention of going but appreciated his response. It was the thermometer she sometimes relied on to measure his intent. He gave her a hug and gathered up his bag, a battered old skid lid and a shabby coat he used to wear in the old days that barely fit him anymore.

"You're not wearing that old thing, are ya?" said Tracey.

"Ronnie's got a new suit and all the old gear. I want to look the part," said Guzzler.

"I know what part you'd look like if you wear that down there," she said.

Guzzler looked her in the eyes before tramping off to change his jacket.

While packing the plastic container in his bag, his eyes were drawn to something inside it. Struck by the fear of a superstition he wasn't sure existed, he refrained from opening it, but instead held it up to the light and shook it around.

"What is that? Is that a…"

Tracey sighed. "It's either that, or you go empty handed. It's your choice."

Guzzler's face was frozen in disappointment. Was there anything in his life that wasn't half-arsed, make-do or flat-out shoddy? Even his best friend's farewell couldn't avoid being tainted in some way, he thought.

"But Trace…"

"You're tipping it in the sea, not carrying it through Westminster Abbey."

In his threadbare flat, Mick stood in front of a canvas print of his old dog, Albie. It hung as the centrepiece of his sparse living room. When Albie died, he took the best part of Mick with him. That dog had provided a pathway to a youthful joy that he had barely experienced as a child. It was eight long years since Albie had passed away and Mick felt every minute of it.

"Farewell, my old friend," he said aloud, as he gave it one more glance, as a lump appeared in his throat. He'd leant on that dog like an old man does a stick. The comfort and companionship he brought Mick helped him through some difficult times, but looking at the picture now, it wasn't the warmth of his body as he'd nuzzled up to him on the sofa that he recalled, or Albie's joyful face as his loyal pup ran, jumped and played, retrieving an outlet of kindness hidden deep within Mick. Now, the only thing he could visualise was Albie's demise. He saw himself perched on an orange plastic chair listening to the Vet twisting and wrenching at his heart whilst trying to convince him that paying another hefty bill might secure a few more weeks of a diminished existence. All of this to the soundtrack of his whimpering, dying pal, having convulsions in a pen a few paces away. Even at the thought of the unbearable pain their separation would bring him, he knew the Vet's half-promises and vague assumptions were nothing more than an opportunistic attempt at extortion. He didn't have the money, but he'd have broken into the Tower of London and stolen the Queen's jewels, if that was required to really save him. He was all too aware of Albie's fate long before he'd carried him into the minicab, on that fateful journey to the pet surgery.

If Mick's flat was sparse before, now it was simply barren. The telescope, computer and much of the furniture was gone. He'd eaten his breakfast off of an upturned box that morning, much in a way that someone just moving in might have. He emptied the place, but still it hung heavy with ghosts.

Mick had lived in the same flat all his life, except for a six-month spell living with a girlfriend, back in the late nineteen-eighties. He inherited the flat from his mum when she died. The council tried to evict him, claiming they couldn't justify letting a three-bedroom property to a single occupant. He tried to dig his heels in, refusing to move, but eventually they gave him the ultimatum of moving out or buying the place at a reduced rate. It was property boom time and people everywhere were trumpeting the benefits of being homeowners. What was once the drudgery of an eighth-floor rabbit hutch was now being proffered as a cosy home with penthouse views of London. Along with about twenty other suckers in his block, Mick fell for the spiel. It felt good to be a homeowner, he felt like he was suddenly on the up. He was eight floors up without a parachute. He had big plans for the place. He ripped down the old-fashioned wallpaper and threw out most of his mum's old clutter, but the bachelor pad he envisaged only ever existed in his mind.

Taking a crowbar to the electric meter in the hall, Mick watched as coins tumbled to the floor. 'Is this the sum of my life's endeavours?' He thought to himself. He was so skint, he'd thought about selling his old Scooter but wondered whether the petrol it carried would be worth more than the bike itself, so he kept it. The mortgage was in arrears and as sellable as a broken fax machine. Outwardly he'd allotted responsibility, for his failure, to anyone and everyone but, when he tallied it all up, he knew he only needed to raise his head to see the finger of blame pointing his way.

The estate had a reputation for generating chancers, drug-pushers and no-hopers, but there were plenty of hard-working folk here too. He reflected on the moments when he stood and caught a cold while others caught a wave. It was the quick and the dead and so often he'd been left floundering in the pits, while his contemporaries were already on their second lap. He felt this way about Ronnie. Nobody wanted to feel left behind and so if you couldn't join them, you'd beat them by taking pot shots at their character. The green-eyed monster had an endless list of reasons for other people's successes.

Ronnie was pumped up like an over-inflated effigy of himself. It was happening. His dream of Brighton and the Aces reunion was on the verge of being realised. He knocked on Mick's front door, excitedly, like he had when he was eight, asking if he wanted to come to the park and play football. As young lads, they'd done everything together. From swapping football stickers to lending records, sharing their first cigarette and sampling their first taste of alcohol.

They shared a paper round, a car cleaning rouse and split their takings on the annual 'Penny for the guy' operation. At the age of fourteen they became blood brothers, although the soft flesh of the thumbs they sacrificed to establish this warrior-like gesture of friendship, were quickly infected by the rusty Stanley knife they used for the hastily arranged ceremony.

Before he had a chance to knock on the door again, it burst open and an edgy looking Mick slipped out holding a bag and a crash helmet. Eyes everywhere, Mick yanked the door closed and swiftly knelt down to do his shoelaces up before heading for the lift.

"I was starting to think you were blowing us out," said Ronnie.

"What? And miss out on this pantomime?" said Mick.

Mick took off, three paces ahead of Ronnie, in a hurry to get anywhere but there. He stood, hovering by the stairwell at the end of the walkway, waiting for Ronnie, his eyes darting around like he was tracking an airborne battle between two flies.

Ronnie, still sold on what he saw as the romantic nature of the adventure, had not quite taken Mick's temperature, awarding him a congratulatory pat on his back as they made their way down the piss-stained stairs.

"Last of the mavericks, eh? I mean, you answer to no-one..." said Ronnie.

"You havin' a laugh?"

Ronnie smiled, oblivious to the stark irony of his words.

"Nah, The world's your oyster."

Mick shook his head and, on spotting some used syringes in his path, cleared them out of the way with a flick of his right foot.

"Yeah, world's me oyster," he said.

The closer they got to the ground floor the stronger the stench of refuse became. Ronnie noticed that someone had jammed an old table in one of the rubbish chutes and bags of refuse had built up, some had split open, carpeting the area with used nappies, half-empty tins of beans and mouldy bread. The majority of the people who lived there were decent folk, but it took less than a handful of lazy deadbeats to invite the squalor. Mick didn't bat an eye lid as they made their way past it and out in to the open.

"Where's your Scoot?" asked Ronnie.

"Garages," said Mick.

Ronnie turned one way and halted as Mick took off in the opposite direction.

"I thought you said the garages?" said Ronnie.

Mick kept walking.

"The garages are right there," said Ronnie, puzzled as to why they weren't taking the direct route to get to their destination.

Ronnie pointed towards a little inlet that had rows of up and over garage doors, some completely removed, most adorned with scribbly graffiti, as if the little ones from the local nursey had been kitted out with aerosol cans and told to go nuts.

Mick, head down and silent, tensed up but continued walking. Mick's fists gripped thin air tightly. Ronnie followed a couple of paces behind. They reached an alleyway that led to the rear of the garages. Ronnie was still puzzled at the route they had taken, which was about five times as long as it needed to be.

"What's up with..." Suddenly Ronnie fell silent mid-sentence.

He felt his whole-body recoil in shame. How could he have forgotten? How could he be so insensitive? Mick's indirect journey to the garages was a conscious move to avoid the spot where his sister, Eve, had thrown herself to her death from the roof of the flats. Ronnie considered apologising but thought better of it. Mick never talked publicly about Eve, let alone about what happened to her. It was a fire Ronnie had no intention of stoking. After her suicide, it was like she never existed. At the time Mick and Ronnie's relationship had cooled and it wasn't long before Ronnie departed to new shores.

It dawned on Ronnie just how self-obsessed he had become. Mick was one of his best mates years ago. He wasn't going to be sitting around alongside Guzzler, Bulldog et al, revving up their scooters just waiting for Ronnie's homecoming party. Their lives hadn't stopped the day Ronnie exited stage left. Ronnie worked hard to attain the comfortable existence he enjoyed, but he had also been lucky. Mick could have told him that and probably would, given half a chance. Fate was anything but even-handed. Mick was certainly the architect of most of his own failures, but no-one could accuse him of enjoying the rub of the green.

Eve was three years younger than him, extraordinarily pretty with natural blonde hair. She wasn't just stunningly beautiful; she had an aura about her. The letches around here made it impossible for her to simply nip to the shops, without facing some form of unwanted attention. They came out of the woodwork like cockroaches in a drug den, the moment her feet touched the pavement.

Being that attractive around here could be a curse. She seemed to do everything to downplay it, dyeing her hair black and dressing like a Goth. She was the first self-harmer Ronnie had known, mangling up her hands and forearms with cuts. She was a troubled soul, outwardly naïve. Today she'd have been diagnosed with a mental health condition, but back then they'd just say, 'She wasn't the full shilling.'

For Mick, Eve had been something of a burden. He had been charged to look after her by their mother, but he had his own life to lead. He'd warded off bad choices in the boyfriend department but resented being expected to watch over her morning, noon and night.

The Dopeheads loved to get 'sky high', lolloping around on the roof smoking weed. They broke the lock off the hatch door. One day Eve climbed up the wall ladder and used their route to gain access to the roof. Ronnie stole a quick glance at the top of the flats. It was sixteen floors up. He thought about how frightened she must have been as she took those final fateful steps. He felt a shiver chill him to the bone.

The funeral had been a small private affair, just a handful of close family members. Mick had seen his Dad for the first time in years. It almost turned into a brawl as his father repeated some of the nonsense printed in the tabloids. They had a field day, callously blaming his mother for what had happened. One red top was touting around the estate for pictures of her; top dollar for the person who could supply a picture of Eve in a bikini. Their lives were squeezed in a vice with no way of alleviating the pressure.

Mick's mum was broken by it all, and although her death certificate recorded heart failure as the cause, everyone knew it was Eve's death and its aftermath that killed her. She was smouldering in her own personal Hiroshima. If the blast didn't wipe her out, the radiation was sure to get her. Mick blamed himself for not protecting his sister. His rage would be set on a hair trigger after that. He could always handle himself, but fighting didn't exactly come as second nature to him the way it did with some of the roughhouses he took on. He became fearless and somewhat reckless, one misplaced comment, a slight on her mental fragility and Mick would explode, often getting battered by people he had no business fronting.

CHAPTER 12.
The Road to Brighton is paved with good intentions.

The sun glistened on the two scooters parked outside the Lost Angel pub. They looked like religious relics next to a shiny new bubble-shaped Mini. Ronnie was outside perched on the edge of a table, supping his beer. His Mod Parka was strewn over his Scooter, like a tarpaulin. In the shadow of the Tavern's doorway, Mick shifted about like a man in desperate need to relieve himself of his surroundings.
"They were supposed to be here ages ago," grumped Mick.
"No rush, is there?" said Ronnie.
"I thought you wanted to get down there pronto?" said Mick.
"I do, but let's enjoy the first beer of the day, eh?" said Ronnie.
"Can't leave this shithole soon enough," mumbled Mick. He aggressively eyed out a small group of young black men, who sloped-by clowning around with each other. One of them met his eyes, caught his drift and returned the compliment.
"Try me, go on, just fuckin' try me," uttered Mick, under his breath.

Ronnie noticed there was something untoward going on but packaged that malevolent puzzle up for a conversation on a later date.

"Here come the Cavalry," said a delighted Ronnie, keen to bury his earlier faux pas in the comfort of more company.

Bulldog and Guzzler breezed in on their scooters and Ronnie delighted at the aroma of a fresh waft of two-stroke oil and petrol. To Ronnie, it was the scent of adventure.

Guzzler beamed like a Bingo winner as he dismounted Arnie's prized Vespa, while Bulldog, clambered off Guzzler's old Lambretta that had seen better days. He was lifted by being with the gang of friends. For once he felt part of something bigger than himself.

Bulldog gave Ronnie's retro Mod vibe the once-over. He thought he looked to all the world a B-Movie superstar, in his Paul Smith mohair suit and Hush Puppies. Ronnie couldn't bring himself to return the compliment. Bulldog wore his usual faded red Puffer Jacket and Jeans that had gone AWOL on wash days. He had the dog-end of a cigarette in his mouth that would only go half-way to explain the yellowness of his teeth.

Bulldog pulled out his mobile phone and took a few snaps.

"What you havin'? I'll shout 'em up," said Ronnie, who was rediscovering the rough edges to his Cockney accent.

"Let's not let the grass grow, eh?" said Mick.

"One for the road, an' all that," said Guzzler, perplexed at Mick's attempt to set the tone.

"Come on, I wanna get out of this fuckin' place," said Mick.

His agitation was coming to the fore.

"So, what's the plan of action? You got a route all mapped out, food breaks and fuel stops?" asked Bulldog.

"When did we ever need a plan? We're shooting off to the seaside not delivering parcels for Amazon," snapped Mick. Bulldog looked at Ronnie and raised his eyebrows in acknowledgement of the negative vibes emanating from their obstinate friend. Ronnie was convinced that once they'd advanced on Sussex and Brighton's brisk sea air had blown away the cloud of smog that hovered around Mick, like soot on a coalminer, he would rediscover his old self and fervently share in Ronnie's rose-tinted vision of the Aces' long-over-due reunion.

Ronnie, Guzzler and Mick mounted their scooters. It couldn't match the deep roar of a convoy of Harley Davidsons, but there was something exciting about the combined sound of their machines, it brought them the looks from passers-by that they had once revelled in.
"Come on, twist your wrists," shouted Mick.
Bulldog straddled Guzzler's old Scooter and felt something of his old self as he revved it up.
The old friends set off through the streets of Battersham, like they'd burst through the vista from a bygone age. Most of the teenagers they passed would have probably never even heard of Mods. Youth culture had come from the street back then, with its accessible styles and local customs, but it had long since been hijacked by faceless multi-million-pound corporations and now, except for the rare few, most youths wore identikit clothes from high street brands. No invention or imagination, the fun had been ripped out of street fashion.
Ronnie rode up front like the general he aspired to be. They had only been on the road for a short while when the Lambretta Bulldog was riding, petered out. It was as if the old thing had got a whiff of their intentions and decided to

bail. Coughing and spluttering it came to a shuddering halt in front of some bemused customers sat outside a roadside café in Balham. Mick took one look in his mirrors and, not wanting to put his name in the hat for an extra passenger to contend with, he continued along the road.

This really was like the old days. There were always casualties on the way to the south-coast scooter runs. Ronnie and the boys would often see dismantled machines strewn out on grass verges on the side of the road, with their bewildered riders scratching their heads and waiting for the more mechanically savvy members of their crew to rock up. Arnie and Bulldog would count up who had taken the most casualties, Vespa's or Lambrettas. Although Vespas were more numerical, it was Lambrettas that got the reputation for unreliability.

Guzzler checked the scooter over.

Ronnie manoeuvred his scooter back to where Guzzler had pulled in to help.

"What's the diagnosis?" asked Bulldog.

"Sorry mate, the old girl's well and truly had her day," said Guzzler.

"Can you patch her up?" asked Ronnie.

Guzzler was clearly disheartened. He clunked around in the side panel before declaring its death notice.

"She's not gonna make it to Brighton this time," he said.

"D'you want me to push it around the corner?" asked Bulldog.

"Nah, just leave 'er to the crows," said Guzzler.

"Back in a minute," said Ronnie.

He tootled off, in the direction they'd come from. He stopped a few streets away and parked his scoot outside an army surplus store. A couple of minutes later he re-emerged with a carrier bag.

On return, Ronnie found Bulldog sitting on the curb smoking a roll-up, alongside a daydreaming Guzzler.
"Ronnie, D'ya reckon you could -" said Bulldog, in a pleading tone.
Ronnie cut him off. "- One condition."
Bulldog shrugged his shoulders.
"You wear this," said Ronnie, as he threw him the carrier bag. Bulldog pulled out a khaki green, heavily padded, US Airforce Flight jacket. It was not too unlike what Mick had on, except Mick's was adorned with the odd splattering of paint.
"Cheers, Ronnie, you're a Diamond," said Bulldog, remembering an overused cheesy line from the old days.
"It ain't a Parka, but it's better than that monstrosity," said Ronnie, pointing at Bulldog's red puffer coat that was so scruffy and worn, Ronnie thought it would probably melt if they encountered rain. It offered about as much protection as a silk crash-helmet.
Ronnie ushered Bulldog on to his scooter, enduring a few wobbles before finally readjusting for his passenger. Bulldog's spindly hands held on to Ronnie, as they sped off, doing their best to catch up with Mick. He'd have rather ridden solo to Brighton, but in hindsight he thought it was likely that both Bulldog and his Scooter were going to run out of puff long before they got anywhere near the South Downs.
Ronnie spotted a skip by the side of the road and, without stopping, he managed to pull out Bulldog's old coat and hurl it on top of a mound of broken up plasterboard and disabled office furniture. Bulldog considered protesting but said nothing. The deed was done. 'It's alright for you, you flash git, you could buy a new coat for every day of the

year and not feel the dent in your pocket,' Bulldog thought to himself.

Guzzler, Mick and Ronnie with Bulldog riding pillion, drove their scooters along empty country roads to the backdrop of the gently sloping hills of Sussex. Swirling winds made the crops dance and sway as the gang glided by.

As they were held up at a set of temporary traffic lights, in a quaint little village, not unlike Arksdean, three children, all wearing ear bud headphones, were sticking their tongues out at them through the back window of a car. Ronnie looked to Mick and they shared a smile. As the lights turned green, Ronnie pulled the throttle back and moved to the front to lead the pack, it wasn't quite the convoy of fifty-odd scooters he commanded in the nineteen eighties, but it gave him a little buzz, nonetheless.

Sitting at a garish yellow plastic table, in a burger bar that looked like the set of Sesame Street, the four friends hunched over their hamburgers. Guzzler was devouring his food while keeping more than an eye on Bulldog who only picked at his.

"D'you remember the first time we rode through that big arch thing, into Brighton. Scooters everywhere. That was the time to be a Mod," said Ronnie.

"Except when the Skinheads arrived," said Mick.

"Yeah, that was a bit unhealthy," said Guzzler

"They kept you fit. All that running you did," said Mick, mocking Guzzler.

While Mick was talking reportage, Ronnie was in Hollywood. The memories playing out in his mind had edited out all those unwelcome shots. Damp beds, black eyes, heavy rain, police aggression, extortionate beer tabs and getting thrown out of pubs. All of those negatives ended up on the cutting room floor, but without them the good times wouldn't have felt so special.

"All those Mod girls. The music, mini-skirts and mayhem. We looked the business eh?" said Ronnie, re-establishing his line of thought.

"Look at us now," said Bulldog.

"If I could, I'd go back there in a shot. Best days of our lives," said Ronnie.

"Maybe, but what sort of future can you have if your head is stuck in the past," said Guzzler. Just for a moment, the others caught a glimpse of the imposter Jason. That soon evaporated as Guzzler returned to demolish Bulldog's half-eaten burger and fries.

Ronnie was leaning against his scooter, waiting for Bulldog to return from the men's room, Guzzler was busy texting Tracey while perched on his, and Mick was rummaging in his sports bag. A waitress came rushing out of the restaurant waving at them.

"You didn't stiff them on the bill? You old miser," said Mick to Guzzler.

"I don't know, Mick, they're probably still counting out the coins from your penny jar," said Guzzler.

"One of you gen-tel-men lose you bag?" said the woman, in broken English.

Guzzler took a swift glance at his luggage rack then grimaced.

"Arnie," he said, louder than he had intended to.

"You left Arnie in the burger bar?" quizzed Ronnie, in a mocking tone.

"You idiot," said Mick.

"What? I didn't know, did I?" said Guzzler, Squirming.

Guzzler reached out his hands to retrieve the bag, but Ronnie intercepted it.
"Maybe Arnie should ride with me," he said
The waitress, a recent arrival from Eastern Europe, was doubly puzzled by their conversation, wondering what on earth an 'Arnie' was. Ronnie thanked her while Guzzler continued to protest.
"I would have realised," said Guzzler.
Ronnie pulled the Tupperware box out of the carrier bag and peeled open the top.
"What you doing?" Guzzler protested angrily.
Ronnie replaced the lid and secured it in his sports bag.
Bulldog appeared and Ronnie thought he looked like death. He wondered whether bringing him to Brighton was such a good idea.
"Everyone good to go?" asked Mick.
"All good," said Ronnie, who gave a sheepish Guzzler a sceptical look before heading off.

CHAPTER 13.   Pride of Brighton.

The Battersham aces arrived in Brighton. At a major junction Ronnie spotted a group of Scooterists heading for the seafront. One of the riders gave Ronnie a thumbs up and he soon signalled the others to follow. Brighton was bustling with crowds of people overflowing on the streets. There were stewards waving the Scooterists through and an enthusiastic Ronnie was leading his own crew along behind them. It was a good omen, thought Ronnie. It was some kind of street festival. Brighton was opening up its arms and welcoming them home.

The sun was beaming down, and the party mood was tangible. Ronnie felt an extra jolt of excitement when he caught a glimpse of the calm sea and frothy waves of the English Channel.

The Bank holiday dash to the seaside had a long tradition in working class communities. A chance to escape the smog of the city, away from the grind of daily life. Ronnie had memories of his family invading Brighton in the early seventies with sozzled aunties, grumpy uncles, his mum, dad, cousins and neighbours. When they knocked the terraced houses down to make way for the skyscrapers a lot of those folk were dispersed to other places. Family ties were ripped up or at best loosened. The army of children, togged out with buckets and spades, soon became depleted. Bulldog caught a glimpse of the words 'Pink Panther Scooter Club' written across the wheel covers on the back of one of the immaculate scooters in front of him. Brighton was a riot of colours, the other Scooterists had dressed themselves and their machines in flamboyant pink and yellow dayglo tones.

As they edged out onto the seafront, the Aces found they had joined an enormous parade that seemed to stretch as far as the eye could see. People lined the streets, clapping, hooting and waving. Bulldog was reciprocating their enthusiastic applause with the occasional thumbs up. It was a jamboree of high-spirits, noise and colour. The Scooterists playfully tooted their horns at the Cheerleaders in front of them. Ronnie's face dropped when one of the cheerleaders turned around and blew him a kiss. The Cheerleader in question was a bearded man with a fat hairy belly poking through some kind of shocking pink tutu number. Ronnie, becoming more flustered by the minute, called over his shoulder to Bulldog, holding tight to Ronnie on the back saddle.

"If you take a selfie now, I'll bloody murder you," he shouted.

Behind them he could now see an enormous rainbow flag being unveiled along the procession. Everyone was camping it up with whistles, plastic trumpets and streamers. Ronnie led his friends away up a back street at the earliest opportunity. Bulldog was disappointed to leave, whereas Mick was enjoying winding up Ronnie.

"Why did you really bring us down here, Ronnie?" he said. Ronnie felt embarrassed. This wasn't in the script. He didn't have an issue with homosexuals, he tried to explain, it's just this wasn't his party, and he would carry flags for no-one.

They parked up and Guzzler tucked into a big ice cream as they all sauntered along the promenade. Children screamed with joy as a whirly contraption flung them up into the sky at the funfair on Brighton Pier. Ronnie felt it looked much as it had when he was last here, decades ago.

While Mick, Bulldog and Guzzler crowded around the concierge's desk, in the lobby of the Ocean hotel, Ronnie drifted quietly away to slip a bad penny or two into a nearby pay phone. The receptionist was pulling a face as blank as a list of honest politicians.

"What's he up to?" said Mick, looking over at Ronnie.

"Probably calling HQ," said Guzzler.

Mick raised a suspicious eyebrow.

"On a pay phone?"

The look on Ronnie's face informed them that he had returned from the call box short changed. They too, looked less than delighted with their current predicament.

"What's up? asked Ronnie.

"They've got no free rooms until tomorrow," said Bulldog.

"It's not like it's the only hotel in Brighton," said Ronnie, in a condescending manner.

"They've searched all over the city, not so much as a broom cupboard vacant," said Bulldog.

Mick was standing, arms folded. "It's Bank holiday," he said.

"And it's Gay Pride Day," said Guzzler.

"So what?" replied Ronnie.

"I knew we should have booked online," said Guzzler.

"We never had to book before," replied Ronnie, feeling the heat of their collective scorn.

"'Course we didn't. We never even have credit cards then, let alone the bloody internet and mobile phones," pronounced Mick.

Ronnie was starting to feel a bit narked with them.

"Well, there's only one thing for it then, ain't there?" said Ronnie.

"What's that then?" said Mick.

"Think about it," said Ronnie. "What would Arnie do?"

Ronnie took off at pace, like someone trying to shake off a bad smell. The others followed on, as he reasoned they would, to a nearby pub.

After drinking their way through half a dozen hostelries, supping a pint per pub, they ended up in a rough looking backstreet drinkerie called The Pickled Goat. It was a spit and sawdust establishment with a three-piece house band. Ronnie and the guys had just caught the last couple of songs before the interval. At the bar Ronnie got chatting with the singer, who ribbed him about his Parka. His older brother had been a Mod and so conversed in a common tongue when it came to music. He had a decent singing voice, and the band were competent but gave a rather static performance. On hearing that they played a couple of Who numbers Ronnie interrogated the singer, convincing him that a Mod-themed second set was the order of the day and if he had to grease his palm to make it happen, he would. Ronnie pulled out a handful of notes.

"Hundred quid if your second set is full of stuff we like."

He didn't need to ask twice, the money disappeared from Ronnie's fist within a blink of an opportunistic eye.

The change of direction wasn't to everyone's liking, but the old Battersham boys were in seventh heaven. They drank and danced, jumped and pranced their way through classic numbers by The Who, The Small Faces, The Kinks and a couple of songs from The Jam.

Half-way through a rendition of the Jam's 'Strange town,' Ronnie plucked up the courage to join the singer on stage. It wasn't a giant leap, the stage was a six-inch platform, and the singer was hardly likely to object now that Ronnie had crossed his palm with silver. Ronnie was away. For a brief time, he was performing with Weller, Foxton and Buckler at a packed-out gig at The Rainbow Theatre, in North London. None of the many drinks he'd throw back on this long hot summer's night would taste as sweet as this moment. It even came with the ego-boosting attention from a couple of middle-aged women who'd been watching him throughout. They sidled up to him when the music had died off.

At the end of the night, Ronnie, Guzzler, Bulldog and Mick fell out on to the street, like dirty suds from a wash pale, all a bit wrong footed and over-watered.
"I thought you were gonna pull then," said Bulldog to Ronnie.
"I reckon she'd have let us all kip on her floor," said Mick.
"Or in her bed," said Bulldog.
"Leave it out. I've seen Hedgehogs with less stubble," said Mick.
"He ain't come down here to chase women. Have you Ron?" protested Guzzler.
"Unless they're called Roxy," said Bulldog, as he whipped out a scrap of paper with Roxy's number on it and dangled it in front of Ronnie, who tried unsuccessfully to grab it back.
"Oi. Where'd you get that? You bloody tea leaf." said Ronnie.
"Fell out your pocket," said Bulldog, with a grin.
Ronnie gave him a suspicious look and gave up trying to grab the note back. Ron and Roxy, thought Mick, that was an old chestnut worth leaving, undisturbed, in the shrubbery of ancient history.
"Unfinished business, aye, Ron?" quipped Mick.

"I said I'd give her a call if I ever came down to Brighton. That's all."

"Give him the number, Bulldog. Roxy's bound to let us stay round hers," said Guzzler.

Ronnie shared his frustration.

"Don't matter anyway, it was a wrong number. It was some health club or something. They'd never heard of her," he said.

Like a twenty-first century Hansel and Gretel, they followed the electric breadcrumbs that guided them back to Brighton's famous pier. As each step brought them closer, so its majesty fell away to reveal what was nothing more than a tacky fairground on wooden stilts.

Bulldog halted the march of the drunks and turned to correct Ronnie.

"She don't call herself Roxy no more."

"Oh yeah. It's Jenny or Joanna or something," Guzzler interjected excitedly.

Ronnie grimaced.

"Fat lot of good that is to us now. What we gonna do walk up and down the seafront shouting 'Jenny' or 'Joanna' or 'Roxy?' said Mick.

Trying to look at the situation positively, Bulldog thought about how warm it was and on reflection of his lack of funds he declared, "Let's sleep on the beach, I mean it'd save us a few quid."

"Freeze our bollocks off, more like," responded a less than impressed Guzzler.

"Bulldog's right, it'll be just like the old days," said Ronnie, finding a new wind at the suggestion.

"Back then I always had a bird to keep me warm," insisted Mick.

"Guzzler'll do you a turn if you buy him some chips," said Ronnie, sniggering.
"Oi, don't take the piss," said Guzzler.
Bulldog tugged at a packet of cigarettes and lit one up. Guzzler spotted that it wasn't his usual brand.
"Where d'ya get them, then?" asked Guzzler.
"Bloke at the bar, said I could help meself," he said, with a cheeky grin.
"You're sommink else, you are," said Guzzler.
"Wonder what ever happened to Big Sarah? she knew how to keep a lad warm," said Mick, as he found the more amorous rooms of his memory suddenly unlocking.
"She's a traffic warden," said Bulldog.
"How do you know?" said Mick.
"I bet he let her take down his particulars," said Guzzler.
"We're Facebook friends," said Bulldog.
Guzzler, having no time for social media himself, mocked Bulldog. He was always banging on about it being the place for the vaingloriously ignorant with their deep opinions of themselves and shallow attention spans. Tracey thought of it as a window to the world, he thought that if that was what the world looked like, he'd rather draw the curtains. Guzzler did, however, plug Tracey for a regular rundown of the local gossip it spewed out.
"I know you still use pigeon post, but this is the twenty first century, Guzz," said Bulldog.
"They're not real friends. You can't dance with them, you can't kiss them," said Guzzler.
"You can if you try the right places," said Ronnie.
"Everyone does it. That's life," said Bulldog, who always seemed to be on the back foot in group conversations.
"It's just fakery," said Guzzler, who was hell-bent on having the last word.

"Hark at him," said Mick, teasing him.

"Fakery? Is that even a word?" said Bulldog

"I don't know, why don't you ask Mark Zuckerberg," said Guzzler.

Bulldog pulled the bottle of spirits out of his inside pocket that he'd been hoping to keep to himself.

"Cuddle up to this if you want?" he said.

"You could steal the eyebrows off a Russian, you little tea leaf," said Mick, as he grabbed the bottle and took the first swig.

CHAPTER 14.   Under the Stars.

A gentle ripple of waves lapped at the giant wooden supports of the pier, on the pebbled beach, a few metres from Ronnie, Mick, Guzzler and Bulldog, who were stretched out under the stars. The temperature had dipped but it was still warm enough to be out. Ronnie took a swig of booze and passed the bottle to Guzzler.
"You know, When I think back there's one night that always makes the hairs on the back of my neck stand up, said Ronnie.
"When you pulled that Tranny in Blackpool?" said Guzzler, mischievously.
"I never pulled no Tranny," said Ronnie, determined to snuff out the fuse on that anecdote.
"You talking about when that drunken Irish bloke tried to nick your scooter?" asked Mick.
"Oh yeah," said Guzzler. "I remember that."
"No. He wasn't trying to nick it. The twat just sat on it and was trying to find a coin slot to get it working," said Ronnie.
"He was proper blotto," said Mick.
"Be fair, you were parked outside Amusement arcade," added Bulldog, smirking.
"Weren't amusing for me, I had to try and get the fat fucker off it," said Ronnie.

"Was when…" said Guzzler, struggling to get the words out as he set off a ripple of drunken laughter. "He keeled over," Guzzler was in hysterics.

"Not as funny as that time when Guzz burned that house down?" said Bulldog.

"How was I supposed to know that can of silly string would explode?" said Guzzler.

"You had to give Peckham a proper swerve after that. That big bastard would have killed you Guzz, if he wasn't running in and out of his house trying to save his record collection," said Ronnie.

The bottle was lubricating their excursion to the nostalgia comedy club. Even Mick began to thaw.

"Remember the *May Day* bash, hundred club? That was some night," said Mick, a satisfied glow on his face.

"That was the night we caned those lary Soulboys," said Ronnie.

"I can still see their smug faces drop, when they realised, they'd bitten off more than they could chew," said Mick.

"We were invincible that night," said Guzzler.

"Yeah, invincible…Except for Bulldog who was trying to be invisible," said Mick

"Oh yeah, he ran off and ended up wrestling with a double-decker bus," said Guzzler.

Everyone chuckled, intoxicated by their collective history. Everyone except Bulldog.

Ronnie beamed. "The stuff of legends."

"Mick tried to throw a moped through that pub window," said Bulldog.

"Nah, that weren't me, it was Ronnie," said Mick.

"One minute we were supping a pint, the next we were starting a revolution," said Guzzler.

"It was the rise of the Battersham Aces," said Ronnie.

"Yeah, what ever happened to them?" said Guzzler.
"*They* ended up in a cell," said Ronnie.
"Yeah, the accommodation was a bit lacking that night as I recall," said Mick.
"At least they put us all in together," said Ronnie.
"We laughed like schoolboys that night. Didn't we, aye?" said Mick.

This immersion into past glories radiated a warm feeling and reminded them of their baptism into a gang culture. In an ugly foreboding world, it felt good to be part of a tribe. A skinny man, in tight silver shorts and vest combo, minced by, shooting them a look. Ronnie thought he'd watched too many 'Carry on' films. He was such a caricature. His presence was like a windscreen wiper erasing their macho mist of yesteryear and replacing it with a more sobering taste of someone else's reality. Mick thought the guy was trying a bit too hard. Suddenly it seemed the wind had gotten its bite back.

Bulldog got to his feet, readjusting himself for balance on the sloping carpet of large pebbles.

"Gotta be a garage open 'round here, get some fags," said Bulldog.
"You said you were giving up?" said Guzzler.

Bulldog shrugged his shoulders.

"What, you turned into me mum all of a sudden?"

Bulldog trailed off. Guzzler half-heartedly motioned to get up.

"I'll come along with you," said Guzzler.
"I'll get you something, if you want?" said Bulldog.

Guzzler, knackered from the day, happily slumped back down in the groove he'd made for himself.

"Bring us back a Mars bar…and Jelly babies…oh and some crisps."

Bulldog cadged money from all of them and attempted a mental list of confectionary and soft drinks. He took a quick swig of booze, before disappearing across the pebbles and into the night. Guzzler took a swig and handed the bottle to Mick.

"D'you feel that?" said Mick.

Guzzler sat up at the sound of a rumble in the sky.

"Abandon ship."

Within a matter of seconds a few specs of rain turned into a torrential downpour. The three old friends, struggled to gather their belongings up, before rushing for cover.

"Every Mod for himself," charged Ronnie, laughing while he stumbled, across the pebbled terrain, towards the shelter of the pier.

Ronnie tried to gain entry to some storage huts. Next to a shopping trolley containing bags of old clothes, he found one that wasn't locked. He managed to get the door wedged open enough to squeeze in, tripping over something and crashing to the floor in a bundle.

"Fuckin' 'ell," he grumbled, but his grievance just encouraged the other two to fall about laughing.

As uncomfortable as it was, none of them had any intention of moving anywhere else. They were out of the rain and wind; an evening's heavy drinking would take care of the insulation and after the days' antics, it wouldn't be long before they'd formed a snoring chorus to compliment the soundscape of crashing waves outside.

Squawking Gulls filled the air, as the sea crashed in and filtered back out through the pebbled beach, each wave brushing a million stone teeth. Luminous joggers ate up the tarmac on the seafront, accompanied by early morning roller-skaters as a bright blue sky dominated the vista like a start flag heralding the beginning of something positively exhilarating. An instant uplift for those who chose this day to experience the seaside. Dog walkers scurried past dossers, and weekend stop-outs, who were stationed in an array of Victorian shelters like human bin bags.

It was pitch black inside the beach hut when Guzzler was woken by strange shuffling sounds. He sat up and scratched his weary head, an aching, from tip to toe, pounced on him as if biding its time for when the cushion of alcoholic analgesic had worn off. What could pass as a place to sleep now, was very different than it was as a teenager. He hadn't slept on the concrete floor it had slept on him. He wondered if the scraping noise existed outside of his head. A scuffling sound, audible and close, soon solved the puzzle.

"What the hell?" Guzzler said, aloud.

Unnerved, Guzzler nudged Mick, gently calling his name, trying not wake the bear with a start.

"What?" grouched Mick, as he lashed out into thin air, trying to tame the source of the prodding but only finding the unfamiliar impression of the cracked and dirty stone floor.

"There's something in here," said Guzzler.

"Piss off Guzz," said Mick.

Ronnie stirred, addressing the shape he could barely make out as Guzzler.

"What's up?"

"I swear I just saw a face with a beard hovering over me," said Guzzler.

"He's dreaming about that cheerleader on the parade, you know, Widow Twanky." said Mick, now fully awake and doing a quick mental rewind to explain to himself his current physical predicament.

The sound of water trickling prompted Ronnie to flick his phone screen on, softly illuminating the naked backside of a Tramp urinating into a bottle a few feet away. As the light travelled to the vagrant's saggy eyes, it sounded like he'd become engaged in a heated, if slightly muted, argument with himself, as he pulled his trousers up.

"Urgh," said Ronnie, Mick and Guzzler in unison.

It was enough to send their hangovers into overdrive. The tramp, who was only a few years older than themselves, gathered up his meagre possessions and shuffled off towards the exit.

"Bloody tourists," grumbled the vagrant.

As he opened the door his silhouette was swallowed up into a stark beam of daylight that stung their eyes. Mick and Ronnie looked at each other and burst out laughing.

"What's so funny?" said Guzzler.

"I don't know, but do you think you could have a word with reception about the room service," said Ronnie, barely able to get his words out while being overwhelmed by a bout of the giggles.

CHAPTER 15.
Morning After the Night Before.

Mick wondered whether this whole adventure was some kind of reality TV gig. They'd run the gauntlet of the carnival queens, survived the night with *Stig of the Dump*, and for that feat of endurance Ronnie was rewarding them with a greasy fry up, in the only eatery in Brighton where not only the décor, but the menu, had endured since the nineteen eighties. The only thing missing was the ash trays. Bulldog had been voted off by a baying audience of millions of losers with nothing better to do with their Friday evenings, wilfully abetted by a panel of judges made up of minor celebrities with just enough savvy to read a cue card or two of patronising put-downs and double-entendres.
They finished at the greasy spoon just in time to check-in at the Ocean hotel, have a shit, shower and a shave, before reporting to Ringmaster Ron, for the next challenge.

Guzzler pulled the key card out of the door and the bedroom lock sprung open. He stepped in tentatively, like he was expecting to be jumped by a Bogeyman. The contents of a holdall had been emptied on to one of the twin beds.
"Bulldog?" called Guzzler.
"In here," came a groggy voice from the bathroom.

Guzzler didn't know whether he'd find Bulldog on the floor attached to a needle or half-asleep in the bath. He extended his neck around the bathroom door to find his friend shivering, while sitting on the closed lid of the toilet.
"Mate, you look rough," said Guzzler.
Bulldog groaned. Guzzler picked up some tablets lying next to a toiletry bag.
"Oh, mate," said Guzzler.
Bulldog snatched them from him.
"What do you think you're doing?" said Guzzler.
"Aye?" said Bulldog.
"No fuckin' drugs," said Guzzler.
Bulldog found some energy from somewhere, enough to fire off a defensive volley.
"Drugs? Oh, I get it. Boing, boing, it's Judge Jason from the Kangaroo court."
Guzzler wasn't buying it.
"Fuck off. I ain't come down here to say farewell to you 'n all," said Guzzler.
"Okay. You got me bang to rights. I have to confess that I have taken some drugs," said Bulldog.
Guzzler sighed as his heart dropped. Bulldog rifled in his toiletry bag and started pulling out various pill bottles.
"These are for my anxiety," he said.
He slammed them on the side and pulled out another bottle.
"These are for my blood pressure."
"Alright, mate," said Guzzler, verbally retreating.
"I've been clean for five years," said Bulldog.
Guzzler wasn't sure whether Bulldog was being totally up front with him and even if he was, history had justified Guzzler's lack of faith. There are no ifs or buts, Junkies are notorious liars and his friend had been guilty of telling

many a porky in the cause of concealing his habit. Bulldog returned to the toiletry bag.

"These are..." Bulldog smiled, suddenly recognising the bottle. "These are my Rocket Boosters."

He had a closer look at the 'use by' date on the bottle.

"Viagra?" Exclaimed Guzzler.

"Dunno what I was thinking when I got these. Can't remember the last time I went into Orbit," said Bulldog.

"Just promise me you don't get them mixed up, I don't want any surprises in the middle of the night, if you know what I mean?" said Guzzler, finding his sense of humour returning.

Ronnie and Mick were sitting on a table looking out, beyond the coastal road, at the sea. Dirty plates and half-drunk coffee cups were scattered across the table before them. If there was an art installation created as a homage to Mick's life, this could be it. The pattern on the tablecloth was so close to that of Mick's shirt, from some angles it was hard to tell where the table ended, and Mick began.

"I'm mesmerised by the ocean," said Ronnie. "The sheer enormity of it makes me feel like our existence here, on this planet, is as significant, in the scheme of things, as flotsam frothing at the heel of this giant rock, we call England. Take Brighton, it's amazing. The architecture. The wide, open space. The aura of the place. Even the people are different," said Ronnie, like he suddenly found himself fronting a TV travelogue.

Mick, still weary from last night's insomnia contest, was boring holes in the linoleum while Ronnie was boring holes in his brain. His words reminded him of school where he suffered regular bouts of library fatigue. He grunted a vague acknowledgement to Ronnie, who he could see was waiting for the starting pistol to release another round of backstreet philosophy.

"On the other hand, I see this vast stretch of sea and get a rushing sense of opportunity, like the great expanse was telling me endless possibilities are out there waiting to be discovered," said Ronnie.

Mick wondered whether Ronnie wrote the blurb on the back of DVDs in his spare time.

"What the fuckin' hell are you on about? Someone put something in your tea?" said Mick.

"I know, I know, I'm waffling," said Ronnie.

"You wanna know what I like about Brighton?" asked Mick.

"What?" said Ronnie.

"There ain't no Blacks," said Mick, jamming Ronnie's pastel coloured transmission.

Ronnie was totally thrown by his comment.

"What's that supposed to mean?" said Ronnie.

"I'm just saying," replied Mick.

Confrontation was bubbling under a well-rehearsed sneer. Ronnie was relieved when the waitress came over to clear the dirty plates away, hoping she would also clear the venomous air before disappearing back off to the kitchen. Mick pointed at two men in Parka coats, crudely decorated with brightly coloured badges and patches, gliding along the sea front on well-tended scooters.

"You order a Mod-o-gram?" Asked Mick.

Ronnie's face lit up. "Living the dream, eh?"

They parked up near the Café, giving Ronnie and Mick a good view of their original VBB Vespas, that had been polished to within an inch of their lives.

As they casually sauntered past the café's partly steamed windows, they took their crash helmets off to reveal themselves as a couple of OAPs with Paul Weller haircuts in a fine shade of 'Father Christmas grey'. It was like Mick Jagger and Keith Richards sponsored by Vespa.

"Well, bugger me," said Ronnie. "Look how old they are."

"Easy with your language, mate," said Mick.

"Err, yeah," said Ronnie, clocking the grumpy face of a mother sitting with her children on a nearby table.

"This is Brighton remember. Half the café thought you just issued an invitation," said Mick with a caustic smile.

"So, you're a homophobe too, now?" said Ronnie.

It seemed the more time he spent with Mick, the more his old friend was desperate to play the bald man at a curly hair contest.

"It's a joke, Ron. Remember we used to have them in the eighties before laughter was made illegal," said Mick. "Anyway, you think them two are ancient. Have you looked in the mirror lately?"

Mick paused, waiting for the full force of reality to claim his friend. But any epiphany visited upon Ronnie, found the shutters down.

"Cool scooters, though," said Ronnie, reaffirming his rose-tinted mission.

"What was it exactly that you were hoping to find here, Ron?" said Mick.

Ronnie shrugged his shoulders.

"Because if our younger selves were here now, they'd laugh us out of town."

Mick gave Ronnie an affectionate slap on the back.

"Still have a laugh, though, eh?"

"We're not too old for that," replied Ronnie, as he left the table to use the café's pay phone.

Guzzler bounded through the door and joined Mick at the table.

"No Bulldog?" asked Mick.

"He's sleeping it off at the hotel. He kipped in a shop doorway last night. Got hassled silly. Bulldog's pretty liberal minded but even he baulked at some of the propositions he was getting," said Guzzler.

"Took a long time considering them though, eh?"

Guzzler nodded in the direction of Ronnie at the pay phone.

"What's his game?"

"Well, it ain't Trivial Pursuit."

"He can't have forgotten how it ended with her," said Guzzler.

"The less said about that the better," said Mick, scrunching up his face.

Ronnie left the phone booth, with an extra skip in his step, and headed towards the door. He felt eyes, like lasers, burning into his back and turned to his friends. He reached out and picked up Guzzler's skid lid.

"Don't mind if I…" Ronnie trailed off as he headed for the street. Guzzler followed him to the door.

"Where you going?"

Ronnie slipped his helmet on and mounted his scooter. He kicked it over and it burst into life on the first kick, with the same urgency and lust for life as its rider.

"Bird watching," said Ronnie.

Ronnie headed off along the seafront, fuelled-up and over-revved with excitement.

"Watch out for those birds of prey," said Guzzler, under his breath.

CHAPTER 16. Beautyfools.

Ronnie felt like a film star. The synchronisation of the traffic made him feel like it was parting for him, as he glided on an uninhibited path through Brighton. On hearing the fizz and pop of his Vespa, strangers gave him the thumbs up and even traffic lights turned to green on his approach. Inside his mood reflected the cloudless blue sky above, on the short trip to finally meet up with Roxy. The hangover and aches from last night's accommodation were washed away within the surge of nervous energy now consuming him. He had found the single-minded, live-in-the-moment attitude of his youth and it felt good.

Roxy was waiting for Ronnie as he pulled up in front of the 'Beautyfools' salon. It was a classy looking outfit, with frosted windows and bold artworks, built into an imposing, four storey, Georgian house, on the corner of a row of fancy boutiques. This was posh Brighton. No candyfloss, kiss-me-quick hats and chip wrappers here.

Three youths standing on the corner watched him as he got off his scooter. They were sniggering at his Parka with its bright coloured patches and pin badges.

"He looks like a Christmas tree," said the tallest one, deliberately loud enough for Ronnie and Roxy to hear. It would take a lot more than that to burst Ronnie's bubble today. He ignored them and headed into the building with Roxy.

Roxy led Ronnie past reception and up the stairs. Her stunning figure and the way it moved was mesmerising. He enjoyed the view so much he was hoping the stairs would go on forever. They reached their destination on the second level while indulging in small talk.

"Have you had this place long?" Asked Ronnie.

"Must be about twelve years, now. It was an old youth hostel when I bought it. I had everything ripped out and knocked into shape," said Roxy.

"It's in magnificent shape," he said, still imagining her unwrapped

"Thanks. I've got another one west from here, and I'm in the process of setting up a salon in Cornwall," she said.

The place was classy but artificial. It was tastefully furnished, the cross between an upmarket hotel and a film set. A gentle aroma of lavender, eucalyptus and lemon hung delicately in the air, complimented by piped relaxation music playing tranquilly in the background. It all felt so expensive, thought Ronnie. The kind of place where a glass of lemon and cucumber infused water cost more than you were hoping to pay for the treatment.

Ronnie couldn't keep his eyes off Roxy's sleek curves, accentuated by her figure-hugging skirt and blouse. No matter where she stood the subtle spotlights seemed to follow Roxy, illuming her like she was in a photoshoot for Vogue magazine.

He tried to play it cool and hoped his tongue wouldn't snag on his amorous daydreams.

"I always knew you'd do well," said Ronnie.

Her expression told a different story.

"Huh, I wish you'd leant me your crystal ball, might have saved me a lot of anguish," she said.

"You always had such drive and self-belief," he said.

"I reckon we're two of a kind then. I have to admit, though, I never dreamed you'd move from building houses to selling them. Shrewd move," said Roxy.

"You see an opportunity; you've got to grab it," said Ronnie.

They both wondered if he was still talking about selling houses. He followed her into a large office with enormous, glazed windows looking out over Brighton's famous pier.

"Wow. That is some vista you've got here," said Ronnie.

"That's the money shot, as they say in the trade."

Suddenly, he had his Estate Agent's head on. He couldn't help himself, it had become second nature. She is sitting on a goldmine here, the view alone would rake in a large slice of green, he thought. He pictured it as his own office. To be working away at your desk and just tilt your head and be able to take in such a stunning view, that could do wonders for your state of mind.

"It's a long way from Battersham..." she replied.

Ronnie turned to face her.

"I reckon Battersham gave you that vision long before you ever stood at this window," he said.

He knew what he was struggling to say, it sounded better in his head than when he said it out loud, but he hoped she'd fill in the blanks.

"I remember listening to this guy on the radio, I can't even remember his name, but he said, A roast dinner tastes its best when you've had three weeks of beans on toast, I heard that, and I made it my own personal edict," said Roxy.

"That's Battersham. Love it or loathe it, it'll always be a part of who you are," said Ronnie.

The wave of nostalgia Ronnie surfed in on made Roxy play-out a familiar film through her mind's eye. It was always available on loop for when she needed reminding of the magnitude of her own journey.

"I remember looking out on those dreary concrete blocks," she said. "Some days you couldn't tell where they ended, and the grey sky began. The constant volcanic eruptions next door and the old man upstairs trying to cough up an ace, twenty-four-seven. And if he wasn't coughing, he was crying. I promised myself then that I'd never end up doing life there."

"You must have landed some smart punches to get this far," said Ronnie.

Roxy smiled, she loved how he set up her lines like she was the leading lady in a movie. "You know me, a white flag was never my style."

Roxy gathered up some paperwork on her desk and placed it in an organised pile. Everything about her screamed 'neat,' She was smart, erudite and decisive. Ronnie found himself thinking like the head of her personal marketing department. He was sold.

"It's great to see you've lost none of that Roxy magic," said Ronnie.

"Oh, I buried Roxy a long time ago," she said.

Ronnie was puzzled. The script had been going swimmingly, suddenly it felt like someone had thrown a piano into the pool.

"I think my mum pictured some bohemian darling, tip-toeing through a field of daisies when she christened me," she said. "When I hear that name, I see 'Red light Roxy,' a two-bob stripper tripping over dirty needles in the gutter. Pitied, plucked then pawned."

Ronnie was a little taken aback, his perception had done a one-hundred-and-eighty-degree turn. "Wow. I never knew you felt so strongly about it," he said, in a light tone that she clearly didn't appreciate.

"It's alright for you, you had the Krays protecting your name," she snapped, with an aversion to the cheap image her teenage years had, in her mind at least, been awarded to her by her peers.

Roxy laid her cards out, clear as day. "Can I get you a drink?"

Ronnie suddenly remembered his hangover. "Black Coffee would be nice. Thanks."

"You given up the Ribena with Lucozade then?" she joked.

Ronnie rebalanced himself with a little chuckle.

"I'd forgotten all about that," he said.

Roxy put on an exaggerated male Cockney voice. "Tea and coffee are for Wimps. Real men drink Ribena. That's what you used to say, wasn't it?"

Ronnie held his head in his hands in self-mocking shame.

She picked up the phone and asked reception to rustle up some drinks.

Roxy nodded at his Mod attire. "What's with the fancy dress then?"

"Fancy dress?" said Ronnie, trying to hide his hurt pride.

"I take it you don't wear that every day?" she said.

"We were coming down here on scooters and I just thought...why not? Be like the old days," said Ronnie.

Roxy enjoyed a wry smile. Ronnie looked into her eyes and was suddenly hit by a wave of uncertainty, a swift self-conscious reassessment of himself, of where he was at that precise moment in time.

Ronnie hid behind the mask of the wide boy. "Thought it'd be a laugh, y'know."

Roxy reached out a hand, burst through the veneer, and gently squeezed his arm.

"It's good to see you... Coat and all," she said.

There was a knock at the door, followed by the appearance of Penny, a woman in her late thirties, who carried a tray of drinks to the desk.

"Was there anything else, Joanna?" asked Penny.

Roxy gave a small shake of her head. Penny was about to leave when Roxy decided to introduce her. "Penny, this is Ronnie."

Ronnie and Penny shook hands politely, both self-conscious for different reasons.

"I've heard so much about you," said Penny.

Ever since he got there, his lift had been heading for the top floor, his ego was being courted in style and he was loving it. He came with strings attached, Roxy was well aware of that, but today she had decided she would play the puppet master. He was the pursuer but there was no doubt that it was Roxy who was the power broker. She gave him a flirtatious smile, keeping her eyes fixed squarely on his. "Ronnie and I go way, way back, don't we Ronnie?" she said.

CHAPTER 17.   Beach Babes.

Riding as a passenger on a scooter was an opportunity to get up close and personal in a way that was accomplished more subtlety than the request of a slow dance at a night club. Roxy held on tight to Ronnie, keeping her face out of the wind, as they travelled along the coastal route through Peacehaven and Seaford, towards Beachy Head, about fifteen miles outside of Brighton. It reminded him of their early courtship when he was about fifteen. They'd been clowning around, and she accepted his offer of a piggyback. It was all light-hearted fun, but the physical closeness was tantalising and led to their vey first kiss. They left the scooter and made their way along a winding path that took them to a secluded beach at the foot of some imposing chalk cliffs. Roxy stretched out on a large flat rock, using his jacket as a pillow. Seductively, her hair danced, and her blouse lightly swelled in the breeze. Ronnie was sitting up beside her, hugging his knees as if forming a shape that would conceal something of himself. For Ronnie, pursuing Roxy was like watching his favourite film on a second-rate Television, the vision was plagued with interference. There were so many personal reminders of Hazel, Ronnie found it hard to focus on the narrative. He had noticed a woman with the same coat as Hazel, driven past an old haunt of theirs, heard a shared song on the radio of a passing car that was entangled with memories of a past summer of frivolity. The song had become one of their personal anthems. Even when he thought he had a clear run, the set suffered badly from intermittent ghosting. Seagulls were swooping in the air, gliding, carefree, on an upsurge of sea breeze. The famous white cliffs that intermittently spanned the south coast, loomed behind them, like the edge of an enormous platform shoe. Ronnie could see the phallic shape of the red and white striped lighthouse jutting out of the calm blue sea before them. Beachy head was a famous beauty spot with a black history of suicides. It had become a waste ground of spurned lovers, terminally ill patients, people considered bankrupts, both morally and financially, and others generally crippled by life. Many travelled from far and wide to launch themselves from the precipice to claim the ultimate ticket out of here that only comes with death. It was a place of dark tourism, attracting those who revelled in a fascination for its macabre notoriety. Among the hundred or so deaths each year, there were many who, in the age of the selfie, had gone in search of a daring photograph or two, and had fallen foul of the perilous crumbling cliff edges and lost their footing on their way to an unwelcome and thoroughly unexpected early grave.

For Ronnie the place was an iconic landmark of Mod folklore. The Who's feature film, Quadrophenia, featured a Mod gang led by a troubled teenage character, with a split personality, named Jimmy. Auteur Franc Roddam had his director of photography, Brian Tufano, capture the young actor, Phil Daniels, driving a Scooter over the grassy perimeter, the camera following the GS Vespa as it began disintegrating on the jagged rocks below.

Quality coming of age films were rare, and almost always set in New York or Los Angeles. Here was a British film that spanned the cults and captured the working-class teenage zeitgeist at its most fervent. The film had a profound effect on Ronnie and the many youths up and down the country who became second generation Mods, in the wake of its cinema release.

Roxy enjoyed Ronnie watching her. She didn't need a science degree to recognise the fizzing chemistry that had reignited between them. When she processed her initial readings, at Arnie's wake, the current was off the scale. She knew he was a man of means, he could move mountains should he so wish. She was sure that if he succumbed to temptation, they could carve out a future together. Unlike Ronnie, she had very little to lose, except perhaps, her heart.

The gentle gusts, warm sunrays and the sound of the waves were intoxicating, it felt to Ronnie like a massage of all his senses. It papered over all the little hindrances that had seeped, like spilt ink on Bond paper, into the plans for his dream return to Brighton.

"I've been all over the world, Thailand, the Gold Coast and the beaches of California, but nothing compares to this."

Roxy smiled.

"Maybe because in those places I'm just a visitor. This... This feels like home, where my heart belongs," said Ronnie.

Roxy looked a little bewildered.

His mind had wondered off and got caught up in a forest of jumbled words.

"Perhaps it's just the company," he said trying to right himself.

"I'm glad you came," said Roxy, as she reached out and gently caressed his forearm, sending a little spark of excitement racing up his spine.

"I promised I would, didn't I. I'm a man of my word, if anything," he bumbled.

He was rambling, and he knew it. He thought about gathering her up in a passionate embrace but didn't want to misjudge the moment, or rush things. He was nervously making excuses to himself, but at the same time, delighting in the anticipation of what might lay before them.

Like a fire alarm at a wedding ceremony, the sound of Ronnie's mobile phone ringtone gate-crashed the party. He pulled it out of his pocket and recognised the digital display. It read 'Hazey fantayzee calling'. It was another prick to his conscience.

"Someone wants you," said Roxy, who had felt his phone vibrate in his jacket, at least two or three times on the journey from Brighton.

"It's just work. It can wait," said Ronnie.

Ronnie pretended to fumble with the phone.

He pressed the 'reject call' button and placed the phone back in his pocket.

They both knew it was Hazel on the other end of the line. Estate Agents, although open on Saturdays, couldn't push anything through until business resumed on Monday, when solicitors and HM Land Registry were operating.

Roxy rolled over onto her side. Resting on her elbow she propped her head up with her hand, light strands of hair danced around her face. Ronnie thought she looked magnificent.

The phone rang again.

Roxy joined in the charade. "Could be important."

"Don't want anything to spoil our little adventure," said Ronnie.

Roxy appeased him with a half-smile which faded at the sound of his phone.

Ronnie felt like the ringing was becoming louder as he fumbled with the phone, planning on switching it to silent mode, he inadvertently pressed the answer button and an irritated voice burst forth from the tinny speaker.
"Ronnie… Ronnie… are you there?" asked Hazel.
Tentatively, Ronnie put the phone to his ear, he sprang up and took a few paces away from Roxy.
"Hello, err, Oh, Hi Hazel," he stumbled.
"Where the hell are you? I've been trying to get a hold of you," said Hazel.
Hazel was like his personal Augur and right now that scared him. She only needed to garnish a look or listen to him breathe to know whether a deal had gone flat, or if he was anxious about a health issue or was concealing something. She could take his temperature from the way he wore a tie. Even the fact that he had addressed her as Hazel, and not his usual Haze or Hazey, was a warning blip on her radar. Amongst all the hullaballoo of his mid-life crisis, or whatever it was he was going through, she sensed danger.
"I've been out on me scootah," said Ronnie, a little too brazenly.
"Owt on me scoo-tah," she mimicked, in an exaggerated tone. "Listen to yourself, Ronnie."
"What's that, I can't really, I can't really hear you," he said in the kind of voice commonly used to give directions to foreign tourists.
Ronnie bluffed her off with complaints of a bad phone line, in an attempt to save face with Roxy. In doing so, he risked lighting the kind of emergency warning flares, for Hazel, that would render the nearby lighthouse redundant. He turned his phone off and placed it back in his pocket.

"No more disruptions," he declared, rather pathetically, as he returned to his perch on a rock.

Like a bomb scare in a crowded restaurant, the unwelcome interruption had murdered the atmosphere on the beach. Both Roxy and Ronnie found themselves back at the starting line. Hazel's spectre hung there like a paralysis, freezing them in time.

Roxy broke the silence.

"I was just trying to recall, was it you who fell off the back of a scooter, drunk as a skunk, in front of the police in Margate?"

"Oh yeah, that was Arnie, how he got away with that I'll never know," said Ronnie.

"So tragic about Arnie," said Roxy, successfully easing the conversation onto neutral ground. "He was one of the really good guys. Always made me feel like one of the gang," she replied.

Changing the conversation to their dead friend was preferable to thinking about his very much alive wife. Ronnie suddenly thought about Arnie's ashes and made a mental note to plan some kind of tribute as soon as he was back with his friends in Brighton.

"The man was a legend," said Ronnie.

"He was a real gent," said Roxy. "We could have a conversation without it being some cheesy attempt to get me into bed. We'd talk about all sorts of things. Faye didn't like that much. I think most of the other girls hated me."

"They didn't hate you," said Ronnie.

The look Roxy gave him convinced him otherwise.

"I couldn't care less. Their spite just bounces off the bonnet of my Mercedes A-Class."

"I thought you might be settled down with a lorry load of kids by now?" said Ronnie.

"This is the twenty-first century. No-one has kids by choice, Ronnie," said Roxy.

Ronnie was reminded that a lorry load of kids was exactly what he and Hazel had been desperate for. Before he could ponder the thought any further, Roxy sprang to her feet, and flicked her immaculate long blonde hair out of her face to reveal a beaming child-like smile.

"Race you to the sea," she said.

Roxy had changed gear and Ronnie had no time to do anything but succumb to her will.

"Come on," she shouted.

He clambered over the rocks to where the beach turned to a fine golden plain, and found Roxy waiting to playfully kick sand at him, giggling as she headed for the little waves that were effortlessly tumbling over each other a few yards away. Thoughts of Hazel suddenly receded like an ebbing tide.

CHAPTER 18. Playtime.

"He made such a fuss about reuniting the Aces. And who's sat here holding the baby?... Not him, that's for sure," grumped Mick, to Guzzler and Bulldog, as he picked over a carton of fish and chips, on a rickety old wooden bench, on Brighton's promenade.
"Well, what else would you be doing this weekend?" said Guzzler.
"I'm glad *I* came," said Bulldog.
"You still getting work from that courier firm in the West End?" Guzzler asked Mick.
"It's a right racket," said Mick. "Their operation is so cliquey. Sometimes it feels like a club I'm not a member of. I get a bit of painting work, toshing up warehouses with Billy the Fish."
"I could do with a bit of an upgrade on the old job front, meself," said Guzzler.
"Food taster for Greggs Bakeries," joked Bulldog.
"Don't you think he's got enough on his plate already?" said Mick
"Hilarious. No, I'm sick of the grind. I wouldn't mind working in a book shop or a Library."
"You don't want to work in a Library, mate," said Mick. "They're going the way of the fax machine and the Dodo."

The unmistakable sound of a Vespa approaching drew their attention. Ronnie and Roxy made a sudden appearance.

They pulled up on the Scooter in front of the Fish and Chips stand. Roxy winked as Bulldog snapped a photo of the couple just before they dismounted. Mick felt it was more of a statement than a mere arrival.

"Hello boys," said Roxy.

"Well fancy seeing you here," said Mick, sarcastically.

Bulldog gave Ronnie a knowing look. "Someone did."

Guzzler was prodding a wooden fork into polythene plates of chips, when Ronnie helped himself to a handful.

"Get yer own," he grunted.

Ronnie laughed. Guzzler would give you his last ha'penny but would begrudge parting with a morsel of anything that was destined for his belly.

"Hiya Roxy," said Guzzler, with his mouth full, now quaffing his grub at speed, for fear of another hostile raid on his fries.

"It's Joanna," said Ronnie, as if his pronouncement was an act of defending her honour.

"Jo will suffice," said Roxy, casually.

"*Jo*... has sorted us out some tickets for a club tomorrow night," said Ronnie.

"Cheers, Rox... I mean Jo," said Guzzler.

Bulldog flashed a handful of tickets before them.

"What, you mean these tickets?" he said, laughing.

"He'd steal the sand from between your toes," said Ronnie.

Just then Penny arrived, and Roxy duly introduced her to the gang.

Ronnie threw his arms out wide.

"What say we go hit the arcades?" he said, like the head boy from a bus load of raucous school children.

Like a moody teenager, Mick shrugged his shoulders nonchalantly, but followed along anyway.

Ronnie and Roxy sat side by side on a racing car game, Mick was pouring coins into a fruit machine and Bulldog and Penny were posting two pence pieces into a money drop game. Guzzler was content chomping on some radioactive-looking candy floss. When a group of children came in looking for some play time, they soon backtracked at the sight of these overgrown teenagers whooping and hollering as they hogged the machines.

"Guzz, you got a quid on ya?" said Mick.

"What happened to that sack of coins you had yesterday?" Said Guzzler.

"I'm not gonna walk around like a bloody charity bucket, am I? I left 'em in the hotel."

"You're like a living, breathing, black hole when it comes to dosh," replied Bulldog.

"Giz a minute," said Guzzler, trying to clean himself up by licking the sticky residue of candyfloss from his hands and making a bigger mess.

"Come on, Guzz. I'm on for the jackpot," said Mick.

Penny threw him a two-pound coin and he caught it, keeping his eye on her the whole time it travelled through the air. Her gesture took him by surprise, it was like he had suddenly noticed she was there.

"Cheers…umm," said Mick.

"Penny," she said with a smile.

"Cheers, Penny," said Mick.

Penny came and stood by the machine as Mick placed the coin into the slot.

"One condition," said Penny.

"That's a bit sneaky, I've already put it in the machine," pleaded Mick.

"You've got no choice then," said Penny.

"Go on then, name your price," said Mick.

"Take me on the Waltzer if you win," said Penny.
Mick smiled, suddenly hoping that what she'd said had been a euphemism, as he set the wheels in motion by slapping the flashing play button on the Fruit machine. They spun to a blur and then, one by one, came to a shuddering halt. He got a duck, and two oranges, worth a big fat zero. Guzzler, who'd been watching from the corner of his eye, shook his head. He had one final credit left but Penny stole in and set it rolling. Clunk, Clunk, Clunk. Three Melons appeared in a line. Suddenly the machine looked like it was going to take off, with all the flashing lights, buzzing and melodic alarms that were ringing, along with the sweet sound of an avalanche of coins hitting the tray.
Penny whooped with joy. "Five hundred quid. Wow,"
"I can't believe it. I mean, I never win, do I Guzz?" said Mick, who was so ecstatic it looked as if his face would crack under the weight of his grin.
"He's right. His family crest is a duck with a wooden spoon in its mouth," said Guzzler.
Before he knew it, Mick had given Penny a bear hug.
"Oh, we've only just started," said Penny, trying to get her breath back.
Mick couldn't remember the last time he'd shared anything resembling fun with a woman. She was breezy, fresh and a little flirty. And underneath it all, Mick had an overwhelming sense that there was something indelibly good about her. Maybe she might prove to be good for him. Penny was younger than him, and because of her weight probably overlooked in a line-up of Roxys. Mick wondered what on earth he could offer her. Truth be told, the way his life was of late, he hadn't been looking for anything more than an exit strategy.

CHAPTER 19.   The Last Post.

Hazel spent the morning staring into a long mirror wishing her dresses onto her. No matter what angle she took, they refused to conform to her desires. Hope knew better than to ever consult a measuring tape. Between the mirror and her brain something had got lost in translation. Her mind clung on to the image of herself as a twenty-year-old; pretty, slim and carefree, with a glint of gaiety in her eye. What she attained from this new reflection was about as welcome as a parking ticket on your birthday. How had she allowed herself to get so….old?

Dressing had become some kind of Chinese puzzle where she performed conjuring tricks to hide the bad and signpost the good. In her mind, the signposts were becoming more and more redundant. Why was will power doled out in buckets when she had no need for it, but now in her time of desperation, it seemed as rare as Phoenix eggs?

She marked the death of her figure by mostly wearing black. A widow to more obliging times. Hazel was regularly complimented for her style and poise but felt overly conscious of the maxim 'the mirror never lies'. She still drew rave reviews, but she never read her own press. A lifetime of Woman's magazines, crass advertising and male expectation had warped her reality.

Whenever she fell out with Ronnie, it always felt like she was running on the wrong fuel. Her capacity shrank until normal service could resume between them.

Ronnie wasn't taking her calls and for their one brief conversation, he had clearly answered the phone unwittingly. Perhaps, she thought, he needed a reason to be upset with her. That worried her further.

In a depressed state, she ventured downstairs and did what every self-respecting woman in her position could do. Hazel opened the fridge and devoured the chocolate cake she'd been keeping for later. Just as her mouth was at maximum satisfaction, packed with sugary goodness, the doorbell chimed. She was irked that she now had to rush to swallow it all.

Hazel opened her front door and met with a whirlwind of gossip on her doorstep. Jane burst in with tales from the riverbank. Barely taking a breath, she rattled through the local news headlines like a modern-day Town Crier on speed.

"Jonathan Sutherland, you know, *that* Jonathan, has been expelled from School. His Dad. Gone crackers. The Vicar is in trouble for telling a group of children that they should find love in their hearts for all criminals. Can you believe it? Parents up in arms. The Gamekeeper, Clawfinger Johnson is in bother, shot a dog by accident on a Fox Hunt. Not even supposed to be Fox Hunting. He's in, well…And Ray Stone, went gaga, didn't he. On gardening leave. Lost the plot and now having his head seen to at the funny farm. Two teenage daughters will do that to you. And the pothole in the middle of the village is so big now, Hawkington-Stanley says the council have received planning permission for a Ferry terminal."

The bulletin came to a shuddering halt, she had discarded the gossip column before the ink was even dry. Hazel was used to these outbursts and knew you weren't supposed to join in or respond with anything more than a cursory nod.

It was like she was coughing up fur balls and had to get it all up in one go.

Jane took one long breath then became someone entirely different.

"So, how are you?" said Jane

"I'm alright." said Hazel, in a tone that intimated the opposite.

She walked through to the plush kitchen and flicked the kettle on. Jane followed behind, like a saggy helium balloon, gently exhaling the remnants of her pent-up energy.

"Now tell me, what do you fancy? That new Daniel Craig film, Dennis playing pub rock at the Arms, or a table at the new Italian in Bawden?" asked Jane, born again.

Hazel shrugged her shoulders.

Jane got a whiff of discontent as Hazel handed her a cup of coffee.

"You, ok?"

"Sure… It's just…Oh, I don't know."

"What is it, Haze?" said Jane.

Outwardly, Hazel had her face on, calmly sipping her coffee at the breakfast bar, but mentally she was pacing the room in anguish.

"I know he's only been gone a few days, but I woke up this morning with this unsettling feeling that he had been suddenly cut from my life. It was horrible."

"You not heard from him?"

"No, but his friend Bulldog posts regular updates on Facebook. I think they slept in a shop doorway last night," said Hazel.

"Sounds delightful," chirped Jane.

Hazel opened up the laptop and spun it around, so Jane could see the pictures too. They chuckled as Hazel flicked through the images of their journey down to Brighton and various photos of the beach, pier and even a couple of the Pride parade, with all its rainbow colours and bombastic exuberance. Their smiles swiftly diminished as the picture of Ronnie, with a beaming Roxy on the back of his scooter, appeared like a telegram from the devil himself. For a moment they sat in stunned silence. Roxy looked like the cat who'd got the cream. Eighty miles away, in Arksdean, Hazel was curdling. She felt a hurt travel from her gut to her brain, where it exploded into an inferno of humiliation.

"Who the bloody hell does she think *she* is?" said Jane.

"Roxy Nostos." Hazel mumbled under her breath.

"You actually know her?" said Jane.

"She's an old flame of Ronnie's, snuffed out a long time ago, or so I thought. I might have known that tart would be part of his stumble down memory lane."

Jane could see it was tearing Hazel apart so tried tentatively peddling backwards.

"It could all be innocent," she said.

Hazel looked at Jane with raised eyebrows.

"Come on, Ronnie's not like that," said Jane.

"He's a man, isn't he?" said Hazel.

Jane's mind was racing, she sprung into practical mode, like they'd been set a challenge to cook up a new recipe, one where Roxy ended up as mincemeat.

"Call him," insisted Jane.

Hazel was scanning through the history of her married life, searching for chinks in her armour. Something to blame herself for. 'She'd put on weight, maybe got a bit too comfy around the house,' she thought.

"Haze, call him," said Jane, with a heightened appetite for the drama.

Hazel paused the film projection in her mind and picked up her mobile phone and rang him. The video now playing in her head was now urgently scrubbing through his behaviour, for any signs of infidelity. Suddenly, the decades of intimacy slipped from her conscience and she began questioning whether she even knew the real Ronnie. The phone just went straight to his answer machine. She hadn't enough composure to leave a message. She started to wonder whether she was overreacting. It wasn't nice seeing him with Roxy but perhaps, as Jane had said, there was an innocent explanation.

"If you're really worried about it, don't stew up here, go down there," said Jane.

Hazel picked up their coffee cups and deposited them in the sink. She gazed out across the fields.

"He couldn't just let sleeping bitches lie," she muttered to herself.

CHAPTER 20.
Beside the Seaside, Beside the Sea.

On Brighton seafront, Ronnie handed a photographer some coins before pushing his head through an old-fashioned painted picture board featuring a buxom woman and a scrawny man in Victorian bathing suits. Roxy joined him, giddily sliding her head into a hole above the picture of the man, as the cameraman readied himself to take the snap. Roxy was intent on making the most of it. She had cancelled a date with a guy called Steve, whose only contact had been via an online dating app.

When it came to the opposite sex, Roxy had endured a long line of disappointments. If you were looking for romance, the internet was a liar's lair. If there was any resemblance in real life, to that of the person in their profile photo, it was generally considered a bonus. Six-foot sports champions appeared as balding sofa-slobs or pale skinned nerds and this was after she'd filtered out the perverts who messaged a menu of sexual requests that would probably make a porn star blush. She doubted that those twisted fantasists had the means, let alone the appetite, to live up to their bluster, but they were unwelcome all the same.

The whole thing was the antithesis of the real world. She wished it would return to a time when finding someone meant the heady enjoyment of risk and anticipation followed by a honeymoon of exploration. In this alternative universe, they drafted their positive attributes, like they were issuing certificates and bonds, only for their validation to fail as, one by one, you discovered each boastful declaration belonged in the second-hand fiction section. Roxy doubted whether Steve would be any different. Just another unlucky dip in love's bargain bucket. Another unwanted product of the lonely-hearts fire sale. Reconnecting with Ronnie, a married man with deep roots a hundred miles away, might not have been Roxy's fairy-tale adventure, but there was something special about spending time with a person who shared your youthful history, particularly if, like Ronnie, much of it had been rewritten to fit a new rose-tinted agenda where you were cast as the belle of the ball.

Mick and Penny were an instant hit, giggling like giddy children as they threw their hands in the air while the Waltzer spun them around like a human tumble dryer. It felt so alien to Mick, laughing had been an optional extra, a subscription that his meagre budget could never stretch to. Mick felt like he was holding on to something far more substantial than handlebars, as the shiny little car threw them one way and another. They were surrounded by children of all ages, lost in the hullabaloo of unadulterated joy. Clocking up airmiles on the various fairground thrill-machines, they matched the youngsters for gusto, until finally they ran out of puff.
After exhausting the fair rides, they moved along the seafront arcades competing at everything from shoot 'em ups and hoop shoots to horse racing games and digital dance-offs. The two lovebirds were carefree, in the busy

throng of holiday makers and day-trippers from the capital, they soon found that they had eyes for nothing but each other.

Guzzler and Bulldog made their way along the promenade and were stopped by a couple of actors, in full costume, reciting a scene from the theatrical production they were promoting. It was an ambush of sorts, having been given a prop to hold, Bulldog had no way of escaping without destroying the rendition. Rather than look awkward, as Guzzler thought he might, Bulldog joined in the spirit of it, interacting with the thespians. By the time the performance was over, about twenty holiday makers had gathered to watch and applaud before leaving with leaflets and balloons advertising the show, handed out by Disco Dames on roller skates.

Guzzler loved the seaside, having had a run of eight summers at a chalet in Herne bay, owned by Tracey's folks. He could think of nothing more enjoyable than sitting on its veranda, with his feet up, reading a book while Tracey was off shopping in Margate. He thought about his reading history. It always seemed to be in spite of his circumstances. A guilty pleasure. At work reading a paperback in a toilet cubicle, on holidays, when Tracey was out with the children and in Arnie's garage, which he'd surely lose now his friend was gone. Ronnie and the boys were more sophisticated these days but as teenagers he would have retained more credibility if he'd hidden his reading material behind a porn magazine, not the other way around.

Guzzler and Bulldog made their way further down the beach where they stood aimlessly lobbing pebbles into the sea. Bulldog soon ran out of puff and slumped onto the stones, cursing their choice of Brighton as the most uncomfortable beach in Britain. Guzzler threw a few more. Snatching a quick glance at Bulldog to see that he hadn't nodded off, Guzzler returned his gaze towards the English Channel and began reciting a poem.

"Drop your anchor, dip your toe,
But don't whistle up a storm,
For there is none mightier than me,
I will carry you on deep tides of blue,
Or shatter your dreams into floating matchwood,
A current like a thousand grasping arms
Dragging you down…"

"What you on about?" said Bulldog, rudely interrupting.
"It's a poem," said Guzzler.
"You do look a bit like him, but what you done with the real Guzzler?" said Bulldog.
Guzzler couldn't have felt more embarrassed if he'd walked into the pub with his lower half unclothed. He thought, if any of the old crew would appreciate a bit of culture, it would be Bulldog. He had clearly miscalculated the situation. Maybe Guzzler was rehearsing a role for someone else's life, there certainly didn't seem to be an outlet for this kind of thing in his.
He shrugged his shoulders.
"Oh, Fuck off, will ya," said Guzzler. "You're worse than Tracey, I wrote one for her and she laughed in my face."
"You wrote Tracey a poem?"
"I, errm, I read her a poem," said Guzzler.
"But you just said you…"
"Just drop it, will ya?" said Guzzler.
Guzzler fiddled with the laces on his shoes.
"Who was that then, Shakespeare?" asked Bulldog.

"Dunno, I can't remember," said Guzzler, wishing he could erase the last few minutes.

He knew only too well who the writer was. It was himself. Guzzler sloped off further down the beach and returned to flinging pebbles into the sea. He picked up a handful of smoothed flint and tried his luck at skimming stones.

"A six-er," called Guzzler, keen to paper over his little venture into verse.

Bulldog came down and joined him.

"Do you think Ronnie's used us?" he said.

"How?"

"I get the feeling that we're playing the beard for him," said Bulldog.

"He's become a bit unfamiliar with himself, you know," said Guzzler. "He probably came down here because he thinks this is where the trail went cold."

"And Roxy's gonna help him warm it up?" said Bulldog.

"Well, I hope he has a change of heart," said Guzzler, thinking about the dire consequences he'd face if he was in Ronnie's position.

"Ronnie's changed," said Bulldog.

"We all change," said Guzzler.

"You haven't," said Bulldog.

Bulldog's comment irritated Guzzler.

"Once a clown always a clown. Is that it?" said Guzzler.

He picked up a large pebble and hurled it into the sea.

"No-one's saying you're a clown," said Bulldog.

Guzzler gave him a look.

"You're the soundest bloke I know," said Bulldog.

Bulldog got to his feet and they both resumed stone throwing, both imagining hurling the bad bits of themselves into the frothing sea.

"I've made a total mess of my life," said Bulldog.

"You're still here though, ain't ya," said Guzzler.
"Sometimes I think I should just leave Battersham, and never go back."
"What you talkin ' about? Where would you go?" said Guzzler.
"Me mum, she ain't getting any younger. I just wanna give her a chance to live a bit. She deserves that. All the shit I've dragged her through," said Bulldog.
"That's all behind you now, though ain't it," said Guzzler.
He'd be a rich man if he'd had a pound for every time someone said that to him, Bulldog thought to himself. He picked up a large boulder but struggled to hurl it very far. It made a deep thud and skidded along some pebbles to its watery grave.
"I can deal with my past, it's the future that scares me," said Bulldog.

CHAPTER 21.   Confessions.

At the salon, Roxy led Ronnie into a treatment room. The temperature was deliberately warm, the lighting was low-key, and the gentle sound of relaxation music was being piped through speakers on the wall. He slipped his big green Mod coat off and lay it over a bamboo screen.
"You're going to lose that when we go to the club, won't you?" said Roxy, in a tone that indicated that she was tiring of the joke, if it was one.
Ronnie tried to hide his bruised ego.
"Oh yeah. Course." He mumbled unconvincingly.
"Take your shirt off and make yourself comfortable on the bed. I'll be back in a minute,"
Roxy closed the door behind her and Ronnie self-consciously undressed. He winced as he caught sight of his saggy torso in the smoky black mirror. His comfort layer had expanded of late, it was a losing battle with a slowing metabolism and self-restraint being trounced by a simple desire to eat nice things that he could afford in abundance. In the reflection he saw a face with so many laughter lines it was surely due a stint at the London Palladium. He stretched out, face down on the treatment table. Roxy returned. She had changed into a loose tunic with Japanese-style three quarter length trousers and white towelling sauna slippers.

"You okay? Would you like a drink or anything?" she asked, in a whispered, slightly husky tone.
He could have murdered a triple vodka and coke, but he declined the offer.
Roxy started caressing some fancy smelling cream into his upper back. It felt wonderfully sensual and anxiously daring.
"Just relax. You're all tense," said Roxy.
Her voice had taken on a softer more drawn-out timbre. He tried to calm himself and exhaled a pleasurably measured breath, before regulating a calming pace.
"You always were good with your hands," he muttered.
She smiled to herself, leaned in close, an inch or so away from his head, lightly brushing her breasts into his back as she tenderly kneaded his shoulders. She talked to him in an ever-gentler whisper.
"Someone's got a good memory," she said.
"I could never forget you as long as I live," he said.
A long pause dared him to be a little bolder.
"So many times, it's really puzzled me about how things were back then," he said.
"We were just kids," said Roxy.
"I know, yeah, but I never did understand why we split-up," said Ronnie.
"Old tales best forgotten, eh?" she said.
Suddenly Roxy felt she was receiving mixed signals. Where was he going with this?
"I know it's all water under the bridge, now," he said, more reassuringly for Roxy.
She poured cream from a different bottle onto his back and he flinched at its coldness. He thought he could recognise an aroma of lavender as she started massaging his lower back.

"You probably forgot for a good reason," she said, trying to padlock the door he seemed intent on prizing open.

"Oh, I know, it won't change anything, just be nice to know, that's all," said Ronnie, not giving up.

"You sure you want to go there?" said Roxy, hoping to avoid a mood transplant.

"Can't hurt, can it," he said with an assuredness he couldn't possibly know.

His persistence irritated Roxy. A void opened up in the conversation. Everything she did failed to bridge it. She was weighing it up and decided against her own instinct that it might be a good idea to clear the air and build the relationship on a more honest footing rather than risk a later a revelation that could suddenly threaten to sour things.

"If you really want to know, it was true. I was with another guy that night," she said, wincing at how unintentionally blunt the words sounded now they had left her mouth. She felt his response in the sudden rigidity of his muscles, but she carried on massaging him as before.

"I was told that you had started seeing someone else," she said.

"Well, I wasn't," he said sharply.

Although he wasn't being totally honest as, although they hadn't properly dated, he had begun pursuing Hazel at the time.

Roxy kept the pressure on his back, ensuring he stayed face down. She would avoid eye contact until they were out of this tricky terrain.

"I know that now, but at the time it felt real. I was told all the details by someone I trusted, someone who I thought had no reason to bullshit me," she said, opening up the wound a little further.

Ronnie was rattled, he wanted to sit up and face her, but she hadn't stopped manipulating his skin, his added layers gave her more flesh to play with and so she carried on like a cat with its claws satisfyingly kneading soft flesh.

"Who was this, this... shit-stirrer?" pressed Ronnie.

"Ronnie, you've got to understand, I was confused. I was head over heels with you and I thought you were too," said Roxy.

"I was," he replied, bluntly.

Any perception of sensuality had evaporated almost as quickly as the cream she'd been applying vanished into the coarseness of his overtly dry skin.

"I didn't know what to think. He got me when my guard was down. He offered me a drink and I took the bait and drowned my sorrows. And... well, I ended up spending the night at his," she said.

It was too much for Ronnie, he sat up and span around to face her.

"Who?" he demanded.

"I don't think I should say. There's just no point in causing any more trouble," said Roxy.

Ronnie was past any sense of courtesy; he knew it would eat him up.

"No. You gotta tell me now. You can't just..."

"I told you we should have just left it alone, didn't I? But you pushed and pushed," she said.

The room hung heavy with the thick stench of animosity. Ronnie was killing his dream and Roxy was re-evaluating hers.

"Who was it, Roxy?"

He tried to catch a direct line of sight, but she was hiding, adjusting bottles of ointments and creams. He tugged at her arm.

"Who was it, Roxy?" he said, in a slightly more measured tone.

She'd backed herself into a quandary, and there was no way out but the cold harsh truth. She could only imagine how much that was going to sting. Roxy hoped his anger would be vented towards the guilty party and not at her. So, she blurted it out.

"It was Mick," she said, closing her eyes to the distress.

"Mick?" said Ronnie, his voice rising.

She drew him close to her, an attempt to cool his temper and avoid looking him in the eye. His head was spinning faster than a carousel on overdrive. His whole body was in the grip of a jumble of emotions. She couldn't stand the silence, it was barbaric.

"I woke up in the morning to see the smug grin on his face and I threw up all over his bedroom floor and scarpered," she said, in a genuinely sorry tone.

Roxy was annoyed with herself for allowing their conversation to take such a drastic nosedive. She was also miffed with him for making her feel bad about something that happened so long ago. Ronnie was shocked and angry, felt physically vulnerable and the touch of her body through the silk tunic, only moments ago unequivocally erotic, was now somehow unsavoury and thoroughly inappropriate for the current mood in the room.

"The fuckin' bastard. We were supposed to be mates...blood brothers," he railed.

She held him tightly and kissed his neck, it was like kissing wood.

"Please, don't be angry."

"He was supposed to be my best mate," said Ronnie.

"I know that better than anyone. I made a mistake. I had a mad night because you made me mad. I could never come between you two, you wouldn't have believed me, so when I was offered a place at college, it seemed like the best solution for everyone that I left."

"I had no fuckin' idea," he said.

"I tell you one thing, I've never been hoodwinked by a man since," she said, reasserting herself. She needed to regain control. No matter what, this had to stop right here, right now.

"Fuckin' bastard. I can't fuckin' believe it," said Ronnie, chewing his bottom lip.

"Promise me you won't say anything," said Roxy.

"Say anything? I ought to throw him off the end of the fuckin' pier."

"Promise me…. please Ronnie."

Roxy loosened her grip enough to rest her head on his.

"You broke my heart, Rox," he said.

"You broke mine too. When I heard you were going out with Hazel, I thought what he'd said must have been true."

There was a knock on the door.

"One minute," said Roxy, her voice faltering slightly. As she pulled away from him and straightened her outfit. Ronnie turned his back on the door and, catching an eyeful of his topless self in the mirror, hastily pulled his shirt on. His head was in disarray. A whole chapter of his life had been reauthored and he'd been none the wiser.

Carly, one of Roxy's young assistants, all bright nails and eyelashes, poked her head around the door.

"You okay, Joanna?"

Roxy nodded.

"There's a Steve on the phone."

"Get Sharna to deal with it," barked Roxy.

"He said he only wanted to speak to you."

"Okay, okay," huffed Roxy, doing her best to look unflustered.

Carly hesitated a second and Roxy looked up at her, clearly an instruction to get the hell out and so she swiftly backed out of the door with an urgent apology imprinted across her face.

CHAPTER 22.
Penny for your thoughts.

Once the sugar-rush of the arcades was over, Mick and Penny recharged their batteries on a couple of deck chairs that were sunk down in the pebbly beach. Around them children played as multi-coloured kites soared way up in the sky, sometimes crashing down in a tumbled mess of string and nylon as the wind changed direction. Knackered-out parents were slumped on the beach giving competing impressions of lobsters.

Without the hullabaloo of the flashing lights, novelty tones and other funfair distractions, Mick found himself a little lost for words. They both had ice cream cones, but while she chomped at hers, he threw his to the gulls, who picked and fought over it.

He leaned across and fingered the cross pendant she was wearing around her neck.

"It's to scare away vampires," she said.

"Should I be worried then?" joked Mick.

"Some might say," she said.

"Must be nice to have something to believe in," said Mick. "I used to believe in myself and Chelsea football club, but they both let me down."

"So, you don't believe in God, then?" she asked.

"I don't think God's the problem, it's his salesmen I have an issue with," said Mick.

"I don't really go to church, but I like to think that something's out there," said Penny.
"I did enter a church once," said Mick. "I was outside stripping off the lead and fell through the roof."
He laughed, and she followed suit.
"I'm only kidding," he said.
She wasn't sure that he was kidding, but she was becoming happily cushioned by his charm.
"You're a bit nutty, but I like you," said Penny.
"I'll take it as a compliment, then shall I?" asked Mick.
They exchanged self-conscious smiles.
"Your friend, Ronnie, is he a Mod then?"
"When the fancy takes him," said Mick.
"It's all a bit before my time, really. We have Mods scooting around here sometimes, but I think they all go to Margate when Gay Pride is on," said Penny.
She pulled out her phone for a selfie.
"Don't you start, I get all that from Bulldog, snapping away all the time. He says it's good for his health, but it drives the rest of us crackers," said Mick.
"I won't post it if you don't want me to," said Penny, wondering if there was an ulterior motive to his camera shyness.
"Post what you like. It don't bother me."
He leaned over and their cheeks touched as she took the snap.
"So, there's no-one waiting for you back in London?" she tentatively pried.
"As a matter of fact, there is," he said.
Penny's heart sunk, but she tried not to show her disappointment.
"I've got any number of fella's, pursuing me at the moment," said Mick, with a straight face.

"Oh," said Penny.
"Probably waiting for me at my flat as we speak. That's why I agreed to come down here. Get a bit of peace," said Mick, leading her on.
A sheen of disappointment pulsed across Penny's face.
"Typical. Well done, Penny. I find a bloke I like and he's not into women. I shouldn't be surprised. That's what you get for looking for a straight date in the Gay capital of England, I guess."
Mick rocked his head back and chuckled.
"It's alright, I ain't, y'know a Queer or nothin'... I'm skint."
She shot him a puzzled look.
"My pursuers, they're loan sharks and bailiffs. They're after my bank balance, not my body, although they will probably steamroll over that if I don't cough up," he said.
She play-hit him and he laughed.
"I'll bloody steamroll you, you rotten sod."
As the tide gradually advanced on them, they exchanged the kind of biographies that would have had Charles Dickens scurrying for his quill. It was a tennis match of hard luck stories, but the accompanying tears had long since dried up. Over the years they had each discharged enough futile energy in the quagmire of self-pity that they knew how to avoid the signposts that led to those particular dead-end streets.
Penny was dumped in a children's home by her mother. It hurt her greatly, but the biggest scar was created by not knowing why she'd been abandoned. Carrying around an unanswerable 'Why?' was soul destroying. He put the jokes on hold and offered an empathetic ear. It was all fits and starts. She put the brakes on with an uncertainty of herself that he recognised as an invite for his own

testimony. They were refreshingly open, but there was only so much vulnerability that each of them were prepared to risk in one sitting.

His tales of high jinks with the Battersham Aces were told in a self-effacing manner that was the antithesis of Ronnie's rose-tinted folk hero hype. He counted his time working as a Repo Man as a dark milestone of his personal demise.

She had excluded the abuse she suffered in the children's home and he avoided the trauma of his sister's untimely death, but they were each able to get an inkling for the horror stories lurking between the lines.

Mick had always used anger to confirm his existence, but it had aged him in more than just appearance. Neither of them was seeking sympathy but, subconsciously, they had begun to weave a mutually agreeable understanding. Circumstances brought him to Brighton, but now he had met Penny, the chaos of Battersham seemed more distant and his return there, something he didn't want to think about.

A football suddenly bounced off Mick's head, knocking his pill shaped sunglasses clear off his face and forcing him to stumble his words, while he was recanting an anecdote about the day he got roaringly drunk and took a disastrous decision to redecorate his friends' house, while his friend was away on holiday. The boy who'd kicked the football, a little West Indian in a bright red Manchester United shirt, stood there frozen to the spot. Mick's reactive triggers of aggression seemed to have been disarmed and he just burst out laughing, throwing the ball back to the anxious lad and his apologetic father who came rushing over to scold his child.

He didn't exactly work hard at it, but Mick had been searching for a sea change for quite some time and perhaps now here it was. He had nothing to lose. Brighton was endearing itself to him and he was opening his arms to embrace it.

CHAPTER 23. Mick's Dark Secret.

Bulldog and Guzzler were lounging around in the hotel bar, the place had the atmosphere of a bank, and the prices of the drinks reflected an expense account that was way beyond their means. They were talking football and whenever they did, Bulldog knew he was on a hiding to nothing. In the early eighties he'd bucked the trend and decided not to follow the local team. He was the only member of the Aces who didn't support Chelsea. On the back of their successive European cup triumphs, he had chosen Nottingham Forest. He was branded a glory hunter and their taunting got more persistent the further Forest eventually fell from grace. Once Footballing giants, managed by the mercurial genius, Brian Clough, they became perennial strugglers slugging it out at the wrong end of the less fashionable divisions. Bulldog let it wash over him. He spent his time anxiously worrying about another kind of scoring entirely.

The lift opened and out walked Mick in a slim-cut Mohair suit. It was an old outfit but something about the way he wore it was definitely new. Bulldog and Guzzler looked up as he tugged at the lapels of his suit jacket and announced with as much swagger as he could muster.

"Alright, boys. There's a town out there desperate to meet us."

"He's thawed out a bit, ain't he?" said Guzzler turning to Bulldog

"The ice caps have melted, watch out for the flood," said Bulldog.

Bulldog and Guzzler unruffled themselves and made to follow Mick, who was heading for the main entrance.

"So, where we off to then?" said Bulldog.

Mick stopped and turned to them.

"I don't know which dag-pit you two losers are haunting tonight, but *I* have got a date."

"What about, Ronnie?" said Guzzler.

"What about him?" replied Mick.

"Ain't you gonna wait for him?" said Bulldog.

Mick looked at his left wrist out of habit, the lack of a watch was a reminder of his personal dose of austerity.

"Time's up," he said.

Mick playfully slapped Guzzler on both cheeks.

"I'll see you chaps later."

He bounded out of the hotel, trying to keep up with the new spring in his step.

Guzzler watched him as he disappeared into the warm evening air.

"Yep, something's definitely up with him, he's got the Polar bear walk," said Guzzler.

"I haven't seen him this chipper since… well, I haven't seen him this chipper," said Bulldog.

"Poor boy's in love… God help her, eh?" said Guzzler.

"So, what we gonna do, then?" asked Bulldog.

"We're in Brighton, city of culture, they'll be music, theatre, cabaret…or, we could just go out and get bladdered," said Guzzler.

"Bladdered it is then," confirmed Bulldog.

Just as they had decided to give their livers a caning, Ronnie appeared. Sizing him up, Guzzler thought he looked like he'd travelled a fair distance since they last clapped eyes on him. Guzzler and Bulldog waited while Ronnie went off to freshen up.

In his hotel room, Ronnie dunked his face in the sink and stood looking at himself in the bathroom mirror and at the droplets of water running down his face. Whatever it was he was trying to dislodge was refusing to budge. He felt a seething rage inside at Mick's betrayal but knew that nothing good could come from confronting him. He would have to let it pass, but at that moment the prospect felt tantamount to swallowing a double decker bus. He tried to sooth his pride with the knowledge that he'd not been totally above board with Roxy, at the time in question he had been a hair's breadth from playing away with Hazel. Regardless of the hypocrisy of misogyny, it brought him no comfort. He opened a can of beer and gulped it down in an attempt to douse the flames of contempt.

Rationality was the name of the game when he dealt with problems at work and maybe a dose of that was needed now, he thought, as he made his way to the lift. He was responsible for this trip, Bulldog and Guzzler weren't party to the treachery and Ronnie couldn't allow anything taint their tribute to Arnie.

The three friends left the hotel and made their way along the seafront, refuelling at various bars along the way. Before heading in the direction of the train station, they stopped in a backstreet pub next to the Brighton Conference Centre. Back in December 1982, it had been the venue for The Jam's last stand. The acrimonious split of the nation's favourite pop group.

"I remember that night like it was yesterday," said Ronnie, who had been obsessive about the three-piece band at the time.

"We walked out of there at the end and it was like our lives was over," said Bulldog.

"You might have walked out of there. I hopped. I lost a bleedin' shoe dancin' to *Town called Malice*, didn't I," said Ronnie, with a grin. "Couldn't find it anywhere, then something flew past my head and I'm sure it was my shoe being hurled at Paul Weller."

"I remember someone throwing a bottle at the stage, that just missed Weller," said Bulldog, who was exhibiting the occasional shiver, despite the fact that it was twenty-eight degrees outside.

"A lot of pissed-off people that night. I mean, it was a right downer, knowing there'd never be another gig like it. People were crying," said Ronnie.

"How long ago was that? And we're still waiting for the reunion," said Guzzler.

"It pains me to say it, but I think he did the right thing in the end. I mean, that stuff he did with the Style Council was shit," said Ronnie. "The Jam, they'll always be legends, know what I mean?"

"Maybe, but if they announced a tour tomorrow, guarantee I'd see you two lunatics at the front of the queue for tickets," said Guzzler.

They drank up their memories and moved north, following the train arches to a large boozer off the beaten track. It wasn't too busy and had a decent sized garden that housed a couple of vintage cars. Ronnie's pulse rate had calmed when he was informed that Mick was out on the tiles with Penny.

Sitting in the pub garden, Bulldog and Guzzler indulged Ronnie on another excursions into yesteryear, particularly as he was buying two rounds each for every one they bought.

Bulldog looked a little distracted, chewing gum like a pneumatic drill and constantly searching around to find his focus.

"How was it you never got lumbered with a poxy nick name then Ronnie?" asked Guzzler.

"I had nick names," protested Ronnie.

"I can't remember any," said Bulldog.

"Well, there was Double Diamond," said Ronnie.

"Yeah, but *you* made that one up," said Guzzler.

"So what?" said Ronnie.

"Do you know what it's like being a grown man called Guzzler?"

"What about me? Do I look like a Bulldog?"

"Dunno, but if you don't get a round in, I'll find something worse to call you," said Ronnie.

Bulldog trudged off to the bar.

"Is he alright?" said Ronnie.

They both turned to look at him at the bar.

"You noticed it too?" said Guzzler.

"He looks like he's dishonoured the Mafioso and he's waiting for the henchmen to arrive," said Ronnie.

"He's struggling. When I found him in the hotel room this morning he was shaking. This is his reality now, he lives on the edge of disaster," said Guzzler.

Bulldog returned with the drinks and Ronnie and Guzzler swiftly changed the subject.

"Do you remember when he had a thing for that Lisa Taylor and he was trying to impress her and drove his scooter through the kids paddling pool?" said Ronnie, pointing at Bulldog.

"Liked to make a bit of a splash with the ladies, didn't you, mate," said Guzzler.

"She was alright, little Lise." said Ronnie.

"Ain't so little now though," said Guzzler.

"I wouldn't climb over her to get to you," said Bulldog.

"That's alright then, 'cause you'd need a fuckin' big ladder if you wanted to," said Guzzler.

"Mick seems quite taken with that Penny bird," said Bulldog.

"I thought you and Roxy would be making up a foursome with them, what with them being mates and that," said Guzzler.

"I wanted a night out with the lads, didn't I, know what I mean?" said Ronnie, bluffing out his angst. He now desperately wished he hadn't soured things with Roxy. 'I couldn't just let it be', he tormented himself.

"Mick always did have an eye for the birds," said Guzzler. "Remember how he used to drive around on his scooter, we all had fox's tails on our aerials, and he'd have the knickers of his latest conquest unceremoniously tied to his."

"Last of the romantics, aye?" said Bulldog.

"It's great to be down here, ain't it. I love Brighton. Shame Mick's not with us tonight," said Bulldog, telling Ronnie what he thought he wanted to hear but winding him up in the process.

"What, 'cos there ain't no Blacks?" said Ronnie, who couldn't hold back getting a dig in on Mick. The irony was lost on his friends.

"What you talking about, Blacks? What Blacks?" said Guzzler.

"Nothing. It was just something Mick said. He keeps coming out with all this racist shit," said Ronnie.

Bulldog met Guzzler's eyes and instantly read his thoughts.

"He doesn't know," said Guzzler.

"Know what?" said Ronnie.

Guzzler leaned into Ronnie. In a quiet tone he said, "If I tell you this you've got to swear you don't repeat it to anyone…ever."

Ronnie was suddenly transported to a makeshift treehouse in Battersham park, about to be let in on the secret that the eight-year-old Guzzler had pilfered a fiver in coins from his Dad's coat and trouser pockets and thus set up a council of friends to debate how best to spend it and thereby share the guilt.

"Go on," said Ronnie, intrigued.

"You swear?" said Guzzler.

"I swear," said Ronnie.

"After, you know, what happened to Eve…" said Guzzler.

Guzzler couldn't bring himself to furnish his words with any detail for the fear of reawakening his sickening nightmares of Mick's Sister's corpse mangled in a bloody heap on the concrete floor. It was an image that tortured him when he was at his most vulnerable.

"Her suicide, yeah," said Ronnie.

"Sometime later, Mick unearthed her Diary. From what he had pieced together, it looked like she made arrangements to meet a bloke called Aston Shetani, a right piece of shit," said Guzzler.

"Fuckin' low-life," said Bulldog.

"Yeah, I think I know who you mean," said Ronnie.

"Eve weren't the full shilling, as you know. Mick thinks he lured her somewhere and she was gang raped," said Guzzler.

It felt, to Ronnie, like the Juke box had suddenly been switched to mute and the sounds of Summer drinkers, the chatter of two young lovers cavorting at a nearby table, a rugby bore and the clatter of the bar staff collecting empties, swirled into a sickly blurred cacophony, like some kind of aural flu. His mind pulled up the draw bridge and blocked his ears with an emergency broadcast of Tinnitus.

"Oh, that's evil," said Ronnie shaking his head.

Ronnie was subdued to the point of breathlessness, such was the assault this information had on his cognition.

"That Shetani was a Class-A wrong 'un," said Bulldog

"By the time Mick had pieced it all together, Shetani had been knifed to death in some gang feud," said Guzzler.

Ronnie's head lifted to regain eye contact.

"Good riddance to bad rubbish, eh?" he said.

"That's the thing. Mick would have killed him, and it might have gone some way to tame the seething monster inside him. It might have cost him his liberty or maybe even his own life, but he'd have done it with a firm hand," said Guzzler.

Ronnie nodded, while a flood of unbearable images of violence and hatred invaded his mind.

"So, he's left like an angry bee in a bottle. He never found out who the others were or what they looked like. He beat the shit out of one bloke, only to find out later that he wasn't even living in the country at the time it all happened. He was properly out of control. And that Shetani didn't even have the decency to be buried. His ashes were scattered in Barbados by all accounts. No grave or headstone exists, so Mick has nothing to pummel 'cept his own sanity," said Guzzler.

"Poor bastard," said Ronnie.

"He only told us the full story about five years ago," said Bulldog.

Ronnie thought about his faux par when walking to get Mick's Scooter and grimaced.

"He's alright most of the time, but sometimes it comes out in rants, normally about the Blacks or the Muslims. If you try to point out how irrational he's being, he just thinks you're siding with his sisters' rapists. I tell ya, you can't win," said Guzzler.

"But what about Oxford? I saw them talking at the funeral. You can't get blacker than 'im," said Ronnie.

"He says Oxford is different. He's one of us," said Bulldog.

"Remember, he used to get called a coconut for hanging around with us," said Ronnie.

None of them wanted the conversation about Mick's sister to drag on but finding a gear change to that kind of journey wasn't easy.

Ronnie took a swig of beer. Bloody hell, he thought, as he realised his grievance with Mick had been usurped.

Pandora had done a right number on him since he began searching for the lost strands of his youth, but this was into another Stratosphere.

Guzzler saw him brooding on it and so tried to add a little rationality where very little existed.

"Listen, if Shetani had been a milkman, or an Arsenal fan, he'd have hated them instead, know what I mean?"

"I think his anger has run out of energy. Best just avoid the subject," said Bulldog.

"Let's be honest here, his life is a fuckin' disaster," said Guzzler, who suddenly wondered to himself if he was talking about Mick or Bulldog.

"He's as sour as a kiss from a geriatric auntie and his love life wilted faster than a bunch of forecourt flowers. I guess the old Mick is in there somewhere, but he's been buzzing in that bottle for a very long time. God help anyone attempting to flip open that lid."

"I had no idea," said Ronnie.

"Why would you?" snapped Guzzler.

Ronnie thought Guzzler's last comment was an honest statement wrapped in a slight. He shrugged his shoulders and a state of limbo ensued. It was going to be a job to rescue this evening from the black hole it had fallen into. As for his grievance with Mick, if Ronnie was going salvage anything from his time away with his old mates, he realised he'd have to swallow that one. As choking as he found it, it was nothing compared with the sewage pipe Mick's jaws had been locked around since his sister's death.

Ronnie's mobile phone started ringing. It was Hazel. This was an escape route from a conversation that should have come with a health warning. He rose from his seat.

"I better get this," said Ronnie, as he made his way to the end of the pub garden and sat down on a giant wooden toadstool that was part of a children's play area.

He attempted to nullify Hazel's frostiness by being outwardly bubbly, switching it on like he was performing in a show. It took a great effort for very little reward. Ronnie wondered if his day could get any worse.

"I think you've got some explaining to do, don't you?" said Hazel.

"Explaining?"

"I saw the photos," said Hazel.

"What photos?" said Ronnie, his mind racing through his memory bank like a burglar trying to beat an alarm system he'd just activated. His own charge sheet came up blank. He had no idea what she was talking about.

"The ones on Facebook of you with *your* friends, of the sea front at Brighton, Guzzler eating a massive ice cream…oh and you and your ex-girlfriend huddled together on a fucking Scooter," she raged.

There were now two conversations going on in Ronnie's head, the silent one with himself, 'How the hell did she get to see that?' and the one he was vocalising with Hazel.

"Oh that. That's nothing," he said.

"It didn't exactly look like nothing," she snarled.

The countdown was on. Ronnie had milliseconds to placate her, his mind racing like a super-computer searching for the correct equation.

"No, that was just Guzzler. He offered to take Roxy for a ride," he said, making it up as he went along.

"Yeah, I bet he did," she said.

"Come on Hazel don't be like that. His scooter was playing up, so he said I'd do it."

"What's *she* doing down there, anyway? You never said there were any women going to Brighton," said Hazel.

"There weren't. Roxy lives down here. We just bumped into her," said Ronnie, desperately hoping he was winning the PR war. Hazel took umbrage with Roxy's name coming out of his mouth.

"How very convenient," she said.

"Straight up," he replied.

Ronnie took the slight gap in her onslaught as a sign that she might be softening. She'd confronted him head on and he had directed her down a blind alley. Now it wasn't about facts it was about choices.

"You better not be bullshitting me, Ronnie."

"'course I'm not," he said.

"Why didn't you take my calls?" she said.

"My phone's been playing up. That's why I haven't called you."

"You just behave yourself. You hear me?" she said.

"I love you, Hazey," said Ronnie.

Ronnie gritted his teeth and waited. Only a second or two passed but to Ronnie it felt like a lifetime.

"I love you too," said Hazel.

With that, she was gone. His shoulders eased, and he let out a sigh and wondered how, in the space of a day, he had coped with this emotional triathlon. His heart couldn't take it. Any more of this and they'd be using a very different kind of ticker tape at his finish line.

Before re-joining Bulldog and Guzzler, Ronnie pondered a moment. What was he doing here? What exactly were his intentions with Roxy? It wasn't simply a sexual desire, although that was certainly part of it.

When he returned to the bar, Ronnie was pleased to see the conversation had moved on.

"Arnie or Oxford?" said Bulldog as he tussled with Guzzler over the correct details from another page of Aces folklore.

"Who had their scooter cemented to the floor? Arnie or Oxford?' said Guzzler.

"Well, that's easy," said Ronnie, as his two grinning friends waited for the answer.

"It was Pete," said Ronnie.

Bulldog and Guzzler gaped at each other and laughed.

"It was after he nicked Lumper's bird, Sue…err.. you know," Ronnie was wracking his brains.

"Susie Baker," said Bulldog, putting him out of his misery.

The mists of time lifted and each of them played out their version of the legend in their heads.

"He was something else, that bloke. Everyone loved him but if you were out with a bird, you had to cone the area off if you went for a piss or up the bar for another round," said Ronnie, with a smile.

"So, what we gonna do about Arnie's ashes?" asked Bulldog.

"Yeah, I thought you had some big plan?" said Guzzler.

"Trust me, boys. I do," said Ronnie. "I want to give him a send-off fit for a Mod."

Bulldog headed for the lavatories while Ronnie went for refills. By then the pub had filled up, mostly with people their age. Guzzler indulged himself with one of his favourite pastimes. He had always been a people watcher, not the twisted voyeurism of Mick's telescopic escapades. He held a genuine belief that he could read faces and attach an imagined background story to each of them.

Bulldog was sitting in a cubicle in the washroom, a phone in his hand flicking through his photo's. He was chewing gum like a hammer drill. He tried to focus his concentration on the images, but it wasn't easy.

When Ronnie returned with the beers, Guzzler was still in *Soothsayer* mode.

"You ever, y'know, size people up, think about who they are, what their lives are like?" said Guzzler.

"Course," said Ronnie. "Every day someone walks into my place looking to buy a house. I've got maybe ten seconds to work out if they're going to buy a flat, house or a mansion and whether they're gonna have the readies to back all of that up."

"I ain't talking about what's in their wallet," said Guzzler. He gave Ronnie a run down on his chosen subjects.

"Take the bloke in the red shirt, playing it cool but inside he's bricking it. The kind of fella that arrives late for everything, bought a cheap Betamax player when VHS had already won the home video war. That woman he's with has issues about her big hooter. Likes to be in charge because if the pendulum swings, she falls to pieces, probably works as a teacher or a nurse."
"Is that right?" said Ronnie, feigning interest.
"You have a go," said Guzzler.
"Alright. See if you can guess who this is. Big fella, looks a bit pissed, talking bollocks to his mate…"
"Where? Who you talking about?" said Guzzler, enthralled that someone was taking him seriously.
"He's a fat fuck who thinks he's a bleedin' Mystic Meg," said Ronnie, as he leaned back on his chair laughing.
"Fuck off, Ronnie," said Guzzler.
"I'm only 'avin' a laugh, mate. Don't get a mood on, you touchy sod."
Bulldog returned to the table.
"Where you been? We was about to send out a search party," said Guzzler.
"Fuck me. Can't a bloke have a *Tom Tit* without having to answer for himself?"
"Cor, it's like a night out with Victor Meldrew and Basil fuckin' Fawlty," said Ronnie.
"Who got these?" said Bulldog, as he picked up his pint.
"I did. Claire's getting the next round," said Ronnie.
"Claire?" said Bulldog, puzzled.
Ronnie throws a thumb in Guzzler's direction.
"Clairvoyant, here."

CHAPTER 24.
Flashback at Paparazzi's

Ronnie and Guzzler were sitting at a table in the hotel's bland dining hall, with its flax-coloured walls, humdrum paintings and the kind of air-conditioning that favours bacteria over living beings. They were nursing the sort of hangovers that are only just sufferable if they prevented you from remembering anything from the night that preceded them. Ronnie was still in last night's shirt and hid his eyes behind a pair of Ray Bann sunglasses. Bulldog hadn't managed to surface for the late breakfast. The table was a bombsite of egg splattered plates and near-empty cups and looked as stale as they did. The only other people present were the staff who were collecting dirty dishes and re-setting the tables for dinner. Ronnie was on his third black coffee while Guzzler was demolishing his second breakfast. Ronnie knew it would take more than a greasy fry-up and toast to soak up last night's overindulgence. Just as he was feeling like he was coming around he would jar himself on a sharp thought from yesterday's revelations. He tried to put them out of his mind. Deliberating anything more than where the paracetamol was kept, on a hangover like this, was as pointless as driving with your eyes closed. He couldn't remember how he got back to the hotel the previous night and why there was a half-eaten Kebab and a traffic cone in his bed.

The day drew past like a slow cloud. There'd been no sign of Mick, but Bulldog did make an appearance later on. He looked worse than Ronnie felt, but didn't he look like that on most of the days he'd seen him of late, thought Ronnie. In an attempt to avoid her number appearing on his phone bill, Ronnie had neglected to give Roxy his mobile phone number, so she had no way of contacting him. He wasn't sure how he felt about her and what, if anything, she would be thinking about him. He tried to convince himself that he had been angry with Mick and not her. His rancour for Mick had been tempered by his sister's ordeal, and what it had done to him. He wanted Roxy to be a part of what they were doing in Brighton, but the whole thing had been derailed. After all he'd gone through, Ronnie knew he couldn't allow this trip to die like this.

Ronnie felt he had the antidote for his woes. He stuck the traffic cone in the hotel lift and sent it to the tenth floor. Back in his room he kicked off his shoes, plugged a pair of headphones into his mobile phone and lay back on his hotel bed and listened to the soundtrack of his life. The musical restoration was almost complete, so he called and had room service bring up some soft drinks that would accompany the bottle of vodka he still had in his bag. He supped and nodded himself into a new headspace.

Ronnie stood up by the window, looking out at the big wheel with all its happy punters, all grabbing their best shots of the aerial views. When he looked out first thing in the morning it was almost vomit inducing, spinning in sync with the booze-driven machinations in his head, now it felt therapeutic.

Another cool tune from Modern World, that threatened the pop charts in the early eighties, exploded into his ears in tandem with a boost of vodka flooding his brain. Ronnie started singing along.

"Clothes half-inched from a market stall,
White socks and shoes that you wore to School,
Scar on your cheek, cut on your lip,
Says today you're nobody's fool,
Making roll-ups from discarded fags,
Because you know that you gotta make do,
But when Saturday comes, it's like the change of the guard,
Because you're one of the chosen few,
1,2,3,4,
Saturday's for Heroes,
Gonna make your dreams come true,
Saturday's for Heroes,
On the backstreets baby, with the chosen few."

"I fuckin' love this song," he said out loud, as the sunshine poured in through the window and a gentle summer breeze shifted his worries off across the blue yonder.

By the time Ronnie, Bulldog and Guzzler arrived at Paparazzi's night club, Ronnie was half-cut, all the bum notes edited out of his dreams. Bulldog was snapping everything with his camera phone and Guzzler had spent the afternoon browsing the boutiques in the Brighton Lanes, where he felt he was in heaven surrounded by rare and interesting books and deliciously enticing cakes. He was a little off the pace on the boozing stakes but was determined to catch up.

As they finally got into the ballroom, after queuing and being searched by the meatheads on the door, Ronnie had a flashback to his last visit here, where sharp suited Mods out ranked the other revellers, or so it had seemed. A few things had been updated but by and by it was pretty much the same. The main glaring difference was that half of the people here were the same age as he was in his flashback. It was eighties night, so at least the playlist was from their era, even if was a little more mainstream than Ronnie would have liked.

Bulldog and Guzzler manned a little table in one of the venue's alcoves while Ronnie headed to the bar. It was rammed. He stood, self-consciously waving a twenty-pound note like a starting flag. He felt someone theatrically embrace his shoulder and he swivelled around to see Mick with a beaming smile on his face.

"I'll get these, Ronnie." he said, as he squeezed his way to the front row.

Ronnie clocked that Mick had called him Ronnie, he never called him Ronnie, always Ron.

"Good luck getting served this side of midnight," said Ronnie.

Mick rested one arm around Ronnie's shoulder, like he had as a lad when they'd walked home, muddy, knackered and bruised, from another 20-a-side football match in the park.

"I wanna thank you for dragging me down here. I know I wasn't, y'know…"

"It's all right," said Ronnie, not knowing what had engineered this change of tact.

"You've been a mate I haven't always deserved… I missed ya," said Mick.

Was it drink that had fuelled this metamorphosis? Ronnie doubted it.

"I missed you to," said Ronnie, the words threatening to choke him.

Neither of them had noticed the young barmaid behind the bar, awaiting their order, who had temporarily paused to tune into their bromance.

"Ahhh, that's really sweet. Now what can I get you, gentlemen," said the barmaid.

Mick ordered the drinks and they watched as the barmaid scurried around filling glasses like some kind of Octopus circus act.

"How's it going with...err," Ronnie had forgotten her name.

"Penny, yeah. She's safe as houses," said Mick.

Between them, they gathered up the drinks and made their way to the table.

The dance floor was filling up, dominated mostly by the female of the species. Madonna, Culture club and Wham seemed to be the DJ's staple diet. Although Ronnie sometimes found himself subconsciously humming along to some of these songs in the car, he considered it plastic music. Tunes with a dollar sign was where the heart should have been. They were played so much on radio and TV it was impossible to keep them out of your head. He didn't expect wall to wall Mod music of course, but the odd Jam song would have made a pleasant change. By all means throw in a bit of Madness, Bad Manners or even Adam and the Ants, if it meant he didn't have endure Michael Jackson or Prince. He remembered how, as a teenager, cult loyalty had defined what music he could confess to appreciating. If it wasn't remotely Mod, it had to remain a guilty pleasure. He could get away with raving about Kim Wilde or Blondie because their appeal was more than just musical, there was a sexual precursor to liking them. To casually admit to enjoying Phil Collins or Duran Duran was social suicide. Praising Bronski Beat or Frankie goes to Hollywood could get you beaten up.

Back at the table they found Penny with Bulldog and Guzzler. She was chatting away as if she'd known them for years. Penny was genuine and good hearted, and Ronnie hoped that whatever it was between her and Mick, might be more than just a holiday romance.

Roxy was missing from the picture, but he wasn't going to quiz Penny about her in front of the others. The drinks kept coming and Penny was educated in some of the more ridiculous antics that the Battersham Aces had got up to in the past, via a tennis match of daft stories, jibes and piss-takes.

Ronnie was staring into thin air, his eyes glazed over, when Bulldog spotted Roxy.

"Oi, oi, here comes trouble," said Guzzler, nudging Ronnie.

Ronnie watched her making her way down from the DJ's booth. Moving through a diagonal shaft of purple light, she looked stunning, dressed in a lightly checked, sixties-style, mini-dress that showed off her pins to perfection. She had a confidence that made it look like the management had designed the lighting solely for her arrival.

The DJ made an announcement. "This next song goes out to Robbie and the Petersham Aces."

Ronnie and Mick mouthed the words 'Petersham', mocking the DJ's error.

"Let's see you move to this one. It's 'One of us' by Modern World," said the DJ.

The song started up and caused an instant reaction from Ronnie, who was already pretty lubricated. He tore off his jacket and threw it towards a seat next to Bulldog.

"Come on lads," said Ronnie. Guzzler tried to encourage Bulldog, but he was not interested.

"I'll join you in a minute," said Bulldog.

Guzzler decided not to waste any more time on him.

Roxy met Ronnie half-way across the dancefloor. The place had virtually emptied out, the edginess of the first few chords of Pop-Punk, ripping into the candy-coated blandness of the disco tunes that preceded it. Ronnie and Roxy embraced, before she made her way to the side of the dance hall where she encountered Penny.

"You certainly know how to make an entrance."

"Watch and learn, my friend. Watch and learn," said Roxy.

Guzzler, Mick and Ronnie were jumping around to the song. For that one moment, Ronnie felt teenage once more. His legs ached, his back was sore, but his spirit was free.

Bulldog picked Ronnie's jacket up from the floor and placed it on the seat. As he did, a pair of sunglasses and a bulging wallet fell out.

The song was only three minutes long but already Ronnie, Guzzler and Mick were feeling jaded by the alcohol and the effort.

Lights flashed and tilted while illuminated shapes whirled and whizzed as they were sprayed across the walls and ceiling. There was an erratic intensity to Ronnie. He threw an embracing arm around Mick's neck, and they sung along to the music in a performance befitting one of the band's live shows.

"When you realise you're not on your own,
Choose your own path, you won't be their clone
You didn't fall off no production line
Try to give you their bull, they're just wasting your time"

Guzzler barrels in and joins them on the chorus.

"No mess, no fuss, you're one of us,

Your schools, our rules, our syllabus,
Two hearts, one beat, my kith and kin,
Mates to the end, through thick and thin."

"They wrote this one for us, eh, blood brother?" Mick shouted in Ronnie's ear.

Looking pretty puffed out they stopped jumping around, arms aloft, they settled for a football terrace-style sing along. In the old days, Ronnie could jump around to a set of twenty-odd songs and barely break sweat, but here he was half-way through a single tune and thinking about his life insurance. They continued to chant along in unison.

"You look down at me, but this is what I chose,
New vision, new boots, new fancy clothes,
Dress right, stay smart, take the world by storm,
I don't wanna be you 'cos your life is a yawn."

Bulldog pulled out his phone and took some photos of the Aces singing to each other. As the song faded into a more commercial disco number, Roxy was waiting in the wings to take Ronnie's arm and led him back to their alcove.

"Did you like the dedication, then?" asked Roxy.

"Yeah, If I'm ever in Petersham, I'll be sure to tell Robbie they were asking for him," said Ronnie.

They both laughed, and it went some way to dress the wound left festering since their last encounter. Whatever had happened in the past, it was obvious that something still fizzed between them. As the night wore on, they simply relaxed into each other.

Mick and Penny were among a throng of people smooching to a slow song. Guzzler was sitting back and taking it all in. He didn't much like discotheques, but he could enjoy the eye-candy and be entertained by some of the over-exuberant, would-be groovers, who with a confidence undeserving of their rhythmic ability, looked like they'd invented new ways of dancing that could make anyone, with a camera phone handy, a pretty packet on YouTube.

Bulldog had disappeared off on one of his extended visits to the toilets. Guzzler tried to reason with himself that his friend had probably lost track of time, perhaps crashed out asleep or sitting on the toilet scrolling through the endless pages of brain-numbing nonsense on Facebook.

An upbeat Northern Soul track came on and Roxy's face lit up like a child who has just caught wind of the distant sound of the ice-cream van's melodic chimes.

"It's Jo-time," she announced.

Ronnie followed as Roxy made her way to the dancefloor which she had almost entirely to herself. He stood around the edge mesmerised as she glided across the floor, her hips swinging and feet shuffling, she oozed sensuality. It felt as choreographed as an intricate ice-skating routine. She stole the floor, putting on the performance of her life, improvising little kicks and twists. Ronnie couldn't take his eyes off her.

As the song came to a close, he felt an urge to applaud her, but restrained himself. She floated back over to him, glowing. There were plenty of admiring glances, but only one judge, and his face told her she'd just achieved top marks.

"Wow. That was amazing," said Ronnie.

"Thanks," said Roxy, barely out of breath.

"You're full of surprises," said Ronnie.

Roxy leaned in and gave him a gentle kiss on the ear and whispered, "I keep the best to last."

She gave him a saucy smile and strode back to the table, safe in the knowledge that Ronnie would be at her heel, captivated by her exaggerated swagger.

CHAPTER 25. Family Albums

With Ronnie being away most of the week, Jane was keen to come over and keep Hazel company. Prior to her turning up, Hazel had a quick clean around. She'd loosened her belt and let the place breathe a bit while Ronnie was away. It had been a pyjama party for one.

Hazel reflected on the fact that Ronnie and her barely had a few days apart each year, and even when they were separated, they spent much of that time on the phone to each other. It would have suffocated most relationships, but their closeness was the fuel to their fire.

Before Hazel completed her blitz on the house, she found Ronnie's photo albums and began slowly leafing through them. Almost every page ambushed her with a different emotion. It was clear why Ronnie may have been tempted to go in search of those days once more. They were full of adventure. Ronnie always seemed to be the centre of attention, playing up to the camera. Always the one the others were looking at to make things happen. Amongst the happy recollections, there were moments when she had little flushes of envy.

The photographs were not so kind to Guzzler. It seemed like every time the camera clicked, it caught Guzzler with his mouth open or his face contorted in some strange or unattractive way.

They enjoyed some wonderful times, care-free days of fun, love and lunacy. She knew Ronnie was being ruled by his heart, and if he'd listened to his head, he might have heard it warn him, 'never haunt your past'.

Her heart strings were pulled at the sight of Arnie, his arms around Ronnie and Guzzler, a beaming friendly smile. Maybe it was in hindsight, but she felt he'd always been keeping an eye out for everyone. It was strange, looking at photographs of a person, someone so full of life in her memories, that no longer existed in the flesh. Her life in Battersham was so long ago that it was unlikely she would have ever seen Arnie again, but the fact that he had died somehow made it all feel so different.

Her emotion soon changed from sympathy to scorn, when she saw an old snap of Roxy with her arm around Ronnie. She couldn't remember seeing it before. She was sure she'd purged Roxy from all their photo albums years ago. The doorbell chimed, and Hazel cursed aloud for allowing herself to wander down the long-forgotten back alleys of her mind.

"Just a minute," she shouted.

She hated entertaining in a messy home and so launched into a mini offensive, chucking clothes into wardrobes and magazines into draws, before dashing to let in her friend. Hazel pulled the door open and prepared for the usual high velocity verbal onslaught of new gripes, old grudges and juicy gossip, but it never came. Jane was strangely subdued. Her husband Anthony, or as Ronnie called him, 'Safe Bet', had put a halt to her spending.

"It's a disaster," she said.

Of course, the two weeks in the Algarve was still on and there was a hefty balance remaining on the fuel card, but he told her that he could no longer pull Fabergé rabbits out of his magic hat.

He had these little knee jerk reactions every few years, usually after her spending had broken new records. Jane had always managed to reinstate the status quo, but sometimes it took a little time. It was a while before he noticed that some of his comforts had been withdrawn, but once he started to feel the pinch, he normally reneged, and the austerity measures were washed away with some love, attention and his favourite bottle of claret.

Hazel and Jane spent the evening not watching a film Hazel had downloaded. They chatted and swapped stories, the only time they paid any notice to the film was when the volume of the music, that accompanied the end credits, started competing with their conversation.

When Hazel disappeared upstairs to the bathroom, Jane spotted Ronnie's photo albums and started eagerly flicking through. On returning, Hazel pretended she wasn't bothered, but inside she was a little peeved at the uninvited nature of the intrusion from one of life's biggest gossips. There was nothing shameful in the photos, but Hazel didn't want to think about those days in the context of her life in Arksdean. The Hazel then and the Hazel now were two very different creatures.

Hazel reminded herself that she shouldn't have expected any less from the village prier. Added to the ample glasses of vino they'd downed, it was foregone conclusion.

Hazel felt obliged to talk her through some of the stories behind the photos, and the faces that made them.

"I was warned off him by everyone. My family, my friends, even some of his friends, although they may have had ulterior motives, if you know what I mean?" said Hazel.

Jane was all ears, totally enthralled.

"He was a bit crazy and I was well aware that he'd been around the block. They used to say, 'You'll never change that one,' and all I could think was 'Why would I want to?' I liked him how he was. The more I saw of him the more I liked. Then one day he said he had finished with his girlfriend, because he said he wanted to do things properly, and would I go out with him?" She paused, as if to breathe in the aroma of that precious memory.

"That night, I was so happy, I did cartwheels in the street, all the way home. My best mate, Mandy, thought I'd gone bonkers."

Hazel was grinning, almost oblivious to Jane's presence in the room. She found herself becoming unexpectedly uplifted by the anecdotes of her early life with Ronnie. Suddenly, she was back in his corner singing his praises.

"You looked amazing, Haze. You definitely loved your mini-skirts," said Jane.

"To be honest with you, I only really had about three outfits back then."

They carried on flicking through the pages, giggling at the clothes and old-style haircuts until she stumbled upon the photo that had upset Hazel earlier on. She wished she'd ripped it up when she saw it.

Jane recognised Roxy in the photo.

"Is that the woman who -"

"- The bitch. Yeah. I told you about Ronnie's excuse," said Hazel.

"Yeah," said Jane, in a manner that suggested she felt the onus of truth was leaning away from Ronnie.

"I don't even know where this picture came from."

"Bulldog?" Jane was fishing but Hazel had already lost herself in a train of thought that was heading for the buffers. Jane motioned to the laptop on the coffee table. "Have you checked your Facebook for any updates?"
"I'm not sure I want to look," said Hazel, in an irked tone.
"Sorry Haze…"
Jane left the question mark hanging in the air and it was growing by the second.
"No. You are right. I should check. Got every right to know what he's up to."
Hazel pulled the laptop over and opened the lid. Jane was virtually licking her lips with anticipation. She didn't wish her friend any harm, but she was drawn to life's dramas like a rubbernecker to an eight-car pile-up.
Sure enough, there in Bulldog's social media feed, was a photo of Roxy, smiling gushingly at Ronnie while gently caressing his forearm. The other guilty party, in sickness and in health, was reciprocating with a flirty grin. Ronnie was in a Night Club with 'Poxy' Roxy Nostos. There was no way he'd bumped into her by chance, she thought to herself.
Slightly blurred, in the background of the picture was a couple, arms and legs entwined, exchanging tongues. It was seeing this that tipped Hazel over the edge.
"The bastard," she said.
"Oh, Haze," said Jane, sympathetically.
Hazel was generating a resentment like a house-fire generates heat.
"The treacherous, bullshitting, slimy worm."
"Haze, I feel so bad. I wish I hadn't said anything," said Jane, who was thinking the exact opposite.

CHAPTER 26. Disco Nightmare

At Paparazzi's night club, the music was in full swing. Outside the male washrooms, Brett and Harvey, two men in their early thirties, were partaking in a guarded conversation with Bulldog. They parted company with him and made a beeline for Penny, who was standing by the dance floor on her own. Brett tentatively approached from behind and shoved his hand up her skirt and she spun around to face him.
"What the fuck?" spat Penny.
Some revellers nearby moved away while others just assumed, although clearly in bad taste, it was just a joke between friends, particularly as she obviously knew him. Penny's head dropped when she recognised who it was that had accosted her. She tried to escape but found her way blocked by Harvey.
"Allow me to introduce you to the fourth emergency service," said a drunken Brett to his equally out-of-it friend. They both sniggered, like idiots tormenting a cat they'd cornered.
"Just let me go, will you?" said Penny, struggling to free herself.
"Lively, isn't she?" said Harvey.
Brett reached out and attempted to jokingly weigh her breasts in his hands.

"Do anything for a little white powder, wouldn't you, you little slut?" said Brett.
She shirked him off again and lashed out at his smug face, but he easily caught her flailing hand.
"Get off me," said Penny.
"You didn't say that last time we met," sneered Brett.
This was Brett's favourite drug. Bullying gave him such a kick, particularly when he could show off to someone as half-witted as Harvey, who was impressed by the smallest of things. Mick arrived, quickly dispensed with the drinks he'd been carrying and reared up.
"These arseholes bothering you?" he said.
"You didn't say you brought your fuckin' Dad with ya?" said Harvey to Penny.
Her anguished face hadn't yet decided whether it was going to explode in fury or deflate into a sobbing mess. She positioned herself closely behind Mick and felt how tensed his body was.
Clearly fancying his chances against the older man, Brett fronted Mick. Brett was a fan of hooligan lit and had watched too many Guy Richie movies.
"Want some, do you?" said Brett.
Mick had no time for chit chat and reacted instinctively, with a stinging right jab that caught Brett clean on the nose, leaving him stunned. As he followed that up with a raging left hook, Harvey launched a heavy blow on the side of Mick's head, forcing him to stumble over.
"Please don't. He's not worth it. Just leave it, Micky," pleaded Penny.
Mick gathered himself up.
"It's alright, Penny," said Mick.
He held out his right hand, his thumb and forefinger, an inch apart, in a pinch position.

"I've got the measure of these wankers."

Brett wiped some blood off his face, readying himself to take on Mick again.

"You chose the wrong..." Smack! Brett was interrupted by Ronnie, who had arrived and tore into Brett with a barrage of fists. Brett, who only usually ventured into conflicts he could dominate with his mouth, collapsed under the weight of the blows. Mick and Harvey were still eye to eye. A circle in the crowd had formed, frightened punters made way for rubberneckers who rushed to catch a piece of the action. Guzzler was by Mick's side now. The spectacle had become too much for Penny, a flood of tears propelling her towards the exit.

Harvey pulled out a blade and there was a communal intake of breath as everyone took a step backwards, much to Harvey's delight. Everyone that is, except Guzzler. He was there for his friends, for Mick and by default for Penny, but he was also there for himself. When he was younger, he'd often battled a reputation for a less than enthusiastic approach to gang fights. There'd been times, even at school, where he'd walked away, not stood up for himself or generally swallowed down vile tasting portions of stark humiliation. After each incident, he had taken flak and the whole thing had quickly become yesterday's news, for everyone except Guzzler. He carried those hurts around like a nail in his boot.

"Leave it, mate," said Ronnie.

Like a ferocious Bear, Guzzler charged forward, throwing out a balled fist that connected sweetly with Harvey's chin. It was enough to lift Harvey off his feet and crumple him to the floor. As he did, the bouncers were waiting for him, like game keepers. The crowd watched as they pounced on him, nullifying the knife threat and manhandling him towards the exit.

"Get off me, you mugs," he was shouting at them.

The Bouncer sporting a goatee beard, head set and arms the size of legs, butted his head into Harvey's face. It was like a boulder meeting a cabbage. The bubbles instantly evaporated from Harvey's fizz.

Mick hurriedly made his way through the maze of revellers, searching for clues to the path Penny had taken. On exiting the club, Mick frantically scanned the area, before he spotted Penny, head down, careering along the seafront. He gave chase, calling out her name, but she ignored him and continued on without breaking her stride. In her mind she was wishing for a giant wave to come and wash everything away. A Tsunami of recompense that could sweep in and drag all the shit from her life back into the darkest recesses of the sea. She wondered how much of herself would still be standing at the end of it, such was her current opinion of herself.

Mick caught up with her, the alcohol and physical exertion playing havoc with his composure.

"Hang on, will ya?"

Penny slowed her pace but kept her eyes glued to the floor, as if searching for a trap door that would release her from the aftermath of another 'shame grenade' that had desecrated her social life once more. Mick persuaded her to take a seat on a bench, in one of the many old Victorian shelters that were deposited along Brighton's seafront. Penny was hiding her face in her hands, scared to look at Mick for fear of recognising the cracks of her own ugly reputation registering on his face. She could see the remnants of her mascara on her hands and knew the mess on her face would be a realistic reflection of her private life right now.

"Why d'you run off like that?" asked Mick.

"I'm sorry, Mickey."

"Sorry? What are you sorry for?"

Her shoulders sagged, and she refused to lift her head.

"You heard what he said."

Penny was drowning in the humiliation.

"Do you think I care what some pissed-up idiot has got to say?"

"I'm bad news, Micky. You're a decent guy. You could do a lot better than me," she mumbled.

Penny was preparing herself for the end of their short but sweet rendezvous. In her mind there was no point in waiting for the inevitable order of the boot. Abandonment was so ingrained that anything else felt alien to her.

"You're a good person," he said.

Penny slowly raised her head and withdrew her hands to reveal her tormented face.

"I'm no good for you. I'm no good for anyone," she said.

"Well, that makes two of us then, eh?" he said. "Look at me. What you see is what I own. When I was younger, I worked my arse off as a decorator, I had big dreams, I was gonna to be the first of us to own a Roller. Now I'm just a painter without a brush... ain't worked in weeks. Even the Jehovah's sidestep me.... but honestly, today has been the most fun I've had in years. That's because of you."

"You're really sweet, and I appreciate it, but if you stay with me, I'll only bring you down," said Penny.

"You can't walk away from me now, we're on a roll...You're my lucky Penny."

Penny perked up a bit and found the courage to seek eye contact with him.

"It's good of you to try and cheer me up," she said.

"I've never been more serious," he said. "Come on, budge up."

She shuffled along to make room for Mick on the bench. Like a curtain of comfort, he put his arm around her and drew her in. She was content to hide her face in his neck. He felt her give a relaxing sigh.

"Can I tell you something?" said Mick.

"It's a free country," she said, trying to regain a little of her charming pluckiness from earlier in the day.

"To be honest with you, I'm only down here to escape the Repo Men. London holds nothing for me now. I like Brighton... and I really like you."

Penny hugged him tighter, his words were an unexpected and very welcome solace, after her humiliation at the disco.

"I like you too," she said softly.

"I'd like to get to know you more. I think Brighton could be good for me," he said.

"Stay with me for a bit if you like?" she said.

Mick pulled her chin up to meet his. Their eyes locked and there was a moment of mutual understanding, that seemed like so much more than desire. They kissed passionately.

CHAPTER 27. Addiction bites

Ronnie, Roxy and Guzzler were sitting at a table in the night club trying to make themselves heard above the music. Ronnie was stroking his right hand and wrist that was still stinging from the fracas. Guzzler refrained from wiping his bloodied hand, deciding to leave it on view like a trophy to his courage.
"Mick seems pretty smitten with your mate," said Guzzler to Roxy.
"She's too good for the likes of him," said Roxy.
"I didn't think there was a surgeon alive that could put a smile back on his face," said Guzzler, ignoring her jibe.
"He always was a miserable bastard," said Ronnie, exhibiting a flash of bitterness brought on by the close proximity of Roxy. He might have decided not to confront him, but Ronnie wasn't going to sit around complimenting him, especially in front of her. There was a brief silence as Guzzler recognised the change in Ronnie's tone. Roxy steered the conversation away from Mick.
"I didn't see Bulldog. Did he get thrown out too?"
"I don't think so," said Ronnie.
Guzzler shrugged his shoulders.
"He was probably waiting for the coast to be clear."
"He always did have a habit of keeping his hands in his pockets when it came to fisticuffs," said Ronnie.

Guzzler downed the remaining gulps of his beer. He placed the empty glass on the table and stood up.

"I better go and look for him," he said.

Guzzler wandered off towards the washrooms.

"Do you remember that fight in here with all them Skinheads. Chairs were flying, all the mirrors got smashed. It was mental, the whole place got trashed. We ended up barricading ourselves in the DJ's booth. All his records got broken and everything," said Ronnie.

"No." said Roxy, abruptly.

Ronnie was puzzled by her answer. "Course you do. The old Bill were gonna arrest Mick, 'cos his hair was really short, and they thought he was one of the Skinheads."

"I think that must have been after my time," said Roxy, her words shooting a bolt of unease across his face, as it dawned on him that it hadn't been Roxy that night, it was Hazel.

"Oh well, it was a mad night anyway," said Ronnie, trying to think of something more appropriate to say.

Guzzler entered the toilets. There were two rows of cubicles and one area with urinals all the way along the wall. They had improved no end since the old days. Back then, there'd been more water on the floor than at the nearby paddling pool. He remembered teenagers smoking and throwing up and one time he smuggled a Mod girl in there and got busy with her in one of the cubicles. It was wild.

All but a handful of the compartments were open. Guzzler listened out for the more unpalatable sounds of life as he walked along. He instinctively stopped at a locked door near the end of the row.

"You in there, Bulldog?" he said.

He was sure that one of these compartments was concealing the booby prize. Guzzler stood on tiptoes to peer over the cubicle door, only to find a teenager, with a straining red face, sitting on the loo, clearly unappreciative of the intrusion.

"What's your game. You fuckin' weirdo," said the teenager, as he tried to throw a toilet roll at Guzzler. Guzzler apologised before trying the doors of the remaining cubicles. On the very last compartment, the door bounced off something and rebound in Guzzler's face. He forced it open. There was Bulldog out cold on the floor, slumped against the toilet bowl, lying in pools of piss, with sick over his face and shirt.

Guzzler hoisted his friend up and dragged him from the cubicle, as the muffled sound of Relax by Frankie goes to Hollywood was pulsating through the walls.

Bulldog was being loaded onto an ambulance outside the night club. Ronnie and Roxy looked on as Guzzler clambered in to join his pal in the back.

"Any news, you call me right away, okay?" said Ronnie. Guzzler tried to force a crestfallen nod but couldn't find any source of positivity in his body. The doors closed, and the vehicle took off at speed, lights and sirens blazing into the night. Ronnie and Roxy walked slowly in the direction of his hotel.

"I feel like the man who poked someone else's stick into a hornet's nest."

"You never put that shit in his veins," said Roxy, in a slightly dismissive tone.

"No, but my money might have paid for it," said Ronnie.

"Once a Junkie always a Junkie," she replied.

Ronnie gave her a look of displeasure.

"Sentiment is no defence against addiction," said Roxy.
"I just want him to be all right," said Ronnie.
"He's in the best place," she replied.
What she meant was he was someone else's responsibility now.
"What a fuckin' nightmare," said Ronnie, shaking his head.
They continued in silence along the road while Roxy searched for a way to salvage the night. Hanging out with Ronnie was like competing in some kind of bizarre game of chess. Her first task was to move the conversation onto happier ground.
"I hope *everything* hasn't disappointed you about Brighton," she said.
She hugged him and, although he reciprocated, there was a hesitancy about his body language. It was an unusual feeling for Roxy, she'd never had to work hard for a man, except at getting rid of the ones who didn't make the grade. Here she was with the only man who had ever rejected her, and once more she felt like she was the one doing the running.

At the hotel, the night duty manager, a young Eastern European woman, was watching a foreign language film on a laptop, she raised her head briefly at the sight of their arrival but swiftly returned to her movie. Ronnie and Roxy headed for the elevator. Roxy released herself from his arm.
"Hold the lift," she said.
Roxy headed for the concierge desk, where she had a brief chat with the night duty manager. She joined Ronnie in the lift, and they headed for his room.
On entering his room, Ronnie vacated to the bathroom. He caught a glimpse of himself in the large wall mounted

mirror as he stood pissing into the toilet bowl. It was far from an admiring glance that came back at him. There was a knock at the bedroom door. Roxy called through to say she'd get it.

He washed his hands and splashed water on his face. Droplets formed and then dribbled down his chin and into the sink. Even though he was still quite drunk, he could see more than the surface representation of himself. Ronnie didn't like what he saw. In his head he could hear his own voice tearing into him. 'What the hell do you think you're doing?' He looked away, took a deep breath, exhaled slowly, then exited the bathroom, his mind in a state of flux.

Roxy ruffled her blonde hair and carefully undid a couple of buttons on her dress. Ronnie stared at her laying on the bed, leaning against the headboard. She looked every bit the goddess of his youthful dreams, yet he couldn't help sensing that there was something vulgar about the whole scene. It was a vulgarity that was emanating from him, not her.

He spotted the Champagne bottle sticking out of an ice bucket. She patted the bed, beckoning him over.

"Come here, you," she said with a smile.

Her beautiful big blue eyes were as inviting as a dip in a swimming pool on a swelteringly hot day. Ronnie moved somewhat mechanically, positioning himself next to her on the bed.

Roxy held up her glass.

"To good times...old and new."

She clinked her glass against Ronnie's bottle then downed the entire contents in one go.

"Whoo," she said, in celebration of her new giddiness.

She was getting in the mood.

She leaned in close and kissed him gently on the lips and they were held in an embrace. Roxy tried not to look disappointed as he hesitated to take proceedings any further. He sat up on the edge of the bed. Again, he gulped a large mouthful of Champagne before she pulled away the bottle and placed it on the floor. She straddled him, kissing him more vigorously on the lips, then she made her way down his neck while unfastening his trousers. She had him where she wanted. She was back in control.

"I got you," she said.

Roxy started slowly gyrating on top of him, but Ronnie flipped her over and buried his face in the pillow next to her on the bed, squeezing his eyes tightly closed.

"I can't do this," he said.

He sat on the edge of the bed with his back to her. He took a big deep breath.

"I'm sorry, I can't do this."

Roxy put a hand on his shoulder, trying to console him. She could see she was at risk of losing him.

"Hey, don't worry, just relax, it's no big deal," she said.

She was offering him a lifeline and the excuse of too much drink, or *Brewers Droop*, to hide his real anguish and allow proceedings to continue in the way she hoped they would.

"You don't understand," he said.

In amongst the haze of booze, melancholy and guilt, he was snatching a fleeting glance at something of great clarity, finding detail in a puzzle that had previously alluded him.

"But why would you?" He murmured mostly to himself.

Ronnie stood up, fastened his trousers and grabbed his jacket and his crash helmet.

Roxy was dumbfounded.

"What? Where are you going?"

This was not part of any plan she'd envisaged.

"Have I done something wrong?" she said.

He reached the door and stopped and calmly turned to her and gave her a warm-hearted smile. Ronnie's eyes betrayed a genuine fondness for her.

"You've got no idea how good you've been for me," he said.

He left nothing of himself in the room and headed out into the corridor. Roxy felt the starkness of the void between them and called out after him.

"But I haven't done anything," she said.

The door clunked shut.

"Don't go, Ronnie," she pleaded. "Please don't go."

Her voice was fading away, as he padded along the corridor.

Roxy had resigned herself to defeat. Sitting on the bed solemnly, she gulped down the rest of her glass of Champagne, before pausing motionlessly as a single tear escaped her right eye and slowly made its way down her cheek. It stung her senses like lemon juice on an open wound. She would never be Ronnie's love, not for one night, not ever.

CHAPTER 28.   Hold on, Farewell.

It was nearing four in the morning and the waste disposal lorries were out, clearing up after another Brighton bacchanal. Broken glass, burger wrappings and sporadic splurges of vomit would be hoovered up and the place would have a fresh round of make up for the avalanche of tourists that would claim the promenade in only a few hours' time. Day and night in the seaside resort were like parallel worlds. Ice creams and deckchairs in the day giving way for drunkenness and debauchery at night.
Ronnie rode his scooter through the empty dark streets of Brighton. He pulled up at some traffic lights that had just changed to red. A sign indicated a left turn for the hospital or ahead for the coastal route out of the city. The lights turned green, but Ronnie hesitated a moment, indecision raking his thoughts. Fragments of his dreams and nightmares were playing havoc with his cognition. Just as the lights turned orange, he revved-up the Vespa, slipped it in gear and took the road to the hospital.
"Hang on in there, mate. Hang on in there," Ronnie said to himself.
Outside the main entrance of the Hospital, Ronnie found a space next to a bright red powerful looking Kawasaki motorbike. It was like a milk float sidling up to a Ferrari.

At the entrance, anxious looking people were pacing and smoking with equal vigour, blatantly contravening a nearby 'no smoking' sign.

Ronnie went searching for Guzzler. He found him munching a family-sized bag of crisps, next to a vending machine in the food court area.

"He might have brain damage," said Guzzler.

Ronnie grimaced and squeezed his eyes shut like he needed to close the information out of his mind. It was too late. The news was an unwelcome addition to the accumulation of disasters he had collected over the last week.

"This is all my fault," said Ronnie.

"This ain't about you," said Guzzler.

Ronnie wondered whether that was meant as a dig or a reprieve. Either way, their mate was in hospital fighting for his life.

"I brought us to Brighton. I really fucked things up for everyone."

"No, mate. This would have happened whether we were in Brighton, Battersham or Bangladesh. It was only a matter of time."

"So, what did they say?" asked Ronnie.

"They ain't saying much. He's in intensive care. Gotta wait until the morning before we find out how he is," said Guzzler.

Ronnie turned to leave.

"Where you goin'?" asked Guzzler.

"Going to do something I should have done ages ago," said Ronnie, as he left at pace.

Ronnie fired-up the Scooter and took off up the road. Out on the main drag he turned away from the city and headed out along the old coastal route. He was thrashing it, the engine was crying out in pain, but Ronnie was in a reckless mood, daring fate to take him out, there and then, and release him from the chaos of his mind.

Ronnie rode along the grassy cliff top at Beachy head. A faint slither of sunshine on the horizon broke the darkness. He headed towards the edge of the cliff and his back wheel spun as he stopped the scooter abruptly. He pondered a while.

He wasn't thinking of any cinematic inspiration from Quadrophenia, or of its lead character, Jimmy. He wasn't thinking of Mods at all. His mind was awash with thoughts of Arnie, Bulldog, Mick and Guzzler, but mostly Hazel. He was thinking of Battersham and Arksdean. He looked out at the uncompromising dark sea and made the engine growl, tears streamed down his face. He switched it off and the engine juddered to a halt. He took the key out of the ignition and pushed himself off the scooter. He let it fall over on to a grassy mound where, its front wheel still spinning, it lay like a helpless tortoise on its back.

Ronnie leaned down and forcefully yanked out the bag containing Arnie's ashes. He stood just staring at the box, his big green parka flapping in the wind. This was all that was left of his dear friend. A life prematurely ended.

"Forgive me, Arnie," muttered Ronnie.

He opened the Tupperware box and, with one meaningful thrust, hoisted its contents towards the edge of the cliff. A swirl of the wind brought most of it right back in the direction of his face. He spat out the bits that had blown into his mouth.

Ronnie made his way to the very brink of the cliff face. Under his feet little chunks of chalk were protruding through the grass. Ahead of him the lighthouse flashed its warning light to alert any wayward vessels of imminent danger.

Ronnie fell to his knees in anguish. His weight forced a little flurry of chalk debris to fall from the precipice. He felt trapped, like the needle of an old record player, having played the song out, jarring endlessly up against the label. He pulled himself back, fists raised to the sky and screamed, "Aaaarrrgggghhhh."

The sound was instantly lost in the blustering wind, as it echoed in his head like the roar of a crowd in a large tunnel.

He hauled himself up from the ground and turned back to the scooter and pulled it upright. Before mounting it, he circled it, eyeing it ferociously, like it was a tribal ritual. Ronnie kick-started it, pulled back the throttle and revved it up. He drove away from the brink of the cliff, the sea to his back.

Suddenly he swung the scooter around, and the machine gave him everything it had as it careered over the lumpy terrain back towards the cliff's edge as fast as it could go. The next few moments seemed to compute to him in slow motion as Ronnie threw open his mouth and roared with the machine on its final voyage.

CHAPTER 29. Pebbles on a beach.

It felt like the Great Britain Olympic team were performing summersaults in her stomach, as Hazel stared out of the car window on her impromptu emergency dash to Brighton. Hazel and Jane set off early and would be on the south coast for breakfast, fried Roxy on toast, the order of the day.

Hazel and Roxy had history. They'd had a mighty row outside a pub in Battersham and, after a feisty encounter, they'd been pulled apart, but not before Hazel had got the better of her. She had no intentions of stooping to those levels now, but she was in no mood to have sand kicked in her face.

Hazel's anger had mostly fizzed into anxiety. She knew whatever she found at the end of this motorway could change her life forever.

"Call it a woman's intuition, but I know he's got an itch that I just can't scratch and I'm sure as hell not going to sit back and let anyone else take their claws to him."

"We'll find him," said Jane.

"I just hope we're not too late," said Hazel.

"He won't be expecting us," said Jane.

"Of that you can be sure," said Hazel.

"Kind of handy that Bulldog guy friended you on Facebook. I mean, we know what hotel he's staying at, which places he's been to and what they ate for their tea," said Jane.

"Yeah, thanks Bulldog," said Hazel.

"What do you think Ronnie will say when he sees you?"

"Sorry, hopefully. He owes me that much. He won't like being henpecked in front of his... *gang*. But I'm not throwing away a good marriage because he can't handle some stupid mid-life wobble," said Hazel.

They passed a sign that said Brighton eighteen miles.

"I can't imagine you in a gang," said Jane.

"What is a gang? It's just a bunch of friends into the same thing," said Hazel.

"What did your dad think?" Asked Jane.

"He liked Ronnie. He used to tease him about how inferior scooters were, compared with his beloved Motorbikes. Ronnie used to drive along my street and as he pulled up my dad would lean out of the window and shout 'Here comes the Moped lad, the Rebel with a flat tyre...'"

Hazel caught a gentle smile on her lips and swiftly reminded herself how upset she was with him. Jane was enthralled to hear about tales from a life so far removed from her own.

"What about all the... you know, aggro?" she said, in a fake Cockney accent.

"My dad? The biggest fights he had were with the Brylcreem bottle."

Jane smiled. "You know what I mean."

"Being a Mod was more about posturing than punch ups. Ronnie knew how to look after himself, but he wasn't a thug. Bank holidays were always kind of wild though," said Hazel.

Looking out the window, Hazel's eyes were fixed on something way off in the distance, as if her thoughts were being projected on the horizon.

"In the midst of all that chaos we would slip away from the others and shelter under the old pier. Sitting there just listening to all his crazy plans and schemes... That's where I really fell in love with him."

Mick and Penny were walking hand in hand along the promenade. They stopped so Mick could kneel down and pet a dog that came running towards them.

"She's beautiful. Aren't you girl," he said.

The golden retriever, with a bright red collar, was enjoying the fuss being made of her. Mick was revelling in the sheer softness of her thick fur.

"You a dog person then?" asked Penny.

"I was. I had a blonde Lab. The best companion you could ever wish for," he said.

He took a deep breath to avoid choking on his words.

"Then she went and..... She broke me heart," he said.

Mick stood up, emotionally dusting himself down.

"That's the price of love," said Penny.

"I guess it is," said Mick.

The owner of the dog, an old woman in her seventies, caught up with them put and the mutt back on its lead.

"Hope she's not bothered you?"

"Are you kidding? She's brightened our day," said Mick.

The dog was getting a dressing down by its owner, as they crossed the road and disappeared into the shadows of a stairwell under one of the large arches.

Mick and Penny continued to saunter along the sea front.

"I think I know what I'll do with my life," said Mick.

"What's that then?" said Penny.

"Something me old schoolteachers used to say to me."
She looked at him keenly awaiting the punchline.
"Rip it up and start again," said Mick.
She smiled at him and, as they walked arm in arm, the gulls whooping and screeching around them, Penny had an overwhelmingly strange feeling that she'd known him for many years and not just a matter of days. She wondered if he really would be the one to unlock the woman she had always dreamed of being.

Hazel walked out of the Ocean hotel, past Arnie's old scooter, and returned to Jane who was leaning against her Mercedes car.
"He's not there," said Hazel.
"Where could he be?" said Jane.
"Apparently, he took off in the middle of the night on his scooter. Guzzler thinks he may have headed out towards Beachy head."
"Beachy head it is then," said Jane.
Jane opened the car door, but Hazel made no attempt to join her.
"Can't walk to Beachy head it's about ten miles away," said Jane.
"We're not going to Beachy Head," said Hazel.
"You don't think you'll find him there?"
"If I truly know Ronnie Diamond, there's only one place he'll be," said Hazel.

Hazel and Jane stalked the seafront, eyes scouting the area for Ronnie. At this point, Jane wasn't sure whether this was a hunting party or a rescue mission.
Hazel stopped dead in her tracks.
"Oh, no," she said.

Jane panicked, looking around for the source of Hazel's distress.

"What? What's up?"

Hazel was looking out with saddened eyes at the dilapidated old pier. Ravaged by time and now just an eroding framework, completely cut off from Brighton by the sea.

"What have they done to our pier?" cried Hazel.

The pier stood there, like a giant piece of conceptual art. For Hazel, it was akin to visiting the house of your birth and finding a supermarket car park had replaced it. 'If I hadn't come down here it would have still existed in my mind,' she thought to herself. When the physical disappears, all you're left with are the shards of time that make up your memories, and they are often no more substantial than a jigsaw made of sand.

Hazel's eyes were drawn to a khaki-green bundle on the beach. She nudged Jane.

Hazel tread purposefully, across the uneven pebbled beach, towards the bundle, calling out Ronnie's name.

"It's Ronnie's parka," she shouted back to Jane, who was holding her position.

Obscured by some old wooden stakes jutting out of the beach. Ronnie was hurling pebbles into the sea.

"Ronnie," called Hazel.

Ronnie turned abruptly and faced her. He shaded his eyes and squinted to get a better focus. He was shocked to see the figure of his wife heading his way.

"Hazel?" he said.

He let the pebble he was holding slip from his hand and crash on to the beach.

Hazel rushed to Ronnie. All the chaos of the last week was stripped away and Hazel found her antagonism strangely calmed by his vulnerability. As she made her way towards him, images of their time here in Brighton flooded her mind. In many ways, the legend had been bigger than its assembled parts, but underneath it all, there was the spark that ignited their passion. It was the place he really chose to show his hand, where the bravado was cast aside, and the earnest man first showed himself.

As Hazel got closer, she found the dark clouds had moved in and visions of Bulldog's Facebook page suddenly flashed before her eyes. When she reached Ronnie, she slapped him across the face. As her warm hand crashed into his cold flesh, she felt the shock of it almost as much as he did. The velocity of the impact was far heavier than she'd intended. Hazel drew her hand up to cover her mouth, wondering how he would respond.

"I'm sorry," said Hazel.

Ronnie waived her apology away.

"I deserved it," he said.

There was a brief moment of hesitancy but as their eyes locked, the ice melted and, almost simultaneously, they flung their arms around each other in a homecoming embrace.

"You scared me, you stupid bastard," said Hazel.

"I love you Hazey."

"I love you too."

They stood there embracing each other for what seemed like an age. To pull away was too daunting for each of them. Eventually Ronnie tried to articulate his swirling thoughts.

"When I was a kid, I just wanted to be a somebody, one of the top boys, a face on the scene," he said.

"Oh, Ronnie, don't," said Hazel.

Hazel feared he was going to give her another life-lesson about the glories of yesteryear.

"Hear me out, please... I always wanted to be a face.... now I realise that the last few months I've been a total arse. So, I just want to say I'm sorry."

"I've been worried about you," said Hazel. "I didn't understand. What were you doing down here?"

"I just needed to scatter the ashes of my past," said Ronnie.

Ronnie didn't need to forget who he once was, but he knew he could never be that man again. Some people only live a half-baked existence but not Ronnie Diamond. He'd been to the top of the mountain and now he had made his descent he realised there were new peaks to scale.

As they slowly made their way from the beach, they held hands with the same self-conscious awkwardness of young lovers. The feeling reminded them both why they'd managed, what seemed like an impossible feat these days, to stay together for so long.

"I saw the pictures on Facebook and there was Roxy," said Hazel, her own sense of worth not permitting it to be swept under the carpet.

"Roxy. Oh, you don't have to worry about her, she's just someone I used to know," he said.

His words hung in the air for a moment or two.

"Where's your scooter?" asked Hazel.

He stopped walking and turned to face her.

"I did what every self-respecting Mod ever dreamed of doing. I drove it over the hallowed cliffs of Beachy head," he said.

"You nutter," she said.

He squeezed her hand tight as they exchanged smiles.

"There's no going back. It's made its final journey," said Ronnie.

"Some people flick through their photo albums and just crack open a bottle of wine and toast to yesterday, not Ronnie Diamond, he has to drive his bloody scooter off a cliff," said Hazel, shaking her head and smiling.
"It's why you married me, isn't it?" said Ronnie.
"Sometimes, I do wonder," said Hazel.
Behind them, Ronnie's beloved Parka lay discarded on the pebbled beach. He'd thrown off the trappings of his youthful identity, but he would always be a Mod at heart. No-one could ever take that away from him, not even old father time.

CHAPTER 30.   The long goodbye.

A beaming couple emerged, through the sliding doors of the hospital entrance, into the bright morning sunshine. They were tenderly carrying their new-born baby. In the other direction a sickly old man coughed and spluttered as he caught the last glimpse of natural daylight that he might ever see as he was wheeled into the artificial luminance of the reception area.

In an isolation room, on the sixth-floor, Bulldog was hooked up to bleeping machines, only the feint signs of a shallow breath alluding to any sign of life. His head resembled a skull doused in porridge, his eyes like two chasms of darkness.

An early death was something he'd been putting off for some time now, and last night he'd bought a ticket to the outer beyond on the expunction express, but for some reason the ambulance had delivered him here, to the Brighton Infirmary, instead.

Ronnie and Mick walked out of Bulldog's room, heads hung low, both choked for words as they re-joined Hazel and Guzzler, who were waiting solemnly in the corridor.

"It's just so heart breaking, he wasn't trying to get high. That was a death wish," said Ronnie.

"I know," said Guzzler.

Hazel collapsed her fingers around his hand, in an attempt to comfort him.

"What did they say?" asked Hazel.

"He's out of immediate danger but it'll be a slow process to get him back on his feet," said Mick.

Ronnie spotted a large see-through bag that Guzzler was holding. It contained some clothes.

"That his stuff?" he asked.

"I said I'd get his clothes cleaned up," said Guzzler.

Guzzler opened the bag up and instantly grimaced at the smell. He had a quick trawl through, pulling out an old appointment card for his addiction counsellor, some chewing gum and a picture of the Aces from 1983.

Guzzler handed Ronnie the crumpled photo. Ronnie felt a twinge of deep understanding and comradery. He realised that Bulldog, Guzzler and even Mick had all felt the same pull to the days of yore. In some ways they were ahead of the game. It was only Ronnie who had donned the Parka, but each one of them had remained Mod in their own way. Those formative years made them who they were. It was more than a drinking club. They were a small gang of mates, but also part of a greater tribe. The life they shared back then couldn't be replicated or easily forgotten and never erased. It was part of them. They still had the resonance of that ideal, but it showed itself in a more individualistic way. The music and the clothes, that was only a small part of it. The Battersham Aces was for life, Ronnie just hoped Bulldog hadn't seen the last of his.

"There's also a letter to his mum," said Guzzler.

"A letter?" said Mick, in a surprised tone.

Guzzler wasn't surprised. He knew Bulldog had been looking for the exit door from the moment they arrived in Brighton.

"What's it say?" asked Mick.

"I don't know, it ain't addressed to me," said Guzzler. "He loves his mum. She has cared for him for years like he was

a bird with a perennial broken wing. She fed and clothed him then became his life support machine. I think he wanted to pull the plug, give her some respite."
The fact that someone they loved wanted away, showed on their faces. It was one of the most crushing aspects of drug addiction, the sheer helplessness and frustration of those who have to stand and watch as they try to hold on to a person they can no longer reach, as he or she disintegrates before their eyes.
"Does his mum know he's here?" asked Hazel.
"Mick called her. She's on her way," said Guzzler.
"I had the feeling she was half expecting it," said Mick. "She's probably rehearsed this moment a thousand times in her head."
"Mick paid for her taxi," said Guzzler.
"From Battersham?" said Ronnie.
"Least I could do," said Mick.
"I can put her up for a couple of days if she somewhere to stay," said Penny, who felt a little awkward being the stranger at such an intimate gathering.
"That's very kind," said Hazel.

Bulldog's mum arrived, looking like the weight of worry was going to topple her. Guzzler spoke to her for some time before handing over the reins.
Outside the Hospital they said their goodbyes. Ronnie gave Guzzler a big hug, he held on to him as much out of affection as to try and compose himself from the raw emotions of Bulldog's situation.
"Keep me posted," said Ronnie.
"Will do," said Guzzler.
"He'll be in our thoughts," said Hazel

"Come 'round anytime? And you Hazel, you're always welcome," said Guzzler.

"I'll call you," said Ronnie.

Mick looked like he sensed that this was more of a farewell than a 'see you later.' Ronnie and Mick gripped each other's hands and pulled in close, in a wrestler-style embrace.

"Think I might stick around here for a while, you know," said Mick.

Ronnie nodded.

"I think the sea air agrees with me," said Mick.

"Everyone deserves a break," said Ronnie.

"Take care of yourself, brother," said Mick.

"Good luck, aye?" said Ronnie.

Ronnie took Hazel's hand and they walked towards the exit.

Guzzler called after them. Ronnie and Hazel turned around.

"Once a Mod always a Mod, eh?" shouted Guzzler.

Ronnie smiled and set off on his way.

"See you Ronnie, have a good life," said Mick under his breath.

Guzzler looked at Mick as it slowly dawned on him that this might just be the final reunion of the Aces.

CHAPTER 31. No place like Home.

For Ronnie and Hazel's love affair, the recent debacle in Brighton had become just another blip on the ever-shifting trajectory of their married life. Ronnie would exchange the odd text message with Guzzler, particularly with concern for Bulldog's wellbeing, but it was most likely to be the unwelcome invitation to another funeral before Ronnie would ever head south to his old stomping ground of Battersham.

In their plush living room, Hazel rested her head against Ronnie's chest, her legs stretched out along the sofa. Outside their window the sky was a fusion of deep orange and purple, delivering a strange twilight glow to their beautiful garden. The TV was on, and David Attenborough was on another worthy venture overseas. He could make the digestive system of a Camel something you felt you really needed to know. If only Attenborough had written the school curriculum, Ronnie thought, perhaps he would have paid a bit more attention in class. The credits rolled and Hazel reached out to grab the remote and switch the television off. They sat in silence for a minute or two.

"It's weird, about Brighton," said Ronnie.

"What is?" said Hazel.

"Some people go to confessional…"

She interrupted him. They still retained that uncanny knack of knowing each other's minds.

"You're going to tell me it was all some kind of religious pilgrimage?" said Hazel.
"Exactly. I took the road to Damascus.... The costal route via Brighton," said Ronnie, with a wry smile. She chuckled as he gazed at her kind and knowing face that resembled home more than any bricks and mortar ever could. He leaned closer so they could kiss.

In Arnie's old lock-up, on the Livingstone Estate, in Battersham, Guzzler was sitting in the battered old armchair, scribbling into a notebook. Faye had sold Arnie's scooter, but the lock-up came with the flat at no extra cost, so she told Guzzler he was welcome to use it whenever he wanted. There was a new addition in the form of a large wooden bookshelf. Guzzler could drink as many beers as he wanted but he would never get as pissed as the shelves supporting the collection of his favourite novels.
The shutter door opened, spraying light over this Pirates' lair. The silhouette of a thin figure came into view.
"Tracey said I might find you here."
It was Bulldog's mother.
"Hiya, Kate," said Guzzler, clearing a space for her in the ramshackle hang-out.
"I do believe congratulations are in order," she said with a warm smile.
"Yeah, cheers. I feel ancient. Can't really believe it, to be honest, me a Grandad."
"What they calling him?" asked Kate.
"Little AJ. He's a real smasher, always smiling. I was touched when they told me his middle name was Jason, but I shed a tear when they said his first name was Arnold. Faye is right made up. Her and Arnie been like family to my Ian," said Guzzler, with a little glint in his eye.

"That's a lovely gesture," said Kate.

"He's a good lad, my Ian," said Guzzler.

"So, what you doing yourself?" said Kate, as she nodded at the notebook that he'd been writing in.

"It's for AJ. Y'know, like, when he's a bit older. I'm writing about the escapades of his crazy old grandad, and all his nutty mates. The scooters, the scrapes, the *Full Monty*," said Guzzler.

"Yesterday's heroes, eh?" said Kate.

"Somethin' like that," said Guzzler.

"What a great idea," said Kate.

"So anyway, how's he getting on in rehab?" he asked.

"So far so good. It's an amazing place. He says it's like being on the TV show, I'm a Celebrity get me out of here. He's seen footballers, pop stars, actors, you name it."

"Lording it with the rich and famous, eh?" said Guzzler.

"Keeps him distracted, y'know."

"Give him me best."

"Of course," said Kate.

Kate paused a moment as if somehow lining things up in her head.

"When he gets out, I think we'll be moving away from Battersham."

Her words refocused Guzzler.

"Oh, right," he said both pleased and sad.

"The council said they'd relocate us to a little town in Wiltshire. Fresh start. Hopefully give him a better chance."

"Best of luck, eh? And if you need a help moving your stuff, just let me know."

She pondered a moment.

"You don't know if Pickfords do carrier bags, do you?" She said with a smile.

"New beginnings, eh?" he said.

"You'll come down and visit?" said Kate.

"Yeah, I'll have to. Be no-one left in Battersham soon. You and Bulldog are off, Mick's in Brighton."

"How's he doing?" asked Kate.

"Lovin' it. He's got to stay off the grid, y'know, so his work options are a bit limited, but he's got himself a little cash job on the Fairground. And Penny, she's worked wonders on him, he's got his mojo back," he said.

She pointed to her head. "Just needed to catch a bit of peace, didn't he, aye?"

Guzzler acknowledged her with a nod.

"D'you hear much from Ronnie?" she asked.

"I got a text from him, couple of weeks back. He was asking about Bulldog," said Guzzler.

"I'll be forever grateful for what he's done. We would have never been able to afford that place without him," said Kate.

"I told him that. He just says, 'What are mates for?'" said Guzzler.

"He's a good 'un, that Ronnie," she said.

"Yeah, he is," replied Guzzler.

"But if it wasn't for you, my boy probably wouldn't even be here," said Kate.

"Main thing is, he's not giving up the fight because the alternative's not much to write home about." said Guzzler.

In Arksdean, Ronnie's garage door was wide open, his scooter was conspicuous by its absence. He was not without space, but yet boxes seemed to congregate in the dark corners of his garage like a cluster of Spiders making themselves at home. As Ronnie tidied up the place, he felt it was no longer a place from where adventures sprung, just four walls and a roof that stored tools he knew he would never use.

Ronnie crossed the yard and peered into a large, green-lidded dustbin, marked recycling. From in amongst plastic milk cartons and old newspapers, he fished out a copy of Scootering magazine, that had been deposited there during a post-Brighton purge. He dusted it down and took it back to the garage where he perched on some boxes and marvelled at the pictures of classic Italian-made scooters.

**If you enjoyed *The Pebble in my shoe*,
please leave a review on Amazon.
It's always very helpful.
Also check out my other books at**
www.Paulrunewood.com

For my son, Sam, who never met Freddie Read-Jahn, but has many of the charming qualities of his maternal grandfather.

For Brian, enjoy the read!
Shirley Read-Jahn

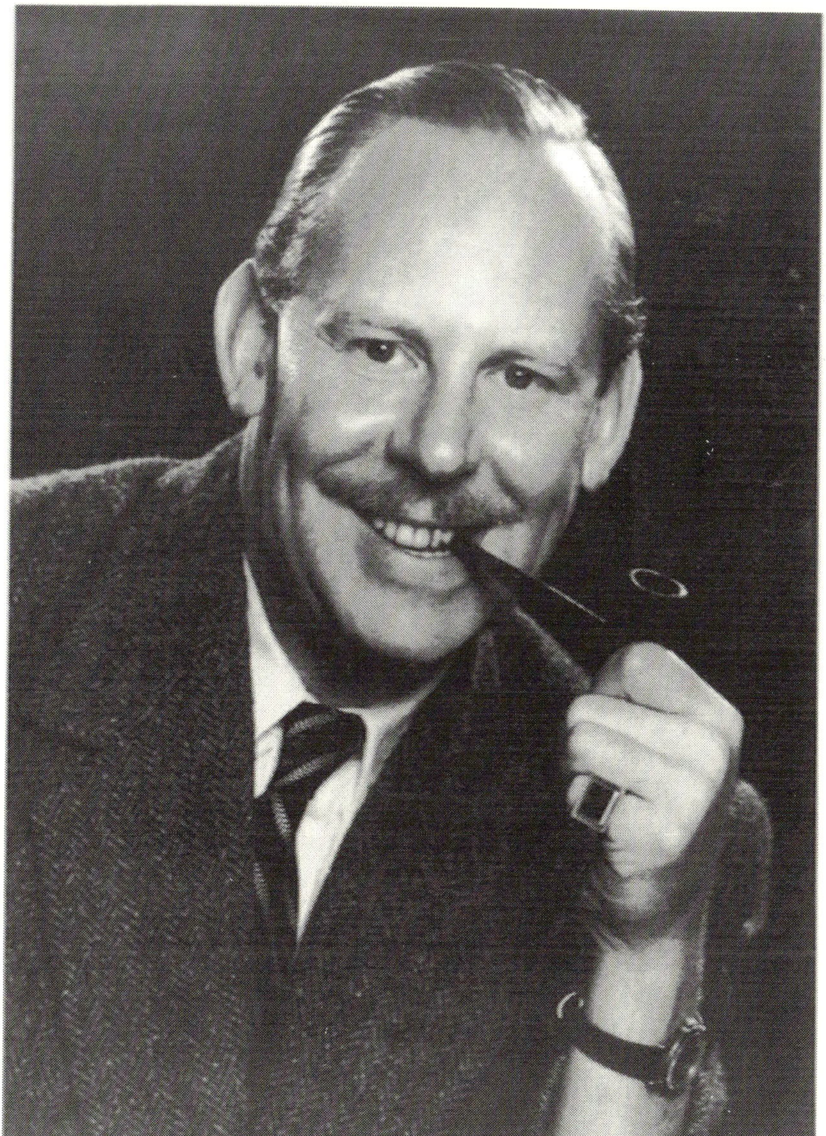

Chapter 1

**Winter, 1980
Shanghai**

Swirling white fog crept its clammy fingers down the neck of the tall young man's greatcoat, seeped under the trilby pulled slightly down over his ears. Horns from ships wailed and honked in the night as the ferryboat pulled across the dark, oily waters of Shanghai port's harbour. Suddenly the young man saw him—a very old, bent-over, short Chinese man shuffling from the stern out of the fog toward him on the deck.

"Fleddie!" the old man breathed up at the young man, breath rank from cigarettes, stabbing his finger into Fred's nephew's broad chest. "It's you, Fleddie," he wheezed up at him, "I'd know you anywhere."

The younger man frowned down at the wizened Chinese man and pulled himself imperceptibly back toward the boat's railings.

"No, I'm not, I'm not Freddie."

"Ah, that voice, that gravelly voice! But you've worn well,

Fleddie, you don't look old, not like me. Still the same deep voice! Same red moustache. Why you here? You remember me, Shanghai Joe! You here with Robeson?"

"Robeson? Who?"

"Robeson! You know, Morgan's man?" said Shanghai Joe.

"I don't know what you're talking about. No, no, I'm afraid you're confusing me with someone else," said the younger man, hurrying away to avoid the little man, glancing back once over his shoulder. He stood there, the old man, both hands gesturing up and out in perplexed question at the younger man's retreating back.

Then Stephen got it. He strode to the ferry's bows where he stood stock still, thinking about the odd encounter. Freddie? Him? Of course! It had to be Fred, who'd spied for British Military Intelligence and the Foreign Office during WWII. That old Chinese fellow had confused him with his relative, for he'd been told occasionally that he did look and sound quite a bit like Fred. Now he wanted to know more. Who was this wizened little man? Damn! He shouldn't have hurried away. What could he tell him about secretive Fred, who'd never told him anything much about his war activities? Intrigued, he hurried back to the stern, peering through the smoke from the funnel and the billowing fog. He was gone. He clattered down the boat's stairs to the ferry's lounge, but no old Chinese man. He'd vanished into thin air.

All Stephen really knew was that Fred had taken an epic journey during World War II to get to the British Embassy in Moscow, having to avoid mined seas and German-occupied territory. He had been an Army intelligence agent—that much was certain. Whom was Fred meeting on his journey? What was he doing *en route*, aside from making connections? Passing messages? What would he be doing once he arrived in the Soviet Union?

But Fred was by now gone. Died early, suddenly, in Geneva, at only 68 years of age. Throwing himself into a deckchair, the young man began to think, wondering how it had all begun, thinking of the bits and pieces a couple of relatives had told him. He knew Fred's daughter Shirley had talked to Fred a lot more than anyone else. When he got back to England, he'd contact her; find out what more she knew. Up to now he'd never given it that much thought, but now, after this encounter, his interest was piqued. He really wanted to know the story.

He jumped up from the deckchair, strode across the deck, and hurried down the gangplank, the ferry now docked and bumping its fenders against the rotting old Shanghai quayside, black water slurping and splashing as the boat rolled gently in place and the halyards of nearby yachts rhythmically slapped against their masts in the slight swell.

Glancing around, still no sign of the old man.

He'd ring Shirley as soon as he was home in England.

Chapter 2

1911-1940
Fred is Born, Works in Berlin,
Courts and Weds Molly, and Becomes a Spy

When Stephen arrived back in London from Shanghai, the first thing he did was ring Shirley. They discussed Fred's death and that his body had been cremated in Switzerland. Fred's secretary, Lexi, had brought the urn back to England, with Fred's passport, per border-crossing requirements. Strange as it may seem, an urn of ashes cannot travel without its passport! The two arranged a meeting to talk about what Shirley knew about her father, and from the research she'd already done.

Fred Read-Jahn died on 13th March, 1980, 40 years after he'd married Molly Sutton, Shirley's mother.

The meeting between Stephen and Shirley took place in London after the funeral, when the long story began to emerge, and was to spread over many days, with many coffees and glasses of wine shared companionably together. By then Stephen had done some research, too, and together with what Shirley already knew, there was, indeed, a story to tell.

Shirley drove down to Worthing, Sussex, where her mother was in an old folks' home, after suffering seven strokes over the past few years. After therapy she was again able to speak, albeit with a slight slur, and offered some insight about Fred, along with her memories.

"Darling," she told Shirley, making a huge effort to talk, after her latest big stroke. But, with her usual gap-toothed endearing grin, she managed to say, "I found copies of my love letters to Fred that I've kept all my life. We always used carbon paper in the war to have a copy in case they never arrived. How about that, then! Think they'd be of any help to you?" Molly's latest stroke precluded her from talking too much anymore.

Holding on to this unexpected treasure trove of memories, Shirley drove back up to London to continue work on her book. The next part was obviously going to be about Fred's and his brother's births. She'd get to her mother's letters all in good time. She felt a wave of excitement wash over her.

Before Fred's birth in London his father, Friedrich Ludwig Jahn, had been Editor in Berlin of the Berliner Zeitung newspaper, then, at the age of 23, had moved to England to work at the London Times, met a wonderful Englishwoman called Clara, and married her. Friedrich's own father had been quite a character. In the Jahn family's lore, it was said that Fred's grandfather had been the inventor of the Army's jumping-jacks physical exercises, bane of all boot-camp soldiers, but that could just as easily have been another yarn from the Jahns—who were known for their sly sense of humour.

The 10th August, 1911 was one of those rare torrid days in London. Temperatures topped 100 Fahrenheit (almost 38 Celsius), breaking all previous records. Clara Mabel Rebecca Read (listed on her son's birth certificate as Clara Jahn) lay panting in her Islington hospital bed, giving birth to her first son. The only relief she could get from the heat in the stuffy ward was a gentle breeze wafting from the north through her open window, stirring the white institutional gauze curtain.

Hours later, the heavy baby, weighing over 10 pounds, came squalling into the world. Fritz Otto Willie Jahn was named after his German father, Friedrich Ludwig Jahn, albeit with the diminutive Fritz for Friedrich. Clara, thoroughly English, thought his name sounded too German, so Fritz became known in his family home as "Fred" or "Freddie". When he'd grown up he liked to mischievously claim he was a true Cockney inasmuch as he was born in Islington "within the sound of Bow Bells", but, of course, there was absolutely nothing about him, especially his King's English, that made him sound anything like a Cockney!

Clara was vastly relieved three and a half years later for the weather to be rather mild in February, alternating between sunny and wet days while she went through the ninth month of her second pregnancy in London. "So different from Freddie's hot birthday", she smiled to her husband.

Friedrich tapped his ever-present pipe on the armrest of the hospital chair he'd pulled up next to her bed and gazed indulgently at his beloved wife. This second son arrived on 7th February, 1915 and they named him Hermann, with Clara saying his name was Herman, to make it sound more English.

For his work, Mr. Jahn relocated his little family from London back to Berlin in the mid-1920s. Clara never learned much German, insisting on English being spoken at home. She had a few sentences under her belt, but only enough for shopping and emergencies. She felt more comfortable around British people so, even though Fred's father was German, to please Clara, the family went to live in the British enclave in Schöneberg, an upmarket area of Berlin, and the boys attended the enclave's Anglican school. Having spoken German at home with their father and on the streets of Berlin, and English with their mother and at school, the boys were now bilingual.

This British enclave was filled with ex-pat businessmen and diplomats. There were many places in Schöneberg where young Fred and Herman used to "hang out" after their studies, meet fascinating people and, unwittingly at the time, develop future useful German contacts—setting them up for the spying careers they would both eventually follow.

Starting in the 1920s the Schöneberg area of Berlin became the "gay" area of Berlin, filled with nightclubs. Neither Fred nor Herman was gay but they both loved to dance and enjoy the social life. It was already known as the cultural hub of Berlin. There was an aura of Bohemianism there, too, an artsy-craftsy feel to the place, and always with the sound of music pouring out from the night clubs. Famous people came to live there; names Fred and Herman knew. The boys loved it all, as, wandering from club to club in the evenings they'd see famous people such as the German actress and *chanteuse*, Marlene Dietrich. Fred told how they even got to talk to her one evening at a club and ask her about her fascinating life.

Marlene told them, "I was born in Schöneberg in 1901, but a lady is not supposed to tell her age, so you didn't hear that from me!" They both laughed with her and bought her a drink as she leaned her head to one side with a naughty wink and went on to flirtatiously tell them, "Bet you boys didn't know I'm both German and American, eh? Really, I'm a cosmopolitan woman because I'm also going off to Paris whenever I can. J'adore Paris. You should come with me one day. Young men like you always love gay Pareee —and its women—*nicht wahr*?!" To both brothers Marlene Dietrich seemed very attractive, a decade or so older, for sure, but so worldly, and with a gorgeous, husky, sexy voice they'd never forget.

In 1927, as soon as he left the Anglican school in Schöneberg at the age of 16, Freddie joined the British Embassy on Wilhelmstrasse in Berlin and worked in the Commercial department. Herman joined his brother at the Embassy in 1931, when he got out of school himself. Both brothers' command of German and English was useful. Eventually their superiors recognised that these two young men could act as a German or an English gentleman at will. Not only that, but Fred had quickly picked up French, too. He thought he'd need it if he ever went over to Paris for a weekend to look up Marlene Dietrich!

Fred told his brother, "I say! If you suddenly tread on someone's toes, all you have to do is listen to what language shoots out of their mouth, and you'll know if they really are English, or German, won't you!"

In his case, Fred had trained himself to be whichever nationality was required at that moment. He found it great fun being different characters. He reckoned he'd have made a good actor. They talked together about their future and both boys excitedly saw a future in espionage, with the way Europe's politics were going and a war pretty much certain on the horizon.

Trusted by the British Embassy in Berlin, where he'd spent nearly eight years, Fred left there in 1935 and was steered by the British Embassy and Foreign Office to work as a spy in Berlin, planted in a private prestigious international high-tech commercial engineering company called Morgan Crucible Company, Ltd., which had its head offices back in Battersea, London.

Fred was planted to work for Morgan's in Berlin as Deputy Manager in a department called "Zk". He said it stood for "Zukauf", the German for purchasing or acquisitions, a sub-department of Morgan's Department Z which stood for Zweckforschung, or, in English, Applied Research.

In 1904 Morgan's had set up this applied research division called Department Z, moving by the 1930s from non-ferrous crucible construction into high-tech engineering including making many other items out of a variety of metals, all of which would be useful in the war. What was of interest to the British Embassy, the Foreign Office, and the British military, was that this department worked with the German military. What better idea than to plant a young man fluent in both languages into Department Zk?

Morgan Crucible, Berlin, had become financially stable because of its military contracts in World War I. It had major customers across Europe including AEG, Siemens, Daimler-Benz, Spies-Hecker Cologne, and the Chemische Fabrik Hackenin. During World War I they supplied the military of the United Kingdom, the United States of America, and the USSR, continuing on with this supply work right up to World War II.

While working for Morgan's, Berlin, Fred learned a lot about its product. He had an innate talent for retaining information that could be of use in the future. He never forgot a detail. You never knew when something you'd learned years before could be applied to your current situation and, more importantly, used to further the aims of Great Britain when the war eventually came about. He didn't know it then, but it would all serve him very well when he was long gone from Germany and England and was working in Russia.

As a plant in Department Zk in Berlin, he was known to the German companies simply as an important supplier, so he freely visited and talked with impunity to the major munition suppliers to Germany. His fluency in both English and German and, indeed, in French, was of paramount importance, and his previous diplomatic Embassy work, obviously invaluable. He was placed well to find out what those huge firms were doing, planning, developing, and report back to the British. Fred had now become a proper spy.

A Mr. Kenneword worked for Morgan's. Even though Fred didn't know him well while in Department Zk, this man was to become one of Fred's "handlers" when he met him in Kobe, Japan, on his epic journey to the USSR, passing and receiving invaluable information to carry along to his next contact, for Kenneword had recognized a potential intelligence agent when he'd watched Fred, as he did all the time Fred was at Morgan's, Berlin.

In the autumn of 1937 Fred's father, Friedrich Jahn, and his British wife Clara, were living in Neue Mühle, Berlin.

By 1938, Fred's father had become a canny businessman, following politics avidly, working in the newspaper industry. When he realised which way the tide was turning, and being rightfully fearful of Hitler's world plans, he encouraged his sons to leave Berlin for England. There they could become naturalised British citizens. After all, his wife was English, and both boys had been born in London.

Suddenly, on 6th March, 1938 Fred's father, Friedrich Jahn, died at the early age of only 60 years old. That left his English wife, Clara, a widow in Germany with war looming.

By the autumn of 1938 the Munich Crisis had arisen, provoking a major crisis in the command structure of Hitler's German government. The British Embassy was evacuated from Berlin by 30th September, just before Hitler declared he would invade Czechoslovakia on 1st October. The British by then knew there would be no avoidance of war with Germany.

Freddie had already returned to England by then. Soon afterwards, Herman, who hadn't left Berlin, did then leave, followed by Clara.

Later in October of 1938, the crisis was over so the British Embassy staff returned to Wilhelmstrasse, Berlin, including Herman and his mother, Clara.

It seemed that imminent war had been avoided.

Clara, a recent widow and an Englishwoman in Berlin, nevertheless got on well with her late husband's sister, Charlotte, so stayed a while longer in Germany. But, ever aware of what her husband had requested, she decided she'd better return to London, along with Herman, before 1st September, 1939—when Hitler's army marched into Poland in the September Campaign, also known as the 1939 Defensive War. In Germany Hitler's government called it the Poland Campaign or the *Fall Weiss* (the White Plan). Hitler's military High Command had worked on this plan up to 15th June 1939. The armies were then made operational, with the invasion of Poland starting on 1st September. Marching into Poland were the armies of Germany, the Soviet Union, the Free City of Danzig, and a small army of Slovak men. The September Campaign White Plan ran from 1st September, 1939 to 6th October, 1939, with the 1st September invasion day marking the start of World War II.

The boys continued living in London with their mother. The brothers were always very close friends. Once the naturalisation papers were in order, Fred affectionately told Herman, "I say, old man, I'm going to call you 'Bertie', because, you're a real Brit now, just like both Edward VII and George VI, and they're both called Bertie!" Both young men convulsed with laughter when Herman said, "Oh, Freddie, you know they're both really German, well, the family was, you know, through Prince Albert, the House of Wettin, the Hanovers, oh, you know…"

"I know, I know, but then, so are we, ha ha, BERTIE!" laughed Fred.

Even though Fred was no longer working out of Germany when the war started, upon the advice of the Foreign Office in London, he still retained his contacts in Morgan Crucible, Germany, and in Austria. He was a prolific letter-writer and, while the postal system was still in place, he corresponded avidly with his German contacts. Even though censorship of mail had been instituted, the system was quite chaotic at first, so Fred was able to send and receive quite a lot of letters with no censored blue lines struck through any of them.

Fred had made a number of valuable contacts while living and working in Berlin, all of whom he knew he could "mine" in much of his secret work as the war years carried on. One of his main contacts was Delia, the daughter of the owner of the Chemische Fabrik Hackenin, a paint, plastics, and varnish company. This woman was to give his future wife a lot of grief some years hence, but at this time, nobody knew what the future was to bring.

The small Jahn clan was now living in London. War had come on 1st September, 1939, just as his father had predicted. Good thing they were now all safely living in London, and naturalized, thought Fred! He had his "secret" work to do, all very "hush, hush" stuff, but it excited him through and through.

On the evening of 25th February, 1940 Freddie went out. He was a tall man, slender but, back then, already with the start of a barrel chest and broadening shoulders. Being over six feet tall, he was told he could apply to be a guard at Buckingham Palace. He liked to relate that tidbit of information with a grin, saying he did apply but was turned down, because he was half German. "But," he'd mischievously add, "so are the King and Queen!"

His bearing was upright and dignified, his blond-brown hair already starting to recede, but kept neatly combed and swept back. He sported a blond-red moustache, always carefully trimmed, and wore spectacles. Behind these glasses twinkled fun-loving, intelligent, warmly smiling blue eyes. All this lent a Continental effect to his appearance, particularly as he'd stroke his moustache when seemingly lost in thought. Fred also had an energy about him that attracted people—a *joie de vivre*, a merriment that was often contagious. His hands were long, white and obviously had never worked a spade in dirt. On the little finger of his left hand he wore his ever-present gold and blue lapis lazuli heavy square ring.

Feeling ready for fun that evening and wanting to leave the worries of the war behind him for a while, Fred went to the Linguists Club on Grosvenor Place. The Club's French motto was "*Se comprendre, c'est la paix*" meaning "mutual understanding is peace". People went there to practise different languages in classes or social settings. At a dance that very night, 25th February, Fred saw her, Molly. It was love at first sight.

Molly Sutton was petite, with auburn wavy hair just covering her ears and styled in the latest fashion, with a cheeky curl falling down over her right eyebrow. Her face was heart-shaped. He was to learn that she was always dressed in a soignée high style, a real "clothes horse". Anything she wore made her look chic and attractive. She loved high heels, expensive jewellery, and always wore Chanel No. 5 French perfume. He noticed she also wore the same Chanel Red Lantern shade of lipstick as Delia did, that daughter of the owner of the Chemische Fabrik Hackenin. Obviously, the height of ladies' fashion!

Molly had a trim waist, curvaceous hips and an attractive, generous bosom. But it was those legs he could see under her just-below-the-knee-length skirt that Fred's eyes were mostly drawn to—shapely, long, strong legs for a petite girl, and one who'd obviously played hockey in her school days! Her brown eyes, spread quite widely apart, sparkled. And her mouth! She had a gap between her two top front teeth that was instantly alluring to Fred. Her smiling lips looked soft and kissable. Fred had never before been so attracted to a girl.

Fred stared at Molly while watching her chat with another man and a girl, obviously enthralling them with some innate ability to tell a captivating story. She waved her hands around, her wrist sparkling with diamonds, laughing loudly, now and again shooting a coquettish look his way. She emanated an ebullient exuberance. She was mesmerising, just beautiful.

Molly, in turn, was fascinated by this tall stranger, who wouldn't, or couldn't, take his eyes off her. She hoped that by sending him meaningful little glances he'd come over and ask her to dance. She liked his looks, particularly his rakish air. She asked her companions if they knew him.

"Well, I heard he's half German; well, he was, but he's naturalised now so a Brit like us," said her girlfriend, "but he's nice enough, they say. You could practise your German on him!" Molly was always ahead of her friends. When she'd heard her father claim that war was definitely, irrefutably coming, Molly decided it would be a good idea to learn German. Who knows, she thought, perhaps the Germans would invade, and knowing their language would probably save her in certain situations she'd rather not be involved in!

Fred walked over purposefully to Molly and wasn't in the least surprised when she agreed at once to dance with him. He held her in his arms while Vera Lynn's voice crooned over the gramophone, "*A Nightingale Sang in Berkeley Square*". He fox-trotted Molly around the hall while a Ray Noble Orchestra's record spun out, "*The Very Thought of You…I see your face in every flower, your eyes in stars above…*" They spent all evening dancing or chatting together over drinks. They discovered they had much in common, particularly a love of the German language. Molly thought he was the most exciting man she'd ever met. By the time Fred took her back home they were totally smitten with each other. Outside her door, he took Molly in his arms and she let him kiss her.

Their relationship proceeded at a fast pace with picnics in

Richmond Park, in the countryside, and more dances, where he could take her again in his arms and woo her as they spun around the floor, floating in a rainbow bubble nobody else could break into. Soon they were stepping out together seriously, with their respective families beginning to ask questions about their rushed courtship.

One sunny day on a picnic in Surrey just outside London, Fred and Molly sat on the grass on a red and white blanket eating their sandwiches. Suddenly Molly was up on her feet, crying out in dismay as ants scurried up her trouser legs. As she stamped about screaming blue murder, a bull appeared from around some trees, and made a dash toward them. Both Molly and Fred flew across the field, both now panting rapidly as they scrambled over a fence into safety. Gasping, they fell giggling into each other's arms, while the bull snorted white foam from his ringed nose, pawing the ground in a mighty fury on the other side of the fence. As Fred held her tightly in his arms, the spectacles in his top pocket were crushed from the intensity of their embrace and it was then that he proposed to her and she breathlessly accepted.

Within two weeks they decided they would marry on 31st March, 1940. He knew he had to marry her and marry her soon, knowing he was shortly going to be sent away. It was war and he had a duty to perform. He wanted her with every fibre of his being. Molly felt the very same way. They already adored and lusted for each other. Then there was the fact that she came from an upper middle-class family, certainly an attraction for him, which made him feel their future life together would be quite comfortable. He'd always hoped to marry someone of the right class. In general, Fred had always appreciated the finer things in life, including his women! Her enthusiasm for life was another asset for him. Plus, he liked her father. He wasn't too keen on her mother or her sister, but he wasn't marrying the sister…

On Molly's part, Fred's fluent German and his secret work in intelligence completely intrigued her. He told her little of what he was actually doing at work, saying it was "hush, hush" and this made him even more attractive to her. She loved the adventure of it all. She had already met his family and felt comfortable with them.

They seemed to have plenty of money so Fred would be able to provide for her; her father always told her this was very important in a man. He had an upper-class English accent, and was well educated, as was she, so they could talk somewhat knowledgeably and intelligently together. Fred knew Molly wasn't a scholar, even though she'd attended Heath House, a well-known English boarding school. She wasn't totally *au fait* with world politics, but was certainly interested and did read the newspapers, and the rest of her made him equally intrigued. He knew she loved adventure, he knew she flew biplanes—a woman flying planes! He was intrigued by that!

And they were in love; it was as basic as that.

They shared a mischievous streak and made each other laugh. They wanted whatever time they could get together. The thought of not being together was intolerable to both of them, but nobody knew how much time one could have together. This was wartime, after all. It was a matter of *carpe diem* and the hell with what anyone might think of the rush. Molly's father, for one, was Not Pleased, and tried to put her off from marrying Fred.

"Listen, darling," Mr. Sutton had worried out loud to Molly, "the man's half GERMAN, for heaven's sake, works in army intelligence, you say, so could be killed at any moment."

Molly had angrily responded, "But he's naturalised, Dad, he was born in Islington, so how much more English could he be?"

"Oh Molly, maybe I should cut you off without a penny?" growled Mr. Sutton, hoping to change her mind that way.

"Dad, for God's sake, please stop this. You know you won't cut me off! I LOVE Fred, I want to marry him, I'm going to marry him, you know I am!"

Mr. Sutton's final remark before giving in was, "Molly, just think. Think of the pain you'll have to go through if he is killed and you lose him!"

"Dad!" cried Molly, "I could lose ANY man, even any ENGLISH man who goes off to war—and they pretty much ALL have to—so please, please stop this. I'm going to marry him and that's that!"

There were more arguments, certainly, but all the major family members showed up for their wedding in Fulham, London, regardless. Herr Jahn and Mr. Sutton eyed each other, talked together, and finally decided they actually quite admired each other. Friedrich Jahn's English was perfect and he, having been a newspaper editor, was an educated man, somebody Mr. Sutton could also admire.

Molly told her father she would take Fred's surname of Read-Jahn. Her father asked how had Fritz Otto Willie Jahn come by his new hyphenated last name? She told him that Fred, calling himself a "clerk" was to change his name by deed poll on 14th May, 1940 to Fred Willie Read-Jahn. (Somerset House was to record the new name on the 20th May in the newspapers.) She explained that as his mother had been a Read, they'd decided why not just hyphenate the two surnames together and lend it a tad more Englishness? Her father wished the German-sounding Jahn name would just go away and leave them as Reads, but he had no say in the matter.

Even though he wasn't legally Fred Willie Read-Jahn yet, on 31st March, 1940 Molly and Fred were married. She was suffering from the measles but stood happily next to Fred in front of the church (her father off to the side of them, still nervous but attempting a feeble smile). Molly—in her racy black picture hat worn at a coquettish slant and Fred in his very English tweed jacket and Burberry raincoat—were smilingly married, with Molly taking the name Fred planned to have, becoming, absolutely delightedly, Mrs. Edith Marie "Molly" Read-Jahn, and scratching discreetly throughout the service at her itching measles spots.

SHIRLEY READ-JAHN

Molly & Fred 1940 on a picnic. The Day of the Ants!

Fred & Molly wed, 31 March, 1940.

Hidden in Plain Sight

Edith Marie "Molly" Sutton, 1940.

Chapter 3

**1939-1940
Molly in the Civil Air Guard**

Before meeting Freddie and marrying him, Molly Sutton had always wanted to learn to fly. She was bold and headstrong, with a great sense of fun; an adventurous type of girl, always riding horses, her bicycle, and dreaming of things she could do to shock and be considered "different", "a bit of a daredevil". She'd make her beloved father shake his head in mock horror at her antics. The maid in her father's house was always giggling about Molly's near escapes regarding her boyfriends. She'd answer the doorbell at the front of the house, winking at Molly to let her know that one of her many beaux was waiting there to be let in. Molly, in turn, would scamper to the living room to hurriedly escort an earlier visiting beau straight out the back door.

One day in early 1939, well before meeting Fred the following year, she read about aviation lessons at a flying club not far from her home, with lessons for only half-a-crown per hour (2 shillings and 6 pence, the equivalent of approximately 30 cents USD in 1939, or about $8.44 USD in 2018). Flying! Biplanes! What fun! Her adoring father naturally gave in to his favourite daughter's latest whim, bought her the requisite flying outfit, and off she went to start her lessons.

It was cold in those little biplanes. Molly had a "Red Baron" type of close-fitting leather cap that did up under her chin. She had a one-piece flying suit, an aviator's rusty brown corduroy belted jacket with an astrakhan collar, aviator sunglasses, warm fur-lined gloves and boots. When working in the hangar, she also had a military side cap that she wore at a rakish sideways slant atop her head. She was a stylish girl so had her photograph taken wearing one of her flying outfits along with her high heels, just to look a little racy and feminine.

Molly was deadly serious about her flying lessons and became very good. When she heard that women could apply for the Civil Air Guard, she immediately applied and was shortly accepted.

The Civil Air Guard had begun in 1938 as a scheme in which the British government subsidized training fees for members of flying clubs, in return for future military call-up commitments. By 1939 all suitable women could be considered as ferry pilots, air ambulance pilots, or general communications pilots, helping out the Royal Air Force in times of emergency. They were civilian pilots affiliated to flying clubs throughout Great Britain, and they had to be between the ages of 18 and 50. Molly was within this range, being 29 in 1939. She received her flying training for this Guard and instead of paying 2s 6d for a lesson she was now receiving 2s 6d an hour while having fun flying biplanes.

Britain's entry into World War II was announced over the airwaves on 3rd September, 1939 at 11.15 am. Molly had heard this heart-stopping news over the radio that Sunday when she'd arrived home from an early morning flying lesson. Her parents and younger sister, Olive, were hunched around the big, brown family radio. The family's maid stood discreetly just outside the open door, listening. As Molly entered the drawing room, her parents both looked up and shushed her, her father's index finger raised to his lips. The

British Prime Minister, Neville Chamberlain, was announcing to the nation:

"This morning the British Ambassador in Berlin handed the German Government a final note stating that, unless we heard from them by 11 o'clock, they were prepared at once to withdraw their troops from Poland, and a state of war would exist between us. I have to tell you now that no such undertaking has been received, and that consequently this country is at war with Germany."

Before Molly's mother could even give her command to the maid, the girl had rushed below stairs to the kitchen to share the news with the cook and ask her to hurriedly make some strong tea for the whole family.

When war was declared, all civil flying naturally came to a halt. Many of the women in the Civil Air Guard switched over to join the Air Transport Auxiliary. Molly flew for a little while longer but by 25th February, 1940, she had met Freddie Read-Jahn and the romance became serious. With his repeated protestations of worry over her flying, Molly turned in her flying suit and moved on to non-aviation war work.

Molly, 1939 Civil Air Guard.

Chapter 4

March-July, 1940
Fred Prepares to Leave for the USSR

Freddie had met the love of his life, Molly, had married her, and now was in the excruciatingly unenviable position of knowing he was going to have to leave her behind in London while his intel work for the British was moving into high gear.

The Foreign Office was readying Fred to leave for the USSR. They sent him to Scotland Yard to pick up some useful experience he would need for his spying work, including a short study of phrenology, involving the reading of the shape, indentations and size of bumps on the skull to tell a person's character, personality, and mental abilities. Even though phrenology had fallen into disrepute since the mid- to end-1900s, it was known that the Nazis still used phrenology in their determination of people whom, they claimed, rightly or wrongly, belonged to Hitler's supposed Master Race—eventually used against Jews—so it was of interest to Fred's work to understand everything he could about the enemy's "forensic" beliefs.

After the war, holocaust survivors told horrendous tales about Josef Mengele, the sociopathic Nazi Auschwitz doctor known as The Angel of Death, who used phrenology in studying the lower jaws of prisoners, to try to understand the race he declared they belonged to; he even wrote, in all seriousness, a dissertation on the matter!

Another study (nowadays considered rather "wacky" by some but still used in certain areas of forensic science) that Fred was asked to take a cursory look at, was cheiloscopy (the forensic study of the uniqueness of lip prints—studied through a magnifying glass on used coffee cups or wine glasses), and even how to gain information from a person's ears and handshake. He enjoyed shaking hands with young ladies and telling them that their "Mound of Venus", situated just below their right thumb, was full and well-rounded. That meant, he said, in palm reading, that the young lady was a sensuous, hot-blooded, wench. He always left them collapsed in giggles, saying, "Oh do hush, Freddie, that's so silly!"

He learned to take note of a person's ears. If the bottom of the ear went straight into the side of the face, with no separated lower lobe, it meant the person was deceitful. You could never tell whether he was pulling your leg or not…his face remained completely deadpan as he shared these tidbits of information.

He would tell interested people, now seriously, "Listen, you should know that much of forensic science involves fingerprints, hand geometry (also known as palm reading), facial and voice recognition, and even body odour, and, of course, my very favourite —the lip prints. There's also iris recognition, practised for hundreds of years by Chinese medical workers. You can tell a lot about a person's health by the colour of their iris or the whites of their eyes."

Fred sometimes mentioned how to practise more of the "tricks of his trade". He claimed he could read lip prints (cheiloscopy!), so, if he told this to a young lady, she'd say, "Oh Freddie, to do that, do you have to kiss a lot of people?" often again collapsing in giggles.

"No, seriously, young lady; lip prints are quite similar to fingerprints; each person has his or her own unique prints", and grinned. "Not only that, but you can also recognise people by their teeth, you know. Did you know Lord Byron used to claim that a person's lips and mouth will tell you what their tongue and eyes try to conceal. You didn't know that, eh?!"

He always smiled, but enigmatically, when somebody would ask (albeit rarely), if they happened to learn that he was an intelligence officer, "Have you had to kill anyone? What was it like? Do you feel bad about it?"

"There are different types of intelligence agents, those who creep around with guns and knives, those who make "letter-drops" in public bins, and those who pick up secrets via different methods, and pass along the information—all to help the war effort."

"But Fred, which kind were you?"

"What good does it do you to know? It would be as useful as a chocolate teapot! It's nothing for you to worry about; don't trouble yourself about it!" Always accompanied by a mysterious grin.

Thus, as to what he was actually up to, not a true word escaped his lips to the eager questioner, and, fortunately for him, hardly anyone knew what his work really entailed. Even family only knew simply that he was in "military intelligence". He'd learned quickly how useful it was to him to sometimes tell persistent strangers something that didn't make sense, but purported to, in order to avoid giving true answers. He'd do that when it seemed necessary to give some answer. With a serious countenance, he'd then trot out a spurious, even nonsensical answer, often using erudite, arcane, literary words, and then enjoy the confused look on their faces. He found that very funny. A favourite answer he liked sometimes to solemnly intone was *"honi soit qui mal y pense"* (shame on whosoever thinks badly of it) then quietly chuckle to himself when his questioner nodded his head, as people do tend to do, not wanting to look ignorant. Oh, how he loved humankind! What fun to trick 'em, he rather heartlessly chortled.

"Listen", he'd say, "if I tell you anything, I'm actually putting my life in your hands. You can appreciate that."

But sometimes people got angry at him for not telling them what he was up to. "Why are you being so wet, Fred? It all sounds quite windy!"

That remark putting him down, making him sound suspicious (which he actually was!) called for another enigmatic smile from Fred, with a swift sidestep to the question, or perhaps another smart aleck reply, "Remember Socrates said 'the only true wisdom is in knowing you know nothing'" followed by yet another smile. That got Fred what he desired, having caused an annoyed response from his interlocutor, stalking away, muttering, "Take a powder, you dope."

Prior to his departure to Moscow he also learned about gadgets, little hidden cameras, exploding pens, cigarette lighters that could be used as a missile, knives or documents secreted inside umbrella handles, film hidden in the handle cavity of a man's shaving brush, and silk from white or black parachutes that was sewn into women's or men's underclothes as tiny secret pockets. He said, if you wanted to know if somebody had entered your locked room, you'd put a wedge, a tiny piece of paper or even a piece of a toothpick or matchstick, into the door by the lock and if it had fallen down, you knew someone was in the room, or had been in.

For his spying work he had to learn Morse code, up to its most advanced level. He not only learned British Pitman shorthand and American Gregg shorthand, but developed his own system to jot down private notes nobody else could read. He also learned how to shoot a variety of guns, and how to get his own gun swiftly out of its shoulder holster, place one hand over his gun-hand, aim and quickly fire. Then there were the lessons in map-reading and compass points. He learned how to survive in the countryside, what to eat and what not to eat, how to follow tracks and trails, how to tread softly and lightly, making barely a sound in woods or on the city pavement, and even how to mask or remove his footprints to fox anybody pursuing him. He learned how to shadow someone, how to fool somebody following him, how to hide and what to do if caught.

Fred had to get used to lying, tricking and using people, how to use confabulation to mess with another person's mind. Conversely, he had to constantly be on the alert in case he, himself, were to be captured and his own tricks used against him. The most frightening thing he was instructed about was the potassium cyanide vial each agent carried, to be taken only as a suicidal last resort, when he knew he was about to be tortured but preferred to die first. Fred thought about having the tiny capsule inserted into a false tooth in his mouth. There was a potential problem with that. If he were to be hit on the head by an enemy, or even fall with his head banging onto something hard, the tooth could break, the capsule break and pretty instant death for him would follow.

After the war was well over, and after Fred had "become redundant in his diplomatic work" (as he used to say), while working for his new job in the United Kingdom's automobile industry he had the good fortune to be allowed to drive one of the Aston Martin DB5 cars actually used in the James Bond movies—this particular car starred in the 1964 *Goldfinger* film. Freddie was like a kid, delightedly examining its special weaponry and gadgetry, and wishing he'd had a car like this while doing his own intelligence work. There's a family photo of a picnic some time later. He's seated in his own car, with the door open and his legs extended outside, pouring champagne, with a fat Havana cigar stuck out the side of his mouth and a huge grin spreading from ear to ear as he related all the wonders of the James Bond motorcar he'd once test-driven.

During the past months, back to February, 1940, before his marriage on 31st March, the Foreign Office was not only getting Fred ready for this work in the USSR, but also was endeavouring to arrange a passage for him to Moscow where he would work at the British Embassy, carrying on with his Morgan Crucible spying work as well as handling his military diplomatic and intelligence duties.

From his earlier years' work at the British Embassy in Berlin from 1927 to 1935 and from his Morgan Crucible Company work, Fred had made a great number of contacts that would serve him well not only in his future work in the USSR but also on this journey to get to the British Embassy in Moscow. He was told about various contacts and "handlers" he would have to look out for and how he would courier messages from place to place, country to country. But, basically, he was going to have to be his own master on the long journey, making the majority of decisions about his own safety by himself. That, for sure, was a great personal responsibility and put some salt on the freedom he was about to also enjoy. He was slightly worried that his contacts might try to queer his pitch and send him off to places he'd rather not be, but, said Fred to himself, "I've just got to get going, start this trip, and work it all out as I go along. I can do this!"

To get to Moscow, in those troubled times, he was going to have to travel via Scandinavia, leaving approximately 17th April but all would depend on available sailings, as actual letters from the Foreign Office indicated.

Room 19,
The Foreign Office,
London
1st April, 1940

Dear Mr. Jahn,

We are endeavouring to arrange a passage for you to Moscow, via Bergen and Stockholm about the 17th April, but this will depend on the sailings about this date.

In the meantime, will you please complete the enclosed forms, and return them as soon as possible, together with three photographs.

Yours truly,

P. Simpson
Communications Dept.

And soon afterwards, he was handed yet another letter.

3rd April, 1940

Dear Jahn,

There is a sailing from Newcastle to Bergen about the 10th April. After that the next one may not be for 2 or even 3 weeks. Will you let us know if you can get away by the next sailing and we will try and get your visa through.

Yours truly,

P. Simpson
Communications Dept.

Preparing for his journey, he knew he couldn't write much down for fear of being captured by the enemy and their discovering his plans. He therefore decided to write a diary, but in his own special code[1]. He would write minimally in this diary and jot down certain things he'd need to be sure to remember. His mind was agile and very sharp but still, he reasoned, he wouldn't be able to remember everything. He went out to a London stationer's and bought himself a small black book. Next, he pored over both his English and American shorthand system lesson books, and spent hours practising the private code he'd invented. Satisfied only he could interpret his pencilled scribblings, he packed his new diary away in his brown leather suitcase.

In Freddie's diary and letters describing his arduous journey to the British Embassy in Moscow, he notes that he was let in to the USSR from Manchuria in short order because the Russians had immediately figured out that he was somebody they needed to allow in quickly, for the very reason he was ostensibly the supplier of Morgan Crucible engineering parts to the USSR. For Fred, he could therefore work as a spy for the British, through his clever cover work for Morgan Crucible, not only in England, but in every country that he was to travel through to get to the USSR, and then, finally, in Moscow itself.

1. *Years later the author was to try to decipher this shorthand system her father, Fred, had worked out before his trip, but, it wasn't anything like the Pitman shorthand she had been trained in as a young woman, or even the Gregg stenography that she knew a little about from her time working in the United States. When she eventually came to write her father's story and had stolen his letters and obtained the diary, it was a huge relief to find there was a second black-bound copy of the diary in readable English—one can only assume that after the war Fred had intended eventually to write his own story, or to have a secretary write it for him, so had transposed his cryptic markings into legible writing, partly in English and partly in German*

Chapter 5

20th July, 1940
Fred Starts his Journey to the British Mission in Moscow

After letting the Foreign Office know he was free to leave England in mid-April, the FO advised him that the day of departure was now not going to be possible until 20th July.

"Wartime problems, old man, you see", said Mr. Simpson.

Fred tried to look appropriately annoyed. In reality, though, he was ecstatic. Three whole more months with his darling wife!

Saturday, 20th July, 1940 had dawned rainy and dull. Fred had left the arms of Molly with great regret. They finally dressed hurriedly and made their way to Euston train station, he wearing the "civvies" Military Intelligence and the Foreign Office had commanded him to wear in lieu of his uniform; that was to be forwarded to the British Embassy in Moscow in a diplomatic bag, to await his arrival. There would certainly be occasions in the USSR when wearing his uniform would be of importance, Military Intel told him.

Fred held Molly tightly in a passionate embrace then climbed into his compartment. The whistle blew. The conductor leapt onto the slowly moving train. Fred lowered the window to kiss Molly's upturned face. Her lips were parted in a brave smile, revealing the gap between her upper two front teeth that endeared her so much to him. As the train puffed out from under the high, dirty, glassed roof of Euston station, Fred leaned farther out of the window. He watched her bright red coat getting smaller and smaller while her white hanky fluttered its farewell. With a sigh, he turned away and settled into his seat.

It was an uneventful, tiring journey to the Liverpool docks. At the ship's offices prior to boarding his ship he suffered through an hour of tedious cross-examinations about his life and purpose of the journey, wondering why the Foreign Office hadn't given him a special note to avoid this kind of harassment? Perhaps this was part of the plan—to make him look like any other ordinary bloke wearing civilian clothes, off on a long voyage to "do his bit for the war". He already had pangs of loneliness and misery.

At three o'clock in the afternoon Fred was released to walk up the ramp of the "Majestic"[1] and saw it was quite a sizeable liner; 27,000 tonnes, he'd heard. His cabin was on "D" deck in a 4-berth cabin that he'd learned he'd be sharing with only one other chap. That meant lots more room than he'd expected.

Fred was neat and organised. He carefully stowed his belongings away and sat down at the cabin desk to write to the most beloved people in his life: Molly, his darling wife; his very dear mother; and his only sibling, his younger brother, Herman, working in the same kind of Army intelligence work as he, but not in the USSR.

Interestingly, in a letter this same day of 20th July, 1940, Fred wrote to Molly on letterhead stating he was travelling on the Cunard White Star "Britannic" rather than the "Majestic". This was an intentional "mistake" in the event his letter fell into the wrong hands…and, on 26th of July he wrote to his mother also stating he was aboard the "Britannic".

3:15 pm 20th July, 1940

Molly, my little Darling,

Well, here I am just settled down nicely. I've a D deck cabin with four berths, sharing it with one other chap who has not yet turned up. I was lucky to get through the various cross-examinations without much trouble. It would not be me if I hadn't forgotten something. My raincoat! Maybe my sweet wife will bring it along with her? I could not buy a mack in Liverpool as the train ran right onto the quai [sic; dock] and you are not allowed to go out into the town. So I shall have to buy one in New York. The second mishap was the small brown bag. The handle gave way and I had to mend it with string. In spite of these two minor tragedies I'm feeling fine, that is, as fine as I can feel under the circumstances.

The train journey was uneventful and tiring. We did not get in to Liverpool until 2 pm. Had a very poor lunch on the train which cost me three shillings and fourpence. Just 3/- more than it was worth. Now aboard ship, I'm going to have tea and dinner will be served at 7.30. Breakfast is at 9 am and lunch 1.30 pm. It's a nice spacy boat and the swimming pool is near to my cabin. But at this moment there's no water in it.

I did not speak a word to anybody in my compartment although once or twice they tried to start a conversation. I was too busy thinking of you and Mum and trying to get the picture of you, sweetheart, standing on the platform, MOLLY DARLING, with your sweet little cerise coat and shining true, faithful eyes. Oh, it does feel terrible to be quite alone again. Nobody to talk to. But I guess I'll have to get used to it. The weather isn't very promising; it's raining nearly all the time. I hope you have a spot of sunshine so that you enjoy your visit to Mrs. Lendrum.[2] This will be the last letter from old England's shores. The next will come from the New World. Now, my brave darling wife, cheerio, look after yourself and don't forget your Freddie who loves you so terribly and is thinking of you every second of the day.[3]

Going upstairs later into the dining room to get a cup of tea, he was introduced to his cabin-mate, a man called Mr. Fred Happlegate, working in the fur trade, who, funnily enough, lived in Chessington, close to Malden, Surrey, where Molly's parents lived.

"Chessington, eh? How interesting," Fred said. "My wife and I wanted to go to the Chessington Zoo on one of our outings." He realised, with an inward smile, that this was the first time he'd called Molly his "wife" to a stranger.

Mr. Happlegate stroked his beard, and rather pompously told Fred, "Well, sir, you may not know, but back in 1931 an animal enthusiast called Reginald opened the zoo naming it after a mansion in the area called Chessington Lodge, built way, way back in 1348. Imagine that! Perhaps you are acquainted with the Lodge?"

"No, I don't know it, and, 1348, eh? So long ago! What I do know is the reason why the zoo is now closed, actually since 1939, when the powers that be saw this wretched war was definitely on the horizon. I heard that's when the government laid out restrictions preventing large crowds from gathering at any entertainment venue, so Chessington was temporarily closed to the public, too. My *wife* (again that inward smile) was quite upset; she loves exotic, actually all animals, and was so looking forward to going. But you probably knew that about the zoo's closure, anyway."

"Indeed, sir, I had heard of the closure."

Silence. Fred sipped his tea. He thought he had two choices. One, to warm this pompous Happlegate fellow up, to have more fun on this part of his journey. Make him laugh, perhaps. Or, simply ignore the chap. Hmmm, he thought, probably best to wait and see…

Fred, tall and slender, was always bespectacled. This look served him well. People took him seriously. He was, indeed, a serious young man who, underneath this veneer, sported a droll sense of humour, and who had a definite sense of sophistication. He was fond of good food and drink and was already quite a connoisseur of all "nice things", as he liked to say, and already knew a lot about the wines of the world. Thus, in the diary he determined to keep of this "adventure" of his, he was planning to note down just about every meal he enjoyed. This day he had "a nice dinner" of hors d'oeuvres, halibut, roast chicken, pudding and coffee. His notes were all in code, anyway, but it amused him that instead of only writing coded information about how to locate his contacts, he was also noting down all the fat pullets he would hopefully consume on board! If the enemy were ever to break his very technical code, he wondered wryly what they'd think of his delicious chickens.

There were many foreigners on board, mostly women and children. After all, the majority of the menfolk were already off fighting the war. The captain's mate called for a "passenger muster" over the speakers. Fred and Happlegate walked speedily belowdecks to their cabin to put on their lifebelts. Up on deck they were told that a long blast of the ship's horn would indicate an emergency at which time all passengers were to report on deck at their emergency station. Short pips would indicate an air raid, in which case all passengers must return to their cabins and stay put. As the two men stood on the deck in their lifebelts near all those women and children, Fred muttered out of the side of his mouth to Happlegate, "My God, if anything *should* happen, it's going to be really awful, really unpleasant, with all these women and kids on board."

Happlegate nodded, with a concerned look on his own face. "Fred," said Freddie, "I can't call you Fred, it's too confusing since we've both got the same name. If you don't mind, you're going to be Happlegate; okay by you?"

"Fine by me, Fred. I can't call you by your Read-Jahn surname, it's too difficult for me to wrap my mouth around!"

Fred privately thought to himself, "and you think your name's not! Happlegate! My foot!"

Later on, Fred strolled around the decks and saw that the "Majestic" had two guns on board and a detachment of naval ratings travelling along. That made for a slightly more secure feeling about being on the high seas in wartime.

After dinner Fred and his now more relaxed cabin-mate retired to the smoking room, enjoying a chat and a Worthington cigar that, as he told his diary, only cost sixpence as against one and threepence on the train. Cigarettes, too, were much cheaper: a shilling against one and five pence. At 11 pm they were offered sandwiches and then withdrew to their cabin at 11:30 pm. He began to think that he'd better be approached soon by a contact with a real secret message or his diary would be turning into nothing but a shipboard menu!

Fred Read-Jahn in British army uniform, 1940. He wore civilian clothes while on his epic journey to the USSR but had it sent on to the British Embassy, to wear as required.

---

1. *The Majestic was launched in 1914 and scrapped in 1943. A black steamer with three orange-and-red smoke stacks.*
2. *Mrs. Lendrum, the wealthy wife of Lendrum & Company's name partner, the first British waste paper recycling firm, where Molly's father was a director.*
3. *During the war it was not permitted by the government censors to put any hugs or kisses abbreviations on any correspondence, or even knitting-patterns, or anything that could be construed as a code.*

Chapter 6

July, 1940
Fred at Sea

While Molly remained behind in London, and, staying up far too late—missing Freddie as only a newlywed can—Fred was *en route* to the USSR on what was to turn out to be an epic journey.

Molly sat at her kitchen table in Cheniston Gardens, chewing her pencil. She'd rather not use a pencil but it was messy using a fountain pen. Besides, buying ink for her little bronze inkwell her father had given her for her last birthday had become too expensive. She owned a ballpoint biro, given to her by her younger sister, Olive, when it first came out in 1938. But, of course, she sighed to herself, she'd run out of refills, hadn't she, and just didn't want to spend unnecessary money for more. So, a pencil it would have to be, she grimaced, sticking its rubbery end back into her mouth while pondering what to tell Freddie. Pulling a carbon copy paper out of her letter-writing kit, she placed it between two thin light blue airmail sheets and started writing.

SHIRLEY READ-JAHN

Sunday, 21st July, 1940
Letter Number ONE!!!!

My dearest dear,

Oh, Freddie, I'm missing you so and you only just left yesterday. I dreamed of you all last night so hardly slept a wink. Did you dream of me, too?

It was so cold last night and it rained again. We had over .39 inches of rain and the radio said that's over 10 mm. I don't quite understand mm. Mrs. Mullins[1] said it means millimetres. I immediately thought of centipedes and millipedes. Daft, aren't I?! I sloshed about in my wellies and mack this morning when I went out. I wanted to read the pillar box to see how often they collect the post these days. I'm going to try to write to you every day so I hope it won't be boring for you! It's a good idea to make carbon copies of our letters in case one goes astray.

Back to work tomorrow. The bank's handyman/janitor/guard, or whatever he is at work, says he'll mend my bike's tyres any time for me. You see, I cycle through all those roads that have bomb craters and there's bits of stuff all over the place. So far he's mended two flat tyres for me. He's given me sticky black tape squares to carry with me, to put over any hole, then I pump it up again, and wobble into work where he checks I did it right. I think he likes me! But you're not to be jealous. You know you, only you, hold my poor broken heart. We should write a song with that title; it's rather good, don't you think?!

Mr. Fairweather at the bank says Jerry's only bombing London intermittently. But you know that. He says towns like Liverpool and Birmingham are getting it more than us in London. But the papers say London's been bombed since the beginning of July. Some people have already been killed, I can attest to that, because I've seen it myself.

Mr. F. has bought reels and reels of sticky tape to crisscross all the bank's windows to help prevent the panes from shattering if a bomb were to explode nearby. He's not sticking it on himself, oh no, he's the manager! He's having an underling do it; glad he didn't ask ME!

Mr. F. reckons Hitler's getting ready for "something big" probably in a couple of months. Wonder how HE knows, but then, he is the bank manager and seems to have lots of closed-door meetings with other bank managers who come to see him.

But darling, you mustn't worry about me at all. I take great care, you know I do. I worry about YOU on all those ships, with German subs about. You will take care, too, I know. Freddie darling, we know our love is so great it will see us through this beastly war. We have a star shining over us, so I can't really worry because I know we'll survive it all.

Can't wait for your first letter. You said the Foreign Office will let me know when the diplomatic bag's arrived and I have post. How exciting that will be. Me and my bike will tear over to the FO to pick it up!!!

Dad said they've got rid of the Duke of Windsor and sent him off to be governor of the Bahamas. Not a bad job, the sunny BAHAMAS! Poor man! (said she, sarcastically!) They think he's a Nazi, Fred, they really do. But you probably know all this, don't you? You haven't told me really what you know, you see, so I don't know what you know…

I love you, forever,

Molly

PS The other thing in the papers was that the government's told us we should start wearing shoes with flatter heels. That's to conserve wood. You know how I love my high heels so it's going to be hard for me, but I'll do my bit. I always do!

PPS Oh Freddie-lein, when you were whispering your sweet nothings into my ear, I felt each one dart like Cupid's arrow straight into my heart, my very soul.

PPPS I love you so much. Kisses and hugs flying your way.

On Monday, 22nd July, 1940, after a long exhausting night's sleep, Fred awoke feeling quite upset. He had, indeed, dreamed of being held in Molly's arms, smiling contentedly in his sleep. The emotions of the last few weeks had tired him out and soon his sweet dream had turned into a nightmare as he saw Molly in her little red coat disappearing from sight as his train chugged farther and farther from her. The train rocked from side to side, black smoke billowed through the open window. He tried to get up to shut it but kept being thrown back. He leaned out of the window and saw her red coat floating now higher and higher up into the black clouds. But, where was she? Just the coat, swirling and twirling higher and higher. He awoke, sweating.

"Listen, old chap," complained Happlegate the next morning. "I had to put ear plugs in my ears last night due to your moaning and groaning in your sleep."

Fred thought he'd have to learn to control his emotions now even in his sleep, for heaven's sake!

In surprise, he saw that it was a beautiful day with a fairly calm sea. He discovered they had left Ireland and Scotland well behind. No rocking of the ship at all. So…just a nightmare he'd had. As he walked around the decks his anxiety disappeared as he got a great feeling of safety watching the other liners so nearby and the two destroyers closing around the "Majestic" he was on. Looking up, he saw a coastal command bomber and a seaplane flying around above them. The seaplane dropped lower to almost glide close over the sea and the people on board waved down to Fred, making him smile.

He chummed up with a naval chap who was going to New York to join his ship. This was immense fun for Fred because this sailor could read the signals the destroyer was making to the convoy boats. He relayed them to Fred as they both happily leaned on the ship's rails amusing themselves with these "ships' conversations" between each other.

That night in the Smoke Room he learned how to play a card game called cribbage. He also played keno, losing three shillings, to his dismay. Next there was dancing but it was a flat affair for Fred, not having Molly there to hold in his arms.

The next few days passed uneventfully enough, with films to watch, deck tennis to play, and many other games schemed up by the ship's entertainment people to amuse the passengers. He told his diary about having Roast Saucy Chicken one evening, simply for sentimental reasons. Molly was never far from his mind. The food on board was really quite excellent, the weather was good, but the sea was now getting rougher.

As they sailed farther north it became cold and showery. Being British, the rain didn't put them off their games on the deck! The ship even had a band to play for them and eventually he regularly joined in the evening dancing, really just "to keep his oar in" so he'd be on top of his toes, he laughingly thought, when he was reunited with his Molly. He continued with his betting on horse-racing, joining a syndicate, and did win three times, but the odds were too low.

On Thursday, 25th July, 1940 he saw a truly wonderful sight of 69 ships moving along in a convoy together. The children on board delightedly peered under, through, and over the ship's railings, chanting out a number for each ship in turn as it steamed past them. Their mothers assured each other the kids were having a lesson in maths as they encouraged their kids to count them forwards, backwards and multiply them by one, two, three and four. Everyone had a grand time that day, each kid trying to outdo the other.

As they neared the Newfoundland banks the "Majestic" was shrouded in fog outside and Fred sat shrouded in smoke inside, paying great attention to the Purser's tales about his time in Port Said. In the afternoon, feeling hemmed in, Fred exercised for hours in the ship's gymnasium then drank and danced the evening away till 1 am at a very lively and noisy party. This sort of behaviour helped him keep his anxious thoughts at bay about Molly's wellbeing in London.

At one point he stepped outside for some air on deck. He'd been wondering whether his "bosses" back home had arranged for him to "do some work for them" aboard this ship. He'd been warned in his preparation conversations for his work on his journey, and in the USSR itself, that it would be far too risky to meet the same agent over and over, that he'd probably only meet one at a time, perhaps receive a message to pass on, then never see him or her again. He was to learn to operate on his own but always, always to do exactly what he was told to do. Never to think he was far cleverer than his handlers. Much later on, he'd learned that that wasn't always to be the case; he'd by that time become trusted to do exactly as HE thought best. But, right now, he felt like an innocent, guileless, greenhorn neophyte of an intel man, but definitely inquisitive. Lighting up, he still felt ready for whatever was to come along…

Fred was leaning against the deck rails of the alleged "Britannic" (actually the "Majestic") smoking his cigarette when the well-known Noël Coward[2] loomed out of a now light fog swirling around the ship and came to join him looking out across the sea. Everyone knew who he was but not of his "secret life". Fred knew; that was one of the secret bits of information he'd been instructed in back in London. The world only knew Coward as an English playwright, actor, director, singer, even a composer. He had an insouciant manner, was a witty, flamboyant show-off, yet got away with it by displaying an endearing cheekiness combined with great poise and chic.

Music floated toward them each time somebody opened a door onto the deck. They had already met and somehow intuited that they shared the same bond and *raison d'être* for this journey. Fred wondered if this man was his new contact; perhaps Coward was thinking the same thing as they eyed each other off. Both were dressed for dinner, with Coward sporting a wild cravat and a heavy gold-chained bracelet. Fred, ever observant, also noticed Coward's gold cufflinks, smiling slightly to himself as he glanced down at his own links that matched his ever-present gold-and-lapis lazuli ring.

Their talk was desultory as they verbally circled each other, puffing on their fags and dropping a careful word now and again, both already somewhat experienced in discovering what they needed to know, whether they could be of use to each other. After a short while, they both tossed their cigarette butts into the sea, shook hands meaningfully, winked conspiratorially, and went into dinner. Fred knew he would be given a message from this fascinating individual to courier to his next contact. The question always remained, how to recognize the next agent? They would have to make a move toward him, and they would do that, of that he now had no doubt. The Foreign Office and Military Intelligence had assured him there would be nothing to worry about in that area.

That night Fred wrote a letter to his mother, stating he was aboard the Cunard White Star "Britannic" instead of the "Majestic". The following is a shortened version of that letter from Fred to her.

Friday, 26th July, 1940
Aboard Cunard White Star "Britannic"

My dearest Mum,

We have mostly women and hundreds of children on board. It was a wonderful experience to watch how everything was managed but, unfortunately, I cannot write anything about it at this juncture. One thing I think I may say and that is that it does not look much like Germany rules the waves!

Incidentally, we have Noël Coward on board and he is going to sing a few songs on the occasion of a cabaret night to be held on Sunday.

Yours lovingly,
Fred

The days rolled on, one after the other with movies to watch, such as "Hollywood Cavalcade" and "Star Dust" and all the usual card or deck games to play. The sea became calmer, some days as calm as a millpond. It was strangely sunny and foggy at the same time some days. His pals mostly suffered hangovers but Fred never overdid the alcohol, ever on alert to catch a snippet of conversation that could be of use to him. Everything on board became damp from the now humid air. Then it became really hot and dancing was suddenly out —too hot for anyone to move. What was there left to do but drink in the Smoke Room? "White Ladies", "Sidecars" and many other cocktails were dreamt up by the enterprising barmen.

On Sunday, 28th July Fred was pacing the decks when he suddenly spied some fishing smacks just like pictures he'd seen of the "Blue Nose" that plied the Ramsgate waters in the late 19th century. As the "Majestic" steamed past a lightship, Fred knew they were soon likely to see multiple lightships, and if these sentinel beacons were indeed seen, it meant they were coming into the Ambrose Channel, the main shipping channel for the New York Bay's harbour. What a relief that would be, to be over the general *ennui* of this phase of his long journey to Moscow! He made enquiries and learned that, indeed, they should pass the Ambrose light station at four the following morning.

Fred flew back to his cabin to start packing, sweat pouring down his brow. "Happlegate," he cried out, "get packing, old chum, we're almost there!"

The weather was getting even hotter, with great humidity in the air. Happlegate groaned in the heat but hauled his own suitcase out from under his bunk and got packing, too.

That night Noël Coward sang a few songs to cheer up the hot and grumpy passengers. He even pulled off his famous cravat at one point, using it to mop his damp brow. The audience hooted out to him in appreciation, for this was a first for the chic Mr. Coward, they were sure!

Next, a Hungarian violinist called Bela Beyoni sat down to entertain them—and he was very good—but at intermission everyone started drifting away, wanting to pack or get some sleep before they made shore the following day. Bela himself finally packed his violin away in its case, tossed off a smiling "goodnight" to his audience and slipped off to his cabin to sleep.

At one in the morning Fred awoke to note the pilot was being brought on board. He heard some commotion so quickly dressed, without awakening Happlegate. Fred stood at the deck's railings listening to the shouted comments between the pilot and ship's captain, and looking across at the lights of New York City. Then he retired to bed again to grab a few hours' sleep before the next phase of his adventure was to begin.

---

1. *Mrs. Mullins, Molly's Cheniston Gardens landlady.*
2. *After the war, when working at Latimer House, Fred learned that Coward had been trained in espionage at Bletchley Park, along with his good friend Ian Fleming. Coward used his fame as a performer and a playboy as a cover for his antifascist espionage courier work.*

Chapter 7

July, 1940
New York City

It was now Monday, 29th July. Happlegate poked Fred to hurriedly tell him, "Hey, Fred, old man, it's 6 am. We're docking. Get yourself out of bed and up on deck!"

Fred leapt out of his bunk, dressed and rushed with Happlegate up the stairs onto the deck to watch the "Majestic" dock at its pier near Brooklyn, New York City.

Immigration Officers climbed aboard at 7 am as the ship crept nearer and nearer to the dock. It was terribly, humidly, hot—102 degrees Fahrenheit (almost 39 Celsius). Through the heat Fred couldn't see much of the Statue of Liberty or the New York skyline. The Captain, aided by the pilot, inched the huge vessel alongside Pier 56 at 14th Street, finally tying up to the capstans at 9 am. Fred loved recording such details in his diary—you never knew when such things would be needed for the future and he was after all, a careful, cautious individual, neat in both physical appearance and mind.

Parting from Fred Happlegate, he got through Customs and Immigration without any difficulties. He was fascinated by how one got around in New York City. He took a taxi, then a bus and a subway to Broadway. For him, the buses were quite different from the London double deckers. These were a single decker and you paid the nickel fare (5¢) as you climbed on board. He learned that if he paid an extra two cents and bought a transfer ticket, he could change onto another bus. He found the New York City subways old-fashioned compared to London's because he had to drop his nickel into a glass receptacle and then pass through a barrier with no ticket issued. When he reached Broadway, he changed £1 in silver and received exactly $2.50 for it.

He then went on to Cunard House at 25 Broadway and met his contacts, a Mr. Hagward and a Mr. Jones, per a "secret" message passed to him from Coward. They were friendly to him and gave him $200, saying he'd need this money for the next stage.

He continued on to Beaver Street to pick up a shipboard friend called Laurie Kingsway. She was a nice girl, friendly, and would probably like Molly. Fred took to girls easier than to men. They were easier to talk to. He liked girls. Some, like this Laurie, were highly intelligent. But if only this Laurie were actually his Molly.

Both of them had lunch at an automat restaurant, the details of which delighted Fred. You got a strip of paper with prices printed on it ranging from 5 to 100 cents. You took a plate and picked up at the counter what you wanted, with the price you had to pay being printed on the card in the respective section.

A detective and business friend of Laurie Kingsway's then took them both to the pier to collect their luggage but the luggage-handlers refused to hand it out, insisting on sending it to the hotel themselves. They took a yellow cab to the hotel that had been recommended to them: the Cornish Arms, W. 23rd Street, 8th Avenue, in the Chelsea district of New York City. His room was noisy and small but it had its own "lav" and only cost him $2 a night, a reasonable price for the New York of the 1940s. When nervous, Fred sometimes suffered from an upset stomach, so, having his own toilet *en suite* was a boon to him.

That afternoon he went to the Canadian Pacific Railroad ticket office at 344 Madison Avenue to order himself a sleeper on the train out of the City, costing him an extra $15. With Molly still so much on his mind, and also wanting to connect with his mother's sister Auntie Ciss in Canada, he cabled them both. He hoped to leave New York around Wednesday, 31st July to get to Calgary on 4th August, spend a few days with Auntie Ciss then carry on to Vancouver.

It was so hot that he and Laura decided to go to the pictures to see "The Life of Tom Brown of Rugby," mainly because it was an air-conditioned theatre where they could escape the humid heatwave. It was 108 Fahrenheit outside the movie theatre (over 42 Celsius). He found it hard to breathe and had perspiration running in rivulets down his body, even as he was walking about in an open-necked shirt with grey flannel trousers, carrying his navy sports jacket. Oh, how good it would be to have lightweight clothing instead. It was far too hot for him to do much sightseeing at all—at first all he managed to do was to creep on the shady side of the street from soda fountain to soda fountain, stopping to hydrate his body, slaking his ever-present thirst. Maybe it was the excessive heat that threw him into a bad mood, confessing to his diary that he didn't much like the Yanks because they were "a rough and tough lot".

Awakening to a new day Fred decided he'd better have at least a quick look around New York in spite of the humid heat. Along with Laura, he went to Times Square then, needing to cool down, they ducked into the Paramount Theater at 10 am and saw "Untamed" for 28¢. This was a stage show with Louis Armstrong's band, consisting completely of men referred to in those days as "negroes". The Paramount was a tremendous, large, theatre, lavishly decorated and the show impressed Fred with its dancers and spiritual songs. He'd never seen anything like it before.

After lunch, Laura went home to the hotel to rest and Fred continued on to 33rd Street to the Empire State Building. He took the express lift for $1.10 up to the 89th storey observatory and, in his ever-detailed fashion, noted it zoomed up 1,000 feet per minute. From there he took another car up to the 102nd storey where he caught a beautiful view over New York City. Berthed at the docks he noted the "Britannic", his own "Majestic", "Cameronia", "Normandie", the "Queen Elizabeth", and even the brand new American liner, the "America". On a clear day you could see ships 50 miles out at sea.

Needing a rest himself, and after collecting his train tickets, he went back to the Cornish Arms. He had the concierge ring upstairs to connect him to Laura's room to see if she was up and about.

"Oh boy, yes, fruit and ice drinks sound wonderful, just perfect," and she ran downstairs to join him in the lounge.

At 7.15 pm Fred Happlegate, his old cabin mate, called for Fred. They went off to the Wilcott Hotel on W 32nd Street, to collect a Miss Larsen, another of their shipboard chums. For Fred, having been used to a rigid blackout back in London, it was strange to see the blazing lights of Times Square at night. He also jumped in alarm every time he heard the cop cars' sirens, so like a London air raid siren. The little group finished up the evening at the Crossroads Café opposite the "Flatiron" building on 42nd Street. The main language he heard amongst the cosmopolitan crowd was Italian, and a rough and impolite lot they were, in their black shirts and yellow ties. The police officers also resembled gangsters to Fred, with their revolvers and cartridges 'round their big stomachs. He'd never seen so many black people in his life. He found the trams queer-looking with their open sides with wire netting.

On the Wednesday, 31st July, after another sleepless night due to the excessive heat, he walked down 8th Avenue and took a tram from Pennsylvania Station for the World's Fair. It only took him 20 minutes and the coaches were roomy and nice and clean but, so hot —no air-conditioning.

His first look at the Fair, even though it was a beautiful sight, had him reckoning that the Paris 1937 Fair had been much better.

Even though he found The British Pavilion to be the best, the Italian Pavilion was very pretty. He noted that Germany, perhaps unsurprisingly, wasn't represented. The "Aquacade" was in a tremendously large open-air theatre with a huge stage in front of which was a long swimming pool, with high diving towers at each side. Eighty girls and 40 men swam in columns to the time of a waltz. Other swimmers dressed as clowns jumped from 60-foot high boards, while one or two of the Olympiade divers showed off some good moves. What a lot to tell Molly about! If only, if only she were here with him!

In the evening he had farewell drinks with Fred Happlegate and Miss Larsen back at Times Square and tried hot dogs and hamburgers for the very first time.

"Sorry, and especially because it's wartime, but I tell you, German Bratwurst is actually quite superior to this so-called hot dog. This is rubbish. And hamburgers? In a bun, a hamburger? You wouldn't catch anyone in Hamburg eating this stuff," Fred huffed in the evening heat. He made a mental note to shut up! No, New York City was too noisy, too hot, filled with rough types, tawdry women and gangsters—no, you could keep New York, he decided.

Tomorrow was going to be another stage of his adventure on the long journey to get to Moscow, so he packed his suitcase at the hotel, wrote up his journal in code and tried to sleep. Tossing and turning in the usual humid heat, he thought about the surprise Auntie Ciss was going to get when he actually showed up on her doorstep in Calgary!

Sunday, 30th July, 1940
Letter Number TEN!!!!

Darlingest Freddie,

You must be in New York by now. Freddie, my Freddie, my dearest husband (mind you, not that I have another one, hahaha!), I still miss you so very much.

I trust you received all my previous letters? I have kept copies of them, via carbon paper, as we'd said we would. I said I'd try to write every night, didn't I!

Do you like New York? Dad says he hated it; too much hustle and bustle and too many people. He says London has all of that but is so much more civilised. He said there's a whole section "uptown" in a place called Harlem which is where hundreds and hundreds of negroes live. I can't imagine that. He says there's a fabulous club there called The Cotton Club. Did you get to go there? It's for white people only but has the best black musicians and dancers. Cab Calloway, Duke Ellington and loads of others. I love all that music; I know you do, too. Dad loved that nightclub.

Remember my tap-dancing, and Mrs. Mullins complained about the noise and used her walking stick to bang on her ceiling? Dad says there are loads of famous tappers at The Cotton Club: the Nicholas Brothers, Sandman Sims, Honi Coles, oh, all the best ones, and all negroes, of course. They're all so young! And they have a much better sense of rhythm that we do. I wonder why?

He also said to tell you it might be closed right now; I wonder if it is, and if so, why? I forgot to ask him. It can't be because of the war because the Americans aren't in it. Yet, Dad said. He knows so much about everything.

If I were there with you, I'd make you take me!

Have you got any of my letters yet? I'm writing frequently, like we said. I've not got anything from you yet. Why? Why? Why? I rang the Foreign Office but they said you're on ships and trains and may not have been able to leave letters for me at a British Consulate. Surely in New York you could? Okay, you'll have done that, I know, so I'll be waiting for one from you. It's awful not hearing from you, just horrid.

Love you, as ever,
Your own Molly

The Cornish Arms Hotel, New York City. Fred's postcard.

Chapter 8

August, 1940
Onward to Canada by Train

On Thursday, 1st August, 1940 Fred dashed over to the British Consulate and left a packet of letters to be sent in the diplomatic bag to his wife in London. The guard said he'd give them to a cultural attaché to take care of the minute the Consulate opened for the day. He planned numbering all his letters from the USSR, as Molly's were and, like her, he also used carbon copies to store in his own letter-writing folder, in the event a letter never showed up. But, he wasn't numbering all his letters and postcards sent *en route*. Maybe this was a mistake. This was wartime and many letters never made it to their destination, sometimes because the Consulate bag was full of "more important" communications. It was true the USA wasn't yet at war with Germany but, certainly, there were many *communiqués* being passed through diplomatic channels between the USA and England.

At 8.50 in the morning the Empire State Express pulled out of

New York for Calgary, in the province of Alberta, Canada. Staring out the train's window Fred saw that they were following the Hudson, a broad New York river, part of which ran along the west side of Manhattan Island. Tugboats spewing black smoke chugged along. Leaving the City behind, he saw proud mansions gracing the riverbanks, their white colonnades peeping through thick brush and tall trees. The scenery was pretty and reminded him of parts of the Rhine.

In his habit for precision and detail (you never knew when facts like this would be useful—his personal mantra) he informed his diary that at 1.30 pm they passed Utica, where he was able to hop off to post a letter to his brother, Herman (no time to find a diplomatic channel to send it through); Syracuse at 2.30 pm; Rochester at 3.45 pm; Buffalo at 4.50 pm, Erie Fort Station at 6 pm, but they just missed going past Niagara Falls—to his great dismay. They went through Passport Control at Erie Fort Station 13 miles farther downriver. That meant they were now in Canada!

To his delight the weather was now grand and not so stinking hot as in New York. He ate trout on the train. He loved trout. The most fun part, after carefully lifting out the whole backbone in one fell swoop, was to scoop out the cheeks of the trout—one of the greatest delicacies of the fish family to savour. He must remember to show Molly how to do that with a special fish knife; but maybe her father had already shown her? Leaning back, he thought about how there was so much he didn't even know about his own wife. With a smile, he happily told himself they had a whole life coming up to learn every detail.

Fred was able to find newspapers at Erie Fort Station and read that the news regarding the USSR and Japan was not too good. He thought about his upcoming work in Russia and wondered how long before Hitler would make a push to reach Moscow and how that would impact his own work. He didn't expect there to be any trusted contacts on board this train for him to discreetly discuss the politics of the war with. He mused that if there were, they'd have to locate him…

At 7.30 pm they steamed through Hamilton and he got a beautiful view of Lake Ontario.

His carriage companion was an older man of mixed race, with long black hair going grey and tied to one side in a plait. Fred was mesmerized by him, never having seen a hairstyle on a man like this before.

"I see ya staring at me, young fellah. Yep, I'm one o' them half-breeds they call us, half white, half American Indian, the Huron people. In my ancestors' tongue, what spoke the Wyandot Iroquoian language, ya know—so ya know what Ontario means?"

"No idea, naturally, but I'd certainly like to know!"

"Weeelllll, we call it 'the Lake of Shining Waters' and, if ya look outta the window at it, ya can sure tell why!"

It was smooth, placid, blue, almost like a skating rink reflecting an azure sky. Fred knew from his earlier mapping out of his journey that Canada lies to the north, east, and southwest of this lake, with New York State situated to the east and south. For his work, it was imperative that Fred knew facts like this, and remembered them. His internal motto was always to "be prepared," just like the Girl Guides in England—as he gave a wry smile—repeating those two words over and over to himself in time to the rhythm of the train's puffing and chugging as its pistons powered it over the rails.

An hour later the train pulled into Toronto, a clean, spacious, modern city, which, having no nightlife to speak of, was therefore called the "good" city. Everyone got out of the train to stretch their legs and stroll around to stare at the nearby houses. At 9.30 pm they were back on the train and at 10.55 pm it puffed its way out of the station. The New York office had recommended Fred take an upper berth, which, to his mind at this point, had been quite foolish, but there was no opportunity now to get a lower berth, all being sold out. All night long he was shaken about as his roped berth swayed from side to side, sometimes even bumping him up toward the carriage ceiling—leaving him feeling in the morning as if he'd slept in a cocktail mixer.

Leaving the compartment to go along to the train's dining car, the Indian man stuck out a huge hand and grasped Fred's.

"Good to meet ya, young fellah. M'name's Tionnontateheronnes. I won't tell ya how to spell it!"

"Well, good to meet you, too, the name's Fred here, F-r-e-d!", grinned Fred, thinking how he was absolutely, certainly 'abroad' now, in a whole different world. The man with the plait grinned back at him, enjoying his humour. Fred thought, Happlegate's name was queer enough, but this fellow's name…well! It made his own Read-Jahn surname seem positively simple to pronounce. On Friday, 2nd August, tired out and annoyed by the high cost of the food on board (breakfast alone cost him 75¢, at par with the English cost of 3 shillings), he cheered up by staring resolutely out the window of the observation car to take in the view. They were steaming past dozens and dozens of small, pretty, rivers and lakes surrounded by pine forests and rocks. The old Indian strolled in and sat across from him.

At 5 pm they reached Lake Superior. Tionnontateheronnes touched his arm to get his attention.

"Didya know that Superior's the only name outta all these lakes that ain't an Indian word? No? Thought ya didn't. Ya needn't be lookin' in that there guide book you got. I can tell ya anything ya wanna know 'bout these parts!"

Fred looked appreciatively at the man, thinking I'll bet he could, he looks pretty darned wise. Must be the long greying hair!

The train continued past the lake as far as Fort Williams, which they reached at 10.05 pm He looked in his guidebook to see that this lake is 360 miles long, and saw the old Indian shaking his head at him. He could see people walking along the lakeside track, which looked very picturesque with its terribly steep precipices. At one point, Fred lowered his window to smell the air, hoping to catch a whiff of pine trees. The air that delightfully invaded his nostrils was wonderfully crisp and invigorating. He felt like a king sitting on the terrace of the observation car and sipping a good cup of coffee.

Suddenly feeling tired again, he got hold of a conductor and was able to talk him into exchanging his upper berth for a lower one. Tionnontateheronnes had disappeared, rather to Fred's relief. He didn't feel like chatting anymore. He fell onto his bunk with a sigh and went straight to sleep to the rocking of the car, and the rhythmic sound of the pistons forcing the train's wheels forward over the joints of the rails: "rat-tat-tat, rat-tat-tat; rat-tat-tat, rat-tat-tat," "Be prepared, be prepared, be prepared, be prepared…".

Fred could tell that Saturday, 3rd August was going to be another scorcher but he'd had a good rest in his lower bunk and was ready for the day. The train pulled into Winnipeg at 9.20 am, where they had a one-hour stop. He walked around outside the station a little and saw that Winnipeg looked like a typical American city—it had no face. He scribbled postcards to his darling Molly and to his mum. At 10.20 am the whistle blew and off they went again.

From his carriage window he saw grassy, flat land and realised they were coming to the prairie. His thoughts flew with excitement to more Indians, to herds of buffalo, to all those exotic people and animals he'd learned inhabited the Canadian prairies. And, oh boy, he'd already met one! One with an appropriately unpronounceable name! Yessir, he was overseas alright. Oh, if only Molly could have met that old chap!

By 4.10 pm they were passing Brandon Broadview. The view outside had become monotonous. He picked up a newspaper he'd bought back in Winnipeg. The news was becoming worse and worse. Lowering the paper onto his lap, he stared sightlessly out the window again, wondering whether he'd actually be able to get to Moscow? What would he do, if not? It was imperative he reach the British Embassy in Moscow to use his knowledge of German, sit at the cypher machines, break codes, and all the other secret intelligence work he'd been trained by the military and Foreign Office to do. Even though having been commanded not to wear his military uniform, he was under the direct command of the British military's intelligence branch, working hand-in-hand with the Foreign Office, and, of course, undercover for Morgan Crucible. He mused that his uniform was on its way in the FO's diplomatic bag to Moscow for any possible military events. Then there was the difficult and highly dangerous job of getting certain people out of Moscow. That was going to be very hard. He'd been told he'd need to learn to ski to handle that job. Thinking about all of that let hour after boring hour pass by.

He left his carriage to stretch his legs. Walking down the train's side-aisle, he noticed some Canadian Airforce and Army officers in another carriage. Searching for information, he casually glanced at them through the window and tried to make eye contact. When one or two of them noticed him and smiled, he slid their door aside to say a friendly hello, and they invited him in. Great! They were drinking. Maybe some information he could use would slip out. A bottle of beer got passed to him and a space created on the long seat by some good-natured shoving and pushing of the young officers. They were a fine crowd, not averse to chatting about the political climate within Canada and the world at war. Fred picked up bits and pieces of some potentially useful information before wandering back to his own carriage. His new civilian carriage companion was feeling a little chatty, too, so Fred was able to also get an idea of how the civilians felt about such matters. He filed away into his head the information he'd gleaned then fell back onto his bunk to read away the rest of the day; writing felt far too strenuous—besides, he didn't feel up to putting the new knowledge into code in his diary quite yet.

Fred's train through Canada.

Hidden in Plain Sight

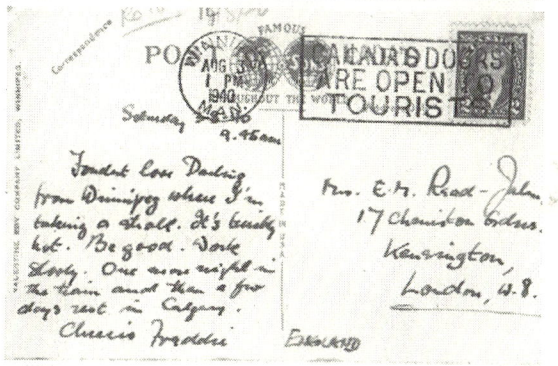

Postcard to Molly from Winnipeg on 3rd August, 1940.

Chapter 9

August, 1940
Calgary, the Prairie, and Banff, Canada

At last they arrived in Calgary, at 8.45 am on 4th August, 1940. The train was divided into three sections here. Calgary didn't look like a very large place at all, from what Fred could see from the train, yet there were crowds of people waiting at the station. When he saw there was nobody there to greet him as he descended from the train, Fred wondered whether Auntie Ciss had even received his cable announcing his intention to visit her briefly. In these wartime days, you could never be sure that letters or cables would get there. Along with a slight worry creasing his forehead, he had to smile as he realised, if that were the case, boy, was she going to get a huge surprise when he rang her doorbell!

He stood on the platform next to his luggage, realizing his aunt and uncle might not even be in Calgary. They could have gone away somewhere; maybe taken a holiday. Who knew? Well, nothing for it but to go to the house and ring the doorbell. He checked his luggage into a locker at the station, not knowing how far he'd have to walk. Outside the station he stood there thinking for a bit then asked a chap nearby for directions. The kindly man immediately offered to take Fred right to the house in his car.

Fred rang the bell, his excitement making his heart race just a little bit. Auntie Ciss opened the door, beamed widely, and embraced him.

"Fred! Oh, Fred, you're here! I'd know you at once, you've not changed a bit. I got your cable. George and Ned went to the station to meet you but must have missed you. Oh dear. Well, they'll be back soon."

Auntie Ciss looked so much like his mother, she could have been her twin sister! In fact, his mother Clara, her sisters Ciss and Ada, all three of his aunts, could have been triplets, they looked so remarkably alike. A slight sob rose in Fred's throat as he held his Aunt in his arms, smelling her lavender scent, so like his mum's.

Ciss's husband, George, and someone called Ned, came rushing in but a few minutes later. They had seen Fred standing outside the station but, because he had had no luggage with him, they presumed it wasn't the right man.

Auntie Ciss prattled on in vast excitement, "Why, it's been 27 whole years since I've seen anyone from 'home'. And here you are, my, oh my, my heart is fluttering with joy, dear Freddie."

"Auntie, you look wonderful, and mum says to give you her warmest love and here, here's the kiss she sends you!"

"Well, I've not slept a single wink since receiving your cable. You know you're the first member of our family I've seen since I left England to come out here to Canada back in 1913. Imagine that!"

"Now Fred, you know my husband, George, and this here's our lodger, Ned. A good chap, you'll get on well with him. Plus, he's going to show you the sights in his old Ford. Ain't we lucky, to have our own chauffeur, eh? Hahaha."

She busied herself making a big breakfast for everyone, chattering, asking after her two sisters, his recent marriage, dropping things, laughing at her butterfingers, bustling about and carrying on in general. Fred found her charming, his heart continuing to ache a little for his beloved mother in England, who was in such wartime danger, and whom Ciss and Ada so much resembled in face and rather plump comfortable figure.

After eating, they all piled into Ned Farrow's car, an old 1930s Ford, and went for a drive Ned expected to be around 160 miles (257 km), following trails all through the prairie. These were only dirt trails, there being no roads built across the prairie. Ned was boarding with Ciss and George and had become a close friend. At one point they got lost, having to find their way back to the right trail. These dirt roads were pretty bumpy but Fred didn't mind one jot—he was in the rumble seat outside at the back of the Ford. It was far better being outside in a car in the fresh air than on that boring, sometimes stiflingly hot, train.

After a picnic lunch brought by Ciss, sitting out on the prairie, they proceeded to the Turner Valley Oilfields. Fred took photos here because he had an inkling this sort of information could serve the British military well, since Canada had become involved in the war in a number of different ways. Auntie Ciss stood at the oilfields, shaking her head and sighing. She'd lost quite a bit of money in speculations at these fields.

Driving on, they crawled past the ranch of an important resident in the area. Ned slowed the old car down further, to yell back at Fred in the rumble seat,

"Hey Fred, that there's the Earl of Egmont's ranch. Bet ya didn't know he was born in a shack on the prairie. Fancy that, an earl born in a prairie shack, eh?!"

Driving on, they came to another stop.

"Okay, Fred, listen up. This ranch here belongs to you'll-never-guess-who...the Duke of Windsor! He got it in 1936 after the, ya know, the royal disaster..."

"Really, Edward VIII's place, honestly?" said Fred, giving the place a good once-over from the car.

"No kiddin', it sure is," commented Ned.

They all sighed and shook their heads.

"Tut, tut, imagine a king of England abdicating his throne. And an affair! With that American, Mrs. Wallis Simpson, a divorcée, yet!

What is the world coming to? Such a scandal!" exclaimed Ciss salaciously.

On they drove, and, to Fred's delight, he saw an old American Indian on a white horse, so quickly snapped a photo.

"Them thar red injuns be of the Sarcee tribe," shouted Ned, from the driver's seat.

Ned suddenly stood on the brakes as a thundering sound approached in a swirling cloud of dust.

"What in the name of God is that?" cried out Fred.

"Buffalo, whole herd gonna pass us by. I'll stay right firm here and they ain't gonna go near us," replied Ned.

When the herd had disappeared like a freight train into the distance in a huge cloud of dust, Fred was keen to drive through the Indian Reserve that George had mentioned. There he saw Indians standing or sitting silently by the side of the dirt track, wrapped in faded old blankets. Still seated in the rumble seat in the back of the old Ford, not only was he getting plenty of fresh air, but a lot more dust. The trail was terribly bumpy, and he thought it a wonder the old car didn't collapse.

When they'd stopped again, he learned from his companions that these Sarcees, and most other Indians, were living in reserves, which cover an area of about 250 square miles (402 sq km) each. The younger generation of Indians spoke English and were educated at the same standard as white men. Their mother tongue was rapidly vanishing, much to the dismay of their elders.

These aboriginal Canadians drove cars and lived in houses, whereas the older generations still hunted, fished, lived in wigwams, and were often very dirty, many suffering from tuberculosis. No alcoholic drink was allowed on the reservations due to a disposition of the Indians to become quarrelsome and run amok.

When out of hearing of any Indians, George told Fred, "These guys tend to want to shoot off guns when under the influence of alcohol. Can get pretty dangerous 'round here. The government's given 'em a small grant of money so many of 'em just laze about. Now, others, for sure, are actually quite good farmers. This should be encouraged, don'tcha say?"

Fred did say, agreeing wholeheartedly, adding, "Back in Old Blighty farmers don't have to sign up for the front, and, as a matter of fact, nor do any chaps with asthma or flat feet. Lucky buggers, in a way, able to miss the whole war, eh?"

They then drove to take a look at the new RCAF aerodrome at Currie Field. This was of much interest, of course, to Fred, ever on the alert for any military knowledge he could gain in his travels. He knew that some of those Canadian Airforce chaps he'd chatted to on the train were on their way here. They weren't deployed there just to sit on their thumbs. Thinking of what he knew about Canada's military efforts in general, he'd learned from his intelligence sources that back in January, 1940 the Canadian Active Service Force's first and second contingents had left for Europe, and that Canada was well involved in the war effort in other ways, too.

He knew that as this year of 1940 progressed, passenger ships had already been converted into warships; that minesweepers and ships including corvettes were being built in the shipyards at Vancouver. In fact, there was a Hero-class ship, the St. Roch, built twelve years earlier also in Vancouver. She was now in operation as a Royal Canadian Mounted Police patrol ship for the Western Arctic operations. With all the imperative security around shipping departures, it hadn't been reported in the papers that she'd sailed out of Vancouver on June 23rd, 1940, heading for Sydney, Nova Scotia and on through the Canadian Arctic, but Fred had heard this from his intelligence sources. This journey was to take two years and Fred had heard that she would be the first vessel to travel both directions of the Northwest Passage. This type of ship was named for personnel from the Mounties, the Canadian Coast Guard, the Canadian fisheries officers, and the Canadian forces in general, all known to have performed heroic acts during their military service.

Fred, ever detail-minded, relished learning all this information, and had enjoyed discovering that the St. Roch was mainly made of thick Douglas Fir, with hard Australian Eucalyptus 'Ironbark' on the outside. For its Arctic voyages, the designers had cleverly ordered its hull to be reinforced with heavy beams that were well able to withstand the Arctic conditions and pressures of solid ice.[1]

The following day, Monday, 5th August, the little clan set off at 10 am for Banff, unfortunately breaking down at Cochrane. Ned and George quite quickly got the old Ford going again, so after a quick lunch they set off for Ghost Dam Power Station. Fred loved its romantic name, snapping his usual photo for possible use at some point further on in the war. Then, at The Great Divide, Alberta, British Columbia, came the Stoney Indian Reserve—and a snap of the monument for posterity. There they took a long winding drive through Banff National Park—with a photo snap of deer (that would be a shot Molly would like, he told Ciss).

So far the old Ford had been carrying them some 85 miles (137 km) from Calgary. Pretty soon they were driving past the Kananaskis Prisoner of War Camp. His guides told him the location had been taken over in September of 1939, just the year before, by the Canadian Department of Defence. They held civilian internees and enemy merchant seamen in there. The guards kept the internees busy by making them clear the valley of brush and trees. Fred also snapped a shot of the monument nearby erected in memory of the first white missionary to the area, a Methodist called John McDougall. Early in life the enterprising young McDougall had taught himself Ojibwa in order to preach and convert the Indians who spoke the indigenous Ojibwa language.

Just before arriving in Banff, the old Ford rocked to one side with a flat tyre. Fred helped change the tyre then off they drove again, to see cavern basins, sulphur springs, and fish hatchings. Fred made a mental note to tell Molly that one day he'd bring her back here because all of these things in this area made Banff a significant place to visit in the Rockies. She'd be fascinated; maybe not by the aerodrome or power station, but definitely by the mountains, the animals, the Indians, and even the POW camp. He looked forward to telling her about the thundering herd of buffalo—she'd be nervous about that and he'd get to hold her tight as his imaginary herd crashed past them—what a thrill that would be!

The little group also looked at the view of the Rockies from the terrace of the Canadian Pacific Railroad's majestic Banff Springs Hotel, and took a look at the Bow River Falls nearby. This really

Hidden in Plain Sight

grand hotel, surrounded by thick forest and rocky mountains, draped in cloaks of green rearing up behind it, was built in 1888 in the Scottish Baronial style. Fred thought to himself that you could perhaps imagine at its opening back then a Scottish piper in his colourful kilt standing at the entrance, playing Scotland the Brave on his bagpipes, while indigenous Indians stood in their next-to-nothings and feathered headdresses shaking their heads in bemused and sorrowful amazement.

There were tales told gleefully to Fred by his Auntie Ciss and George, that "the Castle", as it was known locally, was haunted, including one story that actually told of Fred's imagined Scottish bagpiper playing his pipes, indeed, but headless! Perhaps easier to believe is the most iconic, famous, tale of the hotel's phantom bride. Ciss, with evident relish, rubbing her hands together, intoned to Fred in a suitably gloomy sepulchral voice, "In the early 1930s a young couple had been wedded in Banff, holding their wedding dinner in this grand hotel. Before the wedding feast, the newlywed bride climbed up the marble staircase to join her husband, where he stood at the top awaiting her. As she ascended, her wedding gown brushed against one of the candles lighting the staircase, setting her white gown on fire. In her panic, she tripped on her gown, and tumbled, blazing, down the staircase, to break her neck at the bottom of the marble stairs and die. How about THAT, then?"

"Well", said Fred, "you tell a good tale. Good thing my wedding wasn't held here, wasn't it?!"

The little group had their dinner in the town of Banff. Fred found a shop that sold Indian moccasins so bought a pair for his Molly, imagining her cheeky smile as she'd prance around to show them off to him when next he saw her. Thinking again of the tale of the unfortunate phantom bride, he was glad he and Molly had married in a simple church ceremony near her home in England.

The tremendous snow- and ice-covered mountains of the Rockies staggered Fred. He couldn't get enough of seeing the rushing waters and waterfalls, the truly gorgeous stately pine forests and superb hotels. All its beauty humbled him; he also appreciated that since he was forced to take this circuitous route to get to

Moscow, what a fabulous opportunity he'd received, to see all this beauty.

Auntie Ciss said, "Back when my Will was alive, he brought me to this Banff area. Imagine," she laughed, "how different it was for me after having grown up in the midlands of England. I sure felt my mind had been broadened as wide as the prairie from all this beauty and strangeness!"

At 7.30 pm they all piled back into the Ford, with poor Fred trying to hold warm thoughts of Molly while now suffering the very cold ride in the open rumble seat back to Calgary, which they didn't reach until four freezing hours later.

All in all, they'd driven over 200 miles (322 km) that, in Canada, is considered only a short run. Fred had heard that people thought nothing of travelling 500 miles (805 km) to visit somebody, the distances being so vast in this continent. It amazed him that the distances in Canada are so tremendous that it had taken him $3\frac{1}{2}$ days of continual travelling to get from New York to Calgary. His guide book told him the province of Alberta alone is several times larger than the whole of the British Isles. He found that truly staggering.

On 6th August, a Tuesday, Fred awoke, happy enough, but tired out from his rumble seat sightseeing tour of the day before. He sat around and chatted with his aunt and the others, then went off to chat with a Mr. & Mrs. Maidenhair at the Armouries, very good friends of Ciss's, and a very nice couple Ciss thought he'd enjoy talking with. He had some strong coffee with them then a rousing conversation mainly with Mr. Maidenhair about Social Credit and Technocracy. Again, Fred wondered about the names some of these people had. Maidenhair, indeed! His, of course, was perfectly normal!

"Now listen", he told them. "I simply don't believe that any technical expert élite in the government should be permitted to economically control society or industrial companies. This leads to the poor never getting out of poverty. If a poor person needs an item, he shouldn't be permitted to make small payments against its cost "on credit". Now that's what in England we call the 'the never-

never'. It's becoming much too prevalent in England. It incurs interest, with the idea that finally your debt gets reduced to zero."

Mrs. Maidenhair said, "Well, I couldn't live without my credit card. It's a great new invention!"

Mr. Maidenhair chimed in, "Now see here, Fred, in Canada, oh, and in the great US of A, we all believe firmly in credit. You gotta have a credit card, or you ain't considered a true member of modern society. Ya need one just to even rent a car; bet ya didn't know that?"

Fred said, "No, I didn't, but look, it's okay for people with a good job who can pay the loan back every month, although the interest can be crushing, but, I still insist it's a known fact that poor people have far too difficult a time finding a darned job, and hanging onto it, in these war years, so they shouldn't be allowed to go on the never-never. The poor sods are sent off to fight, and if they even make it home, often the job they'd held before leaving has now gone—been filled by some other lucky bugger. I tell you, I can see how some years down the road and into the future this very thing is going to prove the downfall of these countries' economy. Debt, debt, debt—a dangerous concept."

The conversation continued on, and more coffee was poured.

Tired, once home at his aunt's, but stimulated by his talk with the Maidenhairs and probably wide awake again from all that coffee, he dashed off a letter to his mother in England, noting:

"On Thursday morning I shall leave Calgary for Vancouver and shall look up that business friend of Molly's father. Auntie Ciss has nephews in Vancouver. I might stay with them the night. My boat should sail on Saturday, 10th*, and then I shall be cut off from the world for 10 days."*

Business friends of people he knew were very valuable to Fred. He'd discreetly mine them for information.[2] He had been told by the Foreign Office that the business friend of Molly's father was actually one of his contacts for passing along information on this long journey. Sometimes it turned out that someone would approach him with a message, but often he'd be given a name to watch out for. He knew his mother would pass along any information he gave her to his brother, Herman, who, in turn, would ensure it was whispered into the right ears.

Wednesday, 7th August, dawned bright and clear. After chatting away the morning with his hosts, Fred was driven off by Ned to see the National History Park on St George's Island. There he saw all sorts of Canadian native animals: skunk, timber wolf, bear, coyote, hyena, grizzly bear (huge!), more buffalo, mountain sheep, goats, and antelopes. They even had a skeleton of a dinosaur found in the rocks of Red Deer River that was 150,000,000 years old!

Fred spent that last evening at his aunt's learning more about his family. His mother's mother, Grandma Read, had been a Morley before marriage, and that member of the family was, indeed, a well-known member of parliament. Fred was pleased to realise that if he hadn't made this trip, it was doubtful he'd have found out these nuggets of his family history. After talking into the late evening, Auntie Ciss rummaged around in her "treasure box" and brought out a bracelet made up of eleven pennies. Another gift for his darling Molly!

Hidden in Plain Sight

a) Auntie Ciss & Fred. b) Auntie Ciss, Fred, Uncle George.

Sarcee Indian, Calgary prairie, 4th August, 1940,

SHIRLEY READ-JAHN

Turner Valley Oilfields near Calgary, 4th August, 1940.

The haunted Banff Springs Hotel. Postcard purchased by Fred.

Hidden in Plain Sight

Ghost Dam Power Station near Cochrane, Alberta. 5th August, 1940.

Mr. Ned Farrow outside his 1930s Ford. Auntie Ciss & Uncle George inside the car.

SHIRLEY READ-JAHN

The Great Divide, Alberta, British Columbia.

Buffalo on the Prairie, British Columbia. Postcard purchased by Fred.

1. *The St. Roch made three voyages in all; sailed back to Vancouver in 1954 to be preserved, and in 1962 was Designated a Canadian Historic Site.*
2. *Later in life, well after the war, Fred would laughingly say how he'd trained himself to be excellent as a public relations person. He could talk to anyone, garner information, and remember it all. Before you knew it, you would have told him things that you'd wonder later how he'd got them out of you!*

Chapter 10

August, 1940
Back on Train to Board Ship to Japan

On Thursday, 8th August, 1940 Fred climbed up onto the train again in Calgary. It was hot and sunny. As they chugged through the Rockies he was again much taken with the beautiful scenery. As they rounded bends, he'd lean out a little from his window and see the big black engine gasping smoke up into the air. There were quite a number of carriages for the engine to haul along. He loved watching from his vantage point, the pistons turning, hearing the clackety-clack, clackety-clack, and feeling the cold air rushing through his already-thinning hair. When puffs of engine soot came flying toward him, he hurriedly put his hands over his glasses, and narrowed his eyes for safety.

He wished, for the hundredth, no, the millionth, time, that Molly were there with him to share in all these new experiences. On the other hand, he had to confess to himself that he was relieved she wasn't; he had to be free to talk to his contacts along the way, and the less she knew about his war work, the safer she'd be. But oh, how he wanted her; how he craved for her bubbly personality, raucous happy laugh, and her soft body wrapped around him at night. There was just something so *feminine* about his wife that got him, what was it?—very, very attractive, certainly, but FUN! There it was—Molly was plain fun in everything, as well as, what? yes—he longingly had to admit—she was just plain sexy!

Pulling his head back into the carriage he plonked himself back down onto his seat to distract himself from his urges and started chatting with a local sheriff who'd boarded the train with him. Fred found him to be quick on the draw intellectually so was able to pass the long hours quizzing him discreetly about the area, Canada's politics, and any world matters he could bring up casually. In turn, the sheriff didn't let on why he was heading so far away from his police domain.

The sunset was glorious over the mountains, dark shadows throwing fantastical shapes upon the grassy meadows they chugged through. The train whistled a mournful, long, blast as they entered a black tunnel. Snaking its way out the other side, night had fallen. They came around a bend. Fred lowered the window briefly again to look out and cold air blasted in. All he could see was a long finger of light beaming directly over the tracks, cast forward by the train's engine light. Ghostly shapes and snowy glacial meadows shone whitely in the light of the half moon. He slammed down the window, apologised to the sheriff, and climbed onto his (thank you, Lord!) lower berth to get some sleep.

Up early, breakfast partaken, Fred returned to his carriage. He knew they were almost in Vancouver from the light industrial buildings and train sidings he could see outside the window. The train lurched to a sudden stop. A jovial old gentleman had been leaning in the aisle against their carriage door, which slid open and in he almost fell. Fred and the sheriff both leapt up simultaneously to catch him as he bumbled and staggered from side to side. Fred smelt alcohol on him and realised their new companion had spent the night getting rip-roaring drunk. The old chap produced his almost empty bottle of whisky and was happy to share it with his "saviours", as he slyly called them, pointing and winking at the sheriff's badge. That kindly gentleman, in turn, just shook his head, but Fred was happy enough to accept a wee dram, as he called it. Upon their speedy arrival into Vancouver, the sheriff escorted the old gentleman off the train, his hand firmly and paternally under his elbow.

It was 8.55 am. This Friday, 9th August, was to be filled with "business" for Fred. Upon arrival at the Vancouver Hotel he found cables from Molly and "Jean W" (another agent he had to talk with; interestingly, he saw that not all these were men). He had arranged to speak with "McCanley" (the "business" friend of Molly's father's Masonic Lodge) but when he arrived at his home, only his wife was present. He met up with Ed McCanley at the Metropolitan City Club where part of McCanley's mission was to introduce Fred to his next contact, a Mr. Timmins, Pro-Consul at Kobe, Japan. Things were now moving along. They both knew Kenneword[1] of Morgan Crucible, Fred's colleague at his cover job in London. Kenneword was now the Manager of the Kobe, Japan, branch of Morgan's (and a director of Morgan Crucible), was a friend of Timmins's, and Fred had orders to look him up once in Japan. Fred was also informed he would be travelling on with Timmins to Kobe.

Another person he connected with in Vancouver was a Mr. Pimston of Pacific Paper Mills. After many discussions, at four o'clock a Mr. Fiddilane, a friend of Auntie Ciss's, gave him a tour in his car of Vancouver, where he showed him Stanley Park, the beaches, and took him to Spencer's where he could purchase a raincoat. He'd mistakenly left his behind in London, as he'd told Molly in his first letter back home to England. Ed McCanley had Fred over for dinner and later, after a long, long talk, drove him to the aerodrome hotel for the night.

McCanley told Fred that there would be another "special contact" travelling with him and Timmins, a Mr. Temple. They were all to board the "Empress of Asia" the following day, headed for Japan.

Train & Cathedral Peak, Banff. Postcard of his train, purchased by Fred.

---

1. *This is the first solid mention of Fred's spying work. Fred was listed as a Foreign Office "clerk" when he set off on his journey from London, even though working for British military intelligence. Plus, the Army knew he had ostensibly left Morgan Crucible and quietly started working again for the Foreign Office, where he had worked prior to joining Morgan's. That, in turn, shows us that he had been sent back to Morgan's to start his intelligence work, was now working once more for the Foreign Office, and doubtless using the connections acquired via his Morgan's job for his war job. The fact that Timmins knew Kenneword was significant, showing the connection between the Foreign Office and Morgan's.*

Chapter 11

**August, 1940
Empress of Asia, Heading for Japan**

*17 Cheniston Gardens
Kensington, London, W.8*

Saturday, 10th August, 1940

Letter Number 11

My Own Darling Heart, Bleeding as it is,

I'm including my address on this one because I've heard nothing from you (she wrote, slyly!). Nary a word! Not even a cable. What's happened? I'm starting to worry. I rang the FO but was told, "All is going along according to plan. Fred Read-Jahn is en route, now in Canada. Nothing to worry about, Mrs. R-J." So okay, I won't worry, but I AM worried. You said you'd write every day. I don't understand.

The letters will probably all arrive in one big fat bunch and take me a lovely long week to read, hahaha! And I did like being called "Mrs. R-J"!

Freddie, Mrs. Mullins shared yesterday's newspaper with me and it says Birmingham suffered heavy bombing yesterday. They're calling it the Regenschirm, the Birmingham Blitz (but you know how to translate) but I don't really understand because I thought Regenschirm meant umbrella. I know how they must all feel up there. It's a wonder anyone can get any sleep with all the bombs, the sirens, the awful noise in general, and having to rush to the air-raid shelters at any time of the day or night.

By the way, did you know we all have to carry a gas mask with us, every day and night? They handed them out. They're little cardboard boxes holding the mask, on a rope that goes over your shoulder. They smell horrid, Freddie, of rubber and disinfectant. So far I've not had to put mine on.

Please write to me. I know you have, so where are the darned things?

Jimmie sends you lots of kisses, as I do, but his are wet from his little pink nose and oh boy, his breath is awful! I'd far prefer your kisses, but at least I do have Jimmie's! I'll just have to make do…

With all my love, as ever,

Molly

Saturday, 10th August, 1940 at 10.30 am saw McCanley at the docks to see Fred, Timmins and Temple off. They had a drink together and sailed out of Vancouver at 11 am. Fred leaned over the railings, looking down at the upturned faces, some smiling, some tearful, white handkerchiefs waving, and all the colourful streamers between the ship and the dock being pulled apart as the Empress of Asia[1] gradually separated herself from her moorings and carefully slipped away. It was a pretty scene, thought Fred, as he went down to Cabin No. 203 on B Deck to unpack, a large, airy and spacious cabin, up near the bows and below the first mast.

In the Straits they ran into quite a heavy storm. Fred was instantly seasick, and, groaning, he lay on his berth thinking, "First day you're afraid you'll die, second you are afraid you won't. What a nice way to spend my birthday!"[2]

The next few days on board saw him gradually getting his sea-legs back. He tried to stay out in the fresh air as much as possible, playing deck-tennis and other deck-games.

By Tuesday, 13th August, the weather had turned cold and wet, so he watched another "talkie", a film called "Little Tough Guy", a 1938 movie starring several of the Dead End Kids, then mixed with the crowd of passengers on board. His cabin-mate this time was a Mr. Sims, a reverend heading for Peking as a Missionary. Then there was a Miss Phanerton, on her way to Hong Kong to marry an Englishman in the Chinese Maritime Customs. Fred had a lot of fun with those two, but, more importantly, he continued with his discreet probing and chatting to garner information, particularly from the naval officers. There were many teachers and nurses, all heading for China. His most important chats were with Rear Admiral Sir Geoffrey Layton, on his way to command the Hong Kong garrison. It was through these people that Fred was eventually to make a special Chinese contact, another intelligence man who, years later, was to resurface in Hong Kong and Shanghai and, even later, in London. This contact was nicknamed Shanghai Joe. Fred was to run into him in Japan, and in the Soviet Union, and was to become a trusted colleague since they worked as intelligence agents on the same side.

One morning, strolling the decks, he met up with a small group of the garrison soldiers heading for Hong Kong. They had a Chinese fellow walking with them.

"Hullo, old man. Remember us from the movie night? This 'ere's young Shanghai Joe. Thought you'd like to know him. 'E knows lots of chaps from Old Blighty, believe it or not. Joe, old man, this 'ere's Freddie. Loads of fun, is Freddie. Shake hands and say hullo to each other!"

By Wednesday, the 14th August, it was cold, and windy, too. They were now steaming past the height of the Aleutian Islands, a chain of 14 large and 55 smaller volcanic islands. Fred pored over his world map. The islands marked the divide between the Pacific Ocean to the south and the USSR's Bering Sea to the north—a huge area, for sure.

Feeling much better from his earlier seasickness, he returned to the deck, into the cold and wind, to play all sorts of deck-games with his new-found friends, laughing hilariously as the wind would snatch the table tennis balls or the deck tennis balls out of their hands and cast them all over the deck and even over the side. There, leaning over the deck railings, Fred and his chums placed bets on whose ball would sink, or disappear from sight first. They called this game, "Sinky Da Bloody Ball", that being what Shanghai Joe repeatedly called out as he leant over the railing, nearly toppling over in excitement!

In the evenings Fred took part in Bingo games, mostly good-naturedly losing a bit of money. His two contacts, Timmins and Temple, were nice blokes, except Timmins drank far too much. Fred was much of the opinion that to do intelligence work successfully, you had to be able to hold your liquor and remain on the alert at all times. Opposite, stupid behaviour could well cause one's downfall. He would rather have steered clear of this Timmins chap, yet he knew he had to keep in with him because the plan was for Fred and Timmins both to go to the Kobe British Consulate together, and who knows, Timmins could actually be of great assistance to Fred.

Fred also spent a lot of time talking with a Captain Ranjoyman and a Mr. & Mrs. Lilac based in Shanghai. He soon picked up that these people from the East also drank like fish. He was to discover that most Colonials overseas played Bridge and drank, drank, drank —probably to hide their sorrow at being far from the green fields of their beloved England.

More deck games, and another film, "Moonlight Sonata". Tears filled his eyes in the dark as he remembered Molly playing Beethoven's Moonlight Sonata for him on her father's piano. She was an accomplished pianist. At school she'd played at all the school dances. Her music teacher had encouraged her to continue, saying she was good enough to become a concert pianist. But, her father reckoned she should learn to type instead; just in case any husband she'd eventually marry were to die, leaving her to fend for herself. She became a terrific typist and took up playing the piano accordion for fun. In his mind's eye, he saw his Molly, in her pretty flowery peasant blouse and long skirt, pushing that heavy accordion in and out with her strong arms, grinning from ear to ear, and bursting into song, all just for him. God, he missed her, his clever, his talented, darling wife.

He spent the evening of Thursday, 15th August with a Miss Boston and good old Timmins, as he'd begun to refer to him. For the first time in his life he had the experience of skipping one complete day as they crossed the dateline, meaning that the following day was to be Saturday instead of Friday. Fred found that intriguing. Miss B. was a straight old stick, but good at deck games. Timmins, well, Fred confessed to himself that he was becoming rather fond of the boozy chap.

On the Saturday, yet more games indoors and outside, even with the weather being nastily cold and wet. This time, playing Bingo, he was pleased to win $3. But, his pleasure was quickly dashed, when disquieting news spread through the ship that 2,000 German planes had flown over East Croydon, dropping bombs over this area he knew so well. He remembered that Biggin Hill aerodrome was just south east of East Croydon and wondered whether the Germans had erred in their calculations when dropping their bombs. Biggin Hill was the principal fighter base protecting London and the south east of England from enemy bombers. It also greatly worried him because Molly's family home was in New Malden, to the west of London, between Kingston-upon-Thames and Croydon. All too close for comfort to his Molly and her family.

By Sunday, 18th August, there was so much heavy wind and fog that the ship was making very bad runs and they learned that they wouldn't make Yokohama before Wednesday. Fred's cabin-mate, the Reverend Sims, conducted the Sunday church service. It being so nasty outdoors, another "talkie" film was offered to the bored passengers: MGM's 1939 "Two Bright Boys" with one of the principal actors played by the then famous Freddie Bartholomew, in the tale roaming the country in search of a dishonest dollar.

Fred smilingly thought of himself and his younger brother, Herman, both in the British military intelligence service and the Foreign Office, with Fred now roaming the world, ever with his ears pricked up for useful information. Only the fact was that the brothers would be jolly lucky if they were to make a halfway decent dollar or two; spies weren't paid that much. Smiling grimly to himself he thought how money wasn't a factor to consider in their line of work—staying alive was.

Empress of Asia ship.

---

1. *The Empress of Asia, built 1913. Owned by the Canadian Pacific Steamship Company, she was a Royal Mail Ship, a passenger liner in peace-time and a troop- and passenger-ship in war-time. She was caught in an air raid 5th February, 1942: the ship hit, burned & abandoned. Rescuing ships prevented a loss of life of all crew and passengers. 2,200 troops on board; 1,000 souls in all were saved.*
2. *Fred turned 29 years old on 10th August, 1940.*

Chapter 12

**August, 1940
Japan—Yokohama and Tokyo**

*17 Cheniston Gardens
Kensington, London, W.8*

Monday, 26th August, 1940

Letter Number 12

My Own Darling Heart, No Longer a Bleedin' Heart, hahaha!

I'm sorry I haven't been able to write every night. This bloody Blitz... we have to keep going to the cellar when the siren goes and I get so tired and need to sleep when we are allowed back up.

I've received your first two letters! How wonderful, such a relief. Now

I'm feeling tickety-boo. It will be spiffing to get the rest of your letters; I know you've written me tons more.

The F.O. said their diplomatic bag came from Canada. A plane must have flown it; it came fast, they said. You didn't say where you'd dropped your letters to me off. Must have been at a train station? I envisaged a Consulate man with a big diplomatic bag standing by the train as it slowed down, and you leaning out of the window tossing your letters into the bag. Sort of like catching the brass ring at that funfair carousel we went on. Boy oh boy, we had fun that day, didn't we!

I loved every line you wrote, every loving word. I send you back all my love, too, my darling, and think of you as much as you think of me… no, more, I think of you MORE. Aren't I your silly monkey!

Gosh, the news we've heard is crazy. Yesterday we bombed Berlin. The R.A.F., I mean, not me and Jimmie-dawg in my old biplane…Oh dear, seriously, though, I thought of your old home in Berlin, and your friends there but apparently the R.A.F. didn't do much damage. There wasn't even anyone killed, the papers said. The bank manager told me today that nasty old Hermann Göring definitely got egg on his face because he'd always bragged Berlin would never be bombed! The awful part is, the papers said Hitler's bound to bomb <u>London</u> in retaliation.

And, guess what: today the Canadian Royal Air Force was flying over southern England and saw German planes so there was a sort of dogfight. I wonder what the Canadians were doing there? Checking on our airports in the south, like Bromley's Biggin Hill? But why would they do that? I know you aren't allowed to answer, so I'll ask Dad—my darling Mr. Know-it-all!

Oh and Dad said I should tell you that he's going to convert a lot of his money into platinum and diamond jewellery and keep it all safe in the bank's vault. That's going to be in Lloyds Bank. Only he, Mummy, and I can take it out, not even sis. Well, Olive is younger than me and Dad reckons she's not smart enough to be trusted with the jewellery. There's to be bracelets, earrings and rings. That way, if the worst happens, and he loses his money, at least we'll have the jewellery stashed away for the future and can convert it back into loot after this beastly war is over.

Can't wait for the next batch from you. Let me know you're getting mine? It occurs to me, 'cos you're travelling on boats, trains and things, that you might not get them 'till you get to you-know-where, where you're going. If that's so, you'll be inundated with letters from your loving scribe.

Molly, with all her love.

Wednesday, 21st August arrived. The day and even the night before had been so hot and sticky. Fred had felt tired from the weather, yet excited about the next stage of his journey. He'd never been to the Far East before. He could barely concentrate on the film shown that evening, "To the Victor" with Will Fyffe, the Scottish stage and screen actor playing his usual likeable old codger role. After farewell drinks with his shipboard chums, he filled out all the necessary disembarkation forms for border control, reporting how much money he was bringing in, and the immigration & customs documents.

As he sluggishly awoke and peered out of his porthole, he saw they were off Yokohama. Japan, at last! It was still terribly hot. At 10.30 am they went into quarantine then the tiring procedure from his night-before documents began: customs, immigration, doctor examinations.

Bad news had come over the wireless and spread like wildfire through the passengers, about arrests being made of people trying to disembark. He began to experience nervousness. Could they have got onto him, that he wasn't quite what he appeared to be? He had things he knew that were better off not broadcast, even at this stage of his "work," so made a good attempt to act calm, natural and

SHIRLEY READ-JAHN

casual yet serious. Wearing spectacles, he decided, lent him that useful professorial, academic air—nobody for them to be suspicious of. But, luckily, there was no trouble at all. All the Japanese officials were polite, even social, and spoke pretty good English.

Fred walked off the ship, along with Timmins and his wife, feeling relieved. It had been decided that he would stay with them at the New Grand Hotel in Yokohama. The hotel turned out, indeed, to be quite new as well as fashionable and his room, with bath, only cost him 9 Yen. His luggage was delivered to his room just before lunch—another relief: everything had been gone through but no duty had been charged and nothing had been removed. He'd carried his little black diary in his inside jacket pocket, and nobody had patted him down.

Up on the hotel's roof garden he sat with Timmins and his wife having lunch and looking down at the harbour, where they could see the "Empress of Asia's" grey ship's colour showing up well in the sunlight. It was a tremendously good feeling to be finally off that old barge, yet it was still so terribly hot. Glancing around, he saw everybody was wearing special light clothing. Fred had no white or cream linen suit of his own so felt the heat that much more than the others. Everyone said you had to wear linen, even though it creased easily. He enjoyed the half-Japanese, half-European food provided at lunch, and especially admired the attractive waitresses in their coloured kimonos. It was all most exotic and exciting. Molly would look good in a kimono, he lustily thought to himself, imaging it falling open. No! he mustn't let those thoughts come to him in the daytime —and stared back at the ship below to distract his racing heart.

After lunch he and Timmins went, as ordered, to the British Consulate. There, Fred met up with a Mr. MacDonald.

"You're going on the Trans-Siberian Express next", said Mr. MacDonald. "And I'll tell you, you'd better buy plenty of food to take on board. You'll want to get hold of some jam, marmalade, tea, powdered milk, fruit and 'insect powder'". Insect powder? That didn't bode well at all. Fred decided to keep his mouth shut and just write down the shopping list.

"Some English engineers on their way home from Sweden, old chap" said MacDonald, "reported a shortage of food on the train and that during the last day or two there had been only horseflesh and champagne to choose from." Dear me, thought Fred, horseflesh? That sounded positively nasty. Poor old horses…

Fred went to the Canadian Pacific Railroad office but found no expected mail or cables, so, quite disappointed, he decided to take a look around Yokohama during the morning along with his new shipboard friends Norman and Jean. They had been advised by the British Consulate to let Jean do all the talking as she, coming from Niagara Falls, had the necessary American accent and Americans were not quite so in disgrace as the English were.

He found Yokohama to be a modern city due to the fact that the old city had been completely destroyed by an earthquake in 1923. He could see a great variety of types of Japanese people, most of small physique. The women looked the most attractive. They had jet-black hair piled up atop their heads, gorgeously-coloured kimonos and something like a belt which Jean said was called an obi sash. As they walked along, Fred heard a strange noise he'd never heard before. It went click clack, click clack. He soon realized it was the noise of hundreds of sandals on the asphalt and assumed they had to have been made of wood.

Jean spoke some Japanese. She stopped a sweet-looking lady and her male companion and asked them some questions and received polite answers, with much bowing in between.

"They say that noise you're listening to", said Jean to Fred, "is even louder in rainy weather".

Babies looked as if they were having a rough time of it. They were strapped to the backs of their mothers and got bumped about quite a bit. The polite couple bowed again, telling these foreigners that the authorities were trying to induce women to use prams but so far without great success.

Fred found the way the Japanese greeted each other to be rather odd. They bowed and mumbled words of greeting with their heads right down. Those poor little babies must have got quite seasick!

Jean said it looked to her as if the one who stays down the longest was considered the politest.

"Jean, look at that, look at the men's teeth when they speak or smile. Their mouths are full of glittering gold!" Fred said, "and some of the men are wearing lovely silk jackets with bowler hats!" After bowing again, the Japanese couple told Jean people invested all their savings in their teeth and even covered perfectly good and healthy teeth with a coating of gold to lend them prestige. Some of the men and women wore western garb, but most clacked along in those noisy wooden sandals.

Another thing that made Fred smile when travelling in trams about the city was how everyone gaped at him and his friends. He reckoned that the Japanese thought the Europeans looked like monkeys and they were laughing to themselves about "us funny creatures".

Norman and Jean had arranged to go to Tokyo in the afternoon so Fred promised to meet up with them again at the Imperial Hotel in Tokyo that evening at 7 pm.

Timmins had been "conducting business" at the British Consulate most of the day. Fred joined him there at 4 pm then Timmins drove Fred to the station and bought him a ticket to Tokyo —passing along the secret messages Fred needed to consign to memory for passing on to his next contact.

Fred was then left to his own fate. It was a strange feeling, indeed, when he realised he couldn't understand a single word, couldn't decipher those curious signs and characters on street signs. He eventually managed to find the platform for his train alright and stood there waiting for the Express to Tokyo, when suddenly Jean and Norman turned up. What a happy coincidence! He was very relieved for he certainly felt a little safer when he wasn't quite alone. They were surprised to find that the train was quite modern, electric, only terribly overcrowded, reminding them of dear old London and the tubes. The Japanese seemed to have no problem with "conductors" who bore paddles for pushing and squeezing as many people as possible into one carriage. The little party got into Tokyo within 25 minutes and got out to explore the city.

His first impression of Tokyo was far wider streets than Yokohama, with big office buildings. It seemed very European, except for the women and a part of the men. The first drink the three of them had was typical Japanese of the times: an ice cream soda! After that they tried some Nippon fags, which did not meet their approval—they were truly disgusting cigarettes.

After that little break they passed the Imperial Palace and were greeted by a youngster with "good day how do you do good bye" as the people in Tokyo liked to practise their bit of English in spite of any ill feeling toward the Brits. They then entered a café and had tea, which wasn't too bad. Fred found that Tokyo was obviously built for short people. The chairs were too low and, when washing your hands after using the lavatory, the basin seemed to be fitted far too low on the floor and he nearly turned a somersault bending down to reach it!

Walking by the cinemas they commented on how they were showing chiefly a German documentary about the 1939 Blitzkrieg invasion of Poland, and films such as "Olympia" (a 1938 film by Leni Riefenstahl about the 1936 Summer Olympics in Berlin), and the film "Capriccio". This was a 1938 German historical comedy set in 18th century France, where its star, Lilian Harvey, enjoyed a series of romantic adventures. Lilian Harvey was an Anglo-German actress and singer, who'd lived for years in Germany, and was considered by 1938 one of Germany's major stars. No wonder the Japanese didn't much take to the English. Fred reckoned they were brainwashed to like anything German.

After a lot of asking and losing their way they eventually landed at Tokyo's Imperial Hotel. Fred discovered that the place was built by an American architect.[1] He found it to resemble a mixture of a temple and a villa. Inside it was all stairs, steps and cockeyed corridors, with dim lighting, but very effective. Then, when they'd sat down, they received a terrible shock when ordering three drinks, in being charged an outrageously expensive 3.50 Yen per drink.

At 7 pm Fred met Norman and Jean, as planned, plus a lady passenger from the ship, but he'd unfortunately forgotten her name. He told himself he'd have to rectify that *faux pas* at once. Not only did it show him off badly in her eyes, but, part of Scotland Yard's quick course for him (prior to leaving London and organised through the Foreign Office), had been to teach him to utilise a brain technique called utilisation of mnemonic devices. This was supposed to help his brain encode, remember and recall important names and information. As he sipped his drink, after being reminded of her name, he realised he'd failed that part of his course.

Now, eyeing the lady in question, he quickly ran though in his head the other tricks of the trade he'd been instructed in, such as how to read somebody's handshake; the movements of their facial muscles, particularly their eyes; potential deceit shown in how their ears sloped into the side of the face or whether there was a gap between the lobe of the ear and the face; their breathing; any sweat on their upper lip or forehead; the phrenology of the bumps on their head showing their character and mental abilities (only seen if their hair was thin enough or if he could tell by touching this woman's scalp—hardly likely, he thought!); the gait of their walk; how they held themselves in general…oh, so many tricks. He felt as if he were becoming a bit of a psychologist. All in all, he knew he'd have to subject to memory every single detail of every single thing in this sort of work.

While everyone chatted lightly, he was thinking how he had to be extremely careful how he worded his diary notations, and, particularly, the letters he sent home to his wife, his mother, and his brother. He'd already arranged that certain words he'd write would mean "something special" to them, and, particularly in the case of his brother (also working in intelligence), whether or not something he said would have to be acted upon.

This lady from the ship had brought along her brother to the rooftop dinner, who was with the British Embassy. This was a boon for Fred: another contact to discreetly "interrogate". They dined and talked together on the Imperial Hotel's roof garden, and then watched two "obsolete" American films. One, starring Douglas Fairbanks, was called "The Private Life of Don Juan". He didn't usually cry at films but this one about love, and lovers, did bring tears to his eyes, even though he told himself it was only amusing. That was something else he was going to have to learn to do: control his outward emotions more—he knew he could be a sentimental old fool at times.

At 10 pm an Embassy chap drove them all to the station to return "home" to Yokohama. *En route* they had a glimpse of a fair which was still in full swing at 10.30 pm. It was a formative picture —he now knew people followed different timeframes in Japan, and he'd have to remember that.

As tired as he was, he quickly scribbled a couple of postcard notes to his darling wife, Molly, and by 11.45 pm he'd dropped into his hotel bed absolutely dead tired but feeling much more informed about the Far East.

Wednesday, 21st August, 1940, "Via America"

Molly Darling,

This is where I am staying in Yokohama. From the roof garden you have a lovely view of the harbour. The city is okay, clean and modern. The old one was completely destroyed by 'quake in '23. Hope we don't have one while I'm here. Cheerio! Chin up!

Love, Freddie.

---

1. *American architect Frank Lloyd Wright, June 8, 1867 to April 9, 1959.*

Chapter 13

August, 1940
Kobe & Back to Tokyo

Thursday, 22nd August, 1940 dawned hot, hot, hot. Even though he'd lain in his birthday suit the night before, he still tossed and turned. It had been a terrible night, much too hot and oppressive to sleep. He dunked into a cold bath time and again but each time he crept back into bed the perspiration resumed running in rivulets down his body. His bed sheets were too soon uncomfortably wet through.

Up at dawn he peered out the window to see the sky transforming from mauve to grey to pale blue, then a solid, bright blue as the sun settled firmly in the east and the morning greetings of the chattering birds turned to sudden silence in the heat of the new day. The now crisp sunshine couldn't dispel the loneliness in his heart as he thought, for the millionth time, of his Molly left behind in London. Shaking away these dark thoughts, he washed and shaved, paying particular attention to his neat reddish moustache, thinking, as he wielded his tiny metal scissors, of Agatha Christie's detective character, Hercule Poirot, vain as vain could be about the carefully trimmed and waxed twirly hair on his upper lip. Performing this precise ablution always cleared his mind and made him smile.

He caught the 9:17 am train to Kobe. Once again, he found the train to be overcrowded. They always sold them out in Japan, then had to shove eager travellers on board, making it even more crowded. In the heat they were having it was almost unbearable for Fred, but he felt relieved to even get a second-class ticket and an actual seat.

Timmins and Kenneword were facilitating his journey. Timmins cabled Kenneword at his Osaka office telling him Fred had successfully boarded, was on his way bearing more messages in his head to pass along, and thus was required to be met at the station. Without this sort of help from other agents, Fred knew the whole journey would be far more difficult for him.

It was so hot and so tiring. He was in a Pullman car, a wagon-lit sleeper carriage, and wouldn't he just love to stretch out and get some shuteye. The Japanese lady next to him fidgeted non-stop, exasperating him almost to distraction. He used the occasion to practise a breathing meditation technique to calm himself down, something he'd been taught back in London at the time he'd been coached for this new "job" he'd be doing in Moscow. The darned woman would sit properly for a while then climb up onto the seat and kneel down, as if she were on one of those tatami mats he'd been told the Japanese spread down throughout their houses.

Feeling calmer from his meditation, he stared out the window past her tiny body. The countryside was very pretty with rice fields, lakes, a lot of industry here and there, then mountains—the so-called Japanese Alps. That made him ponder on another aspect of his upcoming Moscow work. He knew he was going to have to learn to ski; he knew there were people over there that he was going to be helping to leave the country—that was going to involve snow, mountains and skiing. Even spending so much of his youth in

Germany, Fred had never learned to ski. He regretted that now, pondering on how hard it was going to be for him to accomplish that part of his mission. With these thoughts slipping in and out of his consciousness, and as they entered and exited one long tunnel after the next, he nodded off, only to awake sneezing from all the dust coming through the open window.

The train ground to a rumbling stop in Osaka with a slowing clank of its engine pistons. His watch told him it was 4.50 pm. Where was that darned Kenneword? His eye roamed up and down the platform, but no Kenneword appeared. Coal smoke briefly obscured his view. Where was that dratted man? Now what was he going to do? Fred was feeling rather uneasy about this, so was deciding he'd have to work out how to get into Kobe by himself, when, the coal smoke clearing, he suddenly spied an obvious Englishman standing there. Fred sauntered over and asked this man if he knew Kenneword. "Yes, saw him this afternoon in the swimming pool." He then told Fred that Kenneword had taken a week's leave to relax at home. He took Fred's name, saying he lived almost next door to Kenneword, so would ask him to pop round to Fred's hotel. That was a stroke of luck! The man also suggested that Fred stay at the Tor Hotel in Kobe. Wondering if this "strange coincidence" were, indeed, a mere coincidence, or somehow just another part of the "management's" taking care of getting him to where he ought to be, Fred rolled with it all, and checked himself into the Tor Hotel. Kenneword failed to ring him up that night, and that was also odd. Perhaps he was just out with friends…he sat down to scribble a quick postcard to his beloved wife.

Thursday, 22-8-40 "Via America"

Dearest Molly,

This is my headquarters in Kobe. The bloke meant to meet me wasn't at the station. If he doesn't pick me up soon shall explore this place on my own.

Cheerio, Freddie.

At 7.30 am on Friday, 23rd August, he awoke to loud knocking on his door. Only in the wee hours of the morning had Fred finally fallen asleep in the awful heat, and now, rudely awakened, hair tousled, and grabbing his glasses, he saw a young boy bowing before him, announcing he was wanted on the hotel telephone. Grabbing his dressing gown, he ran downstairs to find Kenneword had finally (ha!) remembered he was in town and would be at the front of the Tor Hotel to pick him up at 9.15 am.

They went over to Cook's travel agent where he found, to his huge and unpleasant surprise, that his Soviet Union visa wasn't valid from Manchuria but from Riga only. Riga? Good heavens, Riga's in Latvia! Fred rarely swore but, dammit, he protested, when a Mr. Edgar, who could read Russian, spotted it and politely advised him to get himself over PDQ to the British Consulate General. They, in turn, said the visa hadn't been tampered with or altered, as Fred had feared, so there was nothing for it but for Fred to return to the British Embassy in Tokyo and get them busy on correcting the error. BUGGER! said Fred under his breath, what a blow! He then ordered tickets for the Sunday night train back to Tokyo. Hopefully this time he'd be able to sleep in a proper berth overnight. From there he marched over to the Hong Kong bank where he spoke to an agent he'd been put in contact with. This little chap spoke quietly into his ear, while changing $20 USA and $6 Canadian, "Fleddie, here are your instructions...". He conveyed those words into memory while tucking the 105 Yen carefully into his wallet, wondering why that man seemed to be making a point of inappropriately calling him by his first name. Odd. No, not odd. This agent was that little chap he'd met on the Empress of Asia, introduced to him by those English blokes *en route* to the Hong Kong garrison. That's who he was, of course! Joe, wasn't it...Shanghai Joe. Good thing he'd given the Chinese agent a good once-over, in order to recognise him again in the future. Fred muttered to himself, they look so alike, these Oriental chaps. They probably think we all do, too. But how am I going to tell the difference between a Chinese and a Jap? I suppose it's practice, sheer practice. I'll have to work on that. What's Joe doing in Tokyo? I thought he was going to the Hong Kong garrison, not to the Hong Kong bank in Tokyo! Odd, most odd…or, is it?

Kenneword accompanied Fred by train to Shioya where they had a drink at the Beach Club then picked up Mrs. Kenneword, a very pleasant woman. Off they all went to Kenneword's house in the James' Compound. This James, Kenneword told Fred, was a "millionaire businessman No. 1", who had recently been arrested but released again by the time Fred got to this settlement of foreigners. That made Fred somewhat nervous. He looked around but it all just looked plain lovely. James apparently owned it all, all of it on a large hill overlooking the bay. The Shioya Country Club was in the middle and a lovely spot, indeed. He saw that it was all very posh, with its own nice swimming pool. Mrs. Kenneword noticed him eyeing the pool and suggested he have a swim after lunch. The Kennewords' home was a cosily furnished bungalow.

She went in to attend to their lovely little three-month-old baby girl called Anne and organise lunch. Back at the club after lunch, Fred borrowed a swimsuit and had his enjoyable swim then had tea with Kenneword. Back home the men chatted and, when alone, spoke "shop talk" together, particularly to do with his mission regarding his Morgan Crucible connections. The Foreign Office had chosen Kenneword to prep Fred on what he was to do once back in Kobe. On the upcoming 28th August he was to think back about this chat…Meanwhile, with many questions now answered, they had dinner. Fred was back at his hotel by 10 pm, thinking what an extremely nice chap Kenneword was, and how pleased he'd been invited back to lunch on Sunday.

He slept better that night. Awakening early on Saturday, 24th August, by 8 am he was already up, getting his passport snaps taken, then off to the Kamaru Store in Kobe to get a case for his spectacles. That only cost him Y1,40. He was particularly pleased with this case. He could carefully lift the lining and stash an important document in there, replace it, and, hey-ho, nobody would be any the wiser. Pleased with himself how he was managing with his non-Japanese language proficiency, he treated himself to a Panama hat against the sun, for only Y4,80. Next came Cook's again, where he was to pick up his tickets. Then he spent about half an hour trying to mail out a letter to Molly by snail mail. He also posted the postcards he'd written.

Sightseeing time! He caught a tram to Shiru and another tram to the Cable Station and from there he jumped onto a cable car to take him right up to the summit. The view from the Rokko Mountain across the bay to Osaka and Kobe was so picturesque to Fred. He noted its altitude was 3,500 feet. Back down again, he set out to find the Oriental Hotel in Rokko where he'd planned to have lunch. Naturally, there were no street signs in English; he learned that all of those that had been in place before had now been removed, forcing any Englishmen in town to bumble around, trying to find their way—doubtless to great Japanese inward amusement. He met an Austrian woman on the tram. She said she was rather miserable because she had no money. He spoke in German to her, which seemed to cheer her up, and gave her a few Yen. He wondered if she was a connection for him, but she simply simpered at his questioning stare and, startlingly, swiftly jumped off the tram. He sat and pondered on the secrecy surrounding his journey, whom he was to meet, whom he was to talk to, what needed to be discussed. He needed to be ever alert, not knowing what or who was going to approach him next. Be prepared, be prepared, he mouthed silently, just like on the train…

Still searching for the Oriental Hotel, he found he'd gone in the wrong direction when he'd enquired at a post office from a man who spoke a little English. He was starving by then so marched into the Rokkosan Hotel for lunch in their dining room. Before he'd gone two paces into the room a boy bowed then quickly pushed and pulled Fred into a white linen jacket. With Fred properly attired, the boy bowed again, and passed him to a waiter. Now he was permitted to sit down and eat. Good Lord, thought Fred, these people certainly have their rules and protocols!

As he was walking along after lunch, with relief he happened upon the Oriental Hotel, where he now stopped to have a cup of tea. He observed an interesting new game being played. Chaps were throwing clay discs from the top of a hill across a creek, the idea seeming to be that the wind should carry the discs right across. There was an amusing incident next. He asked the hotel receptionist for a postcard. "Yes Sir, five minutes" was the reply, as he disappeared in the back. After five minutes the boy returned. "Car is waiting, Sir." Fortunately, Fred didn't have to pay, explaining the mess up was due to a total misunderstanding in language. "Card not car!" he told the boy's manager, who bowed in apologetic understanding.

He sat on the hotel's terrace for a long time, admiring the view and writing his "Moll" a postcard.

Saturday, 24th August 1940

Hello Sunshine,

I've done a lot of hiking on Mount Rokko near Kobe today. Gorgeous scenery. About 3,500 ft above town. Lovely ride by cable-car. Very hot. Tomorrow Sunday I return to Tokyo. Note new stamps!

Fondest love,
Your Freddie.

On the way "home" he almost bumped into an oriental-looking chap who seemed to appear from nowhere. He said he was from Shanghai but that he was an emigrant from Germany, looking up at Fred, scanning his face for recognition. He spoke first in Chinese, but then tried out his sentence in Japanese, then some German and English on Fred, calling him by his first name, each time saying "Fleddie". Startled, Fred took a good look at this linguistically erudite man and realised within short order this time whom he was. Yes, AGAIN! It was Shanghai Joe, that bloke he'd met on the Empress of Asia, introduced by the young Hong Kong garrison soldiers, then again in the bank, changing his money for him! He'd filed his face and demeanour away in his brain for future need.

"Joe! Shanghai Joe, you rascal. You almost fooled me. Emigrant from Germany, my foot!"

"What wrong with foot, Fleddie? You got bad foot?" grinned Shanghai Joe.

"You're beginning to seem like my guardian angel, you know that? Popping up everywhere out of the blue," said Fred.

"Just the job, Fleddie, just what I got to do. You know that. You know what you do, well me too, I do what you do! We two the angels, good angels, Fleddie, we help the good guys, you know?"

Fred just shook his head then burst out laughing. What a character this Chinese agent is, he thought to himself. Not only that, this man's like the Scarlet Pimpernel, thought Fred, seeking me here, there and simply everywhere! Joe accompanied Fred most of the way back, sharing information he said Fred was supposed to be told. Fred asked him whether he was acquainted with a "rather penniless" lady from Austria he'd run into, but, not surprisingly, the little chap just smiled enigmatically at Fred and strolled away. Now, why, thought Fred, couldn't Kenneword have passed him the information Joe just gave him? It all seemed so excessively secret and exotic...and that Austrian woman...what on earth was that about?

By 7 pm Fred had arrived back at the Tor Hotel in Kobe. He was exhausted from his strenuous walking up and down hills. Before anything else, though, he made it his business to write down, cryptically enough, all that had happened to him that day. After a light dinner he went gratefully to his room. He had to keep batting at the mosquitoes, a thirsty lot, they were. Even with a mosquito net over the bed, the little beasts got through. He had to smile, remembering a philosophical African proverb he'd once been told: "If you think you're too small to make a difference, you've never spent a night with a mosquito"! Wonder if Shanghai Joe thinks that way, ruminated Fred, dozing restlessly, but just before he finally fell fast asleep he recalled one of the Embassy chaps trying to convey the politeness of the Japanese. He'd given Fred an example of an anti-British demonstration. The Embassy would receive a telephone call: "When do you close?" "At 4.40." "Please stay open till 5 pm, we want to demonstrate." What polite nerve, thought Fred! At which point, he gave in to his weariness and finally fell fast asleep.

Sunday, 25th August meant meeting Kenneword again. Fred caught the 10.50 am to Shioya and met the Kennewords at their club. After another welcome swim and another tasty lunch, they swapped showing each other their photographic snaps. The Kennewords' parents had London homes both at Regent's Park and in Wimbledon, and, it turned out, both knew Molly's New Malden area quite well. In the course of the afternoon they dropped formalities and moved straight into what Fred called the German "Du" terms. Now he felt even more comfortable. Kenneword and he talked more, out of his wife's hearing.

He was back in Kobe by 7 pm. He had some dinner then caught the 9.05 pm sleeper train to Tokyo. On the train he met up with his next contact. This was an American friend of "Ken's" whom Fred had briefly seen at the club. Fred chuckled inwardly, thinking how Kenneword had now become Ken to him. It felt nice, in this strange land, to have a real friend. In England Ken had always been Kenneword, or even Mr. Kenneword. Fred and the American talked shop, mostly in the train's corridor, swaying to and fro, to be out of hearing of anyone else. Back in his carriage he tried to sleep but woke up at every single station because the train jerked terribly on pulling up and starting again.

At 8.40 am on the Monday, 26th August, his train pulled into the station at Tokyo. He immediately went to the Station Hotel but it was full up. He had to share a room, to his annoyance. Even getting the room was a long-winded affair. Finally, he got some hot towels for his bath. He requested sandwiches and coffee. What he got was lousy, consisting of sour bread and butter, dry ham, and what he termed filthy coffee. Feeling disappointed, he got a taxi over to the British Embassy. There he met up with "Mr. Straw," a nice enough chap. Fred left his passport there to be given the correct visa to get him into the USSR via Manchuria, not Riga. Mr. Straw sent Fred off to the Sanno Hotel where he could get a room for only Y15,0. After lunch there he met with two foreigners who turned out to be Japanese but didn't look it. They told him where to go to see a Japanese film and a stage show they thought he'd enjoy. The film was all conversation and totally boring to someone who didn't speak the language. The stage show was a peculiar mixture of acrobatics and dancing with a lot of noise. He didn't appreciate any of that, either, so took himself off back to his hotel to write again to Molly.

Monday, 26th August, 1940, Sanno Hotel, Tokyo.

Dearest darling wife,

Left Kobe last night and arrived back in Tokyo this morning where I am staying at above address. Saw Embassy re Russian Visa. Hope I don't have to wait too long. There's a taifun (sic) blowing up. Not too pleasant.

Love and kisses,

Your Freddie.

Then came Tuesday, 27th August. There was no news yet from the Embassy about his visa. He was supposed to meet up with two more contacts in Kobe, one, the Mr. McCanley who lived in Kobe. The other was a director or accountant at Lendrum's[1] in England, a waste paper company where Molly's father was one of the directors. Neither of these contacts was around to Fred's great chagrin. After writing a letter to Mrs. Lendrum to find out where Mr. Lendrum was and for her to notify her husband of Fred's inability to meet with her husband's associate, he had lunch then took himself off to see two more films. Fred really enjoyed the cinema, one reason being there was usually some form of air conditioning in the theatres! This day he saw "Stagecoach" and "Kameraden auf See". Of course, he spoke German. That last flick was a 1938 film, "Comrades at Sea". He then met up with an American he had met at the theatre. They strolled down the Ginza together where all the shops remained open till late at night. Having just seen a German movie he was delighted when they came to a German restaurant on the Ginza called Lohmeyer's. He'd enjoy some genuine German food, so in they went. He was happy to see they had real German beer mats and Steins of cold, frothy, German beer, with Weisswurst, Sauerkraut, and genuine German mustard. What a treat to find these foods of his youth! Fred was a happy, well-fed young man falling asleep that night.

On Wednesday, 28th August, he was in a meeting at the Tokyo British Embassy. It was again strongly suggested that he learn Russian, and fast. Fred was in total agreement, knowing it was going to be a difficult but necessary chore to do his work properly once in Moscow. They said he'd have to take his passport himself to the Soviet Union Consulate to have them change his visa.

He took a taxi to the Soviet Union Consulate, armed with his passport once again. On arrival, when he slammed the old taxi door shut, a windowpane broke. Horrors! The driver pestered and worried at Fred for a long time. Fred tried to mime that it wasn't his fault because of the dilapidated state of the old car. As the driver got ever more annoyed, Fred mimed to him to wait while he dashed into the Consulate and located a Soviet who could speak both English and Japanese. This man was able to interpret for Fred, who ended up having to agree to pay 3 Yen.

Once back inside the Soviet Union Consulate, he discovered he had to get a whole new visa, to let him enter the USSR from Manchuria instead of Riga. They told him they'd have to place a call to the British Embassy in Moscow to alert them they were on the case and Fred would soon be on his way again. The Soviets had told him it would take a few days to acquire his new visa. So…back to the hotel went he, where he lunched, wrote letters, particularly to his brother, Bert.[2] He needed to update him on his activities and contacts, in the code they had agreed upon prior to Fred's departure from England. He also wrote to Mr. Sutton, Molly's father, to let him know he'd been unable to meet with McCanley.

His duty done by 3 pm, and after a chat with the hotel receptionist, he decided he'd go up to the mountains to Nikko to stay at the Kanaya Hotel and report back to Tokyo on the Monday; that should give the Soviets time enough to issue his new visa and it would give him a short holiday...doubtless "a busman's holiday" he thought, ruefully.

After having talked a lot back in Kobe with Mr. Kenneword (the prestigious director of Morgan Crucible, now just 'Ken' to me, grinned Fred), Fred was now considering spending a longer period than planned in Japan in order to do a bit of work in Kobe, or even Nikko, as he told his diary.[3] After further discussions with the British Embassy he returned to the Ginza. There, to his further delight, he found a German bakery. How many Germans were there in Tokyo, he wondered? He met a draper who was happy to give him 70 Yen for $10 US. With that money and feeling quite flush, he strolled up and down the Ginza, finally buying two new shirts. He had so enjoyed Lohmeyer's that he returned for drinks and a delicious Sauerbraten pot roast with vegetables. Then he felt very clever to navigate the Tokyo underground back to Akasaka Mitsuke station in order to return to the Sanno hotel. There he was able to send a cable to his darling Molly and go to bed to dream of holding her once again in his arms.

Hidden in Plain Sight

Oriental Hotel, Rokko, Japan.

Ginza Street, 27th August, 1940.

Kabuki Theatre, 27th August, 1940.

Memorial Gallery of Meiji Shrine, Tokyo, 27th August, 1940). It was a Shinto shrine to the deified spirits of Emperor Meiji and his Empress Shoken, built at an iris garden that the emperor & his wife liked to visit. It was destroyed in a WWII air-raid. A new shrine was completed in 1958 on the site and a few world leaders have since visited it.

Ueno Park, Tokyo, 27th August, 1940.

Tor Hotel, Kobe. Postcard purchased by Fred.

---

1. *Lendrum & Company was the first to start a waste paper business in England*
2. *Fred called his brother Bert or Bertie even though his name was Herman.*
3. *Intelligence work*

Chapter 14

August, 1940
Japan—Nikko, a Short Holiday

Friday, 29th August, 1940 dawned exciting for Fred. He'd decided to treat himself to an actual short holiday and learn more about this fascinating country of Japan by taking the 8.45 am train to Nikko, up in the mountains. Besides, surely it would be a lot cooler up there? Work could wait for a bit.

He couldn't, once again, believe how this country of polite people, bowing and scraping all the time, could gape at him. Either he looked very attractive or totally funny to them! They showed little reserve in staring at his blond hair and blue eyes. All Japanese have brown eyes.

He pulled into Nikko at 12.06 pm and went straight to the Kanaya Hotel by taxi and got himself a nice room with full board for 14 Yen. The hotel was situated on a hill overlooking a river and what they call the "Sacred Bridge". He had his lunch at the hotel then went to see the famous Nikko temples and shrines. They all had the most beautiful eastern art, but strange to his western eyes.

As he gazed at one of the pagodas, thinking he'd like a photograph of himself standing there, to send to Molly, a voice spoke at his elbow. Looking down, he recognized Shanghai Joe. No! It couldn't be! But it was, of course it was—this little fellow popped up everywhere.

"Hello, Fleddie, old man. How you been doing? You got a camera there. Want me take picture of you at pagoda? You send to wife?"

"I certainly would, thanks a lot, Joe! How d'you know I have a wife?"

"I know lots of tings about you, Fleddie. You hafta meet my friend, she help me in all my work."

A beautiful woman approached them from behind the pagoda.

"Zhi Ruo, you come say nice hullo to our Fleddie! Maybe YOU take picture of our Fleddie?"

"Fleddie, Zhi Ruo, she another angel, just like you and me."

"Oh, yes, I see, yes, I understand. She's one of us," he whispered under his breath so only Shanghai Joe could hear.

Fred was knocked out by this exotic, raven-haired Chinese beauty. They shook hands. She took his camera and took a snap of Freddie in front of the pagoda. Upon taking his Brownie camera back and winding on the film, he discovered it had run out of film. Nobody would imagine what was on such an innocuous-looking camera. The sooner he got his snaps developed and sent off to the Foreign Office via the nearest British Consulate, the better.

Zhi Ruo immediately offered to take him to "the right place" where he could "get film developed, very safe". She gazed warmly at him, her even, white teeth sparkling, laying a soft hand on his bare forearm. Shanghai Joe shook his hand and padded silently away in his Chinese soft-bottomed shoes.

"Zhi Ruo", said Fred firmly. "I'm going to send this picture to my wife, and tell her I was thinking of her while that photo was being taken."

"I know, you so lonely," commented Zhi Ruo, looking him up and down with sad approval.

Warning bells went off in Fred's head. He wondered if she wanted more from him than to help him in his courier work. She obviously knew he was an agent, as was Shanghai Joe. As was she! Joe had made that pretty clear. Fred thought he'd be able to use her himself in his work but would have to watch her. It looked like she might have extra-curricular plans for him! She was one heck of a gorgeous gal…with a very light scent, floral. What was it, which flower? His mind raced back to his family's little back garden with its wall of jasmine. Yes, jasmine, that's it!

His mind darted back to Molly. How he missed her! How he wished she were there with him to see with her own eyes all the strangely exotic sites and sights, smell the far eastern food aromas, see those gorgeous colourful kimonos the people wore, their clacking clog-like sandals, their black hair, with the women's swept up high and held with what looked like chopsticks to him—all those things he was experiencing would have been so much sweeter when shared with his darling wife.

Zhi Ruo took him to a hole-in-the-wall shop where his film was taken from him. She assured him he'd get it back "pretty damn quick" and that "someone" would leave it in his hotel room for him. Well, I never, thought Fred, things are becoming more cloak and dagger. He trusted Shanghai Joe, so felt he could also trust this beautiful wench, too.

The weather was dull but yes! much cooler, as he made his way back "home". In the lobby of the hotel he came across some recent German periodicals, and upon sitting down to smoke his pipe and read them, he found himself disappointed at the news therein. Well, naturally, he thought—they were all written from a German viewpoint.

After dinner at the Kanaya, he wrote letters to Molly and, of course, to Ken, to update him on his movements and what he had managed to find out "about matters" to date, using their "agreed-upon" encrypted wording. So much for a short holiday; work always managed to be in the forefront of his mind.

Friday dawned, again with dull weather. Fred took a steep uphill walk to Kirifuri-no-taki or "Mist-Falling Cascade". It was picturesque, a truly beautiful waterfall. On the way there he saw many gorgeous views but became tired out struggling up the stony path he had to pick his way along on. When he finally got there, he saw the rushing water was full of trout (one of his favourite fish!) with deep precipices either side of the cascade. The change of altitude made him terribly sleepy so, back home after lunch, he had a relaxing snooze. Awakened by a discreet tapping at his door, he opened it. A young man bowed, handed him a plain packet, bowed again, and backed away; no words said. Fred carefully opened up the little packet to find two sets of his camera's photos within. No cost to him, either. Well, I never, he once again muttered to himself. He'd send one of his pagoda shots to his mum to see, and she could pass it on to Moll.

Stretching out again on his bed, he lay there thinking about the cable he hoped to receive from Molly. In order to receive it, she'd have to still be living in London. Not knowing was the worst part. He felt so out of it, so out of touch with his loved ones. And… moving farther and farther away as he went on this journey. If only he had his wife with him. His sports jacket needed a complete overhaul. He went downstairs and looked around in Nikko for a tailor to patch his jacket up. Not speaking Japanese and the proprietor not speaking English (or German!) made him resort to miming again. He was getting quite good at this! He looked around the tailor's shop and saw a wall calendar, so was able to point at the 31st to show them that's when he'd need his jacket back. Smiling smugly to himself with his mission accomplished, he set off, only to have the smile wiped off his face as he got caught in a deluge of heavy rain. The kind tailor had seen him getting soaked so had sent his son to run after him with an umbrella and escort him back to his hotel. Back at the hotel he received an expected visit from Temple. Over drinks, they discussed plans and the world situation in general, with Fred mentally storing away every detail passed to him by Temple.

This little sojourn away really is a busman's holiday, thought

Fred, when back at the hotel he was advised in a sealed note left at Reception that Mr. Manson, Private Secretary to His Excellency the British Ambassador, was due to arrive that very day in Nikko, and that Fred would be expected to "hold intelligent conversations" with this individual. Ha! A fine turn of phrase! Looking around the hotel to see where it would be best to accomplish these very private conversations, Fred noticed that the majority of guests were Germans so they'd have to be careful what they said, and where they said it. Perhaps safest of all would be to stroll outside to chat. Interesting, isn't it, he thought, that a mere Foreign Office clerk was going to have "conversations" with HE's Private Secretary! I expect they were going to be highly "intelligent," on all fronts, he smiled wryly to himself!

Friday, 30th August, 1940
The Nikko-Kanaya Hotel, Nikko, Nippon.

My dearest Mum,

I am enjoying the bracing and invigorating mountain air of this beautiful resort. It's a lovely hotel and the food is excellent. There are lots of Buddha [sic] temples and shrines around here, "sacred bridges" and all kinds of interesting things. On Thursday I had my photo taken in front of the Pagoda. A snap like the one I enclose does not give credit to the wonderful colours and art of these old buildings. You see by the photo that I don't look too starved, the only thing that troubles me is the excessive heat and I haven't got the necessary tropical outfit. So I walk about like that. There are lovely walks, waterfalls, lakes, rivers and it would be an ideal spot for a holiday if only I could adopt that holiday spirit. But I'm so worried about you all. These air raids are a beastly affair. Oh Mum dear, I pray you are safe and well. Please do be careful and look after yourself won't you. I don't know whether you are better off in Luton or not. It is awful not being able to hear anything from you. I do hope I can soon get a move on.

I'm so anxious to get to Moscow. I hope I shall find tons of letters from *you all. I cabled Molly on 28th. I hope she gets it. I'm on coals waiting for the reply. On Monday morning I shall return to Tokyo to see whether there is any further development in my visa affair. It's a darn nuisance and it would have to be the Russian one, wouldn't it?*

Goodnight, Mum dear, shall write again soon.

Your loving son, Fred.

The following day, Saturday 31st August, Fred slept in. When he awoke he thought it was still the middle of the night. It was dark and miserable outside and pouring with rain. It was impossible to leave the hotel. "Manson," the man he was supposed to contact that day, managed to get to Fred's hotel and they spoke shop-talk together at length. After Manson had left, Fred moped about the Kanaya Hotel, staring gloomily out the rain-spattered windows. He made cryptic notes to help himself remember his conversation with Manson and how it would impact what he told Temple, whom he expected to see the next day.

The weather, already September now, was getting better. Fortunately, the tailor had had his son deliver his jacket to him. The weather was clearing and Fred was able to go out and have another meeting with Temple. He'd known a Miss Cain (from Tientsin) on the boat, so was pleased to find she was also at the Kanaya. After lunch with her and Temple, Fred took the 4.15 pm express train back to Tokyo and pulled in at Ueno Station at 6.20 pm. He was pleased to get his same room at the Sanno for 4.50 Yen.

That evening Miss Cain agreed to meet him at the Imperial at 8.15 pm. Fred was missing Molly so much, thus enjoyed having a female companion to gad around with for a change. They took a taxi to the Amusement Quarter called Asakusa Ku. There they went into a theatre that they both found very interesting, but afterwards, there were literally thousands of people, so they had great difficulty in hailing a taxi for their return journey. It wasn't raining, which was a blessing. After a lot of talking and arguing with a taxi driver, the man agreed to drive them to the Imperial where Miss Cain was staying. He enjoyed having drinks with her, and hearing all about her doings since the boat, thus he didn't get home till 12 midnight. He just heartily wished Miss Cain had been his Molly. So once again he climbed into bed alone to hug his pillow and drift off dreaming of his darling wife. Visions of Zhi Ruo suddenly floated across his mind. Jerking fully awake, he scolded himself for these thoughts of other women. Dammit, he thought, for the hundredth time, why wasn't Molly with him? A man needs his woman with him. Tossing and turning, he finally drifted off into dreamland.

Monday, 2nd September arrived, and with it, good news! Mr. Straw at the British Embassy said they'd heard Fred's Soviet visa was granted. Fred scuttled over to the Soviet Union Consulate to pick it up but found it still didn't have a visa in it to let him enter the USSR via Manchuria. They told him to get himself over to the Manchurian Embassy & Consulate. After a lot of annoying questions, where he had to think fast on his feet to avoid answering, he managed to get his passport amended, he thought, but then, it turned out that the Manchurian Embassy wouldn't issue the actual visa because his actual route had not yet been fixed. Thus thwarted once again, he cabled his people in Kobe to "do something".

He needed to fill some time pleasantly so picked up Miss Cain to go out for drinks and to lunch. Duly fortified, and in a far better state of mind, at 2.30 he returned to the Soviet Union Embassy, as commanded, to find the Manchurian Consul had fixed up his visa. Finally! At 5 pm he waltzed back into the British Embassy to receive an allowance of 200 Yen. He told them how anxious he was, not having heard from his wife, so they assured him they'd contact the Overseas Department to ensure all was well with Molly and send a cable direct to Kobe for him to receive once he'd got back there. Once again, it was intriguing that a mere "clerk" such as he was getting this kind of attention and care. Obviously, somebody in the British Embassy had been instructed to take care of Freddie Read-Jahn.

Onward, for the next leg of his journey! Back to the hotel to pack and to compose a quick letter to his wife.

SHIRLEY READ-JAHN

THE SANNO HOTEL, TOKYO, JAPAN
Monday, 2nd September, 1940

My precious little Baby,

Good news. My Russian Visa has been granted and I'm off to Kobe tonight. I've had a very hectic day. When they told me at the Embassy this morning that everything was ok, I rushed round to the Russians and from there to the Manchukuoan [sic] Embassy, then to our Consulate. I mentioned to the Consul that I have not received a reply to my cable of Wednesday last and he promised to send one immediately to OD asking for news re my family to be sent direct to Consulate in Kobe. So I hope to hear how you are tomorrow or latest on Wednesday. The Embassy gave me another 200 Yen to carry on with. This working out of my expense sheet is going to be a complicated affair. Last night I wandered round the amusement quarter of Tokyo and went into theatres and studied night life. But it's very tame. It's all over at 11 pm. The problem in this town is getting a taxi. Last night I had to wait over half an hour before finding one and then it took a lot of persuading to get the driver to agree to go further than 2-3 miles. They are so short of petrol.

I shall be so relieved to hear you are safe and well. I'm terribly worried. I must rush off now so good night, Darling.

At 9.40 pm that night he left Tokyo for Kobe again, feeling lucky to be given even an upper berth.

The next few days were a whirl of activity, involving visits to Cook's to arrange his boat ticket to Korea, meeting with a Mr. Edgar, going to Osaka, where he was commanded to pick up his Manchoukno [sic] visa before 12 noon.

At the New Osaka Hotel Fred had some lunch then was picked up by Kenneword at 2 pm. Once again, it was beastly hot, so they decided to hole up in the air conditioning of a cinema. They quietly traded shop-talk together sitting in the back row with nobody in front or to the sides of them while the "Dust Hole" film threw its black and white shadows across the screen in front of them.

There was a public phone in the cinema's lobby so Fred was able to telephone the Tor Hotel for a room reservation and could also ring Timmins. Ken accompanied Fred when they left Osaka at 4 pm, reaching Cook's at 6 pm. There they learned that his tickets were all arranged and everything was therefore AOK. Ken took him to the Shioya Country Club where Fred met up with Timmins, his wife, and another person he had previously been introduced to. After a few drinks they all descended on Ken's house for a 7 pm dinner. Now they were all together, the ladies left the men to smoke, drink, and "shop talk" while they cleaned up in the kitchen. Fred received further instructions for the next leg of his journey. Things were becoming more and more interesting for him. At 10 pm Fred left for Kobe with Ken's promise ringing in his ears that he'd be happy to look after Moll, should she travel out to the USSR to join him via Japan. Feeling he'd got his ducks nicely all lined up in a row now, he fell gratefully asleep back at the Tor Hotel in Kobe, even though it was another terribly hot night, 30 degrees Celsius even up on top of the hill, and with no air conditioning. The fan's blades above his bed turned around desultorily, hardly stirring the thick, hot, air.

The Nikko-Kanaya Hotel, Nikko, Nippon, 30th August, 1940.

Fred at pagoda in Nikko, Japan. Taken by a female agent. Molly's writing on the photo (he'd posted the photo back to England).

Asakusa Ku's shopping gallery. Note the women in kimonos and obis and men in traditional male Japanese garb. 31st August, 1940.

Hidden in Plain Sight

Kirifuri-no-taki or, "Mist falling Cascade". Postcard purchased by Fred.

Nikko Sacred Bridge. Postcard purchased by Fred.

Chapter 15

**September, 1940
Sailing to China Past Korea**

The following day, Wednesday, 4th September, Fred had his baggage sent to the Nekka Maru Japanese ship he would depart on headed for China, passing Korea. He left his hotel and went straight to Cook's to collect his tickets and then met up with Timmins and the British Consul. There had been no reply yet to the Tokyo Consul's cable about Molly but he was assured any reply would be forwarded on to meet him in Dairen[1], or Harbin, or even in Moscow, if it couldn't get to the earlier places to coincide with his arrival. It was also agreed that the British Consul in Dairen (variously known as Dalian or Diaren) would meet Fred at the ship. He was obviously a precious package to be handled; the knowledge he contained in his head of value. Knowing he was to be met at the boat made Fred feel he was going to be alright. Yet the lack of knowledge of Far Eastern languages was a constant frustration and difficulty for him.

At 11 am he embarked and the ship left the dock at twelve.

When he entered his first-class cabin No. 16, he found it had been reserved for a Mr. and Mrs. and the ship's chief purser seemed just as upset as Fred that there was no missus to sleep in the cabin with him. Later the purser decided to put a cabin-mate in the same cabin as Fred. This man turned out to be a German, who seemed to be quite a nice chap. Again, it was useful for Fred, as ever on the alert for any information voluntarily thrown his way.

Lunch gave Fred a queer sensation because he was placed at a table with a small group of Germans returning from Siberia. The atmosphere was peculiar but everyone remained very polite. Fred wondered how it would all go on. One never knew. He would remain polite and as usual, listen to every word spoken. They spoke in German, foolishly not even assuming he could understand. He just nodded and gave a small smile when addressed in English, keeping an impassive countenance while they chatted together, as if not comprehending a word, glancing occasionally down at his magazine, or gazing ruminatively out of the window.

He excused himself after lunch to go outside to smoke. They were passing through the Inland Sea and he could see lots of small islands and very pretty scenery. He stood out on deck watching the shimmering diamond-tipped waves throwing up spume from the ship's bow, thinking how atavistic he'd become, fascinated like all humans with the sea. If he stared long enough, he knew he'd be drawn toward it, closer and closer. Not wanting to think those dark thoughts, he allowed himself to smile as he ran through the men's potentially reckless conversations in his mind. "Loose lips sink ships," he chuckled to himself, while puffing away on his fag.

That evening, over dinner with the same group of Germans, he found the men, well-oiled on beer, to be even more chatty than at lunchtime. Their English had also loosened up and soon they were all talking happily for a long time, with Fred ever careful of what he imparted.

Back in the cabin he again wrote to Moll. He found the cabin to be so far, so good, even though the boat itself was very small.

On Thursday, 5th September he was awakened at 6 am for passport control at Moji, the last Japanese port. There were no difficulties whatsoever; everything seemed to be in order with his papers. He was able to mail off a postcard to Moll from Moji. At noon they left the port and, upon entering the open sea, they ran into rough weather. Fred felt a bit seasick but eating always helped him, so he managed to eat his dinner with no problems. The small ship by then was rolling heavily, upsetting tables and smashing glasses and crockery. He crawled into bed at 9 pm but an hour later his cabin-mate, Herr Schlieb, turned up, so they chatted amicably and inconsequentially in English till midnight.

At 7 am the next morning, Friday 6th, they found they were near the Korean coast in the Yellow Sea, which was calm but muddy-looking. Fred worked on his expense sheet to give to the next British Embassy he came to, which was how he was funding this trip. After lunch he found he needed to sleep again. At 5 pm he was up and about getting ready for a farewell party for his new chums Heinrich, Schlieb and Demby. They all sat around drinking, having a long political discussion, in English, but in a friendly spirit —again, with Fred ever cautious about what he said. He had to laugh when they said he was outnumbered 3 to 1 but as the "enemy" he had fought well in the discussion. All raised their glasses to that remark! They closed down the party at 1 am and he grabbed 4½ hours' sleep because he had to be up again the following morning at 5.30 am. He'd managed not to impart his half-English/half-German surname, which could have raised their suspicions about his "obvious" non-comprehension of the German language.

On Saturday, 7th September he had reached the seaport of Dairen where he encountered no difficulty with passport control. Dairen had been built by the Soviets in 1898 and then had become a territory of Japan, known as Dalian, or Dalniy (now part of China). British Pro Consul Edmondson was at the docks to meet Fred. To his dismay there was no cable from Molly! What was going on? Was she alright? He was very disappointed and quite deflated. They drove together to the British Consulate where the consular clerk was holding an Express ticket for the 10 am train for Fred. Darien was a hot, dusty, fairly busy and rather dirty city located at

SHIRLEY READ-JAHN

the southern end of a peninsula in the Liaoning Province in the landmass mainly belonging to China.

It was a new feeling for Fred to be once again on English soil at the Consulate, even if only for an hour or two. The Consul told him he would cable his people in Harbin, China to meet Fred. Fred hoped an expected cable, or, even better, a letter from Molly would be there.

After breakfast with Consul Foulds, Fred was driven to the station. He got his baggage onto the train only to discover it was the wrong train. Horrors! That train only went as far as Hsungking. He found he was going to have to wait several hours for a connection to Harbin, China. As Fred had tickets for the 4.55 pm train, all he had to do was to get his luggage off and return to the British Consulate. There he met up with a Naval Captain Cayna and went with Edmondson and the Captain to the latter's ship. There they enjoyed a drink together and later returned to the Consulate. At noon they stopped in at some friends of Edmondson's for yet more drinks and some eats and then went on to their Club. Yet more drinks were had. A friend of Edmondson's had a place right on the seashore, so they went off there for more drinks. Edmondson brought him back to the station in time to catch the 4.55 pm train for Harbin. Luckily Fred could hold his drink and was none the worse for wear. He'd been trained well, to sip while others might guzzle, and to drink glasses of water between each alcoholic drink.

Once in Harbin, he knew the next part of his journey was going to be intriguing: he'd be riding on the Trans-Siberian Express. He'd heard about this train and was eager to get aboard and begin the long journey across the whole of China.

17 Cheniston Gardens
Kensington, London, W.8
Sunday, 29th September, 1940
Letter No. 14

Dearest Fred,

I'm in heaven! The Foreign Office rang yesterday and said there was post for me. I jumped on my trusty bike and pedalled like hell to pick it up. It was like that old song we changed the words to, remember?

"Daisy, Daisy the coppers are after you.
If you don't hurry they'll give you a month or two.
They'll tie you up with wire inside a black Maria,
So ring your bell and pedal like hell on a bicycle made for two!"

And TWO letters came from you! Thank you so much, Freddie. It's a relief to know you're alright and on your way still. Such a trip you're having. I read the letters over and over. Oh, and I got the postcards, too, thank you. You're probably much farther now on your trip but, of course, I have no way of knowing because the F.O. won't give me any details and the letters don't match where you are now. But, I know you're still SAFE and that's what counts.

What have I been doing, you ask? Aside from work, I've been knitting. You know how good I am at that (smirk!). I've been knitting socks for the soldiers at the front, and I must say, it does fill these gloomy evenings. It's getting dark at night now, way before summer's 10 pm was doing, so I put on my light, after drawing the black-out curtains. Then I drop a coin into the gas-heater to get at least two bars on. We all have to because of the Blitz; you can imagine. Don't want Jerry's bombers to see even a speck of light.

I do feel clever, Freddie. I don't want to cheat the gas-man so I've drilled a hole in a coin and attached a strong piece of cotton to it. Then I lower the coin into the heater to turn it on then pull it right back up! On the last day of the week when he comes to collect all the coins supposed to be in there, he always looks shocked to find my neatly-folded paper money note in the machine's money place. He raises his eyebrows every week, glares balefully at me, saying, "Mrs. R-J, you are a bleedin' magician. How do you do that, and every time!" He knows how, silly man! I always grin and say, "I dunno, the coins just sort of change themselves into paper, I suppose!"

Fred, I wonder if you heard. Mr. Fairweather at the bank says he heard a couple of days ago that the police in France have been counting up all the Jews there. A sort of census. He says he doesn't like the sound of that. He says he has an auntie who is a Jewess and it's a good thing she doesn't live in Paris. She lives in the south of France, somewhere near Nice; he says it's a beautiful area.

I'm going to be going with a girlfriend to see that new musical, Strike Up the Band, *probably next Saturday. It's got Mickey Rooney and Judy Garland in it. Should be good. I do wish you were here to go with me.*

Remember when we went in April to see Judy Garland in the Wizard of Oz? Holding hands in the back row of the cinema and then you dropped the tin of popcorn and it made such a noise as it rolled away from us? Oh, if only you were here, my darling hubbie. I do miss you so.

Did I already tell you, dear, how all the signposts have been taken down in every town in Britain and the cinemas' posters have the name of the town showing the film obliterated? We don't want Jerry to be able to know where he is, do we! Even if they parachute down they won't know where they are, because we've all been told not to tell 'em!

Yes, the Blitz is still going on, but Jimmy and I are surviving alright. He sends you a wet kiss on your nose. His doggy breath is still awful. I know you're worried about us all. Your mum says she's perfectly fine, and safe, as are Dad and my mother. We all take great care and run to the air-raid shelters when the sirens go off. When you were here, just before you left, I remember how much you hated the sirens on those rare occasions when a Luftwaffe bomber was seen approaching. It's amazing to say but in a way we're all getting so used to the sirens, as horrid as they are. At least they give us time to run to safety in the air raid shelters.

Oh, and I'm not the only one cycling around town. I often see the Home Guard (as well as the Air Raid wardens) on their bikes. They're officially called The Home Guard Defending Forces. They've been taught how to fight the Germans but I tell you, most of them have grey hair and whiskers—obviously too old to go to the front! They cycle along on their bikes and wave and whistle at me as they wobble past me on my bike to wave one-handedly at me. But don't get jealous, hahaha; it's rather uplifting for me to get appreciative wolf-whistles!

Darling, did you hear? The most awful thing happened to the King and Queen. You know on 7th September the Luftwaffe dropped bombs on the East End killing more than 1,000 civilians? You must have heard that. Well, the King and Queen had decided to stay in London at Buck House[2] and a bomb was dropped on their courtyard on 13th September! SHE said she was glad it had happened so she could "look the East End in the face". She's such a wonderful woman is our Queen. Remember Daddy is in the same Masonic Lodge as the King? Well, now they'll really have even more to talk about, won't they; I mean, the King could so easily have been killed. It doesn't bear thinking about. We need the Royal Family; they're the glue that holds our country together. At least, that's my humble opinion!

All my love and kisses,
Mollykins

---

1. *In 1940 the British Embassy Dairen staff was L.H. Fouldsas Consul and G.J. Edmondson as Pro Consul & Clerical Officer. Postwar, this major city and seaport in the Liaoning Province of China had a variety of names: Dalian, Dairen, Dainly, Dalnil, Dalniy and Lueda, but in 1940 it was known as Dairen.*
2. *Buck House = Buckingham Palace.*

Chapter 16

7th September, 1940 to 10th May, 1941
The London Blitz

Fred had set off on his long journey to Moscow on 20th July, 1940. Molly and Fred had only had some three-and-a-half months of bliss together in London. Now Fred had left Molly behind. He promised to send for her once he'd reached the British Embassy in Moscow safely. Meanwhile she was determined to keep herself busy, to write daily, if she could, to her beloved husband, to keep a stiff upper lip, and to carry on!

Not two months after Fred's departure Hitler started his "Blitz" on London. On 7th September, 1940, this "lightning war" included a period of pure terror, when his air force, the Luftwaffe, bombed the city and docks for 11 weeks in a row, day and night bar one, including a huge, dreadful attack on 15th September during the daytime, ending up with one third of London destroyed, much of it in the City and East End.

Molly was serious about "carrying on". After all, she was British, and the Brits weren't going to let that madman in Germany get to them, in all senses of the word. She told anyone doubting her sense in going out to work in wartime England, "Listen! We're English! Have a cuppa tea, keep a stiff upper lip, and just CARRY ON!" That was her pet slogan, used by many other British people, too.

So off Molly cycled every morning from her flat at 17 Cheniston Gardens in Kensington to work at the bank where she'd managed to get a wartime job. She would leave shortly after dawn in order to get there in time because of all the bomb craters she had to gingerly cycle around. As she pedalled along, her local Air Raid Precautions (ARP) warden smartly saluted her, usually with a cheeky smile and a wink. When she'd ride home after work, there he'd be again, going along on his own bicycle, checking blinds were pulled down at dusk, to stop Jerry and his bombers homing in on any lights. People were required to add heavy curtains or shutters to their dwellings, commercial premises, and all factories. If a warden saw any light escaping, he or she would bang on the door or window and yell out, "Put out that light!" A persistent offender was usually reported to the police, and the misdemeanour was considered quite a serious offence.

As the war progressed the ARP wardens dealt with reporting and helping in many aspects of bombing incidents. They also sounded the air raid warning siren, directed people on their street to air raid shelters, checked their gas masks, and sounded the all-clear siren to show when the danger had passed. Then they'd check to see if an incendiary bomb had fallen anywhere on their beat, report it, and organise what to do about it. If people had lost their homes, the wardens helped them find temporary accommodation. In cases of fire or unexploded incendiary bombs, it was also the wardens who notified "Control Centre" for their area, often using Boy Scouts or the Boys Brigade as messengers to run and relay the information and services needed to deal with each event or incident, especially when telephone lines had been cut or come down in a raid.

For Molly's part, she couldn't just stay at home. She had volunteered to help the war effort and banking still had to go on, however many bombs rained down upon London.

Fred had left on his journey to the USSR in July, so had experienced just a smattering of what was to follow for London. His letters reveal how anxious he was to have left Molly alone, without him, during those horrific days of war, but he had to leave. This was war, and his duty had to come first.

He wrote to her from his *Nekka Maru* ship that the sky was a piercingly bright blue, but that the seagulls following the ship were piercing his heart in two with their hungry screeches. His heart felt heavy and black, almost suffocatingly so. Gulping huge breaths of air, he stood at the ship's railing for what seemed like hours, watching the sun go down and the sky transform from yellow to orange to red then purple and finally to black, as black as his heavy heart, but pierced now with stars, as the moon's reflection shimmered and zigzagged in a choppy silvery line across the sea. As he leaned on the railing, day-dreaming, and leaning into the gentle sway of the vessel, his mind moved from Molly back to the carnivals, fairs and drinking bouts with the chums of his youth in Germany. He thought of cornflower blue skies and picnics and wine along the Rhine. He thought of evening parties in beer gardens under velvety dark blue skies, and soon he was swaying to the music in his head of a half-forgotten drinking song about his beloved Rhine and its wine, as the ship swayed with him:

Kornblumenblau
   ist der Himmel am herrlichen Rheine
   Kornblumenblau sind die Augen der Frauen
   beim Weine...

Cornflower blue
   is the heaven above the glorious Rhine
   cornflower blue are the eyes of the ladies
   at wine...

. . .

Fred remembered how the word blue in German also means "drunk" but "depressed" in English. At this point he was most definitely feeling his English genes, so, sighing, he left the ship's railing and swayed his way back to his cabin and onto his bunk.

While Fred was sailing far away, Hitler's bombs continued to rain down from the sky onto the London area. It was the City of London and the East End that felt his force, including Rotherhithe, Poplar, West Ham, Stepney, and Bermondsey, but before long bombs were raining down on Croydon and Tottenham, then Chelsea and Trafalgar Square. The pigeons squawked and chirped in fright, winging up in fluttering dismay around the four huge lion statues of the Square every time an incendiary bomb crashed out of the sky. In September and October Trafalgar Square received hits near St. Martin-in-the-Fields, the South Africa House, and even The National Gallery. 500 lbs. of high explosives fell out of the sky onto Trafalgar Square on 12th October. All of this Molly had to cycle around on her way to her job at the bank.

On the morning of the 12th, as she cycled past Trafalgar Square tube station she saw a scene from hell. She skidded to a stop in the falling dust and watched, mouth agape. A woman stood with her hands over her mouth, emitting a high keening cry. Molly jumped off her bike, pulled the upset woman toward her, encircling her shoulders with one arm, while grasping the bicycle with her other hand. The woman, between gasping sobs, told her that a high explosive bomb had landed on the road right above where the underground's ticket hall was, 40 feet below the ground. All the steel and concrete had collapsed with tons of earth falling down onto the poor people sheltering below, burying some of them alive. A helmeted fire warden approached Molly, asking her and the woman to "move along, move along, nowt to see 'ere, ladies!" Other wardens were trying to shut off a broken main that was spurting and gushing water down into the cracks and hole made by the bomb. Molly gently disengaged herself from the sobbing woman and remounted her bike, all the while murmuring encouraging words to the terrified woman. There was nothing else she could do to help her. She now felt numb herself, unreal, as if she were taking part in a surreal cinema picture.

A little farther on she saw rescue workers already pulling bodies from the huge mound of dirt and debris and laying them onto stretchers.

The victims' faces were white from dust and their bodies looked crushed or mangled, with arms and legs hanging at bizarre angles. Molly suddenly began to retch and hurriedly pushed her bike away from the scene, where she let it fall to the ground while she bent over and brought up all her meagre breakfast, leaning against a brick wall until only dry heaves wracked her body. When she felt a little better, she glanced back toward Trafalgar Square and noticed that the four proud bronze lions around Nelson's Column seemed to have only suffered a few blemishes. Somehow this discovery cheered Molly up no end. On she cycled to work, convinced again that no way was Herr Hitler going to obliterate us British, however hard he tried!

As 1940's last quarter went on, more and more firebombs were dropping onto the City of London. The slogan was "London can take it!" and take it they did, even daring to offer a sigh of relief when it was learned that St. Paul's Cathedral had survived. If their beloved Cathedral had been smashed to smithereens, spirits would have sunk even further. Demolition was everywhere. Piles of bricks and concrete and twisted iron lay in heaps of rubble. Whole facades of houses had slid down off the dwellings, revealing intimate details of homeowners' lives within—a bathtub, a bed, a toilet, a table laid for dinner with four chairs still in place around it.

Each morning people poured out of bomb shelters where they'd spent the night. Exhausted fire-watch wardens sat, smoking cigarettes, at their Auxiliary Fire Service posts, leaning up against tall pillars of sandbags crowned with sheets saying "LONG LIVE THE KING!"

More bricks, beams and pieces of wood, more smashed concrete, dented vehicles, clothing, books and hundreds of pieces of paper were fluttering around in the breeze, or lying, strewn, all over the roads. Women, with their hair covered in cotton turbans, stoically pushed brooms, creating pathways for other women and old men pushing their carts of possessions along, dragging children by the hand, avoiding cracks and holes and all trying to find a place, anywhere, to sleep the next night, to get away.

This was the atmosphere Molly wove her bicycle through each and every morning and late afternoon five days a week, trying to remain cheerful and to get to work "to do her bit". She, along with everyone else—men, women, and often children—carried their own personal small dun-coloured square box held by a thin rope over the shoulder. This box contained an individual gas mask, to be carried at all times.

Owners who chose to stay with their shops taped up the still unharmed glass of their windows with the tic-tac-toe game of noughts and crosses, or, with gritted teeth and a dark glee, taped vile epithets against "the bloody Jerry", all to reduce the effects of bomb blasts they knew were yet to come.

---

17 Cheniston Gardens,
Kensington, London, W.8

Friday, 25th October, 1940

Letter Number 17

Darling Fred,

Today was awful at the bank. This bloody Blitz, Freddie! The siren went off so Mr. Fairweather ordered us all downstairs into the bank's air-raid shelter. I grabbed my smaller piano accordion. You know I have that big one, too? Well, I keep that one at home. Remember I played all those songs for you? I decided to cheer everyone up so played some of our popular tunes. They liked White Cliffs of Dover, *and* I'll be Seeing You. *I had to grit my teeth from not crying, thinking of you as I played it. Mr. Fairweather said he'd think about giving me a Christmas bonus because I was "such a good girl". So, in a quiet moment, when he told me that in my ear (so none of the others could hear) I started to play* White Christmas!

They've got our air-raid shelter under the bank quite nice. There's even a chandelier! I wonder what it was before this. Maybe a wine-tasting room. You can hear the crashes from the bombs up above and the chandelier swings and sometimes the lights go out. That's when I play hardest. Good thing I can play from touch, just like touch-typing. They taught us to touch-type at the typing school by blindfolding us. Good thing, eh?

Your letters aren't numbered, Freddie, but I'm so relieved to hear from you, but I'm hardly getting any letters. Maybe you'll number all the ones you send from Russia once you get there? At least we can do the telegrams. I realized I was only using the 13-word full rate reply telegrams to you, although you said I could do the 25 words Evening Letter Telegram, 'cos it's cheaper. Maybe I'll stick to those when not writing letters. That way, I know you'll hear from me faster. Well, you should do—I so hope you do. Do you?

I love you, my darling Freddie.

Yours forever,
Mollykins

SHIRLEY READ-JAHN

17 Cheniston Gardens, Kensington, London, W.8 (not far from the Royal Albert Hall). Taken years after the War.

Chapter 17

September, 1940
The Trans-Siberian Express Train

On the morning of Saturday, 7th September, 1940, Fred boarded the express train from Dairen (then a Japanese territory) to Harbin, China, in a first class comfortable but very stuffy, non-air-conditioned compartment. Once in Harbin he would connect with the Trans-Siberian Express. The scenery was quite pretty with maize fields, naked children, but filthy little loam houses next to the fields, nearly all looking rain-flooded, or, he wondered, perhaps rice paddies' spillover?

The food on this first train was lousy, the compartments quite dirty, with a strange crowd of passengers: Japanese, Chinese, and Soviets, some very dirty, too, and smelly. Half-undressed women were showing their breasts as they were creeping along the train's corridors. Prostitutes? On the train? He preferred to doubt it...he did wonder what Molly back in London would think of all this?

On this train he met up with a Mr. Eriksen, a Dane of the East India Company. He was a nice chap who knew Harbin's British Consul. He went on and on about the importance of leaving the USSR, and there Fred was, heading for Russia. It made for an uncomfortable feeling, hence a rather worrisome, anxious night in general. Fred fretted a little that once in Harbin there might not actually be someone there from the British Consulate to meet him. You never knew if cables sent would get through alright in this damned war, and, not knowing the language made it so hard. He wished he'd been given the luxury of a linguist-interpreter to be his travelling companion! Rather, he wished he'd had time to learn Russian at the Linguists Club on Grosvenor Place, but he'd got his orders to leave before something like that could happen. He doubted one could learn a language such as Russian in just three months.

The train pulled into Harbin at 8.05 am the following day, Sunday, 8th September. Fred had had a truly dreadful night, all made better with the relief that he was met at the station by a Consulate officer, who, it turned out, knew his brother Herman from Berlin! He'd recognised Fred's unusual surname. After a bath at the Consulate, then breakfast with the very kind British Consul General and his wife, they loaded him up for the next stage of his train journey with fags, fruit, sugar, etc. — everything he'd been already told he would need on the Trans-Siberian Express.

At the train station he was introduced to the American Ambassador to the USSR, Laurence Adolph Steinhardt, with whom he was to travel all the way to Moscow. They both boarded the Trans-Siberian Express, and once aboard, Fred was fortunate to get a compartment to himself.

The journey through Manchuria was monotonous, with endless steppes and tundra country. This land seemed to Fred to be very cold, mostly dry-looking and treeless, with a lot of low, open, herbaceous vegetation. Every 30 to 50 miles he'd see a small settlement, especially near water and where it was greener. There was mile upon mile of brown, yellow and sometimes green land;

wild horses; smallish rivers snaking through flat, rocky, valleys; bluish-grey or yellow treeless crags in the distance; but only occasionally red, orange and yellow riparian trees crowding the edges of rushing streams. If close enough to his train, he glimpsed black-haired men, women and children riding on horseback, wearing brightly-coloured embroidered padded jackets and fur hats, decorated gorgeously and all bearing earflaps. He even saw camels from time to time. When the train rounded a bend through some hills into a valley, there were deer, once even a huge stag with a great rack of antlers following along behind a doe. He made notes of all this to tell Molly and his mother about. Would that they were here, he thought, it's all so foreign!

Once he saw in the distance a squad of military men on motorbikes bumping across the rocky land—they looked like they could have been riflemen. Right after that, he was forcibly commanded to draw his curtains, being told loudly and vehemently by armed Chinese guards that he was not allowed to look out of the windows, or so he presumed from their arm-waving and miming motions. So, he thought, what was one to do? Not wanting to draw any more attention to himself, he obeyed. He slept and managed to get a good night's rest out of it, all the way from 9 pm to 7 the next morning.

Monday, 9th September started with pouring rain, which was quite a blessing as it was terribly dusty. To get any air into the compartments at all you had to slide the windows at least partially down.

Fred had several talks with the United States Ambassador on board the train. The Trans-Siberian Express pulled into Manchouli in Inner Mongolia at 10.55 am. They saw that it was a terribly desolate and broken-down town, on the border with the USSR. The Ambassador seemed interested in Fred and invited him to join him. They went along to the Nikitin Hotel with two secretaries of the president of the South Manchuria Railway, who were acting as escorts for the Ambassador.

Up in one of the hotel rooms the Ambassador invited Fred to

join him in a picnic lunch. He pulled over one of his suitcases on the bed, unpacked a small cooker and started to open tins (what he called cans)—a most unusual behaviour for an Ambassador. But Mr. Steinhardt was a typical American, very humane, quite informal in spite of being a New York City millionaire. When Fred thought of how some of his British "His Excellencies" would behave, he couldn't believe it! They had pork and beans, spaghetti in tomato sauce, raspberries, blackberries, beer, then a truly lovely Bordeaux wine. All followed by biscuits and chocolate; and all that on the edge of civilisation. It was really a thrilling experience for Fred. It changed his mind immediately from his earlier dislike of New Yorkers from when he was over there.

The Ambassador then changed his Yen for him and kindly gave him a very good rate. 40 Yen = 180 Rubles. Now he was all set to start off in the USSR with some real coinage.

Upon arrival in Manchouli, the Japanese Consul sent his car for the Ambassador's little group and they were driven through the "town" that took all of five minutes. As Fred said, "You held your breath, and, by the time you'd exhaled, you were through the whole damn town!" Next they took a short stroll but returned soon to the hotel owing to a sudden burst of heavy rainfall. It had turned even colder. In fact, it was now quite autumnal.

Arriving back at the Manchouli station at 5 pm Fred received a nasty shock. A rumour was going around that they would have to stay in quarantine in Otpor, on the Soviet side of the border for seven whole days as the pest of cholera had broken out in Monteden, Harbin, and Mukden. The Soviet Union Consul, who came to see Ambassador Steinhardt off, confirmed this. Only diplomats were to be permitted to carry on with their journey. Fred was feeling awfully nervous about this. He was no diplomat. He was ostensibly "just a British civilian clerk" on a journey.

They chugged out of Manchouli at 5.40 pm and arrived in Otpor at 6.15 pm. It was true alright, that rumour. The train had huffed and puffed into Otpor station, coming to a jerky, grinding halt with a loud moan, as if it knew it was going to be held up for hours.

All passengers had to leave the train, and railway workers were coming along to fumigate all the carriages' compartments.

Everyone who'd been on the train was locked into the customs office. Then an official from "Intourist" announced in German—since a large number of the passengers were German—that the government had ordered every person be put into quarantine for seven days, until Monday next. That meant being locked up inside the railway cars, which you were not allowed to leave. They were not permitted to wear any clothes other than what they were presently wearing. They were to be allowed to have only one book to read, but nothing else.

The Ambassador, in the meantime, was using all his influence to persuade the customs officers to let Fred carry on with him. Was he just a good chap, a very kind American, or did he have a reason to get Fred going on his journey? Fred wondered about this and decided the Ambassador must "know something" about him, perhaps through his governmental connections with the Brits. Regardless, Fred still spent an anxious two hours waiting for the officials' decision. Fortunately, the Russian interpreter who had come to Otpor to meet Ambassador Steinhardt, succeeded in convincing the lady doctor that Fred was a diplomat and a Very Important Person, so finally she agreed that he may continue on his way. In the meantime, the customs officials had a fine time with his baggage. Every single sheet of paper had been carefully examined. They'd opened his private letters. They also confiscated a book of his, some English information broadsheets, his Japanese papers and his Shorthand System notes[1]. The book was by Webb, about the USSR and absolutely pro-Bolshevik.

After another intervention of the Ambassador and the interpreter he was able to recover his book and Shorthand System. What a relief it was for him to climb up onto the Trans-Siberian Express once more. He was very lucky indeed that Mr. Steinhardt happened to be on the same train with him.

As the train slowly pulled away from Otpor station at 8 pm, they left all the other passengers behind, all upset, some even crying. Fred felt a mixture of relief, yet compassion for them, crowded on the platform about to be pushed back into their carriages, and so many with handkerchiefs held to their eyes.

The food on the train wasn't too bad now that they'd left Manchuria behind. It was better even than in Japan. To his surprise they had gramophone music in every carriage!

The next day was Tuesday, 10th September. Fred upgraded from soft class to 1st class category and paid 200 rubles extra for the luxury. In the China or Mongolia of the 1940s "soft class" was a term referring to 1st class but in the USSR it referred to whether the sleeping shelf was upholstered or hard. So 3rd class sleeping bay benches were called the "hard" class. On a long train journey such as he was doing, one needed 1st class if one could find the rubles to pay for it. His new carriage was well appointed with satin cushions in red and gold and curtains as well as blinds, and with a soft sleeping shelf. The only minor concern was he now had a "cabin mate".

It had largely been an uneventful day for Fred. He read, slept, and chatted with the Ambassador. In the evening he had a long, valuable, discussion with his 1st class cabin mate via the interpreter. He was a young Russian officer who had formerly been a shepherd, and who had fought in Finland in The Winter War. He was a rather educated shepherd, Fred thought. With lots of arm-throwing and excitable gesticulations, he explained to Fred all about the recent history of his land. The Winter War was the military conflict between the Soviet Union and Finland in 1939-1940. It began with the Soviet invasion of Finland on 30th November, 1939. That was just three months after World War II had broken out. It ended on 13th March, 1940 with the Moscow Peace Treaty. It was this Winter War that caused the League of Nations to expel the Soviet Union from the League on 14th December, 1939 because they deemed the attack to be illegal.

Fred was quite impressed with the loquacity of this very young shepherd and mesmerised by his story of fighting in the bitter cold and snow of Finland. His animated talking whiled away some of the long rather tedious journey. He claimed that the Soviet Union wanted Finland to cede over to them a large amount of border territories in exchange for land elsewhere, wanting particularly to protect the city of Leningrad, which was only 20 miles (32 kilometres) from the Finnish border. When Finland refused, in came the Soviet Union army to force the issue. The young officer claimed, darkly, that he reckoned the Soviet Union was actually intending to conquer all of Finland.

Fred also wrote about Wednesday, 11th September in his diary. It was another day where nothing of any real importance had occurred, but, he did have a long talk with a Dr. Buchholz, a German Commercial Secretary returning home from Colombia. It was interesting to Fred how this war had sent him on his own (what was to be three months long) circuitous route from England, and that this German Commercial Secretary had had to take the Trans-Siberian Express up to Moscow in order to get from Colombia back to Germany—he had been travelling for rather a long time, too. Fred noted in his diary how he'd listened carefully, as usual, to what this gentleman had to say, being a German Commercial Secretary, returning to his Fatherland to follow another agenda. Every detail he may have involuntarily imparted, perhaps thoughtlessly, to Fred, would be stored away in Fred's head, or noted in his own peculiar stenography in his diary, to be passed along as appropriate.

From time to time, Fred stretched his legs by sauntering down the train's corridor to Ambassador Steinhardt's carriage for "informational chats". This august gentleman spent some time informing Fred about the new American planes. One of them was the "supercharged Bentley Bomber" which travelled at an altitude of 30,000-35,000 feet. It was a new fighter that could speed through the air at 580 mph. After that conversation, Steinhardt kindly passed Fred a bottle of red Bordeaux. The Ambassador's baggage was certainly stuffed with food and wine delights!

On Thursday, 12th September, Fred was sitting alone at a table in the dining car for dinner when a gunshot was fired at the window right next to him. At the sound, he'd immediately swivelled his head to his window and saw his reflection staring back at him, with total obscurity outside. In an instant, he automatically slid rapidly down as far under the table as he could get, and carefully pulled out his handgun from its shoulder holster under his jacket.

When the excited chatter around him ceased, and he gathered it was now "all clear", he pulled himself up to see that the shooter's bullet had fortunately only penetrated the first pane and cracked the second pane of his window, then buried itself across from him in the wooden panelling. He surreptitiously slid his gun back into its holster.

The train was moving at quite a pace at that point, with darkness outside. At the time of the shot he was illuminated by the lights within the dining car, but he couldn't assume whatsoever that the shot was intended for him. Who would take a pot-shot at him? Surely not? Not here, no, definitely not likely. They must have been racing along next to the train on a motorcycle; it was travelling too fast for a horse to keep up. Thus, he simply finished his meal calmly but quickly, and retired to the relative safety of his compartment, where he planned to keep the curtains tightly closed, just in case. His "cabin mate" the Finnish ex-shepherd, wasn't in the compartment. Probably drinking with his pals in another carriage, assumed Fred.

But, as he entered the compartment he smelled jasmine. Jasmine? That reminded him of someone. There she was, a woman, lying on his bunk smiling slyly up at him. He went for his gun, but she sat up, swinging her long legs down from the bunk, and hurriedly saying, "Shanghai Joe, he sent me; wants to know you safe. You okay, sir?"

"Zhi Ruo", spluttered Freddie, "what the hell are you doing here?"

"I told you, he know you on board. He down other end. He heard you got shot at. Sent me to check you okay?"

"Why didn't he come himself?"

"He keeping eye on somebody else on train. He say you no worry. He got you covered. Here, take this. He give it to me. You give to Big Important Man on train you know, American fellah."

"Will do, Zhi Ruo, thanks, and tell that rascal Shanghai Joe I'm glad he's looking out for me. You're looking lovely, Zhi Ruo, really lovely."

She stood up and put her arms around him. They swayed together briefly to the train's motion, then, after planting a gentle kiss on his chin, she slid daintily from his compartment, her jasmine scent drifting seductively after her. He felt a bit guilty, thinking about Molly, but, as he told himself, there was nothing but a work connection between Zhi Ruo and him.

Thank God that Finn wasn't in here, he also thought, as he lay down himself to get some sleep. He felt a little upset from what had just happened, the shooting, Zhi Ruo. Be prepared, be prepared, be prepared, the train's iron pistons and wheels clattered to him as he fell into a restless sleep. His dreams were all over the place; he just didn't know what he was to be prepared for, or when. The not knowing was so disconcerting.

In the morning, Friday 13th September, he relayed the previous night's gunshot event to Ambassador Steinhardt who responded, while airily waving his hands about, "Well, yes, these sorts of things do happen quite frequently over here, young fellah!"

Fred passed along Shanghai Joe's message to him but didn't think it necessary to mention where he'd got it from. He believed implicitly in the "need-to-know basis". In both his military and espionage training, he'd learned how important it was to restrict very sensitive data information.

Fred wrote in his diary,

"Only another three days to go. Thank goodness. I've had just about enough of trains. I think the gunshot experience has somewhat unsettled me. I cannot but hope the journey ends soon. Three days, only three days more."

Several times during this day the Trans-Siberian Express jerked to a sudden, jolting stop. Armed men dressed in shabby uniforms climbed aboard shouting orders about. They pushed into compartment after compartment, tensely demanding "show papers, please!" while the train stood motionless with steam hissing from its engine. It was all quite nerve-wracking. Fred assumed this was somehow connected to "the shooting" but had no way of knowing.

There had been a sudden change in the weather. It had turned quite muggy and his sleeper compartment was heated. He put that down to the slight flu he'd suddenly come down with. There was no way for him to control the temperature. He asked the fellow in charge of the carriage to do something but the man seemed totally uninterested in helping or understanding him in any way. Fred did his best at miming his problem, wiping his forehead with his handkerchief, opening his jacket, trying to show him that he daren't lower the window or all the dust would fly in. The man just grinned stupidly at him and wiggled his eyebrows, then left the compartment with a shrug.

By now Fred had become tired of his muggy compartment and even chatting to the Finn. He took a stroll down the swaying carriage to see what it was like in the lower-class compartments. He ran into Herr Doktor Buchholz again, obviously going for a stroll himself. Leaning against the carriage windows, they chatted. He told Fred of a most unsettling, sad and rather unpleasant thing. At a point where the weather had recently been very cold indeed—hence the heating of the first-class compartments—he'd learned that the third-class lavatories were so filled with filth and human waste that it was impossible to use them. Thus, the passengers were lowering certain windows and defecating out of the windows as the train chugged or sometimes tore along. It was freezing cold outside.

"Good Lord, man, I sincerely hope the windows downwind were kept closed while that was happening. Those poor people, having to resort to that", said Fred, "we're really on the very edge of civilisation here, eh?"

"Ja", responded the doctor, "but do you really empathise with those poor souls in third-class? I mean, that's what you get in that class, *nicht wahr?*"

"Well, yes", said Fred, "I suppose that's true, isn't it? I mean, these days you're either in first-class or you're not. Sad, but true," he sighed.

Leaving the doctor, he carried on walking down, passing from carriage to carriage, until he'd reached as far down as the third-class compartments. They were jam-packed with people, some even lying on the floor. The smell had become quite unpleasant. He stepped over and around a couple of people resting on the corridor's floor, curious, as ever, to see for himself what it was like. In one compartment the people were singing, a sad, haunting song in Russian. One woman held a child on her lap. Her neighbour held a large wicker basket on hers. He saw the tip of a big watermelon sticking up out of the basket. How clever, he thought, to bring fresh fruit on the journey. They'd surely last fresher that way. He'd no idea you could grow melons in Mongolia! They all looked up and stared at him through the compartment's glass window as he stood, swaying, in the corridor, staring back in at them all. The song faded out and they just stared. Feeling discomfited and out of place he moved away and made his way back to first class.

Back in his compartment and checking his diary, Fred noted it was now Saturday, 14th September. He saw out of the window that the train had just steamed past Ekaterinburg. Ekaterinburg! Russia! That's where, he mused with morbid excitement, the Bolsheviks had murdered Tsar Nicholas II and his Romanov family in that basement on 17th July, 1918 under the orders of the Ural Soviets. In thinking about this, as they were bumping and swaying along the railroad track, and, watching the Ekaterinburg station sign fade off into the distance, he remembered hearing that there was some belief that it was the government in Moscow, specifically Vladimir Lenin and Yakov Sverdlov, who were the savage culprits. They were the two who'd wanted to prevent the White Forces from rescuing the imperial family during the Russian Civil War—attested to by Leon Trotsky in his diary. When Fred had read a copy of that diary it had also said that was disputed by other researchers. "I wonder what the real truth was?" he thought to himself. He'd read as much as he could about the USSR once he'd heard of his upcoming posting there. He knew he should have been learning Russian instead of reading history. But also, he admitted wryly to himself, it wasn't as if he'd had that much time, spending most of his free time locked in Molly's arms, had he?

Fred wrote in his own diary,

"I'm going to be in Moscow. I wonder how long for? A city, and a country, filled with many unknowns, mystery and intrigue."

Then, totally switching gears:

"We English always discuss the weather! Along with my dark thoughts and unwell feeling, it is cold and rainy. I'm feeling rather groggy. The Ambassador and some of his entourage are muttering about the same complaint."

Fred reckoned they'd all got a touch of the flu.

On they went, clickety-clack, clickety-clack, lulling him in and out of feverish sleep.

Fred cheered up, suddenly feeling so much better, as the Trans-Siberian Express pulled into Moscow at 11.30 pm the following day, Sunday, 15th September, 1940. They were two whole hours late. This was slightly annoying to a precise individual such as he, but, far more importantly to him, the news from England was exceedingly upsetting. London had been badly damaged in the Blitz and the population was being generally evacuated. He was now feeling very nervous indeed about Molly, his mother and his brother, Herman. He sincerely hoped he'd find specific news of all three of them when he finally arrived at the British Embassy.

Hidden in Plain Sight

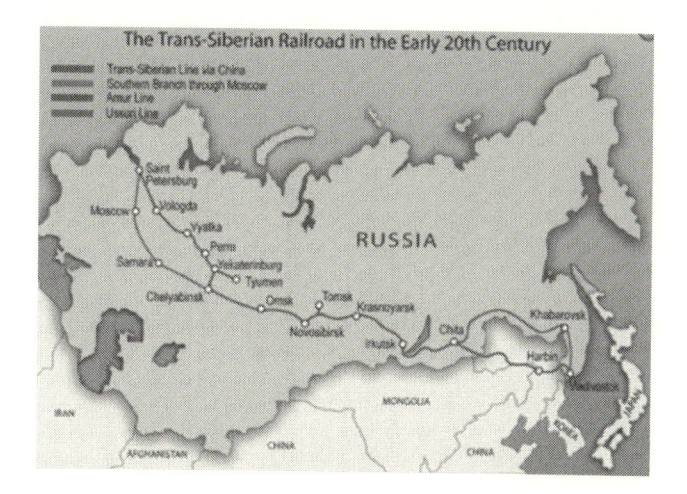

The Trans-Siberian Railroad stops in the Early 20th Century.

1. The plain Shorthand System notes for the system he'd been taught at Scotland Yard before his trip. These notes naturally did not contain any clues to the Code Fred had invented for his own diary notes.

Chapter 18

**September, 1940
Early Days in Moscow**

While Fred had been rattling along on his wearisome journey he'd thought on and on about Molly in London. From newspapers occasionally obtained at stations by the Ambassador, Fred heard ghastly news about the raids on London and other English cities. He hated and feared the idea of his precious wife being out and about in such a hellish wartime environment in London. He couldn't tell her what he was actually up to, she knew that, but he also knew he needed to keep her spirits up, and always let her know in his letters that he was alright and that she shouldn't add to her own burdens by worrying about him. Fred and Molly both felt they'd had so much luck so far, that it couldn't end, not with a love as strong as theirs.

Finally, finally! The Trans-Siberian Express had successfully arrived in Moscow on Sunday, 15th September.

On Thursday 19th, Fred wrote a letter to his mum. As many

people were doing, he now decided he'd better number his letters, both to his mother and to his wife, because one never knew how long it was going to take for a letter to reach them, and they didn't always arrive at their destination in the order sent.

In his Letter No. 1 he told his mother he was feeling extremely fit and ready for work again; how happy he'd been to arrive at the Embassy to find her letter of 30th August plus six big fat letters from Molly awaiting him. It took him half a day to digest all their news. He was relieved that the bombs had spared Luton where his mother was living and he begged her to have his brother, Herman[1], get her out of there to a quieter spot, if bombs were falling on Luton since her last letter. Molly would give her the dough she'd need to find a safer place to live, if necessary. He had to know she was safe.

In those times Fred and his loved ones were also sending telegrams back and forth. There were the Reply Paid Telegrams with 13 words available for a full rate reply, but it was much better to use the ELT kind (Evening Letter Telegram), which was a cheap night telegram on which you could send 25 words, as Molly had mentioned in one of her earlier letters to Fred. Communicating during the war was so difficult, with telephoning having become out of the question, so telegrams were, therefore, the quickest way to let everyone know you were still alive and safe.

When Fred had finally reached the Embassy, they hadn't been expecting him as yet. As he told his wife in his Moscow Letter No. 1 to her, he'd sent the British Embassy in Moscow a telegram from Siberia, but they'd never received it. The British Embassy in Tokyo had earlier informed them that he had arrived in Japan but had omitted to let them know when he'd left again, so, as far as they knew, he could well have been stuck in Japan. Consequently, there was no accommodation prepared for him. The Baltic states of Latvia, Lithuania and Estonia had ceased to exist so half the British Embassy staff from there had arrived in Moscow and taken up all the available accommodation within the Embassy and even the Embassy's flats in the town itself. Fred got lucky in that one of the staff was away in hospital so he was put into that man's flat for the time being. The flat was in a wing of the Embassy.

He sent a photo to Molly of the front of the British Embassy & Mission building. It was a huge, grey, imposing building with an entryway *porte cochère* topped by a broad balcony. The Ambassador's personal quarters were on the top floor. Stepping out onto that balcony the Ambassador could survey everything below and over to the River Moskva. Four Doric pillars flanked the entrance. Fred's office was on the ground floor at the right of the entrance. For his non-cypher work he sat at a window also looking out to the river and the Kremlin. The cypher work was done in a large basement room filled with the necessary espionage equipment.

Fred was immediately immersed in a lot of work. He barely had time to even think about his future accommodation because everything had turned out to be far more complicated and difficult than what he had been told or even imagined. All the staff was expected to provide its own food, linen, towels, crockery, in fact, all the hundred and one things that one would need to run even the smallest flat. He met several nice chaps who agreed to help him out with odds and ends.

He was told he'd eventually be sharing diggings consisting of a small flat with another young chap arriving from Riga—the capital of Latvia—in a day or two. He heard they would each have their individual bedrooms, and share a sitting-cum-drawing room, and would be expected to mess together. And, he knew he was going to have to hire a maid and probably even share a car, if the flat they ended up getting wasn't part of the actual Embassy compound. You'd need a car to get about, he could already tell, because transport was virtually impossible. So, it was all looking to be much more expensive than he'd imagined.

His head was feeling dizzy from everything he had to think about, besides his all-important work. For his personal welfare, one of the first things he was told to do was to send a telegram to Lawn & Alder in London asking them to send him a consignment of tinned food, sugar, tea, flour, drinks, etc. You could hardly buy a thing in Moscow and what he'd received for the Trans-Siberian Express journey was completely gone by now. What they did have was scarce, spare, and of very inferior quality, in all areas. He was fortunate in that the ship bringing provisions hadn't left England yet, so his order would be put on that ship and, all being well, reach him in about a month—if no German submarine got it. All of that consignment was going to cost him about £30-£50.

He'd reached Moscow on Sunday, 15th September and on the Tuesday was introduced to the Ambassador, the Right Honourable Sir Stafford Cripps, CH, FRS[2]. After the pleasantries were over—was Fred satisfied? Comfortable? Anything he needed? Fred raised the question of whether his new wife could be brought over to live with him in Moscow? He reckoned the Ambassador wouldn't object because his own wife, Lady Cripps, was already on her way to the USSR and due to arrive on the 26th. She was travelling along the same route as Fred had taken. The Ambassador certainly understood but would have to consider the matter. He seemed upbeat about the situation, so Fred's hopes were raised.

Fred couldn't tell Molly when exactly she could leave to start the long journey, but he was positive that she should, at least, start preparing her things for the long trip. The weather was expected to be so severe that some of the chaps had suggested she should wait till the following year, after winter, to have a more comfortable journey. There was a potential technical hitch to her coming over. When Fred had been approached by the Foreign Office to go to Moscow as part of his military intelligence job, he had been single, and it was a job for single men only. They preferred not having women in such a dangerous situation—knowing eventually the Germans would in all probability beat their way into Moscow—but, he wanted, no, needed, Molly with him, so he was determined to get over this obstacle any way he could.

He was, as time went by, to learn that some of the men had married Russian wives and lived with them in flats the Embassy provided in the city, but at this time, Fred hadn't known that. This was to prove a potentially explosive situation because some of these women were coerced into spying for the NKVD, which was the Russian abbreviation for the People's Commissariat for Internal Affairs.

Fred fell into a routine at work. He started his day at 10 am,

Hidden in Plain Sight

went to lunch at 2 pm and then picked up working again from 4-8 pm Many times he would have to work after dinner, often until 10.30 at night. Saturdays and Sundays simply weren't known in this establishment. If he managed to get two or three hours off now and then, he felt very lucky. But, he was well aware there was a war going on and, knowing what his wife had to put up with in London made him consider himself most fortunate. He'd already been warned that shortly he and the other fellows were all going to have to be working up to 2 o'clock every morning. That meant they had to get enough rest whenever they could and not plan on going out much at all.

But, to keep himself feeling sane, on his occasional free time he consorted with some very nice people—correspondents and members of other Embassies and Legations. He considered this part of his "work" anyway, always on the alert for news, information, or even gossip, which he could convey to his superiors at the Embassy or relay back to his London "handlers". He even managed to get some dancing in at the Metropol Hotel. He reckoned it was good exercise, and besides, dancing with a female took his mind off his work, and how he was missing Molly, if only for the duration of the quickstep. Aside from those brief respites, his mind these days had to be totally focussed on his work, leaving him little time to daydream; but he could visit her in his dreams when he'd finally climbed into bed.

The Metropol was the only hotel in Moscow the Embassy staff was allowed to go to. At this time Fred hadn't seen one bit of Moscow aside from that hotel and was itching to go out for a simple walk but, so far, nobody was allowed to go outside during the daytime.

Most days were filled not only with work but the ever-present watch for the courier bag to come in. That bag hopefully would hold personal letters for the Embassy staff, apart from the wartime correspondence. The bag service was an on-again, off-again matter, depending on the route it had to take in the world to reach them in Moscow, so lots of nail-biting ensued, lots of frustration, as the day would pass when the bag was expected, and it simply hadn't turned up, so every day thereafter was a potential "family news" day. With luck the bag would come once a week, so Fred wrote his daily letters ready to seal them into the bag with the return mail leaving the Embassy for England—if it showed up when expected.

The Embassy staff got to hear pretty quickly what was going on "back home" and Fred knew that people were having a tough time of it in in the Blitz in Kensington, London, and that Malden, too, in the southwest outer area of London, had suffered quite badly. New Malden was where "Broadmayne" was—Molly's lovely, big, parental home, staffed with a pretty maid in her black dress, white cap and frilly pinafore. He could imagine how trying it must be for all those back in England. He'd listen in to the news mostly from anti-British sources, and many days from the BBC, if they could tune it in okay, and what he'd be hearing made him feel sick and sometimes he was very near on crying, as stalwart as he was. He worried constantly about his wife, and, as he said in part of his first letter home to her on 22nd September,

"Oh Molly Darling you must be having a ghastly time. Sometimes I think I should never have left you. But then, we have had so much luck, I don't see why it shouldn't continue. In the meantime I've heard that John Lewis [department store] *is burnt down and a good many other places round the Circus* [Piccadilly Circus]. *It must be a most distressing and depressing sight for you every morning. And then those beastly night raids. In spite of the nastiness of the situation I couldn't help smiling when I read your reports of your camping at the fire station. I take it it's the one next to Kensington Close, isn't it? And I am ever so pleased that Nita[3] lives so near to you and that you have joined the club. I hope you can enjoy a few nice hours there now and then and forget for a short while all the worries and troubles we have to cope with. That must have been a pretty sight seeing my little wife chasing down into the basement in her nightie. I hope there aren't too many men in your house. You know, sweetheart, it is a beautiful feeling to know that I have such a brave wife who even keeps her humour in the most uncomfortable moments. We are going to get on extremely well together and I think now once and for*

all that I am definitely going to keep you and give up the idea of goldfish.

I was very upset to hear of what has happened to dear old Malden and your house. Your father must be having a terrible time. I do so hope that everyone and everything at Broadmayne are quite okay. Give your parents and sister my fondest love and tell them I am thinking of them all the time and praying that Broadmayne will be spared. Thank goodness I can get the BBC news now and that cheers one up considerably. I get the news every morning at 9.15 am and I am greatly relieved when I hear that bombs were not dropped on the West and South West of London. But then you never know whether the reports are really accurate. So, you're cycling to the bank. Are you sure, Darling, that it won't be too strenuous for you? I am so happy that you are putting on weight so nicely; it would be a pity to cycle it all off again, wouldn't it? But I think you know what you can do and what not. Tell me, Darling, is it really safe for you to stay in London. I feel so nervous about you. Hadn't you better quit your job and evacuate to somewhere quieter? I'm so proud of you being so plucky but do you honestly think it isn't too risky hopping about London these days? But I must leave it to you to decide. The thing you must bear in mind is that I want a safe and sound little wife to come to this place and not a little girl carrying her head under her arm. They don't like cripples out here.

I'm glad you received the moccasins. I wasn't quite sure whether they would get through. And I was rather nervous too as to the size. But they fit and that's okay then. Please excuse my disconnected way of writing but I'm doing this in between work and so I haven't got time to think straight. But you will be able to decipher this into intelligible English I hope.

I'm very glad too that you are happy at Mrs. Mullin's[4]. *Give her my kindest regards and my fondest love to my ladylove, Mrs. Cameron.*[5]

You must have had a very bad time with your toothies, Darling. But it was good to have the job done. So it was your teeth after all which were at the bottom of your losing weight trouble. I suppose I shan't recognize you when I see you. Don't get too fat, will you.

This morning I received a telegram from Mum. She too had overlooked that she could have sent 25 words as ELT. Perhaps you might explain it to her. Mum says she loves you so much Darling and gets on so well with you. I'm so happy about that. And apparently they haven't had any serious air raids in Luton. So it was a good idea that we sent Mum there. She is much safer there than she would be in London.

I was very sorry to hear that poor Doc will have to undergo another operation. It is, indeed, tough luck. Give her my love and wish her all the very best. I'm so grateful to her for the way she is looking after you. She is a real friend."

[LETTER CUTS OFF HERE]

On 25th September Fred had been invited by a couple at the Hungarian Legation to his first Russian ballet, "Don Quixote", and he had much enjoyed the very beautiful dancing. What he didn't like whatsoever was the "peculiar stink you get everywhere out here". He didn't know whether it was the people, their perfume or soap, or what it could be, but it offended his sensitivities. The other Embassy chaps assured him that one got used to it after a while. He learned that his chances of seeing the best ballet, or hearing the best concert music, were all to happen in autumn and winter in Moscow. This is when the dance companies and orchestras were home for the Soviet winter from their spring and summer travel engagements. Now it was wartime he reckoned he'd be luckier still in that they wouldn't be going out of the USSR at all!

Things were looking up a bit for his personal comfort, too. By the 26th, Fred had moved into a small flat. The flat was on the Embassy premises. It had two bedrooms, a kitchen and a bath, and he even had a maid to look after him. She was a Volga German so

Fred felt relieved; at least he could communicate with her in German. Now he had to get on the case to get hold of everything he needed to run this flat. For parties he'd have to get his hands on vodka, black caviar, and western cocktails, aside from the food basics and all the household equipment the maid would need to keep things humming along for him.

He was discovering that his German and French were helping him in many ways, especially when consorting with members of other foreign Legations, but he knew he had to start learning the difficult language of Russian really soon, to get on even better. For his work it was going to be imperative.

British Embassy, Moscow photo sent by Fred to Molly. Her writing on the back states: "Entrance to the Embassy offices on ground floor right. Fred sits at window behind car [half- buried in snow] looking out to river and Kremlin."

Fred could see the Kremlin from his office window.

Fred's East Wing British Embassy flat.

Hidden in Plain Sight

Hotel Metropol, Moscow.

Frozen Moskva River & the Kremlin. The Moskva is a tributary of the Volga River.

---

1. Herman was Fred's brother, in the same military intelligence arena as Fred, MI-19, but based at that time in England. Fred spelled his brother's name in this letter both as Herman and in the German way of Hermann. Also, elsewhere, Fred called his brother Bertie or just plain Bert.
2. The Ambassador, Sir Stafford Cripps was an English country gentleman, a devout Christian, a vegetarian and quite an ascetic. In the 1930s he had been a radical Labour backbencher and considered a bit of an outcast and quite an incongruous figure, doubtless because of his asceticism. His career took an upswing when he landed the position of British Ambassador to the USSR in 1940. It was because of this position he was later able to become a prominent figure in the War Cabinet and even later as a major player in the Labour government of Clement Atlee, who, in

SHIRLEY READ-JAHN

turn, formed his own Ministry in 1945 in the United Kingdom, after succeeding Winston Churchill's government. [Information found on-line.]
3. Nita Sutton Ovington was Molly's cousin.
4. Mrs. Mullins was Molly's landlady at Cheniston Gardens in Kensington, London.
5. Mrs. Cameron was another lodger at Mrs. Mullin's establishment—an elderly lady with whom Fred had innocuously flirted before he'd left London.

Chapter 19

**1940 Moscow,
Autumn Continues On**

The days rolled on, filled with more and more work, fitting out his new flat at the Embassy, and, whenever he could grab a minute, hurrying to write letters to his beloveds in England.

Fred got permission to go out for a walk, not only at night, but also briefly during the daytime, as seen in the following second letter he dashed off to Molly to tell her all about it.

British Embassy,
Moscow
Saturday, September 28th, 1940

Letter No. 2.

His Britannic Majesty's Embassy twerp Freddie presents his compliments to the sweetest girl in the world and has the honour to acknowledge with thanks receipt of her telegram from which he learned with deep satisfaction that the affection of his darling wife is "ditto". A mutual understanding having been reached the matter may now be considered satisfactorily settled.

Molly Darling, your telegram came at the right moment. I just needed cheering up. Have got a nasty cold, a lot of work and feeling terribly lonely. You don't know what those two little words "still safe" mean to me. The worry and uncertainty about you all, sure gets one down. I am so anxious to receive your next letters and read all the news from home. You must be suffering terribly. And your poor parents and all our friends. Do write and tell me how they are getting on.

Today, Saturday, has been extremely busy. The worst rush, however, was on Thursday, which was bag day. You know I'm not used to work anymore and it's a bit tough on a guy at this speed. If you don't hear anything more from me you'll know I've passed out. But I suppose I'll get used to it again. Last night I had the pip and I went out for a stroll. Suddenly I discovered a cinema showing an American film. It happened to be Charlie Chaplin in "Modern Times". I went in and had a good laugh. I felt much better after that.

This afternoon I went to have a look at the shops, which are few and far between. The few articles on display are of terribly inferior qualities and ridiculously expensive. Providing all these thousand and one household things is causing me a great deal of headache. I wish there were a Woolworth's but nothing doing. Dear old London seems from here just like paradise. Fortunately, we have a lot of telegrams to do tonight so won't have time to indulge in gloomy thoughts…

By Sunday, 29th September, Fred could feel that summer was definitely over by now. It had turned wet and cold and was raining all day long. This didn't particularly worry him because he was kept extremely busy. That afternoon at precisely 5 o'clock Ambassador Cripps held a late tea party where all the staff turned up, stood around drinking and eating and moaning to each other about the amount of work they were expected to do. His Excellency was extremely social and a very interesting narrator. The men would stop munching to listen to what he was saying, and stood, fascinated, rooted to the spot in order not to miss a single word.

The British Naval Attaché had a secretary called Bagston. He was an exceedingly decent chap who had taken it upon himself to help Freddie out. They had a small chicken dinner and then went out for what Bagston called "playing". This meant having a drink or two, but all quite harmless. His wife and boy were back in Runnymede, Surrey, their home being right on the banks of the River Thames where the Magna Carta had been signed in 1215 by King John and his Barons. Bagston had been lucky enough to have both his wife and son visit him in Moscow earlier on, but the snag to have them come back out again was not only the war going on, but that Bagston would have to pay the cost for their trip himself this time around.

Whenever Fred grabbed a short break from work to smoke his pipe, his thoughts would turn to home. Molly's playing of the accordion had endeared her even more to Fred. At boarding school she had played the piano and it had been said that she really ought to have become a concert pianist, but he recalled her telling him that her father had realistically insisted that she learn to type instead, saying you should always be equipped to rely upon yourself, in case life served you a rum hand of cards one day. Fred sent Molly a little song he'd come across, the words of which he found very appropriate, and was longing to hear her play it for him one day in the future. He also sent her a passport photo of himself, to show her the sort of rogue she'd married and what he'd looked like when recently in the land of cherry blossoms. He begged her to send him more snaps of herself and reminded her she'd have to get a permit to mail any photos whatsoever to him. He'd been told off by the wife of a Hungarian diplomat for not having a postcard-sized photo of her to show around kept in his pocket.

The news was that people in the heart of London were now safer than those living out in the suburban districts. He asked Molly to send him a detailed report of what bombing was going on, and where, so he could share it also with his colleagues, who would be immensely interested. From this news it was obvious to all of them at the Embassy in Moscow that the Nazis didn't seem to be having it all their own way with the British. The Royal Air Force was doing some wonderful work and *"old Adolf's 'Blitzkrieg' lacks the 'lightning property'* inherent in its name," Fred wrote! After pouring out his heart to his wife, Fred apologised for his "funny" letter and said he was going to sit down to drown his sorrows in Vodka.

By Friday, 11th October, life at the Embassy had become even more hectic. They were all working till one in the morning now and it had become virtually impossible for Fred to find much time off to write long letters. He listened regularly to the Home Service News and, so worried was he, that, even though inundated with work, he was thinking and wondering not only constantly about his wife and mother but also about his brother, Herman, and what kind of work he was doing for Britain. Herman was much involved in espionage, too, but, of course, they had both signed the Official Secrets Act so it was virtually impossible to tell each other any hard details about their work, except for "innocuous" encrypted messages, in words the brothers had fixed on prior to Fred's departure—just as he'd arranged in Japan with the Foreign Office's Kenneword. He was to say post-war that some words definitely were words with an ulterior meaning, which he used in letters to his mother, when asking her to forward certain items to him after speaking to his brother.

It was getting harder and harder for the mail to come through so receiving a telegram now and again saying "am safe and well" really did mean the world to Fred.

Things were developing so rapidly in the war, and Fred knew that now the Japanese had joined the Axis, it could bring all kinds of surprises, and yet more work. He told himself there was nothing to be gained by worrying. All he could do was his very best work, cyphering, translating German and French documents they'd get hold of, keep his nose down, and, as he said, *"nous verons"*. We'll see, indeed, he thought, when discussing another aspect of his work, that of getting certain people out of the USSR—another dangerous project that would be upcoming, and meant he'd first have to learn to ski as soon as enough snow had fallen. It was interesting to him to note how so few of the other Embassy chaps could ski; in fact, he knew of only one, and doubted he was any sort of intelligence agent who could be involved in the upcoming "escapade" with Fred (as Fred humorously thought of it) but, that was something that was always very hard to tell.

At this time Fred had moved again. His new colleague, Michael Crane, had come in from Sweden. They were sharing a flat together, with a bed-sitting room each and a communal dining room. He so wished Molly were there, to help him with fitting out this flat. It needed a woman's touch, plus, he was honestly too busy to pay it much mind. When he wrote to Molly about it, his sense of humour came again to the fore, as he said about her, "*Alas, she's playing hide and seek with ole Adolf's bombers*" so couldn't be with him. He spoke about their courting days back in Richmond, Surrey where they'd walked through Richmond Park then had bread and cheese at the Roebuck pub. Oh, those happy days! They'd loved that old English pub with its hanging baskets filled with red Pelargonium geraniums, white Alyssum and blue Lobelia. Very patriotic, they'd laughed together.

Fred felt so guilty about not writing to Molly's father, sister Olive, and all their friends, but, as he wrote to Molly,

"*...really it's quite impossible at this juncture. I trust they will understand. And the interesting things about this place and in general are not communicationable* [sic]. *Things at the present are so very uncertain that it's no use discussing anything about your coming out here. We must just be very patient and hope that things straighten themselves out in a few months' time. It is d.....*[sic] *rotten that I can't give you any definite promise but you will understand, won't you, Molly Darling. I need you so much, it's ghastly to think that you have to face all these terrible trials alone. I'm so happy to have such a brave wife. It would be awful if you were hysterical and panicky. Are you still working in Oxford Street? Darling, I think I would give it up if I were you. It's so very dangerous and I'm terrified that you might be caught in spite of all your caution and carefulness...*"

[Fred tried not to write swear words to his wife; plus, he was ever aware of wartime censorship, knowing everything he wrote was read by some faceless entity.]

Fred needed another suit and asked Molly to get it from Austin Reed's in London if the place was still standing. He reckoned he might get it in two months' time if the bag service was still operating. He also invented a joke order form for a suit, to amuse Molly in these trying times.

Molly wrote Fred a very long letter in October. She spent a week writing a little more each evening and night, whenever she was sleepless, sometimes hiding under the stairs from the bombs around her, sometimes in the cellar bomb-shelter, and having to write by torchlight.

17 Cheniston Gardens,
Kensington, London, W.8

October, written over many nights, 1940
Letter Number 20.

My dearest dear,

You said I must be having a ghastly time. Don't worry, darling, I'm managing. Don't forget I have Jimmie, as well as Daddy and all our friends! I am safe! Please stop worrying. You'll make yourself ill, darling, you know you will. You know your tummy suffers when you worry.

I want to be with you so much, to take care of you. You've no idea what it's like here now. I know I must be patient, but for how much longer? But it's grand getting cables and the occasional letter from you, Freddie darling. Do keep writing. I live for your letters. I got your Letter Number 2. Thank you!

The rationing is awful. There's a horse-meat shop half-way down the next road for human consumption. I must tell you, I'm so sick and tired of Welsh rarebit for supper so I went to that butcher and splurged on my rations and got some fillet steaks and made bubble and squeak, too, and it wasn't half bad! As of last February, they've only been letting us have a ration of 8 oz of bacon.

I get a ciggie ration of 200 a week. I'm a chain-smoker now, but I have to. Most of the girls at work won't smoke fags anymore. Mr. F. said they're German, made by the Schaeffler Group. I know you and all your pals call all cigarettes fags, but Mr. F. says only those German fags are fags so we should call what we smoke ciggies. Bossy, isn't he!

When I sit at my desk at work, banging away on the old typewriter, the bombs are screaming and the guns roaring, and I hear whistling sounds of them falling in the distance. You mustn't worry, though, I do take care, Freddie, honestly, because really I only hear them when the siren goes and we've all dashed to the bomb shelter. I shouldn't make a joke of it but honestly you can only laugh or cry and I choose to laugh.

At Mrs. Mullins's I've moved my camp-bed under the stairs. Jimmie sleeps with me. It's so comforting when he licks my face and presses his little body up against me. I wish it were yours. He gets so startled by the loud bangs, he trembles, whines, then sometimes starts barking in my face. I hate that, poor little doggie. When it's bad we dash to the cellar's bomb-shelter and I hold him so he can't run away. His breath is still horrible.

I spent last weekend with your mum up at Luton[1]. *She's very kind to me and I'm already fond of her. Bertie says he's keeping a close eye on developments and if it gets worse he's going to evacuate your mum and his wife out of Luton to an even safer spot. He wanted me to go, but I shan't. I need to do my bit for the war effort and the banks have to keep open and they need me. You know that.*

I wish your maid, that Volga German, wasn't living in your house, Freddie. Does she have to? Hasn't she got her own flat? I think I'll call her that Vulgar German, hahaha. You are being faithful to me, I know you are. I love you so much. I'm glad you get to go out sometimes. Remember when we went for those beautiful walks with tea in Kensington Gardens? It's all so different now. Your world over there isn't anything like over here. I'm lonely. I know you are, too. I'm totally faithful to you, darling. Men come on to me but I ignore them and tell 'em I'm MARRIED!

I look at your photo every night before I go to sleep. I've got a torch under the stairs. Well, I have to, to write letters to you. Jimmie looks at your photo, too. He misses you, Freddie. You always called me the "Princess of Kensington" but I don't think I look like one these days. I wish I did but I need more make-up and rationing is no good for that.

Dad says he's terrified now they're bombing the suburbs. "Broadmayne" could be hit. Dad says Mother is so nervous she tells Dad she's going to start drinking. We all know she already does. Sigh. Oh dear! The business is suffering, too. Lendrum's can't be picking up wastepaper when you can't get through half the roads anymore. Dad says it's all very well he's a director at L. but he has to do all the mundane jobs, too, now all of the young 'uns are off at the front, fighting.

You know that red phone booth down the end of Cheniston Gardens? Somebody's taped noughts and crosses over every single pane of glass. All the houses' windows are taped, too, to stop them shattering when bombs come down. Somebody told me there's a phone booth on the Strand where military people can make free phone calls. I'm wondering if I should look for it and try to phone you for free! They said it's near the Savoy Hotel. Remember I told you that's where Daddy threw my 21st birthday party for me. I showed you the photograph of me in that lovely white dress spread all around me as I sat on the floor! But I don't think any of the telephone lines are working. Somebody at work said they keep them all for business and war matters, so nobody can use them for personal phone calls.

Mrs. Mullins says I shouldn't wear trousers to work, but I shall do; they're far more practical, especially 'cos of my bike. What does she know. Honestly, sometimes she isn't quite the full shilling; you know what she's like. Not quite "with it". The trouser flares do get in the way on my bike, so I put rubber bands 'round my ankles. Clever girl, aren't I?!

I'm not sleeping much. I know you remember I told you my toothies had been bad. Doc says it's the wisdom teeth. That's why I was losing weight, he says, but I think I've told you about that before in an earlier letter. If I have them out, I might lose my wisdom, ha ha ha. Oh, and Mrs. Mullins said I should chew marjoram all day to ease the pain. Now, what IS she thinking? Where on earth would I find marjoram these days??? It's odd, isn't it, Freddie, how we tell each other things but then a more recent letter reaches us BEFORE an older one does, so all our news is no longer in the right date order.

Did you hear about the headmaster who said to a class of girls now who can make up a sentence with the word centimetre in it so one girl put up her hand and said I can so she said yesterday my sister was coming home from school and I was sent to meet her. Ha ha ha. What is the difference between an elephant and a pillar box so this kid said I don't know. Well, it's no use sending you to post a letter is it? Oh Freddie, I so miss you. I think of you nearly all the time. I hope my silly jokes cheer you up.

Oh, and remember how I lost a cheque and found it later in my wastepaper basket? I did it again. I must be nuts. I think it's just that my mind is too unfocussed these days, with everything going on, you gone, and the wretched war, the Blitz. Oh Freddie, how I hate Herr Hitler.

Dad says it's good we don't yet have our own house. At least we won't have to worry if that bloody un-Herrlich Adolph smashes it to smithereens. Pardon my French!

I'm glad Crane is a nice quiet boy. If your flat together is in the left wing of the Embassy on the first floor, and your office is the other side of the entryway, you don't have to walk far to work, do you?! You said you have no central heating and have to pay a heavy bill for wood to heat the place and that it costs about 5-6 quid per week. Oh my. If only I were there, I'd talk them down, you know how good I am at that. Oh but I don't speak the lingo.

You said you went to see Prince Igor at the opera. Was he a nice man? Just joking, darling. I'm glad you had a good time. I don't like opera, the violins sound like cats caterwauling to me, except I do like the piano pieces. They played it on the wireless here. I like ballet. When I get out there let's go to the ballet together. I'd enjoy wearing my best frock and the pearls and diamonds Dad gave me. Remember I told you he used to take me riding on Rotten Row in Hyde Park? That seems a world away. Well, it is. Maybe you and I can do it after this beastly war is over. You never told me whether you can ride. Can you?

Freddie, the Greenwoods (that Jewish family) have had so much bad luck and now their home got hit and burnt down. Isn't that awful? Honestly, Freddie, you are naughty telling me that joke. I passed it on at work and the girls all hooted. The manager waggled his finger at me! The one I mean about Adolf saying that the Jews are to be allowed to return to Germany on the condition that they disclose how Moses succeeded in crossing the Red Sea. Some people say it's not nice to tell jokes like that, but honestly, you've got to laugh. People seem so serious so much of the time. If they'd only try smiling or laughing from time to time, everyone would cheer up. We'll get through this, England will. We KNOW we will. Churchill assures us we will, if we only keep a stiff upper lip. Mine is welded into a smile and feels like concrete now. Maybe I'm trying to smile too much! I know it's all so serious, of course

I do, but honestly, Freddie...I'm running on so will stop this vein of talk now.

Back to gossip! You know how Mrs. Balmain-Styne was planning on marrying old Mr. Lendrum? Well, her daughter Maria has caught him instead and Mrs. B-S. is having fits about it. Maria thinks he'll peg out soon. We think when she's got all the money she should put some poison in his tea. So who's being naughty now?!

Darling, when you get my letters is there anything ever scratched out? Those censors read it all, I know. As for the name change, why would you rather do nothing about it for "reasons of registration and other reasons" over there? I wish I knew, but I suppose you can't tell me everything. I suppose it does sound German, well half of it does. Maybe I'll change mine to Mrs. Read-John instead of Read-Jahn. Actually, I already sort of did. When I applied for this bank job the manager said "And what is your name?" You know how careful I am about my new last name so I slowly said, "Mrs. Molly Read...John" and he said, 'No, no, no, we call our superiors by their surname here." Turns out his first name is John! Talk about feeling silly! I say Read-John instead of Read-Jahn to avoid people thinking it's half German, sigh...

I've had all the inoculations ready for Russia. I'm already thinking about packing. Do tell me when I can talk to Cook's about starting the journey. I can't wait to be with you again, my dearest darling hubby.

Oh, and I shall look for a "Walker's" Diary refill for 1941 for you, as you requested. I think I can get it at any stationer's. I'll look for "Loose-Leaf Diary Refill No LL 3." If I find it ok I'll put it in an envelope and send it by the usual courier bag. I'll do it as soon as I can.

I know Dad wrote you that I'm not eating enough, but I am! I also know you don't want me to get too fat.

Your ever faithful wife, Molly

When Fred received this missive from Molly, he laughed and laughed. She was so "in the moment" and always wanted to cheer him up. She came from an upper middle-class family, had received a good education at Heath House, a boarding school for girls in England, she could speak a little German, she liked to read, she played the piano—both classical and jazz—yet she sometimes came across as a bit silly and not terribly sophisticated. Yet underneath all of that she was quite intelligent, read the papers, and was interested in everything going on in the world.

His Molly! In effect, it was Molly who was getting him through "this damned war". It was she who could, albeit sometimes just for a few moments, lift the blackness he felt within his soul. She was quite the lady when she needed to be. Her laugh could be spontaneously loud and somewhat raucous and she could be racy and sometimes even slightly "vulgar" but he loved all that about her. He supposed she'd got that side of her character from her mother, who was her father's second wife, sometime after his first had died. Edith Sutton had been a dancer, a chorus girl, so considered "somewhat common" but John Sutton had fallen in love with her, and she'd borne him two girls. She had the most beautiful peaches-and-cream skin. Molly was her father's favourite, and she knew it. She was upbeat all the time, a real tonic to Fred, as she was to her father. And, she was damned attractive with her little body, so feminine in its curves, and her big grin with that space between her two upper front teeth. Oh, what he'd give to kiss those warm, eager, lips now. Once again, he worried that he'd made a huge mistake leaving her to deal with the trials of wartime alone in London. But their luck would hold, he just knew it would. It had to! Besides, he'd had no choice about leaving her. Sighing, he put her letter down, straightened his tie and went back to the cypher room.

Back upstairs later in his first floor office he stood by the window looking across to the Kremlin. Snow was falling gently, each flake different from the other. He was soon going to have to learn to ski. He pursed his lips as he wondered about the patterning of snowflakes, each one different from the other. Could he use it for espionage purposes? ID cards bearing patterning instead of names?

Was he going off his rocker? God, he was so tired and he hadn't been here that long, just a matter of what? Six weeks or so? He could barely remember. He opened the window a crack and let the flakes settle softly on his finger. Each one so very beautiful. He drew his finger to his mouth and across his deep red moustache and, as the snowflakes settled there, some slid as melted water down into his mouth. They had a metallic taste. He'd better not taste too many. Snowflakes gave you a gippy tummy, he knew that. Turning away, he realised he was letting cold air into his office, so hurriedly closed the window and sat back down to work.

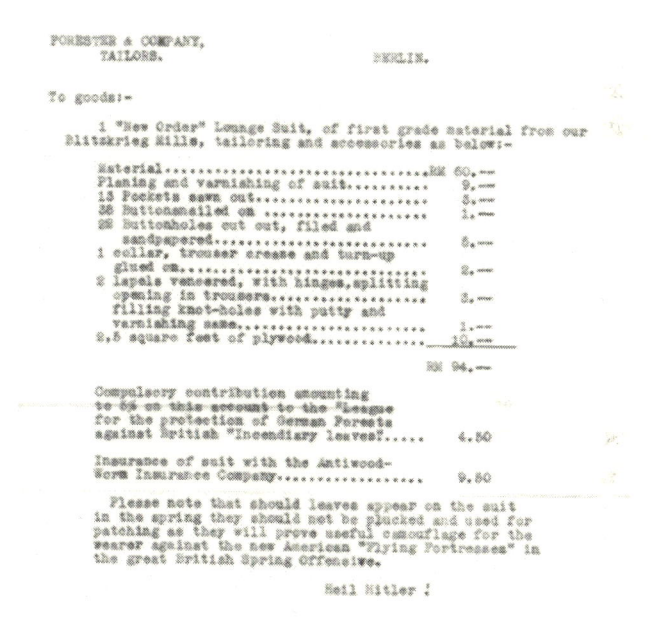

```
FORESTER & COMPANY,
     TAILORS.                          BERLIN.

To goods:-

   1 "New Order" Lounge Suit, of first grade material from our
   Blitzkrieg Mills, tailoring and accessories as below:-
       Material.............................RM 60.--
       Planing and varnishing of suit........   9.--
       13 Pockets sawn out...................   3.--
       36 Buttonsnailed on...................   1.--
       28 Buttonholes cut out, filed and
            sandpapered......................   8.--
       1 collar, trouser crease and turn-up
            glued on.........................   2.--
       2 lapels veneered, with hinges,splitting
            opening in trousers..............   3.--
       filling knot-holes with putty and
            varnishing same..................   1.--
       2.5 square feet of plywood............  10.--
                                            RM 94.--

   Compulsory contribution amounting
   to 6% on this account to the "League
   for the protection of German Forests
   against British "Incendiary leaves"....   4.80

   Insurance of suit with the Antiwood-
   Worm Insurance Company................   9.80

       Please note that should leaves appear on the suit
       in the spring they should not be plucked and used for
       patching as they will prove useful camouflage for the
       wearer against the new American "Flying Fortresses" in
       the great British Spring Offensive.

                        Heil Hitler !
```

Fred's joke Berlin Forester & Co tailor order form for the new suit he wanted Molly to buy for him!

---

1. *Luton, Bedfordshire, north of London.*

Chapter 20

Late 1940, Moscow

The courier bags of mail now came in via Istanbul but it had been a long time since Fred had received news from home. Loneliness engulfed him. He sometimes found himself one step away from tears, choking up his throat from a deep well of anxiety and fear about his own life, his family's Blitz horrors back home, and the war in general. He had to constantly keep a check on his emotions—but, he was trained to control himself, and, like his Molly in London, all one could do was to Carry On!

Meanwhile, to distract themselves, his flatmate Crane and he decided to throw a little housewarming party at their new flat in the Embassy. It was to be a dinner party for some special contacts they had made. They invited two guests from the American Embassy and Captain John Merchant, who was one of Fred's direct superiors at the British Embassy. Captain Merchant was eventually to become the husband of Nina, a Russian citizeness who had been coerced by the NKVD (the People's Commissariat for Internal Affairs) to spy for them—particularly on Captain Merchant—whose espionage activities the Soviets were very interested in. Nina worked most evenings at the Hotel Metropol where she was able to meet, as if by chance, many of the foreigners and diplomats staying or visiting the hotel. The NKVD gave Nina the cover name of Little Bird. They wanted to find out through Nina what they could about an Englishman called John Merchant whom they said was actually a British secret agent with an attaché job at the British Embassy as a blind.

But, much to the Soviets' frustration, Nina and John had fallen in love.

Captain Merchant was due to leave Moscow the next weekend, proceeding to Istanbul and from there flying all the way to the Cape of Good Hope, South Africa, to get on a boat headed for London, eventually to return to Moscow. A roundabout route, but it was wartime and many places were to be avoided. If all went well for him he was expecting to reach London in four to five weeks' time. Fred's letters show that he had many long "chats" with Merchant, who also promised Fred he'd look in on Molly.

Not only was Merchant returning to London and would be able to look Molly up on Fred's behalf, but also could the King's Messenger, one Commander R.C. Harrow. The commander was also leaving Moscow, shortly after Merchant. Thus Molly was going to have two "stand-ins" for her beloved husband, to tell her everything she would need to know about life in Moscow, *if* she were permitted to join him there.

The dinner party was a big success. The five of them managed to drain two bottles of Vodka and also some Russian red and white wines—not too bad, both Fred and Crane thought!

Twenty-three years earlier the country had gone through its civil Revolution and from 7th till 10th of November every year the Soviets celebrated the Revolution's anniversary. It was the biggest holiday of the year and for three solid days nobody worked, except unfortunates such as Fred and his chums toiling away at deciphering "ole Adolf's" messages in the basement of the Embassy. This work was of the utmost importance in that, among other vital information, it meant they could relay to the Allies when the Germans were planning on pushing into Moscow.

During the Revolution's anniversary celebrations Moscow was gaily decorated and there were monuments and pictures of Stalin and Lenin everywhere, covered in a mass of red flags.

The American Embassy overlooked Red Square and they invited the Brits to come on over to their balcony to watch the parade of tanks, equipment, military bands and personnel marching through the cold streets of Moscow. Tribunes had been erected on each side of Lenin's tomb. That was where the parade was going to be taken in the presence of Stalin himself, the Government ministers, the Diplomatic Corps., and all the other worthies in the city. The parade was to commence at 11 am and last till one or two o'clock in the afternoon. It was usually an interesting show, Fred had heard, and he had every intention of being there to watch it in person.

On parade day, 7th November, 1940, Fred got up at 6 am, and, having received permission to have the morning off work, he made sure that he was at the American Embassy by 7.30 am, because he knew all the streets and squares in the vicinity would be closing, so he had no intention of dallying. He had breakfast with the Yanks in their mess hall. They were all pleased that the snow had melted and that it was a lovely sunny day, but it was cold, mighty cold, as the Yanks said, to be standing outside watching a parade. Fred knew to take his little Brownie camera and get as many shots as possible of the USSR's military force on display. You never knew when Stalin might switch allegiance to potentially become an ally of the Axis and then, every bit of information Fred had garnered would come into play. As usual, his mantra was to "be prepared".

From the balcony he saw and photographed hundreds of tanks, armoured cars, lorries, artillery, etc., lined up in front of the American Embassy in a large square. The balcony overlooked the whole area as far as the tomb on top of which Stalin and his generals stood to take the parade. It was all very interesting for Fred. Except for the Cavalry all units were mechanised. There were huge tanks and guns of all descriptions, and the USSR Air Force, too, gave a display.

Standing next to him watching the parade, and, Fred noted, also taking photographs with a discreet, tiny, camera, was a small Chinese official obviously invited from the Chinese legation by the Yanks. He introduced himself as a counsellor from the Chinese Embassy, giving Fred a sly wink. Ha! thought Fred, it's actually our Shanghai Joe, whom he'd last seen in Japan. Here he was yet again, right here in Moscow alongside him! He warmly shook hands with Joe, chuckling inwardly to himself about the movements of this Asian Scarlet Pimpernel—here, there, simply everywhere!

As part of his undercover work, prior to arriving in Moscow Fred had studied a little history of each of the foreign diplomatic legations in Moscow.

Fred knew that since 1928 Sino-Soviet relations had been pretty fractious, but that there was an actual Chinese Embassy in Moscow. He knew that Joseph Stalin's USSR government had given Chiang Kai-shek's Kuomintang government help against Imperial Japan. The small Communist Party of China at that time, led by Mao Zedong, had been warned by Stalin to cooperate with China's Kuomintang government but Mao had gone ahead and attacked Chiang Kai-shek's government anyway. It was an unsuccessful attack and eventually, in 1937, both Chiang Kai-shek and Mao Zedong had got together in order to oppose Japan's invasion of China. That was a little of the history that Fred knew. In 1942 those two Chinese factions were to continue fighting each other, but, meanwhile, in November of 1940, at the time Fred took note yet again of this Chinese counsellor-agent, the small Chinese legation was still on good terms with Stalin.

The military part of the parade was over by 1.30 pm after which the citizens of Moscow—he was told as many as two to three million—filed past the tomb in an endless stream lasting all afternoon. He managed to get home at about 5 pm. So much for "having the morning off"! He knew his superiors realised that everything in the USSR worked in a slower timeframe, with everything starting late—nothing like in England, or, in fact,

Germany. Everything there ran on time. On the whole it was all worth seeing for Fred, although he had seen bigger parades in Germany.

At night-time there was gay dancing and vaudeville in the Moscow streets and everyone did his best to get drunk as soon as possible. Fred, however, preferred to stay at home and miss that part of the celebrations.

After the excitement of the parade, and having taken the previous day completely off work in the end, he was once again bogged down in the daily grind of his job. He began to feel melancholic, realising he was going to be spending Christmas alone, with not one member of his family with him.

The 8th November was the day before Molly's birthday. Knowing this, thinking about it, and aware that "the world outside" was cavorting in the continuing Revolution anniversary celebrations, he and Crane decided to go out after all. They went to Hagshaw's to play darts and poker, meaning they didn't get home till 2.30 in the morning. Fortunately, they could stay in bed till 9 am the following day. Fred reckoned that was the only good thing about working at the Embassy was its civilised morning starting hour of 10 am.

On 9th November, Molly's 30th birthday, once again he and Crane felt the need to celebrate her special day so, after work, at 10 pm, they whipped round to their colleague Scotland's place, armed with three bottles of Champagne. Mrs. Scotland helped them improvise a birthday party where they drank to Molly's health and Fred tried to keep a stiff upper lip in her absence. They played table tennis and mechanical horse-racing and ended up having a jolly enjoyable time altogether.

Fred had sent Molly flowers through Lawn & Alder in London and so hoped she had received the surprise. At that party were a few members from other diplomatic legations, so it was no surprise to Fred to spy "good old Shanghai Joe" (as Fred now privately referred to him) sitting in a corner nursing his drink. When Joe seemed happy to chat with him, Fred was pleased to spend more time talking with him, feeling he was beginning to develop by now quite a good rapport with the man, and that could turn out to be quite useful. "Be prepared…be alert…be ready" said Fred to himself. From that moment on, he and Joe became quite good chums, seeing each other at many of the legations' functions, with Fred observing every move in the room, listening to every conversation he could, remembering every detail that could be of importance to his work.

The 10th November was a Sunday, the day Captain Merchant was leaving Moscow for England, so they all had a very busy day preparing for his departure and all that entailed—notifying his contacts where he would be and what needed to happen when he got there—all done in code, of course. Merchant had his own orders to prepare for, tied into all the different aspects of the espionage he was personally engaged in.

By 10th November a telegram had got through to Fred from Molly. She had received the birthday flowers he'd had Lawn & Alder deliver to her. They had come early so that was an even bigger surprise for her, but it was a relief for her to know that he, too, was alive and well, albeit so very far away from her. The fact she could receive actual fresh flowers in a glorious bouquet during the Blitz made her completely surprised but ecstatically happy! Another reason to try to smile.

By 15th November there was still no bag with personal mail for Fred. He was finding it harder and harder not to be with Molly. He dashed off a letter to put into the courier bag when it eventually showed up:

> *"How I miss you Sweetheart, it's getting worse and worse. To be separated from the sweetest darlingest wife in the world is tough on a guy. Sometimes I get a wee bit anxious you might forget your funny hubby. After all you haven't known him so very long, have you? Well Darling must say cheerio, more work waiting. Be a good girl…Well my dearest there is really nothing to report just now. I love you more than ever and shan't be happy again until I hold you in my arms.*

Your loving and longing Freddie."

November sped on, filled with work, work, and more work, and it got cold, colder, and even colder. Freezing, in fact. The Embassy wasn't heated in every room. Crane and Fred were using up all the logs at a fast rate that they'd brought in earlier to burn in their stove of Dutch tiles in their little flat.

By 15th December Fred took a break in the afternoon and went out for a short walk but was unable to go too far because the temperature had now dropped to 14 degrees Centigrade below zero (57.2 Fahrenheit below) and it was promised to soon reach 30 or even 40 Centigrade below zero! His mind boggled about how cold that was going to be! The Moskva River in front of the Embassy was already frozen over and he could see snow and ice everywhere. This was the true Russia he had read about. It was high time he bought himself a fur cap or his poor ears were going to be frozen stiff. He and a colleague wandered once again around the smelly, poor shops but all they had on offer was still of inferior quality at exorbitant prices. They did manage to find two Astrakhan fur caps and Fred was lucky to get the better of the two, paying 253 roubles (equivalent to 15 quid or, at their current black-market rouble rate, only two pounds ten in British sterling—a real deal!).

His maid, being the German-Russian girl from the Volga River area, was able to speak German but it was no longer that "hot", thus he'd already had a number of frustrating language misunderstandings with his "Volga Boatman" as he called her.

He was quick to explain to Molly in one of his letters about how cold it was, and the purchase of his new hat, and teased her that the "black market" didn't mean that Russian rouble notes were black in colour! Molly was thrilled that she'd get to wear a typically Russian hat once Fred was home with her again. She loved new hats and in wartime England she'd been unable to buy any new clothes whatsoever. Who knows, she mused, her feelings rising—she might even get to wear that same fur hat if she were actually able to be in the USSR next winter!

To keep himself even warmer in Russia's wintertime Fred got his overcoat padded with wadding for the princely sum of £2, but it was going to be worth it, from everything he'd heard the chaps say about the coming further cold. Armed now with a Russian hat and a warmer overcoat he hoped to survive the winter.

The Embassy staff was now aware of a slight Christmas atmosphere pervading Moscow. The shops were displaying a few toys in their windows, along with "Father Christmases". On the squares huge Christmas trees had been erected, with the proverbial "Red Star of the USSR" sparkling on top. Officially being a non-religious country, the Soviets called these trees "New Year Trees" and "Father Christmas" had been converted to "Father Frost". Fred was interested and surprised to find that there were quite a number of churches "operating" in communist Moscow, and which were always crowded. All this was hypocritical to him, but, as well he knew, the USSR was an extremely complex country.

He walked past a number of what he called "Fairs". These were gatherings of stalls selling toys, sweets, etc., with music blaring, and the whole affair decorated by strings of coloured lamps. It reminded him of the "Weihnachtsmarkt" Christmas markets in Berlin only in that the Moscow ones looked far more primitive.

The Home Service on the wireless told him that it had been quieter in London over the last few days, which brought Fred great relief. Touch wood it would last! Michael Crane had got himself a lady friend, so Fred stayed in alone, poring over the snaps of his time with Molly and letting his mind live once again the 146 days together before he had had to leave on his epic journey to the USSR.

By mid-December the courier bags were arriving sporadically but with no personal mail in them whatsoever. This was because things were heating up in the war and the bags were stuffed full with so much official documentation that there was rarely any room for personal mail. Fred hadn't heard from Molly since the beginning of November's mailbag came in. To cheer himself up one night he decided to go to the circus. Soviet circuses were renowned for being quite wonderful. But, he was given so much work to do after dinner that even that distraction was now out.

When he'd first arrived in Moscow on 15th September, 1940 he'd immediately sent off an order to Lawn & Alder in London for a consignment of necessary foodstuffs to be couriered to him. He now saw that these were not going to arrive before Christmas—another big disappointment. He'd be alone, without Molly, and not even have any English goodies with which to celebrate Christmas Day. So much for his order taking one month to reach him.

He did manage to get out one evening to see a Tchaikovsky concert. It was held in a recently-completed, rather nice hall. It had been intended by its architect to be a theatre; a very modern one where they weren't using any scenery whatsoever on the stage, only spotlights turned on the various actors—but, in the meantime, the very famous producer had been "liquidated" meaning, of course, he was probably now in Siberia somewhere breaking rocks. Such was life for artists, authors, and others whom the NKVD considered "undesirables".

Logs piled by British Embassy's porte cochère.

Moscow, 1940 parade for 1917 Russian revolution anniversary.

Hidden in Plain Sight

1917 Russian revolution anniversary parade.

Chapter 21

Moscow, January-July, 1941
Skiing and Code-Breaking

Christmas 1940 had come and gone. Fred—albeit lonelier, yet busier than ever—had survived.

On 18th January, 1941 a telegram from Molly had got through to Fred. If only it had been another of her cheerful uplifting letters, but at least the short telegram told him she had finally left her job at the bank. This was a big relief to him. And the letter he'd received the day before was another relief, showing she was receiving at least some of his letters. He'd been really worried about her cycling to work every day during the Blitz, navigating around bomb craters, and being right in the thick of all the terror. A very few bombs had fallen on London even before the Blitz began, when he was still in London, so he'd known firsthand the mess and destruction she had to cycle around. But the Blitz! On and on it went, with so many bombs falling on London starting in earnest on 7th September, 1940, almost two months after he'd left Old Blighty. He had tossed and turned at night, worrying about her safety.

He immediately sent her a return telegram. It was somewhat more certain that she'd receive this sort of communication rather than letters that did tend to go astray.

By the end of January, 1941 Fred was feeling immensely tired, but a little better in spirits as he wrote in a more encouraging letter to his wife, which revealed his Lawn & Alder goodies had finally reached him.

BRITISH EMBASSY
MOSCOW
27th January, 1941
Letter No. 11

My Darling Molly,

I find that with a spot of luck I can manage another letter to you. The reason being that my fellow-householder Michael Crane is taking this one with him.

I have just had a nice supper with Barclay's beer, and all kinds of English specialities out of the "stores", in other words a sort of rich mix, a real "rill mill". Now I feel much better. You know bag days are like a mixture between a madhouse and a Turkish bath. It's 10 pm and I have retreated to my room, got me old pipe out (some kind chap in a weak moment gave me a tin of lovely Craven tobacco) and on the whole I feel quite pleased with myself. If my sweet wife were here it would be perfect happiness.

Well here are the reasons for my feeling more cheerful than usual: The Embassy have written home requesting the F.O. to grant me £600 and they also say in their letter that "R.J. has worked very well and hard since his arrival" etc. etc. so now Darling if our luck doesn't let us down and you wish strong enough we might be lucky enough to see this request materialise. That would be grand wouldn't it? It would I think make it quite safe for you to give up working and concentrate on looking after yourself, resting and eating and recuperating from the ghastly time you have had and are no doubt still experiencing. They have asked for a telegraphic reply. So maybe I shall soon be able to tell you the result.

The second item is: Your coming out to join me. For obvious reasons I cannot tell you about all the political difficulties obstructing my efforts. But I have achieved this: in principle the Embassy agree that you may come, though I could not get a promise as to when. As far as I can see at the moment there is really only one possible route and that is the same way I came. Apart from the dangerous crossing of the Atlantic it would be enormously expensive. And I fear the F.O. will not stand the costs. In my discussions I hinted that your family might be prepared to help us out in this direction. The costs Darling would be approximately 200 pounds. It might be possible to cut down the expense somewhat but probably not very much, since travelling through so many countries and particularly in the Far East section you have to travel first class. Anyhow I specifically asked whether I may inform my wife that she will be able to join me eventually. And the reply was "Yes". Considering all the hundreds of difficulties that we are up against — many of which, as I already stated, I cannot explain to you — this is a great step forward. And I am living now for the day when I can wire you: Darling pack your bags and come as quick as you can. I'm sure this will be good news for you; so for the moment we must go on hoping and being patient. As regards the financial aspect: Will you think things over and let me know whether, in the case of the F.O. refusing to finance the journey, we could raise the necessary funds somehow.

I see from your telegram of the 18th January that you have received (or better: had received up to that date) my letters Nos. 1 to 5 and 8; I am enclosing therefore confirmation copies of letters, 6, 7, 9. It might be a good idea if you would let me know in your next telegram that you have received all these letters. I hope that this might reach you within a week.

We have lately been receiving a few newspapers and periodicals September-November issues and the pictures therein gave me quite a good idea of what poor old London has gone through. Saw photos of Regent Street and Oxford St. and with the descriptions you have given me I can paint a fairly accurate picture of London life under the "Blitz".

By the way: I haven't yet received my diary and cheque book. Hope they turn up before this year ends.

Incidentally Molly Darling: This firm of Lawn & Alder, 24 Kirby Street, Hatton Garden, London, E.C.1 who have sent me the consignment cater really for any kind of order: from a motor-car down to a stud and shaving cream. It might be a good idea if you were to contact them one of these days. From what I have been told their prices are not higher and in most cases they can obtain things a little cheaper as they are exporters. As I said in my other letter they are licensed to send us tobacco and fags and it would probably save you a lot of time and bother (packing and carrying the parcels to the F.O.) if you instructed them to execute the orders. They know how to deal with everything. I understand from one of their letters that their premises have been badly knocked about; in fact I believe nearly the whole street is down; but I think their office is still operating at the address mentioned. And they have got my name wrong. They have "Readjasn". You might put them right.

I hope you understood my telegram about sending my Mum flowers. It hasn't been edited too smartly. I was trying to explain to you that 31st January was my father's birthday and it would be very nice if Mum had a few flowers on that day to show that we are with her in thought.

Give my love to all at Broadmayne, Darling. I hope your Dad, Mum and Olive are all well. And kind regards to the friends at No. 17.

I am longing for more news from you, sweetest. Be good and don't worry too much about the future. It's going to turn out all right.

Good night Darling. I am dreaming of you by day and by night.

Your loving and longing
Freddie

P.S. Michael Crane is buying a radiogramme. So one of these days you might enclose the "Apple" record in one of the parcels. L & A will see to that.

Snow had fallen steadily as the days and nights got colder and colder. The pile of logs stacked up against the Embassy near the *porte cochère* was rapidly disappearing as the freezing staff ran outside to get armfuls for their Dutch-tiled stoves. The Russians were extremely efficient in clearing away the snow. Thousands of women from the villages around Moscow poured into the city to do this work. Russian women were doing just about all of the physical work, including driving the trams and buses and working as conductoresses and taxi drivers. They took your money at the cinemas, which they called "kinos". They were at the desk of Moscow's newest hotel called the "Mosckva". It even had a roof garden, and it was women who tended the plants up there and protected them from the freezing frost and snow. As Fred walked around, on the little time he had off work, he saw new apartment houses of which the Soviets were immensely proud. They were huge, utilitarian, grey concrete constructions, rather drab to Fred's eyes. The Embassy rented some of these apartments and Fred's colleague was put into one. He said they looked alright from the outside, but the snag was that the lifts, heating and lighting never worked satisfactorily.

All the decrypts that Fred and his cohorts were doing were helping Britain support its Balkan allies, by relaying German military movements to the Yugoslavian and Greek fighters (although it was to turn out that by 1st June, 1941 all of Albania, Yugoslavia and Greece was to be taken by the Axis). But before this takeover occurred, decrypted messages were flying backwards and forwards through the spring of 1941 from Churchill to Stalin, warning him that Hitler's intention was now to grab the Soviet Union. Hitler would then have all of Russia's oil, raw materials, guns of all types, and all its steel to help him hugely in his desire to get into Great Britain to "eliminate the English motherland", as Hitler liked to say over and over.

While all these feverish communications between Great Britain and the British Military Mission were flying in high gear, the Embassy staff was ensconced in Moscow with the spring of 1941 being called one of its coldest ever. Snow still lay thickly on the ground of Moscow. The Russian women continued to work daily like donkeys to clear snow from the streets, dressed in warm coats and scarves and wearing warm babushkas on their heads. No flowers were yet able to push their heads up through the snow. It was so very cold, a truly bone-chilling Russian spring.

When he wasn't at his cypher machine or attending to a myriad of his other duties involving his proficiency in German, Fred spent some of his time in Moscow now finally learning how to ski down the snow-covered roads, mostly empty of vehicles these days, and on the little hills of the city's small parks. It was hard for him, not a sport he'd learned even during his snowy urban youth in Germany's winters. He'd been an urbane city boy, totally not into sports. He knew he had to make time for learning to ski, but what time did he have? He had to hurry up with this project, knowing that certainly the Soviets would soon be in Moscow itself and he had his "extra-curricular" job to accomplish first.

On 26th February, 1941 Fred wrote rather innocently to Clara, his mother in England, from the British Embassy about his taking up skiing, calling it winter rather than spring, although everyone else said it was actually spring.

"Not like spring in England, Crane", he told his flatmate, "with its bluebells, primroses and birds chirping merrily as they build their nests. Here you can't even see a free branch to build on, with all the wretched snow piled on the trees!"

And, more to his mum:

"We are still in the midst of winter. Every now and then it gets a little

warmer and begins to thaw only to turn all the colder again. There is still deep snow and ice everywhere. Recently I took up skiing. Been out a few times and can now even get down a little slope without falling. It's great fun. I borrow the necessary rig-out from Michael (my fellow householder) and the skis from somebody else. If I should be here next winter I shall try and get myself all the ski equipment I'll need."

He was truly exhausted, but, as well he knew, part of his "extra-curricular" work was to facilitate the escape of various individuals[1] needing to get out of the USSR. Certain people had to be removed from the city for a number of highly secret reasons, and the sooner the better.

On 9th March, 1941 he wrote again to his mother:

"I told you in my previous letter that I had been doing a bit of skiing. It appears that my pal Michael took a few snaps without my knowledge. I am sending these snaps home to Moll together with a few of this city which I hope you will be seeing in due course."

Poor Fred was very unhappy in his early ungainly throes of learning to ski, to which some hilarious photos attest, but, in fairly short order, he did master it and was then able to get on with the job of getting "his" evacuees onto a ship and out of the country.

He was the first to admit he wasn't a *"sportif"* man at all, but he'd been told that this work of his could very well necessitate his crossing snowy mountains on skis, hence his efforts to learn. As usual, he'd told himself to be prepared, and to be properly prepared, he was darned well going to have to learn this difficult sport. He only ever discussed whom he was helping, and why, with his immediate superiors. Being so tired, down to his very bones, he fell one day while skiing and broke his arm.

Sometime between his last letter and his next one to her on 18th April, 1941, was when he'd broken his arm, as he explains to his mother:

"As regards my arm the position is the following: It is much better, I can

work again and use it but unfortunately cannot straighten it. So I must have massage treatment and do all kinds of physical jerks at home such as forcing the arm down by a few degrees several times a day in order to expand the muscles. It's going to be a very tedious and tiresome affair, but I hope that in time it will be more or less normal again."

Freddie was officially now listed as a British Embassy "Cypher Officer" in Moscow but this was deceptive. He was doing much, much more than code-breaking and translations and, aside from the cypher work, plus his translations from German and French into English, he was still working for Morgan Crucible—under the cover of the British Embassy—and through his many contacts around Europe managing to get hold of high tech parts for Stalin's Soviet munitions. He obviously wished he could tell his wife so much more than he could, having signed the Official Secrets Act, but a little of what he was doing came through in a "somewhat guarded" letter Fred wrote to Molly on 26th April, 1941 where he told her that Robeson of Morgan's had sent him "a very long and interesting letter" in the official Embassy courier bag—the letter itself having been consigned to memory by Fred then destroyed.

On 3rd May he noted:

"My arm is getting on nicely. I can work and use it but cannot yet get it quite straight. I shall probably be having some kind of electrical treatment in order to revive the muscles again."

By 10th May, 1941 the Ambassador received the wonderful news that Hitler's Blitzkrieg on London was over. A brief party was put together for the staff to celebrate. Everyone heaved huge sighs of relief and a few of the remaining bottles of true Champagne were hauled up from their basement hiding-place and drunk down to a chorus of "God Save the King!"

On 20th May, 1941 Fred told his mother he had been sent off to Stockholm for a few days. He'd flown there on 13th May and had *"met so many interesting and nice people there."* The cover for being in Stockholm was for him to see Swedish doctors about his arm. They thought he ought to have another operation to break and join the bones together again, but the Russian doctor considered it unnecessary. His cover for going to Sweden was his arm, certainly, but in fact, it was an opportunity to meet up with those people who were of paramount importance to many aspects of his job, and particularly to get instructions regarding the people he was now helping to escape from the USSR. The Swedes gave him explicit instructions about how to organise the evacuations.

While in Sweden, Fred ran into Shanghai Joe (surprise, surprise, smirked Fred). He'd by then met up with Joe a few times since the Revolution's anniversary parade, at various diplomatic functions, the occasional party he'd been asked to attend (always to overhear interesting conversations to relay back to the Embassy) and at the Mosckva Hotel. This hotel was similar to the Metropol Hotel, both magnets for all foreign diplomats with even a brief time of respite on their hands. By then Fred considered he and Joe were already quite good chums.

Armed with the information he needed to get "his" secret people out of the USSR, he flew back to Moscow. Flying was very difficult to arrange. "Sweden" told him that for him to accomplish the evacuation of his people, he was going to have to rely on ships, not aeroplanes.

It so happens that some 15 hours by car from Moscow (650 miles [1,046 km] north via the town of Vologda, lies the city of Archangel, situated on the banks of both sides of the Northern Dvina River near where it exits into the White Sea.

The Germans were approaching the Soviet borders, so pressure was mounting on Fred. Broken arm in a sling, he managed the "extra-curricular" job. He had to grit his teeth against the pain and carry on. The British in him rose to the fore as he thought of poor Molly and everyone else over in Blighty having to carry on under far worse situations.

It was the city of Archangel where one of Fred's secret evacuation missions ended up, where he got his escapees onto

English ships and away from the USSR. This is where his skiing did end up coming in handy. The hardest part was skiing with one pole in his one good arm only. Some of the people he was tasked to get out of the USSR were in the hilly, mountainous lands in the farther reaches away from Moscow. He was taken up there by vehicle, bumping, slipping and sliding. The car then dumped him off, having to get back to Moscow poste-haste for another run elsewhere. That's when Fred and a colleague roped in especially for this "escapade" skied along with the evacuees to a village where they could get hold of another volunteered vehicle to get the rest of the way into Archangel. They left their skis with the trusted vehicle driver and followed his instructions to get to a tramcar.

In winter the icy snowy conditions were truly arctic. Once in Archangel the best way to enter the docklands was via tramcar, and from its last stop in those days you had to stumble on foot through knee-high snowdrifts. You could occasionally still see a few dogs running around in Archangel, the snow yellowed in spots from their urine. It was surprising to see animals on the streets because the starving populace had already eaten most of the city's dogs.

The driver of the last car had been another Volga German whom Fred could understand. He told Fred and his colleague in German that there were no dogs whatsoever in the city of Leningrad. Fried dogs were said to taste like mutton; cats said to be far tastier, like rabbit or even chicken. Molly herself had told Fred in one of her letters that she and her neighbours had resorted to eating cats. This was very hard for her, being such an animal-lover and knowing that the cats were probably non-feral pets of people in her immediate area. She was pragmatic, and hungry, with meat hard to come by during the war, as everyone was. Rations didn't go far enough. She also claimed that in her opinion you would be hard pressed to tell the difference between a roasted cat and chicken.

To get onto a ship was hard enough, and sometimes ships were held up for weeks in the iced-in river. But leave they must, and Fred's job was to ensure his evacuees got onto a ship, armed with the correct documentation. Those papers were presented to a grim-faced NKVD officer (basically, the Soviet secret police), usually a stern-faced female, on duty in a wooden hut at the dock. Quite often she had a vicious Alsatian dog at her side. Nobody would be able to get at her dog to eat it! She eyed Fred, his colleague, the evacuees, and the letters of authority to depart. She then checked the photographs against the persons planning to get on the ship, then sent them on to the final checkpoint when everything seemed to her to be in good order. It was all heart-poundingly scary to the little group. Fred kept his wits about him, casually staring off at the other people working around the docks, as if this were something normal, something he did every day, just part of a job. His colleague spoke fluent Russian, hence he accompanied Fred on these missions. Fred just had to pretend he understood, smiling occasionally and nodding his head when it seemed appropriate. Mainly, the NKVD officer hardly gave him much mind, nor seemed much interested in these people who were leaving. She just wanted the papers, the documents, to all be in order so she could do her job, stamping each one with her little rubber stamp and go back into her little wooden shed with her great big dog and sit by her little fire brazier.

The other people around the docks were poor workers, so many of them, all in ragged clothes and shaved heads, obviously starving and forced to work building whatever was needed at the docks. Stalin's USSR held these miserable people in his system in virtual bondage. They were brought to the area to work mainly on the construction of the coastal town of Molotovsk, to the west of Archangel, but some were used on the Archangel docks. Materials during World War II were offloaded from ships at Archangel, or Molotovsk, farther down the river, so the docks were of prime importance to Stalin.

There was a restricted area leading to the ships, surrounded by an electric fence and wooden watchtowers. Armed sentries surveyed the scene below. Even they were mostly women, as far as Fred could see. After scrutinizing the departure papers minutely from their own little wooden hut below, they, too, rubber-stamped them and waved the travellers through. More snowdrifts to stagger through, then the gangplank to safety would come into sight. When you'd made it onto the English ship, you were finally safe. It was easier for Fred and his colleague to just say their farewells quickly and hurry away to get back to Moscow. Their plans were always set in minute detail, covering many contingencies in the event something would go wrong. Best not to sit around in case the guards got too curious.

That was part of what Fred had to contend with, giving him no end of stress, along with the ongoing stress he was experiencing about his wife, mother, and brother back in wartime England, worrying constantly about their safety.

Another major part of his job that gave him ongoing stress was the long hours spent translating at his desk or at his code-breaking machine in the cypher room within the British Mission in Moscow. His desk was on the ground floor to the right of the entryway of the Embassy building. From his desk he spent a bit of time glancing through his window at the Mosckva River while pondering a translation. His arm constantly ached from his fall while skiing. All his different jobs were exhausting, none of which could he tell Molly about.

The stress was something he had to contend with, as did everybody else, and for Fred, the meditation he had learned in his youth was of huge help to him to get through each day. It was a very simple kind of meditation consisting of sitting very still for about a quarter of an hour or so (if he could grab even that much away from work), concentrating on his breathing and on a particular sound which he would repeat over and over until his breathing became calmer and he felt himself sinking into a deeper area of himself. It was a wonderfully relaxing feeling.

In the basement of the Embassy building lay the Operations room, sometimes referred to simply as "Ops.". This is where the progress of the German Army across Europe and toward Moscow itself was plotted. The teletype machine constantly clacked out signals about troop movements, information regarding charts, and any counter-intelligence that needed to be verified. The print-outs were carefully placed on this table or that. Maps were pinned onto walls and tables and a couple of WAAF (Women's Auxiliary Air Force) staff wearing their Royal Airforce uniforms—who'd been brought specially over from England for this job—stuck pins into the appropriate movement locations.

These two WAAFs were highly skilled workers on loan from the Royal Air Force. The British Mission in Moscow felt very blessed to have them on board. Many of them had studied at "Adastral House", Kingsway, London, eventually moving on to Leighton Buzzard in Bedfordshire, England (between Luton and Milton Keynes). There some of them learned to plot on a replica of a fighter command plotting table, all under total secrecy, and all having signed the Official Secrets Act. Some of them had then moved on to train further in Digby, near Lincoln, where they learned about radar and how to recognise different types of bombers. They studied "plan position indicators" and how to get instant plots even when the blips faded in and out, and how to figure out an informed guess at where a bomber was in the sky. All of this was going to be imperative when the Germans got closer to Moscow and raids from the sky were expected to start.

Back in the early days of the war in England, an airman would be seated on a fixed-frame bicycle in a shed outside the building rotating the aerials manually through 360 degrees, with WAAFs running reports back into the Ops room for charting. It certainly wasn't at all like that in the USSR. A man would freeze to death on a bicycle in a shed in Moscow! The two WAAFs kept very much to themselves, housed in a special apartment away from the men so work could be carried on without potential male-female "romantic stuff" getting in the way. Their superiors well realised how sex-starved most of the men working at the Mission were! Overall, everyone appreciated the importance of the girls' work, and left the two girls well alone to get on with it.

The plotting tables were spotlighted almost theatrically, and generally a tense silence pervaded the room, apart from the teletype machines' constant mechanical muttering. The air was clouded thickly with cigarette smoke. Secret orders issued by the officers' curt commands occasionally broke through the mostly silent room, but mainly, the staff at this time remained totally focussed on their work—readying and steadying itself for the certain raids to come.

Off the Ops room was the Cypher room where Fred spent so much of his time. In the Ops room so far there was not yet a lot of action in the sky for Ops to control, but the teletypers clacked on and on, as did Fred's particular cypher machine.

On 22nd June, 1941 the Germans swarmed across the borders into the USSR, with the Soviets still clearly on the side of England. Life in the Embassy and Mission became even more frantic.

On 3rd July, 1941, Fred sent his Letter No. 17 in the courier bag to Clara:

"Mum...I am still in Moscow...things are still quiet here. No raids so far but expect the fun to start any day now. The Germans are advancing in the direction of this place and it might be necessary to leave Moscow and set up office at some provincial town. However, the Russians might stem the advance, which we all hope. I am now living at a country house that belongs to the Embassy. It is about 20 miles out of town... My flat in town has been given to Mr. Cadbury, a partner of the chocolate firm, who is head of the Economic Mission...we have Air, Naval and Military Missions out here."

Not only was Fred fluent in both German and English, with a pretty good working knowledge of French, but naturally, as a Cypher Officer, was highly trained in working on his cypher machine to gain access to secret intelligence messages being used in transit by the Germans. Just like at Bletchley Park in Buckinghamshire, he and his colleagues used the German Enigma-decryption technique and equipment. The kind of information he'd decrypt was of paramount importance in turning the tide of the war in the Allies' favour.

In the Green Belt, not so far from London, some of the stately homes had been taken over by the military for various war work functions, including hospitals for British servicemen brought home to England, or for far more secret activities. The stately home of Bletchley Park was the major secret hub for code-breaking. The German Enigma code cypher machines they used at Bletchley tended to utilise a six-character code, sometimes more, sometimes less, thus incredibly difficult to figure out.

9th July, 1941 was a truly auspicious date. This was when Alan Turing and his cohorts at Bletchley Park in England finally broke the Germans' Enigma Code. They had their own Enigma machines and were now truly "in business" reading the coded messages and translating them. They always ended in "Heil Hitler!" Bletchley Park was now able to submit code-books to people such as Fred far away in the USSR. Fred and his colleagues in Moscow now received the new code every day. There were some 159 million million million different ways of entering the letters. So many millions, it was mind-boggling. Bletchley Park itself was a beautiful Victorian mansion in the green belt, just outside London, set in gracious parklands. These codebreakers were eventually so efficient that they could break and read a German code sent to Hitler from the battlefield before it even reached Hitler!

At the British Embassy in Moscow Fred and his co-workers were using the same type of machines. These had whirling dials on a plug board, a set of rotors and a reflector. Numbers would be matched up in a row of lines, in some ways rather like a typewriter, or one of the "pokie" machines people in modern times use to gamble on. You turned a dial and a light would go on. You'd open the machine by using the code of the day, such as "P175" or "Lazzru". Fred would now receive these codes daily from his English connections. The codes changed frequently, usually daily, as the Germans tried to "fox" and confuse the British whom they knew were attempting to crack their coded messages. The machines were complicated and needed focus and concentration to operate. Enigma, and other decoding machines, "talked" to each other in what resembled unintelligible gibberish on one machine that could only be decoded letter by letter by another such machine. The Germans thought these machines were uncrackable, being so incredibly complex.

It was exhausting work and Fred spent up to fourteen or more hours a day sometimes, finding and translating the messages. His other work, outdoors, helping his secret evacuees to get out of Archangel, was sometimes almost a relief to him. He didn't have to do those missions often but when he did, he was mostly outdoors—freezing, certainly—but away from the clicking and whirring of his Enigma machine, and that, he thought, could be read as a sort of blessing!

With the Germans now within the USSR Churchill continuously sent his encrypted messages useful to Stalin via Bletchley Park's cryptographers in England straight to the British Military Mission in Moscow, where Fred and his colleagues sat, decyphering away as fast as they could. A special liaison officer was then sent over to the Kremlin, bearing these messages for Stalin. They reported on the Panzer divisions Hitler was moving around, to bring them closer and closer to Moscow itself.

On 14th July, 1941 Fred wrote again to his old mother:

"There might be a possibility of my going to Tehran [sic] (Persia) shortly to have my arm mended properly. The Embassy wants me to go but travelling these days from a place like this is not too easy. However, I might not be going for some time yet."

By mid-July the German troops were driving towards Leningrad and Moscow. Everyone in the various legations moved into a feverish crisis mode. Stay or get out of Moscow?

Enigma machines rattled off message after message, each one becoming more important. Fred was working longer and longer hours, sweat pouring from his brow in his concentration to translate each vital message correctly.

On 9th September, Bletchley decrypted the information that the Germans were now preparing the final assault to be made upon Moscow. Orders were immediately radioed to the British Military Mission at the Embassy in Moscow, whose Mission staff then rushed them to the Kremlin. By 20th September, via Enigma, the British learned Moscow was to be attacked in twelve days' time. The head of the Moscow British Mission, General Mason-MacFarlane, had already made the decision to take his Mission out of the capital city in July to the country retreat of Perlovka. It was from that Moscow suburb that Fred sent his 3rd July letter to his mother.

Hidden in Plain Sight

18th January, 1941. Fred's telegram from Moscow to Molly.

New Moscow apartment buildings.

SHIRLEY READ-JAHN

Village women coming to clear snow & do other jobs.

Early days of Fred's learning to ski!

---

1. *Years later the author asked her father who these people were for whom he had to facilitate escapes. He told her he had broken his arm learning to ski because one of his top secret missions was to facilitate escapes of "certain people" before the Soviets made it into Moscow itself, and some of the escapes would involve his knowing how to ski. He just gave his usual enigmatic smile, shook his head and, as to the escapees, said he'd have to take that secret to the grave with him. She wondered whether they were Jews. Many people alleged the Jews were behind the Russian Revolution and held power among the Bolsheviks. Similarly, they reckoned that Jews were behind communism and Marxism. Hitler himself, since the 1920s, had claimed that it was up to the Nazis to destroy what he called Jewish Bolshevism.*

Chapter 22

May, 1941
Rudolf Hess

While Freddie was busy fighting his war in Russia, during this time period another noteworthy event was taking place in Europe, eventually to involve Herman, Fred's brother.

Going back to May, 1941, not only was Heinrich Himmler, Reichsführer of the Schutzstaffel ("SS"), and a senior leading member of the Nazi party in Germany, a follower of astrology, but so was Rudolf Hess, Hitler's Deputy Führer. Both these powerful Nazis looked at the stars to make their decisions. Hess looked at the heavens' rare alignment of planets and celestial bodies in Taurus, his own star sign, to base the date for his flight to Great Britain in order to broker a secret peace deal. He was going to defect; he'd had enough of Hitler's war. He thought he could help bring this beastly conflict to an end. Hess belonged to a secret society of people fascinated by astrology, called the Thule Society. They believed the Aryan race was the only pure race, the original race in our world, and they were alchemists. It was this Society that had eventually grown into the Nazi party.

Hitler had his own personal alchemist, a scientist called Karl Malchus. He told Hitler and the Nazi Party that he was able to turn Munich's Isar River into gold, by using alchemy on its riverbed soil and stones with paraffin. He convinced them that this would provide the Third Reich with the security it needed. Hitler told Himmler to give Malchus his own private lab at Dachau, in the concentration camp, and Malchus was to do all his alchemy work for the Third Reich in that lab, in secret. Sometime later Himmler discovered, to his great fury and red-faced shame, that Malchus was actually an agent working for British Intelligence! Himmler locked Malchus up in Dachau but a few months later freed him, warning him he'd kill him if this shameful conning incident was ever told to anyone.

Britain's intelligence agents were well aware in World War II of the Nazi leaders' interest in astrology so played games with them, to "mess with their heads". They'd gleefully insert fake horoscopes into world-wide newspapers which they knew the Nazis read. They'd claim that Hitler was soon going to die because "Jupiter was in retrograde". In one of these bogus horoscopes the British said Hitler would meet his demise by the last day of April, 1945. Hitler committed suicide on 30th April, 1945 thus one has to wonder whether his belief in astrology had led him to choose this date for his alleged suicidal death.

Freddie's brother, Herman Reade-Jahn was working in bilingual spying at Latimer House and Trent Park. His surname was spelled with an extra "e", different from Fred's Read-Jahn surname. At this time, Herman was known simply as H.R. Jahn, whereas his brother was known as F.W. Read-Jahn.

H.R. Jahn was one of the four principal people involved in the interrogation of Deputy Führer Rudolf Hess. On 10th May, 1941, the date the stars' alignment had led Hess to defect from Germany, Hess flew solo—with temerity, and obviously without Hitler's permission—from Germany to Scotland, where he planned to have peace talks with the Duke of Hamilton, whom he was sure was opposed to Churchill's British government. To Hess' misfortune, a

Spitfire chased him, and Hess, forced to bail out, was arrested upon arrival and taken down from Scotland to England for extensive interrogating at Latimer House in the room next to Colonel Thomas Kendrick's office. . .

Latimer House was one of three secret intelligence sites that Kendrick ran. Across all three (Latimer House, Wilton Park, and Trent Park), 10,000 prisoners' conversations were bugged. One of the highest-ranking prisoners out of the 10,000 who passed through Latimer House was Hitler's deputy leader in the Nazi Party, Rudolf Hess.

After his interrogation at the isolated location of Latimer House, Hess was then transported over to Bletchley Park, and after that on to London to the Tower of London, where H.R. Jahn and three other officers carried on their interrogations.

Winston Churchill ordered Ivone Kirkpatrick, a senior Foreign Office official, to get everything out of Hess that he could, to gain any potential intelligence benefits. H.R. Jahn was listed as the "stenographer" for this high-ranking officer's interrogation. Notes on the interrogation state it was decided as being of "no value", that he had nothing much to report that the Brits didn't already know.

Kirkpatrick was a distinguished diplomat and linguist with postings around the world, including Berlin from 1933-1938. It was in Berlin that he got to know Herman and his brother, Fred (prior to Fred's three-month journey across the world to reach the British Embassy in Moscow later on, in 1940). Kirkpatrick himself was perfect for intelligence work and when he was transferred back to London, he picked some favourite agents attached to the Foreign Office, namely Herman, as well as Fred (but Fred was to come on board a little later, after his return from Russia), to help Kirkpatrick with the interrogation of prisoners of war. This branch of the intelligence service was eventually called MI-19, a sub-set of MI-9, a sub-set of MI-6, with MI-6 standing for Military Intelligence, Section 6—all of it being run by the Secret Service Bureau specialising in foreign intelligence. MI-19 had Combined Services Detailed Interrogation Centres (CSDIC) at a number of British stately homes including Wilton Park and Latimer House, and a number of centres overseas.

Hess was held in custody in the Tower of London until the war finished, when he stood trial at Nuremberg in 1946 as a major war criminal.

A letter found amongst Fred's cache of letters from the war, tells that Herman had taken his family up to Scotland ostensibly "for a holiday". It was there that he was chosen to be involved in the interrogation of Hess.

In the final words of a letter to Clara from the British Embassy, Moscow, dated 26th May, 1941, which he wanted her to pass to his brother, Fred makes an enigmatic comment, *"Mother, what did you think of your friend Hess appearing in Scotland? Strange things happen, don't they?"*

Then he goes on to make a mundane remark, *"The weather is bucking up now. There are buds on the trees and they will soon be green. About time too..."*

There are often a number of perfectly mundane, possibly cryptic, remarks in Fred's letters "home". He did tell the author, his younger daughter, many years later, that many words were in code for his brother to act upon as necessary.

While Hess was in the Tower, a chemist called H.A. Rowe wrote out a sleeping draught prescription of potassium bromide and chloral hydrate for "Herr Rudolph Hess, Deputy Führer, Luftwaffe". Eldred's in Plymouth eventually put this old document up for auction, along with another prescription for another German, the Nazi spy Josef Jakobs. The Tower of London obviously didn't have the relaxing atmosphere of the stately homes of Latimer House, Wilton Park, or Trent Park!

While Freddie's brother, bilingual Herman Reade-Jahn, was splitting his time working at Latimer House and Trent Park, he was also doing bilingual interrogation work at the Tower of London. Josef Jakobs arrived in England in January, 1941, floating down from his plane on a parachute. British intelligence had learned of his planned arrival and a welcoming committee was awaiting him. He was wearing civilian clothing under his German flying suit. He had in his pocket poorly forged documents, 500 British pounds, and a dried German sausage. This very sausage (dry but intact, 77 years on at the time of writing) is still in the hands of a member of the author's family! Josef Jakobs was to be the last person ever executed at the Tower (on 15 August, 1941) and was seated on a rather fine Windsor chair for the military firing squad's brief procedure.

After the war, and after Rudolf Hess was convicted at the Nuremberg Trials of crimes against peace[1], and conspiring with other German leaders to commit crimes, he was sent off to Spandau Prison in West Berlin in 1947. There he remained until 1987 when, after repeated failed attempts by his family and politicians to win his release, Hess committed suicide at the age of 93. Spandau Prison was knocked down after that, mainly in order to prevent it becoming a shrine to neo-Nazis in Germany.

Along with Herman in the initial interrogation of Rudolf Hess was his superior, Ivone Kirkpatrick. Kirkpatrick was a short man, temperamental and outspoken, who believed no leader could "work" with Hitler and that Hitler should actually be "banged on the head". His wartime work and cover were principally and ostensibly as head of the European service of the British Broadcasting Corporation. At the BBC he instituted a campaign called the "V" campaign, which was beamed over the radio to underground fighters and to people in occupied Europe in the Resistance. Kirkpatrick started every broadcast with the opening notes of Beethoven's Fifth Symphony. This was his intention to show Great Britain's faith and belief in gaining an ultimate victory.

---

1. *The definition in international law of "a crime against peace": the planning, preparation, initiation, or waging of wars of aggression, or a war in violation of international treaties, agreements or assurances, or participation in a common plan or conspiracy for the accomplishment of any of the foregoing. [Wikipedia]*

Chapter 23

Perlovka, July, 1941
The Dacha Outside Moscow

While Rudolf Hess was being interrogated in Europe—followed by all the other intelligence work Fred and his brother Herman were later to be involved in—Fred was now, in July, 1941 still based in the Moscow environs.

As Fred had shared in a 3rd July letter to his mother, he himself had been already moved to a country house just outside Moscow. In July the British Embassy, with its British Military Mission, had been obliged to leave Moscow city itself. It had become far too dangerous to stay, with the impending arrival in the city of Moscow of the German army. Nazi Germany had invaded the Soviet Union on 22nd June, 1941, using the code name of "Operation Barbarossa". This was the largest German military operation so far in World War II. Stalin then ordered the legations out of Moscow, expecting street fighting once the Germans had entered the city.

The British Ambassador had decided to move his whole staff to a rather large village called Perlovka, except for two ladies called Nina and Valentina, left behind as Embassy caretakers.

In his July letter to his mum Fred had written, *"I am living at a country house that belongs to the Embassy. It is about 20 miles out of town."*

Prior to the removal of the legation to Perlovka, Fred's superior John Merchant, having returned to Russia from his trip back to England, had now been ordered to get himself back to England at once. He was involved in espionage of the utmost secrecy, involving his speaking directly, himself, to the British military and political nabobs (as he called them), not trusting any other kind of communication at this extremely volatile time of hostilities and bloody conflict.

In discussions with Fred, the two men decided the best way to get out of the USSR at this time was from Archangel, the seaport at the mouth of the Northern Dvina River leading into the White Sea.

So off Merchant went to Archangel, to board a ship there. This is where Fred had been taking people it was considered necessary to get out of the USSR—that highly important and dangerous sideline of his usual work at the Embassy. He knew a lot about how that process worked, so was able to be of great help to Merchant in getting him down to Archangel and onto a ship to be routed circuitously, to be sure, but headed for good old Blighty.

"Sir", said Fred, as he left him at the ship, "you will look up Molly again? You will tell her I'll be home myself just as soon as I can."

"Certainly", replied Merchant, "and I'll tell her, from my pretty reliable sources, that it won't be that much longer and she'll have you in her arms again!"

Regarding the two female caretakers left behind at the British Embassy, before leaving Moscow John Merchant had by then installed one of them, his own Russian love, Nina, to live with him in a British Embassy flat. With the personnel about to be gone from the British Embassy to Perlovka, John Merchant had got permission from the Ambassador to leave Nina actually living in his flat in one of the wings of the Embassy as a caretaker of the premises. The Americans hadn't yet got into the war, so it was to them the responsibility of caring for the British Embassy premises was left. They installed another Russian woman, called Valentina, at the Embassy as the other female caretaker. Nina and Tina became friends. Nina had no idea that Tina was another NKDV spy who had been placed specifically to spy on herself, nicknamed by the Russians "the Little Bird". Very soon, Tina brought a short Japanese man to live with her at the Embassy, and he was the First Secretary of the Japanese Embassy. By October, 1941, both Tina and the Japanese man disappeared from Moscow, turning up in Kuibyshev. Tina was by then dressed in furs and jewellery, her payment for her new job of spying on the Japanese. When Nina heard this, she realized what must have been going on, and was greatly relieved to have Valentina off her back. She was now alone at the British Embassy. Nina wasn't able to leave the USSR herself until June, 1942, but she was eventually able to get out, and was to depart her homeland from yet another seaport, Molotovsk. By then she was the happily legal wife of John Merchant, Fred's British Embassy direct superior, who'd come back to Moscow to get Nina, and marry her aboard the ship on which they were to escape the Soviet Union.

But, back to July, 1941, with Fred's superior John Merchant now gone from the USSR on his Very Secret Mission, Fred was now reporting directly to the British Ambassador. He sent Fred to Perlovka ahead of the entire Embassy staff's removal to the village. Fred was to check out the area, to ensure nobody was lurking around who appeared to be an undercover German or looked suspicious in any other way. All-in-all he was the advance guard. He moved himself into one of the dachas and cabled the Ambassador: "Perlovka still sleepy little village. STOP. Nothing untoward going on. STOP. Full steam ahead. STOP."

The whole staff then packed everything they needed, including their cypher machines, and moved.

This was a quiet country area filled with wooden dachas, those typically Russian countryside log cabins, surrounded by tall pine trees, birches, and gloriously-scented late-blooming mauve and white lilacs. Onion domes decorated the churches above their green steeply slanted roofs. Perlovka is in the Moskovskaya Oblast, and a quiet area in 1941 that wasn't expected to be of particular interest to the Germans, and yet Fred confides in his mother and wife that they *"may have to scuttle the place and relocate to the Near East (perhaps Tehran), or India"*. The reason for that was that nobody knew how close the Germans would get so they'd better follow Fred's favourite maxim to "be prepared".

The Embassy staff was numerous enough to require two dachas to live and work in. Lime trees spread their shade over Fred's dacha. Inside, the wooden dining table was covered with an old cream lace tablecloth tatted in a complex series of knots and loops. An ornate silver samovar sat on a side table to provide tea to the worker bees inside. And work they did—furiously now, sometimes staying up all night, in a continuous beehive buzz of activity.

No more time away for Fred to aid important individuals to get out of the USSR via Archangel. Fred was vastly relieved about this. His arm might now get a chance to heal properly, with no more skiing entailed. Only a short spell for rests was granted to them, and, being British, they used these little breaks for the proverbial cuppa tea.

The rich cordial of tea at the dacha had to be kept burning with coals in the lower section of the gorgeous samovar all day and all night long. Fred was constantly sipping tea in a glass, with an added slice of lemon, in the Soviet manner. The lemon was a treat; hard to come by in those days, but a chum of his had brought a big bag of lemons back after a side visit to Tehran, Persia. One of the Embassy cooks knew how to preserve the lemons "forever" she claimed, by preserving them in a salting process. It took her about three weeks to do it all, around all her other kitchen work, but was well worth it. She ended up with a number of tall jars full of her cut and salted lemons.

As Fred took his quick break, sipping his tea, he ruminated upon all those camels bringing the tea to Russia since the early 19th century, as far as he knew. He'd read how camels had carried the hard-packed huge tea-bricks along what had been called the Tea Road for years, all through Siberia from China. Thousands of tons of tea—mind-boggling, but thank God they did, thought the exhausted Freddie, sipping with relish!

He'd heard that in winter the wooden dachas were covered in snow with icicles dripping their frozen fingers down from the gutters. The only way to get to the dacha village would be by wooden sled, drawn by snorting horses decorated with colourful embroidered and leather trappings, their breath rising up through the light streaming down through the bare-leafed trees around the wooded clearings. One would hear the swishing, hissing, sound of the sled's runners cutting through the icy snow blanketing the dirt roads mingled with the tinkling of the horses' bells, and the rough-voiced barked commands of the Russian driver.

In late summer, which it now was for Fred and his fellow workers, it was still quite hot. The log houses had orchards behind them where the staff could sit for a few minutes' respite from their demanding cypher work. Sometimes you could see a deer cautiously foraging amongst the fruit trees for fallen fruit or hear the peck-peck-peck of a woodpecker searching for insects or sap upon the trees.

Fred entered the orchard to sit and rest for a while upon a rock. There were still late-flowering trees in the orchard, a few of their branches still clothed in pale-pink blooms. As a breeze gently sighed through the orchard, the blossoms wafted gently to the ground like swirling confetti. His thoughts went immediately back to his wedding day when family and friends had thrown confetti and rice at him and Molly as they left the church. He remembered picking it out of her clothing that night as they fell laughing onto their marriage bed, so happy, so very delighted with each other.

As he continued to sit upon a rock under the trees smoking his pipe for a few minutes more that early evening Fred heard Russian balalaika folk music brought to him on the wind. The leaves on the trees shimmered and swayed seemingly in time to the music coming and going. Their susurration whispered to him to dance. To toss away the loneliness engulfing him where he felt but one step away from tears most of the time, to lose the sense of being at breaking point. Move! He commanded himself.

He got up, stretched, placed his pipe on the rock, and took a few hesitant steps in time to the bell-like sounds and soon found himself spinning and dancing there under the trees in joyous abandon. Suddenly he stopped and laughed at himself. So, he still had some energy and the ability to have fun. He wouldn't give in, wouldn't break down. But then, where was Molly? He remembered dancing with her in his arms. Immediately staving off these dangerous thoughts, he grabbed his pipe back up from the rock and hastened back inside to immerse himself once more in work.

One day Fred was granted a much-needed somewhat longer spell off from work. With a colleague who could speak pretty good Russian he visited the 19th century Mytishiasky water pump station, which drew its water from 73 underground springs. By talking further to a local old fellow they got directions to the Rostokinsky Aqueduct near Perlovka, which, the man proudly told them, was also known as the Millionny Bridge, because, he chortled, it had cost 2 million rubles to build. He said Catherine the Great had commissioned its construction over the Yauza River in 1780 and it took until 1804 to finish because of the builders constantly being taken away to fight in different battles! At this nugget of information, the old chap cackled loudly, slapping his thighs in amusement. After his wheezing laughter came to a stop, he added that at one time it had been the city of Moscow's first centralized water supplier, but no longer, he sadly told them. It was interesting to find this local old chap so happily eager to chat because within Moscow city the legation had been advised not to fraternise with the locals, in that they were allegedly a dour, surly lot, suspicious of foreigners, and feeling much hard-done-by. Not hard to believe, for this was wartime, but, here in Perlovka, it was a quite different atmosphere.

But mostly, Fred worked. And worked…

Chapter 24

1942-1944
MI-19 and The Very Secret Places

17 Cheniston Gardens,
Kensington, London, W.8

4th January, 1942
Letter Number 30 (have you got all of mine???)

Darling Fred,

Your mum told me you were going to have to leave Moscow and all of you would be living in the countryside and that it would be much safer. I haven't had a letter from you about this, or a cable. Where are your letters? Probably stuck in Istanbul or Tehran or somewhere!

Freddie, your superior officer, a John Merchant, rang me and invited me for a drink and a pub lunch. He said he couldn't tell me much but did say that your broken arm still bothers you. I'm so sorry to hear that. He said it looks as if it's got a rash on it that could now be psoriasis or eczema. Oh dear. What did the doctor say about it? He said it took him ages to get back to London from Moscow. He seemed very nice, darling, and said I should call him John. He did tell me he was in love with a Russian girl who looked rather like me and how much he misses her. Poor man; I certainly know how he feels. He hinted you might be coming back to England soon. IS THAT TRUE? Oh, Freddie, do write, or better still, send me a telegram about it.

John was quite amusing, darling. He spouted Latin at me…LATIN… as if I'd understand. I mean, we did take some Latin at Heath House school, but honestly, he had to write down what he said to me, so I'd remember it. He solemnly intoned to me, "tempora mutantur, nos et mutamur in illis". You probably got it, but he had to translate it for me! "Times change and we change with them." He was trying to say that you'd be home soon, that the war would be over soon and we should get used to it? I think—or was it in code?! Anyway, he's a clever chappie, isn't he?!

Oh, and you know what else? John said he'd studied classical Greek, too, because when I said, just in general chit-chat, how I so missed swimming in the sea (you know, they don't want us going to the beaches these days because they've built all those wooden groyne fence defences that go down the sides of the beaches through the water, in case Jerry were to attempt to invade by boat) he said that Euripides said "the sea cleanses all mortal ills". Isn't that grand? It certainly always does for me. You know how I love swimming and feel so wonderful after it. Jimmie does, too. I'm sure he misses going for a dip as much as me. John says all this with a straight face but I declare, I think he's taking the Mickey out of me a bit!

Anyway, I've been talking to Dad all about the war. He says it can't go on much longer. We read the papers together and discuss all the news in them. I don't believe everything I read but do feel I'm becoming quite an expert on world affairs, especially in Europe!

Write soon, darling heart. Jimmie and I are still going barmy missing you. He sends you a big wet kiss on your nose. His breath is still ghastly.

All my love, your
Molly

It was now early January, 1942. Fred's Russian days were, indeed, almost over. Six months he'd spent in the countryside. As beautiful as it was, he'd hardly seen much, with the war progressing at great speed meaning more and more work for him and his colleagues. How much more could he take? He thought he was heading for a breakdown. Many of the chaps muttered the same comment, but *sotto voce*, hoping their superiors wouldn't hear them. After all, they shouldn't complain. It was wartime and everyone was in the same boat.

The Ambassador called him into his Perlovka dacha office one morning and announced that Fred's talents were required immediately over in Buckinghamshire, England, at MI-19's base. He'd heard from Colonel Thomas Kendrick, OBE that Fred was to forget his MI-19 work that he'd been doing on the side in the Soviet Union. Kendrick worked for MI-6 at the heart of Great Britain's WWII intelligence. The intelligence agents working for him at this point in time belonged to the sub-set of MI-6 known as MI-19, which, in turn, was a sub-set of MI-9, which Fred did in fact already know. The British intelligence officers working at MI-19 Buckinghamshire base were the vital staff of the Controlled Services Detailed Intelligence Corps (CSD). These were the military personnel who interrogated prisoners of war, known in intel as MI-19 men—a highly secret section of the British Directorate of Military Intelligence, part of the War Office. Kendrick told the Ambassador he'd be running the show at MI-19 in '42 onwards, which was now! And that he was getting his staff together. He wanted the best in the field to help him. He wanted Fred back, and now!

"You realize not only Kendrick's asked specifically for you, but so has Ivone Kirkpatrick? He says he already has your brother in the shop, which should please you, don't you know?!" He went on, "No ship for you. It's got to be an airplane. No time for anything else. The RAF's obliging. I've got that part all arranged. You're a lucky bugger, Read-Jahn! Now off you go."

Fred was utterly thrilled. Molly! He'd have to cable her at once! He was going home!

He immediately started working with the staff on the plan to get him out of Perlovka. He would be taken by the Ambassador's car the very next night (the next night, oh boy, he thought!) to a specific location outside some woods where there was a runway sometimes used by Stalin's troop planes bringing in military support and supplies. The co-ordinates for the pick-up were sent to him via coded radio message. Stealth and meticulous timing were all-important. The aeroplane would land, pick him up, and take off all in a matter of short minutes. You wouldn't want any advance guard of Germans to see what you were up to in the landing clearing near the woods.

Still not knowing precisely where the German troops had got to, he was told to have his handgun at the ready under his civilian jacket. The chap he was working with on this plan commanded him, "Best not to be in uniform, old man. Best to stay incognito. Just in case you get picked up by Jerry. And, if you do, they're not to know where you're going or why. You know the drill. Get your stuff packed and we'll pick you up at 21:00 hours. Carry a torch with you. Got it?"

Fred certainly had got it. With beating heart, he left his radio and cypher machine and hastened to do his packing. He'd spent many a boring night, sleepless, cleaning his handgun, just to "be prepared", so that was all in order. Tomorrow! It couldn't come fast enough for him.

Before darkness fell he stepped outside to watch the sunset and carefully go over his plans. Looking up at the sky he saw the sun disappearing behind the forest. A few streaks of dark orange mixed with dark blue remained. As he stood there in the deep silence the night was rent by a low, steady, continuous noise of flapping wings. Suddenly he realised what it was as he saw a murmuration of starlings wheeling and dipping, regrouping into shape after different shape above him in the fast-fading light. Ah, Fred thought, there's a storm on its way. May it hold off until I'm safely away from this place.

Hours later he was on the aeroplane. Nature's promised storm had moved away. There'd been no hitch whatsoever. Now he sat with some other men listening to the drone of the engine as they flew over the forested land. His heart was in his mouth as he saw brilliant anti-aircraft lights fingering the sky around him.

They flew high over Finland. Swedish military intelligence working with the Allies advised them over the crackling radio to touch down for a brief refuelling in their country. It was too dangerous to refuel in Norway or Denmark—already thick with German troops.

Awakening with a jolt—actually by a sharp elbow bashed into his ribs—he saw a grinning subaltern's face in front of him. "We're in Blighty, sir! Don't you want to get off, sir? Or are you planning on getting off in Germany, hahaha?"

Fred leapt to his feet, grabbed his suitcase, and, with joints aching from the long trip, hurried down the plane's staircase onto the black tarmac. He was home! He could hardly believe it. He wanted to crouch down on his knees and kiss the ground, but the subaltern's stiff salute and hovering smile around his lips precluded that kind of behaviour from a British Army officer!

The subaltern saluted him again at the bottom of the staircase, and Fred started as he swore he saw the cheeky bugger giving him a surreptitious wink. "Sir! Car's awaiting you, sir! Step this way, sir, please."

Good heavens, a car sent for him! They really did need him and his multi-lingual talents. Well, he certainly knew so much about the Germans, and if they'd got German officers locked up, he was the perfect chap to interrogate them. Herman, too. They were, indeed, a perfect team. Hell, they could be German or English at will, he and his brother, the powers-that-be well knew that. He was really looking forward to seeing his brother again…but first, Molly!

He got in the car and gave Molly's new address in Little Chalfont, Buckinghamshire to the driver, who, of course, already had it! Boy oh boy, thought Freddie, these chaps are on top of everything. Molly had moved from London after she'd left the bank, to get away from the Blitz. The Foreign Office had found her a little cottage with a small garden in Buckinghamshire. She was delighted and had been spending much of her days bustling around creating a nest for Fred's return, and hopefully, a family of their own!

The car bringing Freddie to his own private heaven drew up at Molly's cottage. He thanked the driver, leapt out, almost leaving his suitcase behind, opened the low gate, slammed it behind him, and sprinted up the flower-lined pathway. Before he could even bang on the old brass knocker, the door flew open and there she stood, his own sweet Molly! A grin plastered her face, the gap between her two front teeth endearingly drawing his eyes then his lips down to her welcoming mouth.

In his hurry he tossed his suitcase down in the hallway. Placing his hands on either side of her face, he kissed her, long and hard, while pushing her gently backwards into the hallway, and easing the front door shut behind him with his foot.

Splitting apart, they gazed at each other, then, laughing like kids in delight, they took it in turns pulling each other up the short staircase to her bedroom.

That night was most surely the night Molly conceived her first child, to be born in late September, 1942.

Fred and his brother, Herman, had once again with relief been reunited in England. While Fred had been working at his intelligence activities in Russia, Herman had been doing much the same kind of work in England, including the interrogation of Rudolf Hess. After all, Fred and Herman had had much the same training from boyhood on, so it was no surprise they were now called upon to work together.

By 1st May, 1942, Fred's work was gratefully recognised and he was promoted to an Emergency Commission rank of 2nd Lieutenant in the Intelligence Corps., exactly the same as his brother, Herman, but not yet working full-time with MI-19. There was still training to be followed before actual interrogation of German officers was permitted. The work he'd been doing surreptitiously and on the side in the Soviet Union didn't involve interrogations of captured Germans, obviously, because they hadn't arrived in Moscow at that time; Fred's secret MI-19 work over there was getting specific people expeditiously out of the USSR. Now, in England, he was going to be working in a new area for him, interrogating captured German officers, to get important information out of them, all with a view to bringing this damned war to an end, thought Fred to himself.

By 1st November Fred received another promotion, to the rank of War Substantive Lieutenant.

By 16th December he'd been posted as an Intelligence Officer "to be specially employed" at the Controlled Services Detailed Intelligence Corps (CSD)—in other words, to continue to work with Herman, but wholly for MI-19. He was now considered ready for the nerve-wracking, extremely arduous work of interrogation of prisoners, themselves trained in not giving out information.

When Fred started work at MI-19 proper in England, and in the short spaces of free time he had, Fred met up with some fellows from BAAG (the British Army Aid Group), temporarily at Latimer House doing their own research of certain German officers who had connections to China. He was able to ferret out a little information about his old chum, the Chinese agent Shanghai Joe. He'd wondered how it was that he'd turned up in Japan, in Moscow, Hong Kong, and Shanghai, among many other places. Shanghai

Joe himself had never let on to Fred what he was doing, besides obviously passing along messages.

Fred learned that before the war the Chinese spy had been a forerunner agent working for British Army Intelligence "mining" his mostly Asian contacts in different parts of the world, readying for the war the Army knew would eventually come to pass, as, indeed, it did in 1939. It was whispered gravely that Shanghai Joe had also been an ex-POW-turned-agent, helped by BAAG to escape from a Japanese camp back to China. Fred thought it certainly possible. He couldn't find out whether, or even if, Joe had been interned in Japan, because Fred had run into him as a free agent in Japan and Moscow in 1940 and '41, and was told that it wasn't until sometime this year in '42 that the "China" MI-9 unit (later also becoming MI-19), would be doing important work in southern China and was known as the British Army Aid Group.

Part of BAAG's work was to help POWs in Japanese camps escape to China. This Aid Group was very much linked to the Hong Kong Chinese Regiment, and they, in turn, had agents and spies in Shanghai, too, who operated in conjunction with British Military Intelligence. So, thought Fred, it was all deliciously secret about Fred's special Chinese chum, good old Shanghai Joe!

He reckoned that Joe was still attached to the Chinese Regiment while working in the Chinese legation in Moscow and, for reasons known only to himself and his superiors, had been on duty in both China and Japan, eventually receiving orders to base himself in Moscow.

Fred made himself a promise to get the real dope out of Shanghai Joe when next he saw him. He gave a crooked grin, though, realising that Shanghai Joe wouldn't tell him a thing he wasn't supposed to know. He reckoned he, too, followed Fred's own adage, you only reveal something on a "need-to-know" basis.

Fred's MI-19 "special employment" was just the sort of thing he had been doing for the Foreign Office in his undercover work at Morgan Crucible before he left for the USSR, and then in the USSR: spying, as well as doing his cypher clerk work—but this time interrogating and listening in on captured German officers held in the great houses of England.

The British military had commandeered a number of these grand stately homes of England for their own wartime secret activities. At least three of the great houses of Britain were used for spying on German prisoners of war. These three included Latimer House in the Amersham area of Buckinghamshire (where Rudolf Hess was interrogated before being transferred), Wilton Park near Beaconsfield, Buckinghamshire, and Trent Park near Cockfosters in North London.

Another old home commandeered by British military intelligence, called Bletchley Park, was located at Milton Keynes (also in Buckinghamshire, some 54 miles [87 km] by car from London) and specialised in decoding German messages. Bletchley Park was the home of the Government Code & Cypher School, principally using the Enigma codebreaking machine to penetrate the secret communications not only of the Enigma code but also the Lorenz cypher of the Axis Powers.

As we now know, it was the Enigma code that Fred himself had been using to crack German messages by cypher, when he was working in Moscow, down in the basement of the British Embassy's basement Ops Room, where he'd receive decrypted messages from Bletchley Park, and get them sent over to Stalin's people to keep them apprised of the Germans' advance toward the USSR.

When German military personnel were captured they were often held as prisoners of war at one of these stately homes, the German officers particularly at Latimer House. This was the principal location of MI-19 and where Fred and Herman worked. At Latimer House it was more about the captured prisoners and what information could be extracted from them through careful spying. The Germans were often interrogated face-to-face, but only as a cover, in that the really important, useful, information (that would change the actual course of the war) was discovered through secret spying, listening in to them having private chats amongst themselves, making it of vital importance to how Churchill would run the war.

These Buckinghamshire stately homes were gracious very old buildings, homes of the landed gentry and aristocracy lent to the war effort and situated either in north London or in the beautiful parklands and gardens of "the green belt" only about 30 miles distant from London. This was imperative for Winston Churchill's government to be able to have its people come and go within a reasonable time when picking up information to take back to Churchill's underground City of Westminster War Rooms in London. People whispered after WWII was over that much of the spying work done at Latimer House could very well have saved London from eventually being annihilated in the same way as Hiroshima.

Early each morning Fred dressed in his Army officer uniform and mounted his old BSA M20 motorbike to get himself to Latimer House. He left his little family of wife and daughter ensconced in their charming little cottage. Molly's job for the day, besides caring for her little daughter and the house, was to shop daily for food. Rationing was well in place and much of her day was spent standing in lines with her baby on her hip, patiently awaiting her turn at the bakery, greengrocer's or butcher's. The fishmonger was out of business in the village. Nobody had time to fish; the men all having gone off to war. Meat was scarce. Women did all they could in the Women's Land Army, working the soil, raising crops and tending the animals, but food was needed to feed the British military, so not much was left for the elderly, women and children left at home. Molly used all her imagination to make appetizing meals for her precious husband to come home to. She had her own little Victory Garden at the cottage where she grew the vegetables, fruit and herbs that she could to sustain her family, having learned much about gardening from her father. By her post-war years Molly had become a first-rate gardener, tending her gorgeous roses, her dahlia blossoms as big as dinner plates, and her espaliered apple trees. She'd learned to use every garden space to full advantage, producing delicious crop after crop. She was even to successfully grow a variety of succulent mushrooms in the oft-flooded basement of her eventual home on an island in the Thames many years hence.

It was during 1942 onwards now in England that Fred was able to once more put to good use some of those skills that he'd learned in Russia, and that had served him so well over there, helping to get people out of the USSR, decoding messages with his cypher skills, and spying knowledge in general. From all of that work he'd learned how to get along with anybody, to say and do all the right things to further his own cause, and that of Great Britain.

Fred was a true diplomat, a gentleman with impeccable manners. He knew his wines, and cosmopolitan food dishes. He made sure he was conversant with world political and philosophical issues of all kinds. He appreciated classical music. His knowledge of different languages was, naturally, of prime importance. He had a droll sense of humour and was one of those people who could hear a good joke and remember it to pass along. He was tall and distinguished with his barrel chest, his rather reddish hair, and his neatly trimmed moustache. When discussing himself one of his favourite comments about his tall stature was to say that he was too short by only a hair's breadth to become a guard at Buckingham Palace! Fred had extremely intelligent eyes, always twinkling merrily behind his bookish spectacles. He was a graceful dancer for his size. Ladies were always attracted to him. He could wiggle his ears to make people laugh. He'd sustained an injury some years earlier to his right index finger. This he used to great advantage when he'd hold the crooked finger high up in the air to summon a waiter or to draw attention to himself. In short, he was an erudite, funny, clever man whom people much enjoyed being around. This served to endear him to the captured German officers, especially since he could tell them jokes in German, had been to many of their hometowns, and knew so much about their history and culture. After all, he was half German. It was no wonder that both Kirkpatrick and Kendrick valued him and his brother highly.

At Latimer House, as was done at the other stately homes-now-prisons, Kendrick organised eavesdropping of the captured German officers' conversations, often by hiding microphones in the magnificent specimen trees growing in the spacious grounds that the officers were permitted to stroll around in. Here they felt at ease and chatted quite freely with their fellow German officers, much of which chat was picked up and used to stop Britain from suffering further bombing.

The captured German generals thought they had "hit the jackpot" to be forcibly imprisoned at these spacious, stately English homes. The British in charge told the officers that they were being treated according to their high military rank. They were occasionally taken into London to have splendid meals, attend the theatre, and offered other such treats. Soon they'd let their guard down even more, relaxing into their situation, and more valuable information was consequently picked up by British intelligence.

Many of the German generals were held at Trent Park; in fact, eventually there were 59 of them, and they stayed there until the war had ground to a halt. The generals were permitted to have their own personal valets, to drink wine and to eat good food. With hubris they'd laughingly boast to one another about the stupidity of the British. It's said that one general, in a letter home to his family, wrote that he rated his prison so highly, that he wished his family could come to stay with him there for a holiday! But, not only were the trees in the grounds where they walked bugged, but so were the lampshades, the plant pots, and even the billiards tables they loved to play at inside the houses.

What British officers like Freddie and Herman were discovering from all the chit-chat going on amongst the German officers was the basic essential nature of the German leaders, how they were developing their war plans, and many a valuable secret that was then passed along to Winston Churchill and his staff in their secret underground London headquarters where Churchill lived and ran WWII.

Not only did Latimer, Trent, and Wilton Park put up captured German officers but also imprisoned U-Boat submarine crews and Luftwaffe pilots. The submarine crewmen and German pilots were bugged over a fortnight or so before they were removed to more conventional captivity where they saw the war out. They smoked

Hidden in Plain Sight

incessantly and the air in their rooms was clouded with their cigarette smoke and secrets shared, plus an all-pervading, thick, palpable sense of stress and sweaty armpits, as they talked amongst themselves trying to imagine what awaited them next.

The imprisoned Trent Park German generals had much to be thankful for in that they were not held in the Combined Services Detailed Interrogation Centre, known as the "London Cage". These three houses were separated from the rest of the houses by a single strand of barbed-wire fencing. This was another interrogation centre run by MI-19, commanded by Lt. Col. Alexander Scotland, OBE, and which was located in three houses of the exclusive Kensington Palace Gardens in West London. The "hardest to break" captured German military personnel were held there, and after the war criminals from both the Gestapo and the SS insisted they suffered torture while held in the London Cage. The SS was the "Schutzstaffel", German for "Protective Echelon". These men were Hitler's personal bodyguards. Later in the war they had become extremely powerful and feared throughout Nazi Germany. Scotland himself wrote a memoir about his work "breaking" tough German military men, all with a view to finding out how they'd been trained and what they'd been working on regarding military equipment. Scotland felt that if one could discover how a man had been trained and what he'd learned, one could find out the weaknesses in the German military in general, thus how to exploit it to bring the conclusion of the war nearer.

Not only did Fred and Herman interrogate the captured Germans and translate eavesdropped information at Latimer House and Trent Park, but they also consorted with many of the literally thousands of German prisoners of war who had been captured and who had become "German refugees". There were also the Jewish refugees who had got out of Germany just in time. Many of these people began working for British Intelligence and were working at these stately homes of England. Many of these were part of what is now known as the "secret listening machine".

In each of the three stately homes of Latimer House, Wilton Park and Trent Park—now turned into prisons—there was a room called the "M room". This stood for "microphone". In each M room sat the secret listeners with their bugging device monitors, picking up conversations between the Germans via each mic planted in strategic areas within and outside the grand houses. Freddie knew that the information gleaned from the prisoners was so vital that the British government gave their work an unlimited war budget. Without this gleaned intelligence, Britain's winning of the war would have been even more difficult, doubtless taking even more years to accomplish. It was through these overheard conversations at Latimer House that the British first learned about the V1 and V2 bombing aircraft that the Germans were developing, colloquially known as "doodlebugs" in England, which were eventually to drop down onto London in 1944.

One horrible day Fred was summoned into a room at Latimer House to use his fluent German to interrogate a German officer who had just been brought in. He was dismayed to come face-to-face with his German cousin seated obviously anxiously at a beautiful Chippendale table from the 1800s. Fred begged off this particular task and left the room sweating, with the reality of the war lying heavily upon his shoulders. He never discussed what happened to his cousin after that.

That night, Sunday, 23rd May 1943 when Fred came home, he told her, "Molly, I've had a nasty shock today. Let's go out dancing tonight to take my mind off it."

"What on earth happened, Fred, you look quite pale?"

"Just one of those things, darling, involving one of the German officers they brought in. You know we have to interrogate them; that's all I can tell you. But, honestly, it's nothing for you to worry about, but I would really like to go out tonight."

"Okay, I understand. I mustn't ask! You want me to get a babysitter?" asked Molly, "and why, oh why, do you have to work on Sundays? It's supposed to be a day of rest."

"I know it, but you know it's wartime and this is just how it is. So yes, please do get a babysitter. Ask your chums Dora or Dolly? They might not be doing anything on a Sunday night. Let's go to that newish club in London, I heard it's open on Sundays. We can take the old jalopy. They say some chap called Feldman opened the club last October."

"Oh, yes, Dolly told me about it! It's the No. 1 Swing Club. It's in the basement at 100 Oxford Street and yes, that drummer chappie, Robert Feldman, opened it and it's only five shillings a year to join. She knows all the musicians. Dolly says they play ace bebop and swing jazz there and the dancing's just marvellous. She's really good at jiving. She said it's really smoky from all the ciggies but you can see the best jazz musicians play there."

"Right-oh, we'll cut the rug for sure!" said Fred, "and don't worry about making dinner. I heard it's still got 'Macks' restaurant in it, well, that's what the chaps at work told me in passing. And, isn't Feldman a clarinettist not a drummer?"

"Gosh, I don't know, darling, I'm only going by what Dolly says. Apparently, Feldman likes being in the basement there to take his mind off the air-raids! She says it's such hot jazz. Yes, let's go! Um, now what should I wear?"

Months and months went past, with both Fred and Herman working hard listening in to the Germans' conversations at work, and with Fred taking an occasional day or evening off to be at home with Molly and Pam.

By 1944, when his daughter was still little and far too young to have been placed to sit with her father on his motorbike Fred decided to take her for a ride. He swerved and skidded around a corner. She went flying off and landed in a stinging nettle patch. Fred took the screaming toddler home to her mother, feeling totally mortified. Molly was Not Amused. Where was his good sense?

Another part of their looming family troubles was the fact that Fred simply could not tell Molly anything about his work. He'd return home, usually stressed out and so very tired from his day but he couldn't sit down and discuss any of it with his wife. For Molly this was irritating and nerve-wracking. As man and wife, she wanted him to talk to her. All she was told was that Fred was an important cog, along with his brother, in the intelligence wheel, and, as she'd found out that Sunday he'd come back distressed from work in May, 1943, that he was interrogating German officers.

Fred couldn't tell her any of the details of the prisoners who were at the grand houses where he worked. All she could see was that this kind of work was utterly exhausting for Fred, making him irritable and anxious. He told her it was all vitally important. She did truly try to understand, but found it very debilitating. His usual greeting upon returning from work was, "Hello sweetheart. Gosh, I've had a poxy day!" He saw from her reaction that he'd said the wrong thing and he hated himself for it. He berated himself inwardly, "Fred, why are you being so wet? Pull your socks up, keep a stiff upper lip, and stop taking it out on poor old Moll."

But Fred could tell Molly about the beautiful estates he worked at. She listened, enthralled, hoping one day to see these homes of the aristocracy for herself. She came from an upper-middle-class family, but it was the aristocracy (a cut above her class) that had the lineage, the money, and even that "cut glass" accent that so many lower classes took the Mickey out of. Sometimes she'd imitate the aristocracy, making Fred cheer up and roar with laughter. "Dahling", she'd breathe seductively, "I absoloootly adorh you, come to my ahms, you gorjus tigah, you!"

These grand houses were, indeed, beautifully appointed with old, often priceless furnishings, both English and Oriental. At work one day Fred told his brother, "Bertie, I think it's a good thing it's mainly German officers who are held here, and not too many of the lower ranks, or those clods would surely destroy these grand old places, don't you think?"

Fred had a rather lowly opinion of the common soldier's appreciation for anything fine, as did many of his class in those days. As he passed a lit cigarette to Herman, Fred went on, "Have you also noticed, Bertie, that it's the German officers themselves who control the actions of their lower ranks, without us even having to ask them to? Jolly good thing, isn't it!"

"Good Lord!" responded Herman. "Quite so. All we have to do is watch 'em keep their men in line. Quite a relief, I think! It's hard enough doing what we do without having to be bloody baby-sitters, too!"

The brothers' superior, Colonel Kendrick himself, was a fascinating individual with vast experience. In the 1930s he had saved thousands of Jews from the Holocaust while he worked for the British Secret Service in Vienna, Austria. A double agent had betrayed him but he'd managed to eventually get back to England. Kendrick didn't surface in the intelligence world again until he appeared at Latimer House in 1942.

One of the many important jobs of the MI-19 intelligence personnel based at the stately home of Wilton Park was to facilitate the escapes of British prisoners of war from behind enemy lines and enable the return of those who succeeded in evading capture in enemy occupied territory. That meant they had to find ways to communicate with British POWs and to manage to get advice and equipment sent over to them. In effect, this wasn't only the British that MI-19 was aiding—not only shot-down aircrew—but, for example, all those British and Allied stranded soldiers during and after the Battle of Dunkirk (when the defence and evacuation of the British and Allied Forces in Europe took place, from 26th May to 4 June, 1940). They had to be brought home to England, or wherever their home bases were located.

In southern China the MI-9's para-military unit, the British Army Aid Group (BAAG), that helped POWs in Japanese camps escape back to China, was the group who, Fred was pretty sure, had helped Shanghai Joe to escape from internment. MI-9 was, of course, attached to the military and was closely linked to the Hong Kong and Shanghai Chinese Regiment, as Fred had heard. Part of Fred's work was also to stay in touch with Aid Group operatives working through MI-9. To his delight one day his old Chinese chum, Shanghai Joe himself, surfaced at Latimer House. Fred could hardly believe it, but then, as he privately told Herman, "That Chinese pal of mine really is the Scarlet Pimpernel, I tell you. You see him here, you see him there, you see him simply everywhere. Well, eventually you do!"

"Oh Fred, you've got that quote all messed up. Listen, it

should be:

'They seek him here/they seek him there/those Frenchies seek him everywhere/is he in heaven/or is he in hell?/my own elusive Pimpernel."

Fred growled at his younger brother, "Smart ass! I prefer my lines far better!"

To stay in touch with the Aid Group operatives working through MI-9, Fred enlisted the help of Shanghai Joe, who was himself much involved with the British Army Aid Group (BAAG)[1].

MI-19 had to be pretty creative in getting the Allies back home, so looked for people who could be cleverly useful. One of these included a British stage magician called Jasper Maskelyne. He was a master illusionist and could create large-scale ruses, deception, and camouflage. He had worked for MI-9 in Cairo, Egypt, where he invented small devices to help soldiers to escape if captured and where he also gave lectures on how to escape, all based on his magic and illusion expertise. Some of these devices were saws and collapsible shovels that could be hidden inside baseball and cricket bats, maps concealed in packs of playing cards, and even saw blades hidden inside hair combs. He convinced sceptical officers of his camouflage skills by creating the illusion of a German warship steaming down the River Thames. To do that he used a ship model and strategically placed it to look as if it were on the river. He had a team that helped him produce many dummy items including soldiers, steel helmets, guns by the tens of thousands, and even dummy aircraft and shell flashes by the millions. Maskelyne claimed he had also invented a dummy inflatable American Sherman Tank as a camouflage deception.

Fred and Shanghai Joe spent some happy hours working with Jasper Maskelyne. Fred learned some more tricks to add to his own mastery of the "tricks of the trade". Maskelyne showed them how you could make something seemingly disappear. It involved black curtains hung up around a room, and double-sided mirrors facing in different directions. Maskelyne explained to them, "It's just a matter of understanding physics, you chaps. You've got to place your mirrors at right angles. See, watch me." They both watched closely.

"Now", continued Maskelyne, "once positioned at right angles, you have to have their reflective area placed outwards. But! These other two have to have their reflective area facing inwards. Got it?"

"I sort of see," Fred said, "How does it actually work? I mean, how does somebody see the object, then it disappears, um, seemingly...?"

"Ah yes, that's the trick, you know. If they're all placed right, light is allowed to bend around the hidden area revealing the visible object which you've hidden behind this first set of mirrors. Notice each mirror is in two parts, bendable this way or that?" He went on, "the problem is that you have to have the person you're fooling looking at it from just one angle, one line of sight, or it doesn't work."

Fred exhaled, "Whew, sounds complicated, but clever, certainly!"

Shanghai Joe stood there watching, his face as impassive as ever, but with a slow grin slowly appearing as the magician continued showing them more of his tricky repertoire.

Fred, the author's older sister, Pam, and Molly Read-Jahn, about 1944, before the birth of the author.

---

1. After the close of WWII, it was BAAG (the British Army Aid Group) that played an immensely important role in Britain's resumption of its sovereignty over Hong Kong.

Chapter 25

June-September, 1944
Doodlebugs

Fred was working at Latimer House and Trent Park from 1942 to 1944 and part of 1945. Both Fred and Molly were relieved she was no longer living and working in London because, on 13 June, 1944 the first German V1 "Flying Buzz Bomb", known colloquially as the "doodlebug", started dropping down onto targeted areas of London. These were pulse jet-propelled pilotless aircraft that could fly up to 440 mph (708 kph) and launched by a catapult machine from a North Sea German base.

It was its pulse jet-propulsion sound that gave this flying bomb its characteristic buzzing sound. The sound it made was unnerving and rather similar to a pulsating two-stroke motorcycle. If you could hear this sinister engine sound you had nothing to fear, but, once the sound stopped it meant the plane had reached its maximum range, and it was going to drop straight out of the sky with its explosive 1,870 pound (850 kg) bomb load—and God help you if you were right underneath. This V1 was pretty accurate but a lot depended on the weather conditions, including the wind.

The V2 was to come somewhat later. This was a proper rocket carrying a bomb, and it was also unmanned. It was shot 50 miles (80.47 km) up into space, turned in a 120-mile (193 km) trajectory arc coordinated in advance to speed toward its English target. Once its exact fuel-load had run out, down it crashed, with its payload of bomb exploding catastrophically on whatever lay below it on the ground. This rocket was more accurate in reaching its target. Completely silent, you couldn't hear it coming whatsoever, thus absolutely terrifying.

The rocket research for these deadly bombs took place in Peenemünde on the Baltic Sea island of Usedom in northeastern Germany. Starting in September 1944, the Germans sent about 1,500 V2 rockets in a vengeful attempt to annihilate the British, with even more successful hits on London and the southeast in the final months of the war. In all, some 7,250 British lost their lives to the horrific V2s. But, when the Allies eventually discovered where the V2s were emanating from, they successfully managed to bomb the Peenemünde area.

Dr. Werner von Braun was one of the brilliant German scientists working on the V2's development during the war. He managed to avoid the eventual British bombing of the research site. It was he who was one of the rocket scientists whom the Americans talked into relocating to the United States after the war. The rocket science communities throughout the world weren't particularly interested in whether these scientists had been Nazis or not. It was their brilliant knowledge they wished to tap, rather than persecuting them into oblivion.

The German scientists who worked to develop these flying rocket bombs claimed they weren't so interested in their use for destruction either, but were working to advance the science of space flight. This is why, after WWII, not only the Americans, but also the Soviet Union, were so happy to use blackmail, or the threat of persecution, to convince these German rocket scientists to leave their homeland to get them working on furthering all kinds of rocket science outside Germany.

In England, Fred's first daughter was born in the autumn of 1942 so by the time she was two, she wouldn't yet have heard these buzz-bombs flying over. Besides which, she, her mother and father were living in the "Green Belt" outside London, in the pretty village of Little Chalfont in Buckinghamshire, from which Fred would ride his motorbike to work. Very few bombs rained down on this idyllic area of England.

But, one fine autumn day in 1944, when Shirley was still in her mother's womb, and her sister, Pam, just a toddler, sirens to call out the firemen went off, followed by the disturbing sound of a V1 doodlebug steadily approaching. People in the village weren't accustomed to this. They stopped short wherever they were, and, shielding their eyes from the sun, scanned the sky above. When they saw the doodlebug, they ran for their air-raid shelters; people scattering everywhere, like scurrying ants, with the local Postman-cum-Air-Raid-Warden shouting and egging them on to RUN! And all too soon it passed right overhead, moving menacingly farther along the road.

Molly had just stepped outside her house holding her little daughter by the hand. She only had time to grab the child and crouch on top of her to protect her. No time to even run to the shelter. Ten breathless seconds later the plane's engine cut out, followed by twelve terrifyingly endless seconds of an eerie brooding swishing sound, as down it silently soared, to smash explosively, shattering the house at the end of her road. Behind Molly her own house shook; she heard glasses breaking, dishes crashing to the floor —but her home remained standing, with Molly and her daughter lying on the pavement just outside, both miraculously quite unhurt. Then the screaming started.

Years later, Molly told how she staggered to her feet and stood, mouth agape, as both she and the little toddler watched the unfolding scene. A man was emerging from his shattered house, dressed only in his trousers, suspenders and vest. His face was covered on one side with shaving cream, his leather razor polishing strop still clasped in his hand. From all over his face jutted pieces of broken glass. Why hadn't he run for cover? He wouldn't have heard the sinister approach of the doodlebug from inside his house but why hadn't he heard the siren? The wall on one side of his house was completely gone, and you could see the broken mirror in the downstairs bathroom he'd been looking into when the bomb had dropped. As Molly watched in horror, he staggered toward the Air Raid Patrol helmeted street warden, uttering a continuous high-pitched unearthly keening scream.

Over at Latimer House Fred heard the news by telephone. He immediately reported to Colonel Kendrick then rushed to his BSA motorbike, jumped on and tore hell-for-leather back to Little Chalfont. He stopped for a couple of minutes at the smashed house on his road. He noted the Fire Brigade was already there, their hoses running across the road like swollen snakes, as water was poured fast and furiously on the now burning building. He talked to the Air Raid Warden briefly to gather information about the wounded occupant then sped on to his cottage.

Molly was ashen-faced, standing with her little one in her arms at the kitchen range, desultorily stirring a pot of stew. She, still holding her toddler, leant with relief into Fred's safe embrace, and cried her eyes out. Sniffing and hiccupping, she sobbed to him, "Oh Fred, you have no idea. It was ruddy awful, just terrible!"

"What did you hear, I mean, apart from the siren?"

"Well", she hiccupped as she tried talking between sobbing gasps, "it's when you DON'T hear it. Then you know it's coming straight down. Oh Freddie, oh Freddie, when will this wretched, horrid war be over?"

"Darling, it can't go on for much longer. We know. We get all the skinny from intel. It just can't go on too much longer, you'll see."

"Freddie, I've seen so many bomb-craters and destruction before, I mean, I mean, before I left my bank job in London, you remember, but this was so close, too close. It almost hit our house! It could have!"

Molly sobbed uncontrollably against his chest, having turned quickly to set her toddler in her highchair at the kitchen table, where she loudly banged a wooden spoon on her highchair tray, with a look of childish concern on her round face as she stared at her mother.

After sobbing for a while longer, gasping and hiccupping some more while held in his arms, Molly pulled herself together and did what every Englishwoman did in those situations: she went back to her AGA range and made a pot of tea.

As with many other people suffering these sorts of horrors, Molly's hair turned completely grey during the war.

Chapter 26

Late 1944
Shirley is Born, and Pam's Tale

In November, 1944, while Fred was still working as an intelligence agent at Latimer House, Molly gave birth to Fred's second child, a daughter called Shirley [*the author of this book*].

The family was still living in Little Chalfont, Buckinghamshire. Near their village was another village, called Fulmer.

Molly always said she knew Shirley would eventually go off to live in the United States. She called it a "curse" put upon her by Mrs. Eleanor Roosevelt. The problem, though, is that unfortunately, Molly had mixed up the years of Shirley's birth with her older sister's. In fact, the sweet story she used to tell so sincerely about Shirley actually occurred in 1942, her sister Pam's birth year, and not the year of Shirley's birth in 1944. Thus, this story is not actually Shirley's story, as she was the sister who ended up living in the United States, not Pam!

When Pam was born in September, 1942, Eleanor Roosevelt,

the wife of the United States president Franklin Delano Roosevelt (FDR), was on a three-week visit to the United Kingdom. Throughout the war she had been involved in an organisation that helped to have children taken away from the bombing in England to the relative safety of the USA, particularly during the Battle of Britain (10th July, 1940 – 31st October, 1940). She had a great love of babies in general, which Mrs. Churchill (Winston's wife, Clemmie) knew.

Clementine Churchill was the Chairwoman of Fulmer Chase Maternity Hospital for Wives of Junior Officers in Fulmer village.[1] Fulmer was heavily wooded with a serene lake visited by many glorious English birds. Fulmer's name comes from the Old English for "lake frequented by birds".

Clemmie took Mrs. Roosevelt to this lovely village especially to visit Fulmer Chase, the beautiful large Tudor house lent by the Baron cigarette magnate to the military. This was where officers' wives were taken to have their babies safely in the countryside outside London—where bombing was less likely.

Mrs. Roosevelt walked down the ward, saw Molly's daughter, picked her up and placed the little baby in the palm of her hand. She said, per Molly, "My, just you look at her lovely, dark brown hair and violet eyes!"

Holding the child carefully, Mrs. Roosevelt exclaimed further, "Aw, what a cute little baby!"

The problem is that the American president's wife was not holding Shirley but Pam, who was born with blond hair and blue eyes. Molly definitely had got her daughters mixed up!

Molly claimed that on that special day Eleanor had put an American curse on her baby and that she'd end up living in the United States. When Shirley announced to Molly, at the age of 24, that she was going to marry a naval officer from the USA, Molly wasn't one whit surprised, and cackled gleefully, "I always told you so, Shirley, Mrs. Roosevelt put the American curse on you!"

Eleanor Roosevelt wrote a daily newspaper column called *"My Day"*. On 28th October, 1942 her column was despatched to the United States press. She wrote, in part,

"In the afternoon, Mrs. Churchill, Miss Brooks and Lady Portal took us to see a maternity hospital which they have organized for junior officers' wives, in a house lent them by Lady Barron [sic]. They can take 22 girls at a time and I must say it was a pleasant, happy atmosphere and the babies were the loveliest I have ever seen—healthy, placid, and beautifully cared for. Those young mothers live through anxious times with husbands missing, or off in some distant part of the world, and most of them are going through their own ordeal for the first time, yet every one of them could smile and show her baby with pride. There is a little convalescent home nearby also where they go for further training in child care and for the final rest period before returning to their homes."

Molly spent over a month recuperating from the birth, which was normal in those days. After spending around three weeks at Fulmer Chase, the mothers were moved to Fircroft Post-Natal Home nearby in Gerrards Cross for a further two weeks' recuperation. The mothers there would, of course, have been brought to meet the grand lady, Eleanor Roosevelt, on that particular day.

SHIRLEY READ-JAHN

Shirley & Molly, 1945.

Herman & Fred with their mother, England 1945. Fred is at his mother's left.

1. Not long after the war ended, Fulmer Chase, the beautiful old Tudor building where both Molly's girls were born, suffered a fire, not from any sort of bomb explosion but through the thoughtless action of somebody tossing a lighted cigarette down onto the floor. This was a tragic irony in that the Fulmer Chase estate was on a rent-free loan to Clementine Churchill from the London cigarette magnate, Edward Baron.

Chapter 27

**Early 1945
The Channel Islands**

Molly and Fred had their ups and downs, as do all married couples, but overall they had got to know each other well. They were happy enough living as man and wife together in England. Molly naturally continued to be kept out of Fred's secret work, with some resentment, but generally, things were going alright—considering they'd married in such haste in March, 1940 and had been apart so much of their early married life while Fred was in Russia. It was she who had kept Fred's spirits up during his stint in Moscow. He'd placed Molly on a pedestal in his mind while away from her, as she had done for Fred, too. They'd only had such a short period of time together before he'd left for Russia, and that was a honeymoon period for them. So it was no wonder that life, considering the stresses of wartime, was not easy for the couple, now with two children, too. They'd certainly had their usual problems, as do all honest married couples. For example, when Fred seemed so careless to Molly by taking little Pam for a ride on his motorbike and she'd fallen off into a patch of stinging nettles. Obviously they'd had their share of other rows.

By November, 1944, their second daughter, Shirley, had arrived in the family. Molly felt busier than ever. She was relieved that Fred's interrogation of prisoners' work for MI-19 at Latimer House was winding down (not that she actually knew what it was he was doing over at Latimer House) but it had become clearer and clearer that the war was ending soon, in the Allies' favour. She hoped he'd be able to spend much more time now with his little family.

The weather in England, and Europe in general, was terrible. The winter of 1944-45 had been severely cold—with food crops fast being ruined in both England and Germany. Rationing was still in place, and people were fed up with it all. Tired of rationing, tired of all the destruction, tired of all the wounded and dead members of family and friends. As Molly said over and over, along with many others, "I'm just sick and tired of this whole ruddy war." Her life seemed consumed with finding food for her family to eat, aside from what she was continuing to grow herself at home.

For Britain, there was still another governmental problem to look into, that of the Channel Islands' situation. It was decided that Freddie should be sent over briefly in the spring of 1945 to the Channel Islands with a few other MI-19 agents to "check things out more thoroughly", basically, to "take the temperature" of the Islands now that the war appeared to be coming to an end.

There are seven inhabited islands and several uninhabited islands forming The Channel Islands. All the islands lie in the British Channel to the south of England and directly to the north west of France, on a good day perhaps even within view of Cherbourg, but definitely of Carteret, St. Malo and other villages and towns along the north coast of France.

Guernsey and Jersey were the two principal inhabited islands with Sark and Alderney being the third and fourth, smaller inhabited islands. Herm, Jethou and Brechou were even smaller. All the rest in the whole cluster was basically uninhabited except for marine and bird life during World War II.

Germany occupied The Channel Islands from 30th June, 1940 for five years during the war. The British forces didn't think it was possible to defend the islands against Germany after France had fallen to Hitler, thus a sizeable German force had moved in pretty easily. Not only that, but the Channel Islands weren't strategically important to Britain—unlike the very important location of the island of Malta—situated in the Mediterranean between North Africa and Sicily, below the toe of Italy in southern Europe.

The Channel Islands were considered important only inasmuch as they would keep hundreds of German soldiers based there away from the rest of Europe's war arena—not a bad idea, thought the British military! Besides which, to keep a British force there would have been expensive. The British did spend rather a lot of money on building up fortifications prior to the Germans' arrival—in the end, a rather useless investment of funds.

The British, knowing German forces were arriving, had given the inhabitants an early chance to evacuate back to England's mainland, and demilitarised the whole area—only leaving a few of the islands' civil leaders in place to keep an eye on the safety of the remaining British.

Freddie's military intelligence work at Latimer House was widespread. He not only dealt with interrogation of German officers and all that entailed, but also, because of his language abilities in both French and German, he was charged with staying apprised of German shipping and radar on and around the Islands. Since it wasn't considered particularly important to get the Germans out of the Islands only sporadic air attacks were aimed at them there, mainly to keep the Germans "on their toes".

The BBC had reported over the radio that Churchill had sent members of the MI-19 staff to the Channel Islands in order to quietly look for evidence of any collaboration between the civilians left behind and the Germans who still occupied the islands.

This could well be a dangerous mission. Carrying his gun in its hidden shoulder holster, Fred did his work looking for collaborators undercover and principally in Jersey. The operatives needed to silence the whisperings going around the Islands and getting back to the mainland. Speculation had to be silenced. Collaborators with the Germans were traitors. The information was disseminated over the radio because Churchill was trying to prove to the world that Britain would not have surrendered to the Germans if it, the British mainland, had been invaded in the same way as the Channel Islands. Churchill said the Channel Islands had surrendered to Germany because of failures in every level of society, so there must, therefore, have been collaborators. MI-19 agents searched high and low for traitors but, as it turned out, there were very few instances of collaboration with the Germans brought to light on the islands.

Molly only knew that Fred was off on a "secret mission" to the Channel Islands, in the English Channel west of northern France. She and other wives had the kind idea to have him and his colleagues carry Red Cross food parcels with them to help out some of the very hungry inhabitants. This was a particularly noble gesture inasmuch as rationing was still in place in England and food still hard to come by for its inhabitants.

The liberation of the Channel Islands was going to have to wait until the rest of the war throughout Europe had come to an end; it just didn't make sense to end it earlier, for, as Churchill liked to repeat over and over, keeping some of the German soldiers away from the front, "stuck in the Channel Islands", made much more sense to the Brits.

When MI-19 advised Churchill that there was no more collaboration between the residents of Jersey and Guernsey[1] with the occupying German forces, he soon decided to get the remaining Germans out of the Channel Islands. The islands were officially liberated on 9th May, 1945, a full four months before the end of the war was declared on 2nd September, 1945.

Hidden in Plain Sight

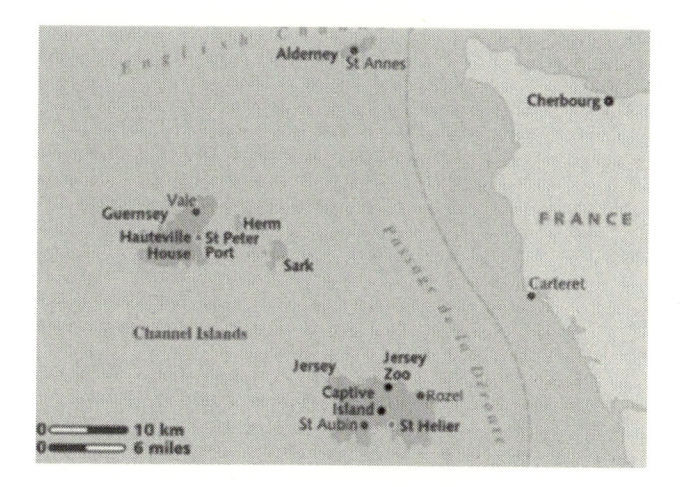

The Channel Islands

Fred and Molly's daughters in Alderney in 1947, one five and the other three years old. Note the tall-backed wicker basket chairs.

---

1. *After the war in 1947, as very young girls, and before their parents split up, Molly and Fred took their daughters to the island of Alderney, where they played on the beach while Molly & Fred sat on huge wicker beach seats with tall protective backs. In 1959, when Shirley was 15 and Pam two years older, Molly took the girls to Guernsey, and mentioned they could well have been visiting places their father had gone to, even though he was principally in Jersey. She wryly commented*

that his movements had obviously all been so secretive during the war, even to her, so she couldn't be certain at all.

Chapter 28

1945-1947
Control Commission World War II

The Allies had definitely won the war. On 8th May, 1945 VE Day was celebrated in England, with VE meaning the marking of the Allied "Victory in Europe". Molly and Fred were ecstatic. Fred rang her from work as soon as he heard the news. Molly had already heard it on the radio. She begged him to come home to celebrate. He roared home on his motorbike. They hugged in relief while Molly repeatedly whispered into his ear, "it's over, oh, it's truly over!" Filled with joyful abandonment they danced madly all around the house while the children stared in wide-eyed wonder at their crazed parents, the baby sucking on her dummy fiercely and energetically.

A couple of hours later, Fred had to return to work. He told Molly that World War II's ending meant a lot of continued work for him and his colleagues. For example, what on earth were they going to do with all the POWs in Latimer House and Trent Park, and all the other venues?

A meeting was arranged by the Allied leaders to sort out details for its ending, both for the war against Japan and the restructuring of both Germany and Eastern Europe. This meeting was named The Potsdam Conference. It was held at Cecilienhof, in occupied Germany, in the home of Crown Prince Wilhelm, and ran from 17th July to 2nd August, 1945. The war was to be declared officially over one month later on 2nd September, 1945. The principal players attending this all-important meeting were the Russian leader, Josef Stalin, the American leader, Harry S. Truman, and Great Britain's Winston S. Churchill. He was replaced on 28th July, 1945 by Clement Attlee as Britain's prime minister.

Both Fred and Molly, along with many others in Great Britain, found it really strange that Churchill's Conservative Party was defeated by Attlee's Labour Party in the 1945 elections in that it was Churchill who had heroically led the Allies to victory in World War II, yet, for many reasons, they and most of England were tired of the Conservatives, who had, in effect, brought them into this bloody Second World War. The people were ready for a new life and their votes proved it. Simply said, the majority of the people believed that Attlee's Labour Party was better able to rebuild England following the War than the Conservatives.

Following the return home of the world leaders, one of the questions not only being discussed by Fred's superiors but the British parliamentarians themselves was precisely what Kendrick and Kirkpatrick had asked on VE Day: "What on earth do we do with all these prisoners of war?"

It was to turn out that even a whole year after the war was over some 402,000 German POWs were still in camps all over Britain. The aristocrats who'd had their estates commandeered for the war effort now wanted their homes back for themselves. It became a political argument among the government representatives as to when the Germans should have their "human rights" respected and be repatriated to Germany. Meanwhile, many of the prisoners were set to work doing road repair, making bricks to rebuild the damaged houses, helping with farm work, and even cleaning up after the wild and ecstatic 8th May, 1945 VE Day celebrations. Many of them were called upon to help construct the buildings for the upcoming 1948 Olympics. Many politicians thought it dangerous to repatriate the ardent Nazis among the prisoners. Plus, just getting all those people sent back to Germany was quite a nightmare for those people in charge of handling transportation plans. All of this continued to be discussed and argued about in the new Labour Party parliament.

Before Fred's sojourn in the Channel Isles in the spring of 1945, he had been approached by Yvone Kirkpatrick.[1] Even as far back as late 1944, it had been obvious to Kirkpatrick that the Allies saw that they were going to win this war, defeating both Germany and Japan, thus the Allies had started work on what was going to have to be done as soon as the war was over. The government had to deal with all of the broader issues, including repatriation of German POWs, but for Kirkpatrick, he wanted to have "his men" placed appropriately and happily into jobs as important and meaningful as they'd been doing to date.

As 1945 moved along, and with Fred back from the Channel Islands, Kirkpatrick had started metaphorically to "move his chessboard around", to prepare his main men for the roles he planned to have them play the minute the war was won and over. He called Fred into his office.

"Captain, good morning. I'll come straight to the point. Looks like things are going well for us in this dashed war. Once it's over come September, we'll be putting good men into highly responsible positions in running the show."

"Quite so, sir", said Fred. "Where were you thinking of placing me, sir?"

"Germany, of course, Read-Jahn, goes without saying. I got used to you and your brother, both dashed good chaps and ones I could always rely on. I've talked to your brother. You won't be in the same place in Germany, but will, nevertheless, be working closely together once again."

More details were given, and Fred left Kirkpatrick's office with a light and buoyant step, feeling hopeful for the first time in a long time. Kirkpatrick was "in" with the powers-that-be, and if he, and they, were absolutely certain the war was about to end, then it was damn certain it was! Fred himself, he quietly chuckled to himself, had heard much the same thing whispered about in the corridors he frequented.

For the Europe theatre, the Allies had already placed Yvone Kirkpatrick in 1944 as Deputy Commissioner of the Inter-Allied Control Commission in Germany, ready for his post-war duties. Kirkpatrick went on to become the British High Commissioner at Allied High Commission. He had known Thomas Kendrick at Latimer House. Kendrick was both Fred and Herman's superior at Latimer. Kirkpatrick had also been a Foreign Office official who had worked at the British Embassy in Berlin in the 1930s and who had known Fred and Herman in those days, with Fred working at the British Embassy in Berlin up to 1935 prior to going to work in England at Morgan Crucible. Kirkpatrick was very familiar with the talents of the brothers Fred Read-Jahn and Herman Reade-Jahn, thus, who better to work for him? It made perfect sense to him to promptly hire them both for the future Control Commission work he and the Allies were planning for the immediate post-war years. Fred would be involved in trade and industry, in which he had developed major contacts.

Thus, as planned, with the ending of hostilities in World War II the Allies put in place their planned European Advisory Commission plus a Far Eastern Advisory Commission. These were called "Control Commissions". The European Control Commission's purpose was to bring Germany back as a fully functioning state, controlled by the Allied Powers. Regarding Germany, the Allies needed to effect military disarmament and establish certain non-rearmament of the losing country.

In early August, 1945, Herman had received orders via Kirkpatrick to immediately join the Central Commission in Berlin. Fred, on the other hand, in September received his orders, also via Kirkpatrick, ordering him off to Cologne as soon as possible to join first the Commercial Branch of the Control Commission and then, in October, to join the Northern Rhine region, and shortly to be upgraded to the rank of Honorary Major.

The Allied Control Council (ACC) oversaw the German Allied Occupation Zones. It was based in Berlin and its members were Great Britain, the USA, France, and the Soviet Union. This was a temporary, provisional, political situation. Decisions were made by consensus but, jumping forward, in the spring of 1948 the Soviet Union's representative was to withdraw and that decision broke the ACC down[2]. This resulted in Germany being partitioned into two states—West and East Germany (including East Berlin), with the East being ruled by the Soviet Control Commission. When Germany became partitioned into those two states the West then became called the Federal Republic of Germany.

But, just before he left England for Cologne, he promised that soon Molly would be able to join him. He'd look for a nice flat or house for them all.

"Meanwhile, darling", he told her, "keep a stiff upper lip, and carry on!"

Molly grimaced. She had been sick and tired of the ruddy war. She was sick and tired of being told to "carry on". What did he think she did each and every day, eh?

"Damn it, Fred", she spluttered, "you know I always bloody carry on! Rationing is still in place, I'm still scrounging around for food. I've got two daughters to take care of. OF COURSE I ruddy carry on!"

"Please, Moll, don't swear so…stop carrying on like that…".

At which point, realizing the pun he'd made, they both collapsed in laughter into each other's arms. Things seemed to still be alright for them both—except, he was about to leave her, yet again.

Yvone Kirkpatrick was to place Fred officially in the Trade and Industry Control Commission on 15th August, 1946, in his, Yvone's, capacity as Commissioner-in-Charge of the Inter-Allied Control Commission in Germany.

But, back to September 1945, Fred was still in the Army, and was still involved in intelligence. He'd followed Kirkpatrick's orders to move himself over to Germany, hopefully to go in September, but, as it happened, he wasn't able to get over there until the beginning of 1946. This meant that Molly was able to spend Christmas 1945 with Fred in England.

Once in Germany, aside from being extraordinarily busy sorting out the trade and industry of the new provisional country of West Germany, he had to stay in touch with his contacts made before and during the war.

Back in Cologne, one of his all-time favourite cities, Fred had many cosy conversations with Konrad Adenauer, one of the city's former mayors. Konrad Adenauer knew many of Fred's contacts, most of whom were in the elite social class that Adenauer himself inhabited.

"When things have settled down, my friend." Adenauer told Fred, "there's no doubt I shall run the new country, the Federal Republic of Germany, West Germany. I happen to know I shall be made Chancellor."

Fred was thrilled. He much admired Adenauer. Fred said,

"Well, this will certainly make my work a lot easier. My superiors will be absolutely delighted. You can smooth things out. There will be a lot of paper to push, a lot of decisions to make, a lot of agreements to work out. You and your friends…yes, if you're at the helm, the whole ship will have smoother sailing. I'm delighted, truly pleased, Konrad!"

Fred had told Molly he'd send for her and the children as soon as he could. Many of her friends had lost their husbands in the war, so Molly had to keep reminding herself that she still had a husband, and to be grateful.

He told her things were going very well for him in Germany, that he'd risen in rank as an intelligence officer from Captain to Major, working at Head Quarters Military Government Northern Rhine Region, then at the Head Quarters Trade and Industry Control Commission. He had settled well into his work in his role. He passed from Assistant Controller to Assistant Instructor (SO2) in Trade and Industry.

Fred telephoned Molly on 25th September, 1946 to say he was now officially "Struck off Strength" from the Army (meaning, ceasing to be the responsibility of the military) as of 17th July, 1946 and was now on the books as holding the rank of full British Army Intelligence Major in the Control Commission, working for the Trade and Industry Control Commission.

September, 1946 onwards saw Fred busy as a bee in Cologne. Molly, on the other hand, was still in England, alone once again, and raising her two daughters by herself. The girls were now four and two years old. She remembered the days of waiting to hear whether she could join him in Russia. Déjà vu for her. But, this time, it was going to be different. The war was over and she WOULD be joining him in Germany. She'd better start brushing up on her German. Now, where was her grammar book?

Fred telephoned her often. Molly was excited to hear that she was to start an adventure with Fred this time around but that she was going to have to wait until January of 1947 to get going to Germany. She knew he was now in a much better position and that meant more food not under rationing, drinks to enjoy, parties, and lots of fun. Fred said they'd even be able to afford a nanny to help take care of the girls. This would free them up for all sorts of good times together.

Thus, it was with conflicted pleasure in December of 1946 that Molly began the packing for this big change in all their lives. She hated leaving her beloved father behind. She cared little for her mother, a nurse and chorus line dancer he'd met up with after the death of his first wife, but still, the mother of both Molly and her sister, Olive. This woman had become very stern, in character and demeanour, with the precise middle parting in her dark hair and the neat bun at the nape of her neck, her long black skirts, and her round gold spectacles. Besides which, she had never offered Molly any affection. Mrs. Sutton's dancing background had done nothing to let her live her life with joy. Any compassion she'd held in her nursing work had evaporated when she'd married and had children. She did have gorgeous long, dark hair—only unpinned at night—and the most beautiful, clear, soft skin. Her complexion glowed with its peaches-and-cream tone, but her hard, mean interior couldn't be disguised by her lovely clear skin—or so Molly always thought. Mrs.

Sutton liked a drink now and again. She'd fallen one evening against the closed-in stove and badly burnt her back. Ever since, she'd stand rigidly, swathed in felt wrappings under her dark clothing. One assumes her sternness could have come from the constant pain she was in, which she tried to assuage with alcohol. Molly tried to feel compassion but couldn't because that stove, oh, that awful stove…

Molly was terrified of that stove. Mrs. Sutton had meanly wrested Molly's favourite soft-toy bunny rabbit one time from her arms, thrown it in the stove, when Molly was sick with a childhood illness, saying, "Molly, you are far too old to have such a ridiculous toy. That's for babies. We're throwing that away immediately. Besides, it's sure to be riddled with your sickness. Out it goes!"

Molly had cried her eyes out and never forgave her mother.

Musing on this and how she'd miss her dear, dear father, Molly thought about her new adventure.

Fred told her he'd arranged boat tickets for her and the girls to cross the Channel in January, 1947. She'd get to practise using the German she'd studied for some years now, ever since meeting Fred in 1940 at the Linguists' Club in London. She gave one of her huge laughs as she remembered those early days, right before the war, falling in love! Instead of being left behind now, while Fred was off on his adventure, she was going to join him, along with their little daughters. She wasn't afraid that the Germans would resent this English family; after all, they'd be protected by the British Army in case of problems because he did hold the rank of Major. And, she was a friendly, sociable young woman, and, surely, they'd appreciate her using all her German. How could this next experience fail?

The European winter of 1946-1947 was yet another ordeal; it was the most severe since 1812-1813. Molly had been a good pianist in her past. She loved music, especially anything with piano in it. When she read in the papers about the winter of 1812 she immediately thought of Tchaikovsky's 1812 Overture, especially when storms were raging outside in her 1946 winter—the crashes of thunder reminding her of cannons and cymbals. She mused as always to herself, "But you can keep those violins…sound like cats caterwauling to me!" And burst out laughing at her own joke…cats caterwauling, hahaha. She must remember to share that one with Freddie when he next rang!

The February 1947 day arrived for their Channel crossing to Germany. Molly led her girls onto the ship on one of the coldest days in recorded history. It was horrendously, freezingly cold, caused by an anti-cyclone moving over from Scandinavia. Temperatures fell to well below freezing. Storms, wind, icy rain, and more snow than had been seen in decades, all whipped at their ship as it valiantly pushed its way across the Channel to the Continent. The ship surged up and down, and even sideways, with the huge waves. The captain ordered all passengers to stay below deck. Molly's youngest daughter got horribly seasick.

As they neared the Continent, the captain announced it was calmer and passengers were now permitted to come up on deck. With relief, Molly dressed the girls warmly in woollen hats, scarves and thick jackets. She held their hands tightly as they lent against the ship's railings, exclaiming in delight at all the miniature blue icebergs and floes drifting past them as they steamed along.

As she stood at the deck's railing holding onto her precious daughters, glancing around her, Molly saw icicles hanging from the ship's portholes and icy snow banked up in every nook and cranny. Molly had a sudden bad intuition that this cold environment boded nothing good for her. She wrote in her diary that night that she had an inkling that Fred's love for her may have grown cold. Now what made her think such a thing, she wondered? A proverb suddenly ran through her head, "Marry in haste, repent at leisure". What was the matter with her? Why was she suddenly anxious about this next adventure?

While Molly was still over in England Fred had been alone in Germany for a few months. He felt a certain relief that he was now no longer an Army man but a civilian working for the Trade and Industry Control Commission, Germany. He took his British Army uniforms to the dry-cleaner to have them pressed and packed away. "Be prepared, always be prepared" he chuckled inwardly, as he carted the big box home to his flat. "You never know when another war comes along, so best to have these all ready. Ye gads, this box looks like a woman's wedding dress box. It even has a 'viewing hole'!" he mused to himself.

Once home, he kept his handgun carefully hidden with its bullets in a separate box, for safety. Again, he muttered to himself, "Once an agent, always an agent, hmmmm?" "Best not to tell anyone I have this. I just might need it. No-one's asked me yet to turn it in, so, I'll hide it right here!" as he selected a good cubbyhole to stash it away in.

Molly, when still living in England, had telephoned Fred in Germany. She was pleased as punch with the news of his officer rank upgrade. "Darling, you'll always be called Major Read-Jahn, but you won't have to do anything military, will you? No more secrets, no more tearing off here and there for the Army, isn't that right?"

"That's it, Moll, old girl. No more secret stuff. Just my work in trade and industry, and you, my sweet, will have to act the part of a successful civilian's wife. That means— a new wardrobe for you— we'll go shopping for it once you're here. What do you say!" "Moll", he added, "I know the head buyer for a big department store in Düsseldorf. Not too far from Cologne. She'll help you choose the most fashionable outfits, you'll see!"

"Freddie, darling, that's terrific news. I'll be giving you the biggest kiss ever when I see you, you wait and see!"

All through the war she'd wanted new makeup, new shoes, new clothes in general. She'd always been fashion-conscious, quite the "clothes-horse" and now, oh joy, she could hit the shops running…"But, the question was", she sighed to Fred, "would they be filled yet with the latest fashions?"

"Probably not yet", said her husband, "but with my new rank, we will be able to afford 'em, if they're even available. I'll have to ask Bertha, one of my contacts who's that chief buyer at the main department store in Düsseldorf!"

Of course, Fred still kept his ear to the ground; this was his training. He may not be in the military anymore but, he still had his contacts to retain, nurture, and milk for whatever information he could use in his new job. He told himself this was just making use of his training. He had his trade and industry work in Germany to sort out. All those company contacts were still going to be of great help to him. One in particular, the Chemische Fabrik Hackenin firm in Cologne, had already proved to be of huge help in his new work. The person he mostly talked to was the beauteous company daughter, the red-haired Delia, a savvy business woman who was helping to run the firm. He didn't want to upset Molly, whom he adored, so he kept this connection quiet. Why rock the boat? It made no sense to; he'd keep all that side of his ongoing work quiet from Molly, and all should go along in the future as before. Besides, what was there really to tell?

Looking into the future, Fred also had an inkling that goods made in the Far East would become more and more important to world trade. They worked for almost nothing over there in Asia, mostly China. He'd seen it for himself, and everyone in business was saying so. Musing on this, he thought of his old pal, Shanghai Joe.

Fred knew that Shanghai Joe was now settled into the Far Eastern Advisory Commission. He and Fred stayed in touch from their respective commissions, even though Fred himself was by now technically out of military intelligence. Shanghai Joe didn't believe for one minute that Fred was now "only a civvie" and teased Fred mercilessly in his messages about this. They were always ribbing and bantering with each other, with Fred constantly haranguing poor old Shanghai Joe over the Far Eastern pronunciation of his name, "Fleddie"!

Having survived the rough, freezing cold, boat journey across the Channel, Molly and the girls were now living with Fred in a capacious flat in Cologne. He had lots of friends, lots of events to attend, and wanted her to accompany him. It was going pretty well, she thought, this new adventure, and 1947 did, indeed, go along well for Fred in his work, too.

But, Molly was not stupid. She'd landed in Germany in

February of that year, and soon picked up that the intuition she'd been having was starting to look right. She was an intelligent woman, with finely-honed intuitional skills. Conversations were stopped when she entered a room where Fred was sitting, black telephone at his ear, or when she entered a room and he had been talking closely to somebody. He had a German secretary with rather bulging "thyroid" eyes whom Molly tried to like, but just couldn't. She wasn't exactly sure why. This other woman was blonde, for a start, and Molly herself was dark-haired. She kept thinking about that adage, "blondes have more fun" every time she saw how well Lexi, the secretary, got along with Fred. This secretary was a married woman, Molly knew, with the intimidating name of Frau Hildegard. No wonder they called her simply "Lexi". Molly began an ongoing worry about Fred and his female friends; a definite underlying feeling of some sort of unease.

---

1. *Later in life Kirkpatrick was knighted, gaining the title of "Sir". He was also known to be a great friend of Germany's Dr. Konrad Adenauer, the post-war Chancellor of the Federal Republic of Germany, serving from 1949-1963. They were both masters of diplomatic manoeuvring and both worked to establish close Anglo-German relations after the War. Kirkpatrick was incredibly astute, intelligent and bright. It's been said of him, "he was so sharp that he cut"! (A saying attributed to Sir Evelyn Shuckburgh, a British diplomat.) It was through Kirkpatrick that Freddie had come to know Dr. Adenauer quite well himself, for whom he, too, had a great respect and affinity of ideas.*
2. *As an afterword here, the ACC did convene again, but not until 1971, to make agreements for transit rights in the split Berlin, and to solve Allied privileges and rights issues in Germany. The ACC was finally disbanded in 1991, two years after the Berlin Wall had come down.*

Chapter 29

**5th April, 1948
Herman Reade-Jahn Dies,
The Berlin Blockade & Airlift**

Molly and Fred seemed to the outsider to be a loving, adoring pair. Everything seemed perfect. They had a wonderful flat in Cologne in the upmarket district of Marienburg.

Fred kept his promise and arranged for Molly to have a nanny for the girls, who were both still too young for school.

Molly began to notice more about Freddie and his "contacts". He seemed to know an awful lot of people and there were so many parties to go to! She became adept at dropping her drinks into indoor palm-trees in pots in people's living rooms. Drinks were constantly pushed into her hands and it became easier to just accept one, then surreptitiously dispose of it, than constantly say "no, no more, thank you" and then have to answer the persistent question, "Oh, you don't drink; good heavens, what's wrong with you; we're over the war now!"

Then there were the women; so many of them draping themselves over her husband, making cow-eyes at him. 1947 passed into 1948, with Fred increasingly tied up with his work. He would tell her here and there about his brother, Herman ("good old Bertie!") who was working in the Control Commission in Berlin. Herman's own little family had come out to Germany from England, too, at the same time as Molly and her girls. Bertie and Fred would speak on the telephone quite frequently and occasionally in the first three months of 1948 get to attend Control Commission meetings together in Berlin where Herman was based.

In late spring of 1948 Fred was moved out of the Control Commission in order to work in Bonn at the British Embassy as a diplomat. Some people say that Embassy diplomats are really "undeclared intelligence officers or agents". In Fred's case this was certainly true. He carried on "relationships with his contacts" in many ways that would further his diplomatic work.

Christmas 1948 came and went. New Year's Eve was another Big Bash, as Fred called these parties. Molly hadn't made many friends. She was lonely, missing her social life (such as it had been during the war!) but it was her one or two girlfriends back home that she mostly missed. She was a bit of an extrovert but just couldn't relate to the other wives and how they partied all the time. She was pleased how her German was picking up. Even her daughters chatted away in German, especially her younger daughter, Shirley, who needed to have her needs met quickly by her German nanny. The family had moved first to Detmold, north-east of Bonn, and then found a more pleasant home in Friesdorf, a small district of Bad Godesberg, Bonn, thus not far from the British Embassy in Bonn, and where many ex-pats lived. Molly hoped to make more friends in this new location.

It wasn't until July, 1949 that Bonn was made the provisional capital of the Federal Republic of Germany. The hope was that when the reunification between the West and East Germany occurred, Berlin would become the capital of all Germany, with Bonn remaining as its second, diplomatic, capital. Adenauer, West

Germany's Chancellor, happened to live in Cologne, fairly near Bonn, which was so helpful for his work commutes.

Over dinner one night in late July, 1949, when the girls were tucked up in bed and the nanny had gone off into her own room for the night, Fred began to tell Molly more about his brother and a little of his fascinating intelligence work. He told her they'd obviously both signed the Official Secrets Act but that the tale he was about to relate was pretty common knowledge by now, having been in all the newspapers.

Tears rose up in his eyes as he related exactly how his brother had died on 5th April, 1948, already over a year ago, and how Herman's wife and children had moved from Germany back to England to live.

As Fred sat talking to her, Molly sat bolt upright, understanding that what her husband was now relating was of great importance not only to the brothers' respective families, but even to international politics, as Fred went along with his tale.

"Damn it, Moll", exclaimed Fred, "My brother Bertie's death actually started the Cold War when you think about it!" "I'll start at the beginning," said Fred. "Look, it's a long story, but you should be aware of the ins and outs of it all; it's no longer a secret, except for parts, and those, well, I simply can't speak about. So, here goes—sometimes I say Bertie and sometimes Herman, but it's all the same—you know it's my dear brother!"

Fred told Molly how Winston Churchill thoroughly appreciated the importance of the work of the military intelligence, thus, throughout the war, he frequently travelled the thirty miles from London to Latimer House to be briefed in person on the latest spying information eavesdropped from the Germans.

"You know Herman and I both worked at Latimer," he told Molly.

He went on that Herman had met Churchill at Latimer House at the time of the Rudolf Hess affair in 1941. They'd got on well and after that meeting, Herman greatly respected the British leader even more.

Herman was the chap who'd volunteered to play the role of Churchill in April, 1948.

"What role?" asked Molly.

"Well, that's the story, you see. There is, there always is, Moll, a different story of what happened…you read some of it in the papers", said Fred.

There were actually many newspaper articles, and even a parliamentary report, on what was to turn out to be a tragic event with major political consequences.

"I have to say," went on Fred, "in an event such as this, even if my story were proven quite true, of course a more "likely" story would have to be presented to the world, you can understand that; it's just the way it is. Politics, you see. And history is what you make it."

Molly chimed in, "I'll totally believe your version, Freddie, because it's so unusual for you to tell me this sort of thing, so it must be true!"

Fred told her that he knew that the "party line" given in Britain was that one of Russia's Yak fighter planes had buzzed the plane that Herman was in over the Berlin Corridor and clipped its wing, causing the crash and Herman's death, along with others in the little plane. Herman had the misfortune to be flying in that particular plane when "the accident" occurred.

Fred's version was that intelligence had learned that the plane Churchill was to fly in to an undisclosed meeting location in Europe was to fly over the Berlin Corridor on 5th April, 1948, and that there was a chance that the Russians might shoot it down. It was imperative that Churchill not be on that plane, but that, for undisclosed, highly secret reasons, it would appear that he was. It was decided that somebody would dress as Churchill, in his wool felt Homburg hat, and, if a thinner man, he would wear a much-padded greatcoat in order to more resemble the stocky Churchill. He would also be seen holding his ever-present cigar, in order to fool anybody watching that Churchill was, indeed, getting on the plane.

"Molly darling", said Fred, "tragically, that is what happened—the BEA Vickers 610 Viking VC1B was brought down and it was Herman, my only brother, the "doppelgänger" who had volunteered for the imposture, who died along with the others in both planes."

He went on to explain to Molly that the Soviets had thought they'd been unfairly treated after the war, feeling they should have gained the whole of Berlin rather than one section only. Thus, from early 1946 onwards, they'd made land crossings to East Berlin more and more difficult and also carried out the buzzing of Allied planes flying over the Berlin air corridor. The month prior to the crash, March, 1948, Allied senior Control Commission staff had met up with the European Advisory Committee in London to try to decide what could be done about the problem of all these planes buzzing Allied planes.

"I even flew over to Berlin and joined Bertie at one of his Control Commission meetings. Fascinating, it was."

"But", interrupted Molly, "what were the land crossings really about?"

"Simple really—lorries were carrying food in to the East Berliners, and then, the Allies were flying food and other supplies in to them. The West Berliners had relatives and friends over in the East and couldn't let 'em starve! The Americans, in particular, were involved in all this."

After the crash it was given out that the British plane was on a scheduled flight from Northolt via Hamburg to Berlin and it had collided during its approach to the RAF Gatow airport with a Soviet Air Force Yakovlev fighter, nicknamed a Yak-3. The Soviet plane was, per the Soviets, performing aerobatics in that area at that time, yet, as Fred pointed out, the British knew the Yaks were buzzing their planes with the intent to encourage them to get out of West Berlin.

"Acrobatics? My foot! Of course they weren't!" exclaimed Fred.

Four crew and ten passengers died in the Viking, as did the sole Soviet pilot in his Yak. The Viking passengers consisted of three of the Control Commission staff ("all in Intel", whispered Fred), and seven other non-intelligence people. In the ensuing uproar, the Soviets claimed the British plane had been outside the air corridor. In the investigation it was established that it was the Soviet's fault, whose actions went completely against the "quadripartite" rules of flying—flying rules that the Soviets had agreed to adhere to.

By this point, Molly's eyes were riveted on her husband. She was relieved to have him explain all these facts to her; she'd indeed read "bits and bobs", as she called them, in the papers, but never properly understood the political ramifications.

After telling Fred this, he touched her arm, and went on with his narrative. Touching someone's arm was a unique quirk of Freddie's. He would touch your arm to get your undivided attention, lock eyes with you, and talk. If what you were telling him was of a serious nature, he'd perform his routine of touching your arm, locking eyes with you, all giving you the impression he was listening intently, that every word you said was of great importance to him. It made one feel very, very special. Women, in particular, loved him for it—in that era used to being considered second class citizens.

Telling this tale, Freddie suddenly became very tired. It took something out of him, talking about his brother like this. Keeping his hand on Molly's arm, Fred told her he'd continue his explanation of these European politics another evening. They were both tired, but she begged him not to stop. She'd been fond of her brother-in-law and wanted to hear how his death had caused such a ruckus.

So, after pouring her an *eau-de-vie*[1], Fred seemed to be lost in thought as he stared at the flocked wallpaper, then, sighing deeply, he went on with the story.

Josef Stalin, the Soviet leader, wanted to force the Allies to give up West Berlin. He blockaded the whole of West Berlin so no cars or trains could come in across the land. He thought the West Berliners would run out of food and fuel and start to riot, thus forcing the Allies to give up their sector. Thus, by 24th June, 1948, the Soviets had completely sealed off the land corridor, and relations with the USSR had dropped to an all-time low. The Soviets were ordered to keep the three air routes open, to allow access across East Germany; this was legally mandated by the Allies' occupation statutes in place following the war.

"Still with me, Moll?" asked Fred.

"Oh yes", she breathed, "don't stop, what happened next?" She moved her feet off her *petit point* footstool and leant forward in eagerness. "As I said, the Allies (primarily the Americans) weren't going to let the West Berliners starve. Think about it, Molly, how hard it was in the war to get food. Why, you even killed pet cats on your street, claiming they were rabbit because you said they did taste like rabbit—you told me so in one of your letters. People were almost starving, and this was now happening after the damn war."

He continued, "The blockade and Berlin Airlift went on from 24th June, 1948 to 12th May, 1949. You read that two months ago in the papers, that it had finally come to an end...so, back to before it stopped..." He told her that they started supplying just over two million hungry Berliners in need, via tiny planes dropping supplies, food, coal, medicine, and fuel. This was called the Berlin Airlift, which was to last just under a year, and ranging from some 2,000 to occasionally 4,700 tons of provisions delivered daily to the starving people below in West Berlin. The little planes used were mostly twin-engine propeller C-54 and DC-3 transport aircraft.

"You can imagine what they were like, Moll, from your own flying days, can't you?"

They flew out from bases in West Germany, primarily Frankfurt's Rhein-Main and Wiesbaden in the American Zone, and Celle and Lübeck in the British sector, bringing in the food and supplies.

By mid-April, 1949, the Berlin Airlift, involving both US and British pilots, had brought an amazingly huge amount of 12,800 tons of freight into beleaguered Berlin. This freight was known as "Care Packages", a word that was to become part of the German language.

Fred paused and relit the pipe he liked to smoke when telling a story. "So, you see, it was this air crash that took my brother's life that became an international incident which, in effect, started the

Airlift, and which, as I've said, led to what the politicos are now calling the Cold War![2]

"Good Lord!" was all Molly could manage, staring at her husband in amazement.

Fred tapped his white Meerschaum pipe on his armrest and blew out a stream of blue-white smoke, then continued on to explain that after this recent year of the land corridor closure, the Soviets faced the fact the Allies weren't backing off by leaving West Berlin, so re-opened the land corridor and declared East Germany was now a separate state, to be known as the German Democratic Republic. In turn, the Allies named West Germany as The Federal Republic of Germany.

"And that, my dear, is why we're now in Bonn[3] at the Embassy. Why I'm shuffling papers from one side of my desk to t'other, in-tray and out-tray, to help this new Germany get back on its feet. And my old pal, Konrad Adenauer, is the Chancellor. We'll be seeing more of him at the Embassy parties, you'll see!"

Having tossed back their drinks, Molly now poured tea for them both. She'd been keeping it hot under a blue quilted tea-cosy Fred's mother had sewn for them as a wedding gift. Fred was looking suddenly very serious and clasped her arm yet again, this time pulling her closer to him. She slid forward on her armchair as he pulled her nearer. She barely heard his quiet words as he sadly whispered, "I was the one who had to identify Bertie's remains, Moll. Remember that day I came back from work in a terrible state? I couldn't even speak to you. It was awful. Well, that's why. Only now can I feel able and permitted to talk about it. They said it was highly confidential and I was to keep my mouth shut. But now… anyway, I could only recognise him by the ring he was wearing and the handcuffs attached to what had been the briefcase "Churchill" was carrying on the flight. I've thought about this a lot, Molly, but if Herman wasn't playing the part of Churchill, one wonders why he had a briefcase cuffed to his wrist? Not the sort of thing he tended to do, you see?"

"My God, Freddie, my dear God, I had no idea…"

Fred sipped some tea, then went on, "Interestingly, the Aviation

Safety Network listed the flight as having aboard an 'International Scheduled Passenger'. Think about it. Had to be Churchill, or that's what we all think, my cronies and me, or why would they word it like that? Lots of us were 'international'. It's just odd wording..."

"And then", Fred continued, "the following month, on 7th May 1948, Churchill himself did successfully fly from Britain, to address the opening session of the Congress of Europe in The Hague, in which he warned of the threat that the Soviet Union represented for the future of European unification. You would have read about that in the papers, too, Molly. Relations between the USSR and Great Britain were at a further all-time low."

Fred then pulled his briefcase toward him and removed some papers, telling Molly that, as he'd mentioned earlier, there is always another "more likely" story explaining the air crash, of course there is. There always is. This one was disseminated to the press and to parliament. The parliamentary version of the tragic collision is in the Hansard papers of British parliamentary proceedings, he told her. He also told her that it's interesting that the final sentence requests that the House should withhold any further speculation or recrimination about this tragedy.

"Don't you think, Molly, that it's pretty obvious that British Intelligence wouldn't want anybody looking further into who was aboard, or why...I mean, the real story looks a bit windy, doesn't it?"

He then handed her The Hansard archives' report to read:

HANSARD 1803–2005 → *1940s* → *1948* → *April 1948* → *6 April 1948* → *Commons Sitting* → *BERLIN*

Chapter 1 British and Russian Aircraft (Collision)
HC Deb 06 April 1948 vol. 449 cc32-332
§*Mr. Churchill*
(by Private Notice) asked the Secretary of State for Foreign Affairs whether

he has any statement to make on the present situation in Berlin, including the destruction of the British passenger aircraft with the loss of 14 lives.

§**The Secretary of State for Foreign Affairs (Mr. Ernest Bevin)**
Yes Sir. I should like, if I may, to answer these two points separately.

As the House will have heard, a British European Airways aircraft was approaching Gatow aerodrome in the British sector of Berlin from Hamburg yesterday afternoon when a Soviet fighter aircraft collided with it. As the result of this both aircraft crashed to the ground and all the occupants were killed. I wish to take this opportunity to express the deepest sympathy of His Majesty's Government, and I am sure, of the House, with the relatives and friends of the victims in this appalling occurrence. The British aircraft fell 2½ miles North-West of the Gatow airfield in the Russian zone, and the Soviet fighter fell just inside the British sector of Berlin close to Gatow airport.

I am awaiting a full account of the disaster. The information which I have received so far shows that the British aircraft was proceeding on the ordinary route, and that according to routine instructions, warning should have been given by the Soviet authorities that their fighter was in the air. No such warning was given. After the crash the Soviet authorities took immediate charge of the British aircraft, and later in the day British representatives went to the scene to investigate and to gain access to the bodies and the baggage. A cordon of British troops has been placed round the Soviet aircraft, with one Soviet sentry.

The Soviet General, with whom the British Commandant in Berlin dealt, expressed a desire to deal with the occurrence with proper calmness. Immediately on hearing of the disaster, the British Commander-in-Chief, General Robertson, communicated with the Soviet Commander-in-Chief, Marshal Sokolovsky. In this communication, after stating the facts that I have given, General Robertson asked for an immediate assurance that Marshal Sokolovsky condemned as strongly as he did that the Soviet aircraft was being flown without prior notification and in a manner to cause the catastrophe. He also requested a positive assurance that British aircraft using the corridor in accordance with our mutual agreement would be immune from molestation. General Robertson also reserved all the rights of His Majesty's Government.

General Robertson also had an interview with Marshal Sokolovsky yesterday evening. General Robertson's actions in this matter have our full approval. At the interview, General Robertson made it plain that he had no wish to prejudge the *cause of the catastrophe until a proper inquiry had been held. The form and scope of this inquiry is at present under consideration. Marshal Sokolovsky then gave General Robertson orally the assurances for which the latter had asked. A written reply to General Robertson's communication is awaited. In view of the assurances which have been received, the British Commander-in-Chief has countermanded the instructions which he gave that British civil aircraft should receive fighter protection. I understand that the United States Commander-in-Chief took similar action.*

I wish to make it clear, pending the results of the inquiry, that I have no information to suggest that the conduct of the Soviet aircraft was in any way the result of direct instructions from the Soviet authorities. Routine flights to and from Berlin by British aircraft are continuing in the normal way.

In view of what I have said, I trust the House will agree that it is undesirable that there should be any further speculation or recrimination about this tragedy. I am pressing for an inquiry to be held as soon as possible, and until the results are known I suggest that judgment should be reserved."[4]

Exhausted from the telling and the listening to this tragic tale, Fred and Molly just gazed at each other, now wordless. Forgetting the tea, they each had a glass of Cognac, then retired to their room to sleep.

---

1. *Colourless light fruit brandy.*
2. *The Cold War remained in place until the Berlin Wall came down on the 9th November, 1989.*
3. *In 1949 Bonn became the* de facto *capital of what was now the newly-formed Federal Republic of Germany. Konrad Adenauer was its first chancellor.*
4. *In the summer of 2008 both the World Tribune and Der Spiegel newspaper printed articles about the Airlift by the Allies for the Luftbrückendank (Air-Bridge-thanks) charity that had been put in place in 1948. Der Spiegel said:*

   "Almost 60 years ago one of the first "battles" of the Cold War took place above the skies of Berlin. A battle fought with candy and coal rather than bullets. On Tuesday German Chancellor Angela Merkel extended warm thanks to veterans of that vital Berlin Airlift at a ceremony to mark the opening of the Berlin Air Show. Merkel, who grew up in the former East Germany, told over 80 veterans who had made the trip to Berlin that without their help "history would have turned out differently."

   Many of the veterans and their families will be staying on in Berlin for the 60th anniversary of the Air Lift in June. The Western allies kept West Berlin alive by flying in supplies for almost a year from June 1948 to May 1949 after the Soviets shut off all ground access to the city. Merkel offered "special thanks, especially to America and Great Britain, that they helped Germany and the city of Berlin in a difficult hour."

   The veterans -- now aged between 83 and 93 -- were delighted to be back in Berlin. "We saved this city without firing a shot," Tom Flowers, a retired Navy officer from Alabama told the Associated Press. Johnny Macia, who had been an airplane mechanic with the US Air Force's 317th Troop Carriers during the airlift, said *"It's a great thing we did here."*

Gail Halvorsen, who became known as the *"Candy Bomber"* because he used to drop sweets attached to parachutes to the children below, is also in Berlin. Halvorsen used to wiggle his little plane's wings to identify himself, which led to his other nickname *"Uncle Wiggly Wings."* The 88-year-old told the DPA news agency that the airlift *"was only possible because of the Berliners' gratitude..."*

Not only had the Airlift dropped daily necessities to the West Berliners, but also candy and sweets for the kids. The children would stand on huge mounds of rubble at the runway approach to Tempelhof Airport, to grab the sweet delights raining down from the sky attached to tiny parachutes. Tempelhof Airport was in south-central Berlin in the borough of Tempelhof-Schöneberg (where Fred & Herman had lived in their school years).

Chapter 30

Molly Moves Back to England,
&
1949 Through the 1950s

In 1949 Fred was now enjoying his work in Bonn as a diplomat working at the British Embassy. He often repeated the words that his wartime military intelligence job had "become redundant".

Now he sat at his Embassy desk shuffling papers and doing what all conquerors of another country have to do to get the defeated country back into safe working order. The lifestyle there was hectic and busy but also exciting for Fred, involving many parties and people to meet—all in an ongoing celebratory mood from winning the war. This included many ladies to catch Fred's eye, and other men interested in Molly.

Fred adored Molly. Even so, after parties, back at their home, they began to argue often because he found it hard when she would complain she had few friends, hated all the drinking, and hadn't much to do. She was a very attractive, vivacious woman, but complained when men made passes at her. He didn't like men to flirt with his wife, but then, women flirted with him all the time. He told her it was just like that in the diplomatic corps; she had to learn to put up or deal with it.

"I don't want to attend these parties at the Embassy anymore", declared Molly.

"Moll", said Fred, "this is the diplomatic corps. The word "precedence" is what it's all about in my career here. It's important that we're included in the most prestigious party lists and whom we're seated next to. It just wouldn't look good for me to show up without you. Damn it, Molly, it would throw their seating lists all out of whack!"

"Seating lists? Do you really care about that sort of thing?"

"Not really", he sighed, "but you can see it would make me look all wet, not being able to get my wife to accompany me, and that just won't do, you must see that. And it helps me to be seated next to important people, such as Adenauer, for example. Please understand what I'm saying, Moll. Getting ahead in my new career depends on all this sort of thing. It all centres around whom you know, you see, and that you stay on people's A-lists".

After yet another argument about the flirting one evening, he sat down alone to smoke his pipe and think this awkward problem over, while Molly stormed off to their bedroom in tears. He thought about following her, but it was always the same. They'd argue some more, they'd eventually make up, make love, and the problem never got solved.

He realized his female contacts tended mostly to be beautiful, cosmopolitan women who had been through a lot of the same experiences as he had during those war years. It wasn't Molly's fault she'd missed out on all of that; he wasn't allowed to tell her anything, anyway, because of the damned Official Secrets Act.

She just hadn't been with him through the majority of the war. It had been hard for them both, separated for so long while he was in Russia. Even when he'd moved back to England and was working at Latimer House and Trent Park, they were long hours and he'd had little time really to be with Molly. It was simply that he just couldn't talk to her; not that he was unable to, but it was that damned Act again that he'd signed. Might as well be called the Official Silence Act, he reckoned, grimacing. He wondered if other couples had falling-outs about this. They'd married in haste. He recognized they'd fallen in love, and in lust, and, dash it, so many other young couples had got married like that. The man was off into the military and so you snatched at life when you could. That wasn't what bothered him. It had just happened like that.

What bothered him was that it was really, he mused, that Molly didn't know a side of him that people who'd known him in the war did. As he knew them—both the female and the male agent contacts; the spies. They knew what it was like to live life on the edge, have your heart pound as someone suspicious followed you, even to be held at gunpoint and be lucky you made it out alive—all this had drawn him closer to these women and men. They knew him in a way Molly couldn't. They'd been with him when he'd been tested, when he'd passed a message to the wrong person (thank God that hadn't happened more than once!), and they'd helped him escape. He ran through all those dangerous occasions in his head. It felt now as if he'd had a whole life already that Moll wasn't part of…and it was true.

Smiling to himself suddenly, he thought how some of those hard, scintillating, brazen, women could drink him under the table. He was very, very practiced at seemingly drinking huge amounts, but never to excess. He remained in control at all times; that was what could save his life, and, in fact, had done so on a few occasions.

Then there were the softies, those cold, hard females who actually had hearts of gold once you got to know 'em. Agent ladies he got close to—but always for a solid reason. A surge of guilt overtook Fred as he thought back to lying in bed with one of those, mining her for knowledge, feeling bad afterwards, but having got what he'd come for, in all ways. He knew he shouldn't feel guilty; it was part of his job, and he knew it. How could he do that when he so loved his wife? It was as if he held a number of different boxes in his heart, each one with someone's name on, and each one never overlapped by another, just held, the one next to another in his heart. That's why it seemed fine to him. Only a tad of guilt, just a very small niggling feeling eating at him occasionally.

He'd never told Molly about these infidelities; they meant nothing. He didn't think of himself as a philanderer, a cad, but as a bit of a rascal, a ladies' man, and, more than anything, so much of it was a means to an end which helped the war effort. He knew he was a bloody good spy. He never slept with a woman just for her sake, or even his own—it was only and always to get information from her. If that made him a cad, so be it. The things he'd found out through pillow talk! His superiors had been eminently pleased with him.

No man, nobody, was perfect, he told himself. There had never been a Monsieur Parfait, even though women constantly told him they were searching for such a perfect man. He knew his faults, if indeed, they should even be considered faults in wartime work. Hmmmm, he thought, he was really a deeply caring, loving, husband. But sometimes in life things you do, or have done, have to be kept quiet.

So Molly mustn't know. It honestly didn't affect his life with her. She was number one in his life. He really did love her. She was already upset over the way women came on to him. She simply mustn't know how close he sometimes had to get, all in the name of "the war effort, for England!". But, those days were surely over? The war was over. His domestic life was in full swing; his daughters now attending the British Army school nearby, Molly at his side nearly all the time. It should all be perfect. But politics and intrigue were never over. He knew that, too. So how does one stop it all? How?

Tamping his Meerschaum down, he mused further.

He had developed close friendships with four principal women. They knew him inside and out, having been with him here and there throughout the war, in England, in Germany, and one of them even seeing him in Moscow of all places—sent there as a courier herself. She was one of Shanghai Joe's agents; that tall, willowy raven-haired beauty from somewhere in Asia, somewhere in China, for sure. He was mesmerised by this beauty, Zhi Ruo. She told him her name stood for herbs, angelica and something called pollia. She said her shiny black hair stood for the fruit of the pollia condensata herb, the shiniest living material in the world. Pollia condensata! She even knew the Latin name. He would love to have shared that with Molly, who was a tremendous gardener. He'd managed to keep Zhi Ruo pretty much at bay, when it was obvious to him that she liked him more than a little, and a smile flashed briefly across his face at the thought.

Musing on about the angelica herb, Fred thought how Molly was his angel, his delight, the love of his life, the mother of his darling girls. He couldn't break her heart by her knowing about these other women. They meant nothing! She must not know, there was no question about it!

Then, there was, no, is, Lexi, his secretary—the completely reliable, faithful Lexi. She'd accompanied him to his desk in the Control Commission, and now to the Embassy in Bonn. A kittenish woman, with a baby-like voice, and that soft, soft skin covered by a fine golden down, but, she was certainly made of steel within. A real asset to have in your corner. He trusted her completely and had thanked Kenneword of Morgan's, in both Germany and England, who had unearthed Lexi to be his trusted companion in his work. He knew she was totally loyal to him, and, pretty obviously, nuts about him. Why, she'd even left her own German husband to work for him. He'd met that man: a studious, academic sort of chap. Boring as all get-out. No wonder she likes me, thought Fred to himself, then immediately felt chagrined. He WAS a cad, wasn't he?

And Betsy in London. Seemed a real housewifely type, but very smart, with a wonderfully sanguine personality. Street-smart. Common as dirt, but that was useful to him, when he needed a female companion to go underground with. She knew 'em all, all those frightful wide boy types he occasionally had to consort with, get information from. Yes, Betsy was also an asset. None of those nose-picking lowlifes scared her. She was swift with a knife, too. No guns for her, but she knew how to handle a flick-knife better than any man he'd ever known. Useful woman, very useful…

And Bertha. Who would ever suspect that this rather rotund,

short, chief ladies' clothes buyer for one of the best department stores in Düsseldorf, with her iron-grey short man's hairstyle, was a first-class agent? She was a whiz at public relations, could talk to anybody, and was from the upper middle class of German society. A Nazi through and through. She had access to many of Germany's military and civilian leaders through their wives, all of whom asked specifically for her services when buying their clothes. She always managed to find something fashionable even during the darkest days of the war when most shops had nothing but dusty, empty shelves. Bertha was a good confidante to have; good with squirreling out secrets and passing them along to him. Very valuable woman, too, his Bertha.

Switching to thinking of genuine upper-class society females, nobody could match Delia. Nobody. Fred was afraid he was half in love with her. Was he? He admired her greatly, but no, he didn't love her. He loved his Molly, and that was certain. Yet Delia, more than anyone else in those days, understood his "German-ness", that side of his heritage that was so alien to his other, British, side. She was German through and through. And she was another Nazi. She was absolutely beautiful, with flaming red hair and Chanel red lantern lipstick and nails. She was elegant, clever, sweet, nasty, all at once. She teased him mercilessly about his upper-class German accent, when she knew he was also half English.

"Freddie, mein Schatzi, you sound so, so German, but how do you do that, you English bastard, you!"

He knew that she knew he was half English but what she did not know, most obviously, was that he was an agent. She could have assumed it but, doubtless because Delia was obviously in love with him, she couldn't entertain the idea. She knew him as a top-end supplier to her family's paint, plastics, and varnish factory, Chemische Fabrik Hackenin. That's all. He'd tested her many times, and each time he knew she hadn't a clue. A big relief to Fred. He grinned when considering the name of her family's factory. Hackenin meant hacker, chopper, or in some vernacular, traitor. Hahaha, he laughed, she didn't know it but SHE was a true Hackenin!

Plus, Delia was ill. That appealed to the softer side in Fred. He sometimes felt he wanted to take care of her. She had Diabetes and he had often helped her to inject herself. She was a tiger in bed. He'd started the affair with her to mine her for information to relay back to England, as with all his "lady contacts". She was a canny businesswoman—the family firm was completely in the hands of the Third Reich. Upon entering her house, her damn Amazonian 60-year-old grey parrot would always eye him balefully, lift one sharp-clawed foot off his perch while squawking a raucous greeting of "Heil Hitler!" at him. Fred reckoned that bloody bird knew exactly who he was. Enough to give a chap the total creeps.

Fred puffed away at his pipe, thinking these thoughts that could never be shared with Molly. It was all part of his job. He knew he'd only get the information he needed by acting in this way with these women, these damn contacts, he swore to himself…but all that was surely now over. Wasn't it?

How can I judge myself, he thought? I'm certainly slightly ashamed of some of my behaviour, and if Molly were to find out, I know how painful it would be for her. But I know she loves me, she knows I'm human. She would love me even if she knew I weren't the purest of men. Wouldn't she?

Oh, Molly, he thought, my dearest Molly. You mustn't find out, you must not know anything, you just mustn't. It's over now, anyway, all that wartime work is over. Surely? Isn't it?

Nevertheless, even <u>not</u> knowing the truth of Fred's past wartime activities, it was all becoming too much for Molly, especially the never-ending parties, the drinking, and other women draping themselves familiarly over her husband. She probably could have stood it all and carried on, as was her wont, but…Molly found out!

Who but another woman would reveal his secrets, claiming she was telling Molly "for her own good"? Who, but Lexi? Lexi wanted much more from Fred. She wanted him all to herself. She wanted his sweet little English wife and those wretched kids gone from

Germany. She decided to tell Molly about Fred's other women, pretending she, herself, was not involved except as his secretary. She told her one day when Fred was away. Lexi was all sweetness and kindness, putting her arm around Molly to whisper about Fred's infidelities and that she, as a loyal secretary, shouldn't tell on him.

"But, you see, you are such a nice lady, so kind, dearest Molly, so I cannot let you suffer. You must know what he does, well, what he did. It was wartime, you see, and you weren't there. He doesn't know I know, but I know everything, as his secretary and his close friend, you understand. I've heard things, so I know. I've got intuition; I've put two and two together. Yes, I know everything! And you, too, should know, my dear, dear Molly! We women must always stick together!"

Molly was completely devastated and could hardly believe it, but, on the other hand, her own intuition, her senses, even the occasional different smells on his skin and clothes, had told her otherwise. Yes, she thought, it's true alright…he has other women, he really does!

From Bonn to Düsseldorf, via Cologne, the drive was only about an hour's commute by car. Fred decided to move the family to Düsseldorf, where both he and Molly hoped the marriage would get back onto a stable footing. More and more arguments were erupting, almost every night when he'd get home from work.

Molly did not tell him yet that she knew about his other women.

Molly hired another nanny for the girls. Theresa was a wonderful cook, too, who loved making doughnuts for her young charges. Molly's youngest, Shirley, was fascinated by the holes in the doughnuts and repeatedly asked where they went to!

"Maybe if I, and not Theresa, did the cooking, that would make for more of a domestic scene, Freddie, don't you think?"

"No, Molly, it's just not the way it's done over here, you know that. Hell, you're a diplomat's wife. We have people to do that sort of thing!" said Fred, to Molly's frustration and dismay.

"Of course, you're right." Molly mentally added that to another reason why she just couldn't fit into this sort of life.

"We have a cook at Dad's house, so I never cook there," added Molly, "but, honestly, if I were running my own home, I'd do all the cooking—just like I did when we were back in Buckinghamshire and you were working at Latimer House—you remember, Freddie, you liked my cooking!"

"So I did, angel, but, as I say, it's just too *infra dig* over here. The other wives would think you were batty!"

More arguments erupted, day after day. Sometimes the girls were nearby and could hear. On one occasion Molly started shouting at Fred. He hurriedly told her, *"Pas devant les enfants!"* She knew some French and both she and he had always said private things in French if the children were in the room. And, she had to agree, it was not a good idea to argue at all in front of the children.

One day, after leaving the warmth and pleasant smells of the kitchen, young Shirley walked into the dining room, following the sound of convulsive, uncontrollable sobbing. There sat her mother at the far end of their long, shiny wooden dining table, her head resting on her bent arms, crying her eyes out. Shirley was terrified; she'd never heard her mother cry like that before. She ran back to the peaceful shelter of Theresa's strong arms and ample bosom, crying herself.

On other days following, both girls found their mother crying, but never when Fred was around.

The family's flat was in a red-brick tall building on Cecilienallee, with views from their windows out at the River Rhine. Horse-chestnut trees lined the river, casting welcome shade in the summer, and, in the autumn providing conker nuts for the girls to play with. They drilled a hole through the middle of each fat shiny chestnut seed and threaded a thin string through it, tying it in a knot at one end and leaving a foot of string to swing. The point of the game was to smash your conker against your opponent's, aiming to break hers into a mess of chestnut shards, and thereby win the game.

Molly and Fred staggered on in their marriage, through 1950 and 1951. Molly tried to get along with the diplomatic crowd, tried to befriend other diplomats' wives, tried hard in many ways to be the "right kind of wife" to Fred. But, the marriage was falling apart. She missed England, her family, friends and mainly, her dear father. And she carried the secret knowledge of Fred's infidelities constantly burning a hole in her heart. She often almost blurted out what she knew but she just didn't want to give Lexi the satisfaction of knowing how hurt she was by her spilling of Fred's secrets.

The girls grew and by 1952, when one was 10 and the other eight, Molly left Fred, and, sad but angry, took the girls with her back to England. She had finally had enough. Lexi had been accompanying them everywhere, to business dinners, to the theatre, to parties, always with the excuse that she was "needed" by him. She became nasty to Molly, ignoring her, or being downright rude. Molly discovered one day that Fred had even been giving Lexi her ciggie ration; no wonder Molly kept running out. What was he thinking? It was downright mean.

One evening Molly came across Lexi leaving the home-office Fred also maintained in the Düsseldorf flat. Molly heard Lexi's "little girl" voice calling Fred by an endearment as he helped her into her fur coat—doubtless bought for her by Fred, Molly groused inwardly to herself. When Lexi had gone, Molly took a deep breath, and accosted Fred. There and then it all came pouring, spewing, out of her, all her anger, misery, recriminations, accusing him of all his lies. Fred was gobsmacked. He held her sobbing body but she was adamant about her decision and pushed him away.

"Fred, I'm leaving you. It's all over. I can't tolerate any of this anymore. We were so in love! Oh, all those wasted years! All those LIES you've told me over all these past years! You're a cad, a rat, Fred Read-Jahn, an absolute monster, the devil himself!"

"Now look here, Moll, you can't do this. You can't just leave. You can't take the girls away from me."

"No, you look here, Fred; it's over and the sooner you recognise that, the better. I'm done. It's over. OVER!"

Giving him a withering look, she ran from the room.

Once again, Molly was packing. Fred was gentlemanly enough to make the booking for her and the girls to return to England.

Over the next few days before they left, he tried again and again to explain himself to Molly. She remained icily calm. She'd tell him she'd given her best to the marriage; she'd been cuckolded. She was totally, irrevocably, outraged by his adultery. He told her he loved her, his only angel, and only her, *only* her, his darling, his sweetest Molly, nobody else mattered, those other women, they weren't important, they never had been, it was just part of his work, over and over, but it was all too late.

The winter of 1952-53 was bitterly cold, similar to the 1946-1947's winter. Molly wanted to be "home" by Christmas, and she had to get out of there so decided to take the girls on the ship anyway, even if it was so freezingly cold.

The ship Molly and the girls were travelling on to cross the Channel back to England was tossed in gigantic storm waves with ice forming, and bitterly cold snow falling. She couldn't believe life could get much worse. All three of them were horribly seasick. Molly lay on her bunk crying silently into her pillow, hoping her daughters wouldn't hear. By the time the ship had docked, she'd become sternly calm and collected, ready for this next phase in her life. The hell with Fred! And, holding the girls firmly by the hand, stalked off the ship, a baggage-handler with all her cases stumbling along as fast as possible behind her retreating back!

Grandpa Sutton met them at the docks in his big black car. The girls piled into the rear seats. Molly sat in the passenger seat and, in a low voice, hurriedly filled him in with more details, aside from her last telephone call to him, on why she'd finally walked out on Fred. Her father nodded, tutting after every word, then said out loud, "Molly, my dear, we've had horrific weather over here, with many tragedies due to the cold. This is the worst winter since '46/7 so I'm putting you up in my "Broadmayne" house until we can find an appropriate place for you and the girls, preferably near a school we'll find for them. Somewhere you'll be cosy and warm and", lowering his voice so only she could hear, "somewhere where that husband of yours won't find you or bother you."

As they got near to London they encountered another horror, for it was one of the days of the Great London Smog, the worst of which engulfed London during the early days of December, 1952, lasting from 5th to 9th, five whole days of thick, green, mucous-like disgusting air you choked on. People in London were still burning coal and wood in their fireplaces, which caused this horrible, stinky, green smog—truly severe air-pollution. Grandpa Sutton explained it to his granddaughters. "When the pollution level gets up this high, and high pressure's compounding it, and an inversion is present, this nasty green smoggy pollution gets trapped near the surface. You know, girls, the air has become so thick you could not only choke on it but chew the dratted stuff!

"Whaaaat? I don't understand", chirped young Shirley, "but it is horrible and stinky, yeuk!"

Scowling at her younger sister, Pam said, "Grandpa, that makes total sense. SHE never understands anything!"

To which, Shirley put her fingers in her ears, flapping them up and down, and stuck out her tongue at Pam.

"Now, then, girls", said Grandpa Sutton, "you take it in turns to sit on the bonnet and wave your white hanky so other cars can see us, and I'll crawl along very, very slowly so you won't fall off, and I'll know whether to turn left or right. You'll see each signpost before I do. The eldest always goes first, remember primogeniture, girls. Hell, Molly, this is the worst pea-souper I can remember!"

"Primo what?" chirped Shirley.

Pam said, "You know, silly, I'm the oldest so it means I go first in everything!"

With glee, Pam then climbed up onto the bonnet of the big car, feeling very important, and started to wave her white hanky with her left hand, so other cars creeping along would, indeed, see her. She hung on to the bonnet's ornament for dear life with her right hand, her legs hanging down over the car's grille in front. When her legs began to cramp, and at Mr. Sutton's command, Pam swapped places with Shirley, who scrambled up like the little monkey she was, and delightedly waved her own white hanky backwards and forwards, yelling out instructions in a high falsetto to her grandfather trying to drive the big car, slowly, so slowly through the nasty thick smog.

Quite some hours later they made it "home" to his house called "Broadmayne", where a maid, in her black dress, little white cap and frilly apron, opened the door to them, holding a hanky against her mouth to keep the green smog out. She bobbed a quick curtsy to Molly and rushed to get the luggage inside before the expected icy rain.

"Oh Daddy, darling", cried Molly, throwing herself into his arms once inside the hallway, "I'm so happy I'm home, I could cry."

"Well now, I shouldn't say this, my girl, but you married in haste and now must repent at leisure," said Mr. Sutton, giving a crooked smile and a grimace.

"Oh Dad, that's so old hat, but", she sobbed, "it is true…at least I've got the girls, though!"

Through the early 1950s Molly continued her life in England, moving from house to house, to escape Fred when he'd somehow discover where they were living and make attempts to see them. The girls changed schools frequently as their home changed location.

There was much excitement in 1952 when King George VI died. The new young monarch, Elizabeth, came hurriedly back from a trip to Africa with her prince to take over from her late father. In 1953 Grandpa Sutton draped the whole of the huge "Broadmayne" home in red, white and blue patriotic flags. Then came the Crowning of Queen Elizabeth II. The girls sat dutifully at the feet of Grandma Sutton, stern and silent as ever, in her long black dress. Molly and her unmarried sister, Olive, sat close to their father, as the whole family watched the ceremony on the first television Mr. Sutton had ever bought.

Molly eventually had a bad reaction to the change in her life and the London weather. She came down with a severe case of pleurisy. Her doctor advised her to take the girls and go off to sea for nearly three months, to get the benefit of fresh, clean, salty air. They were aboard a Holland-America line cargo ship with only twelve passengers. Molly slowly stopped coughing and recovered her health.

Upon their return, in 1954, the girls were packed off to St. Mary's Hall, an English all-girls' church boarding school in Brighton, for the rest of their school life.

When Molly left him, Freddie remained in Germany around the Düsseldorf, Cologne, Bonn, and Bad Godesberg areas, working at the British Embassy until that job, too, "became redundant" some years later.

He then made the move back to London in the 60s, bought a town house in a private cul-de-sac in Ealing, London, and joined the Society of Motor Manufacturers & Traders as their Overseas Press Representative. They are the trade association for the United Kingdom's motor industry with the role of promoting the interests of the UK's automotive industry in Great Britain and abroad. Lexi, as usual, accompanied him, to be his secretary, and this time to live with him as unmarried man and wife. She had got what she wanted.

Chapter 31

1960s
The Berlin Wall—
Fred & his Mother Visit Their
Old Schöneberg Home in Berlin

Molly and the girls had gone from Freddie's life and were living in England. The girls at that time were not permitted to have much contact with him. Herman was dead. The only close family Fred had left in his life was his mother, Herman's wife and her two children, both the same ages as his own children.

Fred knew his mother, Clara, was ageing rapidly and was ill with cancer. She'd long expressed a wish to see her old home again, where she had lived near a small lake with Herr Friedrich Ludwig Jahn, Fred's father, in the upmarket Schöneberg area of West Berlin, long before the Berlin Wall had been built in 1961.

The Berlin Wall was not to come down until November, 1989, but in the early sixties, Fred wasn't to know if or when that could possibly happen. Thus, he decided to take his old mother back to

Berlin while she could still walk, and to help her fulfil this yearned-for wish[1]. To accomplish this, they had to get onto the other side of the Berlin Wall. He talked to his old contacts at the Foreign Office in London, to his contacts at the British Embassy in Bonn, and to contacts he'd met throughout his intel in general—to anyone who would be able to help get him and his mother safely into East Berlin and out again. While the Wall was in place, there was only one road to get into the city, with everyone wishing to enter having to pass through a checkpoint, manned by armed guards.

It was a tricky undertaking and he told his mother the whole project could turn out badly for them both. His mother didn't care; she knew she was ill and she didn't know how long she had to live but intuited that it wasn't very long. In fact, the Berlin Wall wasn't to come down for 24 more years[2], well after Clara had passed on in 1965.

After making his careful plans, Fred drove his mother to the checkpoint at the Wall, showed his passes, and, to his happy surprise and relief, they were both allowed through. Following a map (and trying to remember back to the years of his youth), he finally drove them both successfully to the old family manse in East Berlin.

On the way there, Fred was aware an old black Russian motorcar was following them the whole way, but at a discreet distance. When they had stopped to use a public lavatory, a Soviet man in the proverbial spy's khaki trench coat and black hat followed him into the Men's urinals. It took Fred right back to his spying days and made the hair on the back of his neck stand up. He well knew that every foreigner was followed by NKVD or KGB agents whether in the USSR itself or in any Soviet-held territory. There was no choice; it was simply normal surveillance procedure. He had decided against carrying his handgun under his jacket; if he'd been stopped and searched, carrying the gun wouldn't have gone well for him.

All he could do was maybe shake off the following car—also knowing that it could be dangerous—but he wanted to know, all these years after his war work had ostensibly finished, whether he really was being followed. A light rain was falling. He drove carefully and steadily, not too fast, to see what the car behind would do, and hoping to convince his follower that there would be no sudden moves on his part. As the rain increased, it became harder to see. He put his lights on, as did the car following him at a distance. His wipers beat out a steady clack, clack, clack, clack, as they swept backwards and forwards over the windscreen. He had an idea. Time to get rid of the follower, then he'd know for sure! As they rounded a bend, he saw a road splitting to the left and to the right off the main road. He was driving on the right side of the road, so suddenly swung the car to the left across the other lane, and disappeared into the woods, immediately turning off his lights and engine. He could see very little, totally surrounded by a heavy, grey, wet mist hanging down over the trees.

After some five minutes, glancing sideways, in the gloom he noticed to his surprise that his aged mother was smiling broadly at him. They quietly giggled together, like naughty kids, then Fred gently eased the car into gear, put on the side lights only, successfully turned around, and emerged back onto the road.

As he drove on slowly now through the quite heavy rain with his headlights back on, the other car appeared coming back toward him. It flashed its lights at him and crossed over slightly into his lane, forcing him to slow down. Once alongside, the man in the hat quickly rolled down his window and, leaning forward to avoid Fred's passenger, waggled his index finger at him, then drove on. Fred was sure he'd seen the sides of the man's mouth go up in a slight grin, and, Fred was delighted to see the rain splash into the car right onto the man's face.

Driving on, he heard a squeal of tyres, and in the rear-view mirror saw the lights of the other car as it obviously made a three-point turn to take up its following stance once again. With a sigh, all Fred could do now was to simply carry on. Yes, he was certainly being tailed!

Eventually they rounded a final bend, the mist lifted, the rain stopped, and there stood the old house, almost the same as how both his mother and he had remembered, but obviously older, and now more dilapidated. The two cars parked outside the house but the follower remained in his car, just watching.

The bushes Clara had planted around the garden's perimeters were now almost trees. The garden was a mess; walking slowly around, she could still see some of the plants she'd put in so many years before, but mostly it was all pretty much overgrown. An old man and his wife came outside to talk to Fred and his mother. There were a couple of families living in the house. They said they had been there for years so had every right to be there, even though Fred's mother pointed out she was still the legitimate owner of the house[3].

"Nothing we can do about that so if you've got a problem with it, you can take it to the authorities" said the old man, sniffing and turning away. Clara looked quite discomforted by this exchange of words, as if she might cry, so Fred quickly thanked the house's residents and steered her back into the garden. Fred knew she'd understood the man's German; she could understand so much more than she could speak, just like so many others—hence the tears building up in her eyes.

"Freddie, dear", exclaimed Clara, "look, look over here, oh, and over there. I planted all those so long ago, when your father was alive. He helped me. Oh, we had so much fun in those days, before, before, you know, before he saw the war was coming and before he…before he…died." As she hung onto her son's arm, he noticed a tear rolling down her chubby white cheeks. He squeezed her arm in great affection.

Fred leant somewhat away from her and gave her a long look. His mother, his dear old mother!

"Look at YOU, mother dear! You're like a beautiful old flower yourself, with that glorious wavy white hair crowning your head."

She was really quite tall, Fred thought, and somewhat stocky. She loved to wear flowery prints in her dresses. She'd been a milliner in Luton in her youth. She still occasionally wore hats she'd made herself, felt or straw, trimmed with faux violets, feathers or roses. He'd asked her about them one day. She'd said they were always lined in foulard, so soft, made of silk, satin or cotton. She'd got excited, waving her hands around to show him how long the feathers she'd used were, some even being of ostrich! So exotic, she'd laughed. "And I'd add beads," Clara exclaimed, "making the hat look as if it were decorated with diamonds. Oh my, people paid a fortune for MY hats!"

As Fred drove his mother back toward West Germany, he was again aware of being followed. When they stopped to eat at a small café, the dratted man in the trench coat and black hat also came in, sat at a table at the other end of the café, ate while reading a newspaper, every so often lowering his paper, obviously to keep his eye on them. They drove out of East Berlin with nothing further untoward happening to them, but both with a big sigh of relief to have made it safely back out.

On 26th June, 1963 the American president, John F. Kennedy, made his famous speech at the Schöneberg Town Hall in which he said, in German, "Ich bin ein Berliner" (I am a Berliner). He was giving the United States' policy support to West Germany 22 months after the Communist Soviets had erected their Berlin Wall to stop East Berliners escaping to the West.

In November, 1989 the divisive Berlin Wall was finally brought down, marking the symbolic end of the Cold War, with the Iron Curtain lifted and the citizens of East Berlin and West Berlin once again free to cross the country's borders.

---

1. [Author's note] I do not remember the exact year my father took his mother over into East Berlin. Clara was born in 1877 and died in 1965; was already ill with cancer in her later years, so I believe the visit must have occurred in the early 1960s. The Wall had gone up in 1961 so it was probably in 1962 or 1963 that Fred took his mother to visit her old home in East Berlin. Later on, after his mother had died, Fred was to compare his mother's Berlin house with the house shown in the 1965 *Dr. Zhivago* movie, when Dr. Zhivago himself returns to find strangers crammed into his old Soviet home. It was sadly rather similar.
2. The Berlin Wall came down on 9th November, 1989, on what, coincidentally, would have been Molly's birthday—but Molly had died two years previously, so never knew the Wall had come down.
3. After the Berlin Wall had been knocked down and our parents had died, the author's cousins, her sister and herself, looked into getting their Berlin house legally back from its current residents, but were unsuccessful.

Chapter 32

13th to 21st March, 1980
Fred Dies and
Shirley & Pam Steal his Letters

Many years passed, and lives were lived. For his part, Fred was continuing to live with Lexi in the townhouse he'd bought in the '60s in Ealing, London. She had never divorced her husband in Germany and obviously far preferred Freddie, as many women always did!

Fred continued his work as Overseas Representative for the Society of Motor Manufacturers and Traders. When Fred was working for the SMMT, he was involved in the sale to overseas buyers of high-end British motor cars, such as Rover, Jaguar and Rolls Royce. This meant that Fred could no longer drive his beloved German Mercedes with its open-air roof, but was forced to switch to a deep forest green Rover, albeit with its beautiful all-wood dashboard. Fred always wore leather driving gloves. He also kept a little toy lion called Leo swinging from the Rover's inside rear-view mirror. His star sign was Leo, and he held some superstition, claiming Leo looked out for him and had brought him much luck in surviving the war.

An English girlfriend, Betsy, his old wartime agent quick with a flick knife, lived quite nearby and, such was Fred's charm, it had wrapped itself warmly around both Lexi and Betsy, with both of them not only tolerating each other's company, but seeming to like each other. So, grinned Fred, at least two of his boxes in his heart had now overlapped; fancy that! Betsy had been married to a German at one time. She'd experienced the horrendous Kristallnacht in November of 1938. Betsy had named a daughter Kristal, but tragically, Kristal had died during the war.

On his numerous trips back to Germany on business, Fred would see Bertha, his department store buyer female contact, staying with her in her beautifully appointed flat in a high-rise in Düsseldorf, with its deep red Pelargonium geraniums gorgeously spilling down from her balcony's window boxes. Interestingly, Lexi accompanied him on those trips, too, so it would seem, again thought Fred, that Bertha and Lexi also got along together! His separate heart-boxes were all falling apart, weren't they!

Fred travelled a lot through Europe attending many auto shows, and speaking on television and radio, all to promote the interests of the SMMT. He was in Geneva, Switzerland attending a motor show in March of 1980 when he collapsed. Rushed to hospital, it was discovered he was suffering from pancreatitis. Fred loathed hospitals, and particularly couldn't stand all those tubes connecting him to bottles of life-saving fluids. He was last seen flapping in his open hospital garment down a corridor heading straight for an exit, unattached tubes swinging wildly from his speeding body. As a nurse chased after him, he collapsed, dying immediately from a heart attack. This was on 13th March. Fred was only 68 years old.

His daughters were notified to return to England from, respectively, Australia and the USA to attend their father's funeral. They stayed in their father's house with Lexi.

It was the morning of the day of the funeral on 21st March, 1980. Lexi had gone out by taxi to have her hair done—she had never learned to drive. The girls knew there were letters written by Fred to his mother and his wife during World War II—letters he had told Shirley had to do with his secret undercover work in the agonising days of the war and the history that swirled about them. He'd occasionally referred to these letters and how some of them were coded in phrases that would mean something to the recipient. He'd said that the censors would take his letter requests for certain items to be sent to him at face value, then he chuckled merrily at his memory of deceiving the censors, who read all the post—in his case, those were the diplomatic-bag censors. Knowing this, the girls were intrigued and badly wanted to read these mysterious letters.

The British Embassy in Moscow sent all their mail in a special, sealed bag, heavily protected and guarded on its journey back to Britain, but each letter within was always checked first, just to ensure nothing was written therein that could aid the enemy in the event the courier bag were stolen. Sometimes the bag had to travel in circuitous routes to get back to England, very similar to Fred's 1940 long journey to reach the British Embassy in Moscow. As the war had progressed, the bags took longer and longer to get "home" from Moscow to England or *vice versa*. Molly and Fred had been driven almost crazy with anticipation. Sometimes their numbered letters arrived in one big heap on one day. Sometimes there was no room in the diplomatic bag for personal mail, with it being filled with wartime directives. Those were sad days indeed when the bag would arrive but with no personal mail in it.

Fred's daughters hoped these letters would shed more light on their father's wartime activities because his life had always been kept so very secret. Shirley and Pam were determined to find them and spirit them away.

At the earlier Reading of the Will in the solicitor's office they learned that Fred had left everything to his secretary, Lexi. It was a strange decision and they both decided she shouldn't get the letters. They theorized that she would doubtless toss them away anyway, because so many were to his ex-wife, their mother. They felt Lexi was only interested in Fred's paintings, Persian carpets, and household goods after she had been adamant in telling the girls that they must take nothing from the house, not even a single photo. Shirley knew this for certain because she had overheard Lexi say in a dismaying phone call to a neighbouring German friend, "Ich habe alles gekriegt" (I got everything).

When the taxi bearing Lexi had disappeared down the short road taking her to the hair salon, the girls looked through Fred's office but found nothing. Next, they searched in their father's bedroom. With determination, Shirley lifted a chair up on top of a table and placed two telephone books on top of that. Up she climbed, to feel around in the back of the uppermost cupboard shelf for those mysterious letters. Meanwhile, Pam kept "KV"[1] at the window. Fred lived in a cul-de-sac so there was no way Lexi could come back in a taxi without being seen.

Suddenly the girls froze. Footsteps came creaking up the stairs, closer and closer. Lexi was coming back, and fast approaching the room! A Hitchcockian "movie moment" occurred, as her steps came nearer and nearer. How had she done that? Was there a private back garden entrance they didn't know about?

With heart pounding, Shirley had never moved so fast. Suddenly she spied the pile of letters—there they were! Way up high, wrapped in a ribbon, way at the back of the topmost cupboard shelf. Next to them she felt a cloth bundle. Hurriedly running her fingers over it, she felt the hard shape of a handgun and leather holster.

"Oh my God, I'm leaving his gun right there!" she muttered to herself. "I'll just grab the letters."

She breathed a sigh of relief, but the steps were approaching relentlessly nearer and nearer up the long staircase. She stretched on tiptoes, grabbed the bundle and scrambled speedily and silently back onto the floor. The phone books, the chairs were quickly dismantled and the table was moved quietly, oh-so-quietly back to its appointed place. Now, what to do with the letters? Thinking quickly, she frantically asked herself what should she do? What would her father do? Suddenly it came to her—Fred always used to say if you wanted to hide something, it should always be left right out in the open for anyone to see. She tossed the bundle on top of her open suitcase and hurriedly sat on the bed next to a shaking Pam.

In came Lexi, roving her eyes around Fred's bedroom, surveying the girls suspiciously, flicking her eyes from one face to the other, then all around his room yet again.

She never even saw the letters. Of course she didn't. They were —thanks to their dear father, Major Fred Willie Read-Jahn—totally and completely *hidden in plain sight*!

With the precious bundle of letters now stashed away in Shirley's suitcase, the girls went downstairs to await the Rolls Royce to bear them and Lexi to Fred's funeral. Seated in the comfortable roomy car, their knees covered with a fur blanket, they took it in turns to hold his urn of ashes. Hundreds of people attended Fred's funeral, hardly any of whom the girls knew. Many were from other countries, many connected to his SMMT work, but there were many others, too, dignified military-looking grey-haired men, and a few beautiful older women, dressed impeccably in black, plus obvious "diplomatic types", as Fred used to call them. You could hear English, French, German, even Russian being spoken in a low hum as people softly greeted or introduced each other.

Suddenly, from behind a tall gravestone shuffled a short Chinese man, bent-over, his upturned face lined and creased into a sad frown and down-turned mouth. He seemed to be searching for someone, his eyes nervously darting from person to person, finally settling on the girls' cousin, Stephen. He grabbed Stephen by the arm, pulling him a little away from the gathering of mourners, as a sudden, radiant smile triumphantly crossed his face. Shirley watched, fascinated, remembering how Stephen had told her of his strange experience, much earlier in the winter of that year, of just such a man accosting him on a Shanghai ferryboat.

Shirley moved surreptitiously a little nearer, a lace handkerchief held up to her eyes, her head held down, as if listening to the minister intoning his prayers for the dead. Through the white lace she watched the two men. It had to be Shanghai Joe that Stephen had told her about! She moved behind a gravestone closer to them both, listening intently. She peered around the stone and saw Stephen shaking his head in disbelief.

Shanghai Joe hung onto Stephen's arm, chuckling silently, and whispering hoarsely, "Fleddie, oh Fleddie! You old trickster, you! They think you dead, going in that grave there…but you pulled it off, didn't you! I see Robeson with those Morgan men, and the others all here. They part of this plan, eh? That why they no surprised by you here, eh? You old dog, Fleddie! Look, your grey hair! But, you still look younger than old me, oh yes. You didn't want to know me on the boat in Shanghai, but I know YOU! Come on, you come away with me…what you up to now? It's been YEARS since we proper talk, eh Fleddie! You come tell me. We got so much to catch up on! Let's go talk to the others. THEY know you not dead!"

Stephen raised his hands to his forehead in perplexity, as Shanghai Joe forcefully steered him over to a group of older men respectfully standing in a huddle near the graveside, as the urn was gently interred at the foot of Fred's mother's grave. This group looked up and smilingly acknowledged Shanghai Joe. These were British Embassy, Foreign Office, Army military, and company directors, all of whom had had a part as Fred's MI-19 handlers. They were Robeson (of Morgan Crucible Co.), McCanley (the director friend of Molly's father who had introduced Fred to Timmins), Timmins (Fred's Kobe, Japan pro-consul contact), and Kenneword (of Morgan's and manager of its Kobe subsidiary). The group now exchanged looks with each other, nodded briefly, and took Shanghai Joe's hand in a warm handshake, as Stephen, in turn, offered the group a half smile then quickly backed away. The wartime intelligence officers all stood side by side, staring down at the newly-turned soil now covering Fred's urn, the Englishmen looking serious, and the old Chinese man impassive, certainly, then with a gleeful, knowing little grin hovering over his lips as he glanced up to watch Stephen quietly slipping away behind the gravestones.

Shirley walked quickly after Stephen, pulling Pam with her, and caught the young man before he could enter a waiting car. "Come on, let's all three go for a drink. We've got so much more to tell you about the story! Stephen, you won't believe it but we've found Fred's wartime letters!"

---

1. KV = to keep vigil, quiet surveillance.

Epilogue

Fred died on 13th March, 1980. Many people, especially women, have missed him for many years since.

Molly died in Worthing, Sussex on 3rd October, 1987 thus outliving Fred by seven years. Her daughters buried her ashes next to Fred's and his mother's in Putney Vale Cemetery, Southwest London.

Shanghai Joe ended up moving to the USA, ostensibly leaving the world of espionage, and opening up a Chinese restaurant called Shanghai Joe's Delicious Diner in midtown New York City, where he dishes up "the world's best lobster soup dumplings" (attributed to Shanghai Joe himself).

Stephen ended up in Andorra—where he liked to ski—and hoping to escape the persistent clutches of Shanghai Joe. He wasn't successful. Therein lies another story.

Delia died of Diabetes in a Davos sanatorium high in the Swiss Alps. Her old Amazonian parrot accompanied her but was found one day with his head bashed in after repeatedly squawking "Heil Hitler!"

Zhi Ruo cut off her long, shiny raven hair, and started wearing a bob with a fringe. She married Shanghai Joe's third cousin twice removed. The happy couple went to live in Formosa, now Taiwan. Zhi Ruo became a housewife and refused to ever say what she'd done in the war.

Betsy eventually died of a stroke, after successfully wielding off a home-attacker with her trusty flick knife.

Bertha disappeared from the high-end fashion world in the 1990s. She was last seen on 26th December, 1991 at the finish of the Cold War, boarding a plane to the USSR.

Lexi sold Fred's house and all his possessions and returned to Germany. She was pleased with herself; she'd done well. The girls never spoke to her again.

Pam and Shirley both ended up moving far, far away from England to Down Under—to the other side of the world.

Acknowledgments

I want to thank my husband, Horst Reimann, who had such patience with me as I waded through reams of paperwork and research, and who never faltered once in his encouragement. I also acknowledge with sincere thanks the input of my sister and my cousin whose own research was invaluable.

Author's Note

This book follows my father's life from his youth to when he entered the world of spying, his journey to his base, the British Embassy in Moscow during World War II, and, as much as I could fathom, or imagine, of what I believe went on at the Embassy and elsewhere. Interwoven is some of Freddie Read-Jahn's later life, and some of his wife's, my mother's, story as it concerned her husband.

Some names have been changed to preserve anonymity.

As the younger daughter of Freddie Read-Jahn, I wrote this book because I had always dreamed of retracing my father's 1940 journey from London to Moscow, with its inherent wartime dangers. I would follow the same routes by ship and train, even ride the Trans-Siberian Express, as he did—but, life got in the way—now I can only write from memory of the conversations my father and I had prior to his death, and from looking at his diary, papers, album photographs, military records, and his letters, the latter discovered and spirited to safety by me and my sister on the day of his funeral in London on 21st March, 1980.

For the conversations, situations and events I could not have known about—not having been there with my father—I have had to rely on my own imagination and research.

At the age of 12 my parents' divorce had hit me like a ton of bricks. I had been born in England in 1944, with ¼ German and ¾ English blood. My early years had been spent in Germany. Indeed, my first language had been German as well as English. One day, when I'd turned 12, a bowler-hatted, pin-striped English solicitor had been shown into my English boarding school's study where he advised me, because of their coming divorce, that it was now the time to choose whether I wished to live permanently with my mother or my father. "If you choose your mother, you will continue to be brought up as an English girl. If you choose your father, you

Author's Note

will move to Germany and be brought up as a German." I sat there, gobsmacked, trying not to cry. Upon seeing my distress, this kind grey-haired old gentleman leant forward and whispered in my ear, "Mind you, I am absolutely forbidden by law to tell you that your sister chose your mother." Not wanting to be parted from my only sibling, I made my choice, to continue on as an English girl, but with a love of most things German for the rest of my life. Indeed, my Australian husband is of German birth.

In the late 1950s and 1960s, when I was in my late teens and early 20s, I occasionally flew to Germany or France to be Fred's hostess at different diplomatic or business functions, since he and my mother were by then divorced and he said he enjoyed having me at his side rather than one of his female friends.

Twenty-two years later, I was planning on going through a divorce myself from my first husband, an American. I had flown home from California where I then lived, to talk to my parents, both then living separately in England, to seek their opinion on my potential break-up and its ramifications. I particularly wanted to find out how they had got through their own traumatic divorce. I was unable to question my mother too closely because of a recent stroke she'd sustained, but did gain some documents from her.

Up until then, I'd not been really close to my father. I admired him, loved his sense of humour, the twinkle in his eye, his knowledge of fine wines, and his debonair worldliness in general. My father sat me down in his London study and offered me a whisky. That was an absolute first. Fred obviously now considered me a grown-up. We talked. He gave me advice. I asked him if his extraordinary, secretive, work had been the real cause of my mother's leaving him. There was a long pause, then my father, between sips of whisky, started to tell me bits and pieces of his time working for the Foreign Office in London, and for British military intelligence in the Soviet Union in World War II, and mentioned how that period had impacted his whole life. He said he'd have to take most of what happened with him to his grave, in that he had signed the Official Secrets Act—but, he did give me intriguing snippets of information which I have now used to create this book.

I was flattered that he'd opened up to me somewhat, recognising me as an adult. I didn't judge him for his infidelities to my mother. God knows, I was married to a man whose work often kept him away from home so I knew how hard it must have been for my father, and for my mother, over their long separation during wartime. Neither of them had ever remarried. I think that says a lot. It was a marriage of passionate attraction, hastened because of the war, but still, a very deep love story. He'd had his affairs. I only knew of a handful of other men who had intrigued my mother in her life, and only of one "date" she'd been on after her divorce—with a man whose right hand was perpetually and mysteriously held inside a black leather glove. Of course, growing up I was away in boarding school for seven years, only home for brief periods between school terms, and doubtless she was very discreet. Besides, it wasn't anything a rather private Englishwoman like Molly would share with her children.

Fred and Molly's love was, like many others, a casualty of the war. I do think Fred thought of the other women in his life as all part of his "job" and, that, I believe was obviously the root cause of their eventual split-up. Molly could not tolerate the other women or the diplomatic lifestyle Fred expected her to live.

As I grew up, I picked up a certain bitterness she held toward my father. She kept us children away from our cousins. She had to legally let us see Fred here and there, but didn't like it. We were subconsciously led to believe he was not a good man and, over the years, he was always referred to at home as the DH, an acronym for the Devil Himself. To me, that actually made him more intriguing; a conflicting situation because I was also rather afraid of him, and, when still a youngster, would balk at being made to see him. I know Molly was always after him to provide for us children and had a hard time accomplishing it. I can now understand her great frustration.

On Fred's side, I picked up a certain bemusement he held about my mother. My sister and I rarely saw them together but when they were, he seemed still to be quite fond of her. I think he couldn't understand why she wasn't still in love with him. He obviously still

Author's Note

liked her and she still made him smile. It didn't seem like arrogance on his part. Putting myself in his shoes, I could see that those other women had all been part of his work, hadn't they! I have a vivid recollection of when guests arrived for my first wedding in England. Friends of my mother were seated on one side of the church and friends of my father on the other, rather than friends of the bride on one side and friends of the groom on the other.

My mother was always an attractive, vivacious, character, but as she aged she became quite quirky, and rather reclusive. When she left my father, she was obliged to return to work. I'm sure she was then rather sadly relieved that her father had forced her to give up playing the piano and learn shorthand and typing instead.

Many years have passed since World War II became history, and some stories have now been released, which Fred doubtless knew would eventually occur. It is only quite recently that I have learned that my father, and his brother, were both part of the highly secretive MI-19 section of British Intelligence.

The author of this book, Fred's younger daughter, Shirley, with her father on 6th October, 1966, as a hostess for Fred at a Society of Motor Manufacturers' reception in Paris, France.

About the Author

Shirley Read-Jahn was born during World War II and educated in England before becoming a hippy and living in an ancient Roman burial tomb in Matala, Crete. She went on to take up many different colourful careers, including swimwear model, interpreter, landscape designer, paralegal and events organiser. She also co-founded the highly-successful SFJAZZ (the San Francisco Jazz Festival) as well as running her own landscape business in the United States. Shirley has belly-danced since her thirties, still plays table-tennis, and now lives in Australia. In retirement, she has finally found time to devote to her passion for writing and the books swirling around in her head.

Email: shirleyreadjahnbooks@gmail.com
Facebook: https://www.facebook.com/srjpublications/

Other Books by Shirley Read-Jahn

The Prince Oliver Penguin Trilogy for Children:
Volume 1: *Prince Oliver and his Friend, Olivia.*
Volume 2: *Olivia and Prince Oliver's Penguins.*
Volume 3: *Prince Oliver & the Penguin Chicks.*

Made in the USA
Middletown, DE
05 April 2019